ECHOES OF THE PAST

BY ZOE SAADIA

Beyond the Great River
The Foreigner
Troubled Waters
The Warpath
Echoes of the Past

Two Rivers
Across the Great Sparkling Water
The Great Law of Peace
The Peacekeeper

At Road's End
The Young Jaguar
The Jaguar Warrior
The Warrior's Way

The Highlander
Crossing Worlds
The Emperor's Second Wife
Currents of War
The Fall of the Empire
The Sword
The Triple Alliance

Obsidian Puma
Field of Fire
Heart of the Battle
Warrior Beast
Morning Star
Valley of Shadows

ECHOES OF THE PAST

People of the Longhouse, Book 5

ZOE SAADIA

For more information about this book, the author and her work, visit www.zoesaadia.com

ISBN: 153965107X
ISBN-13: 978-1539651079

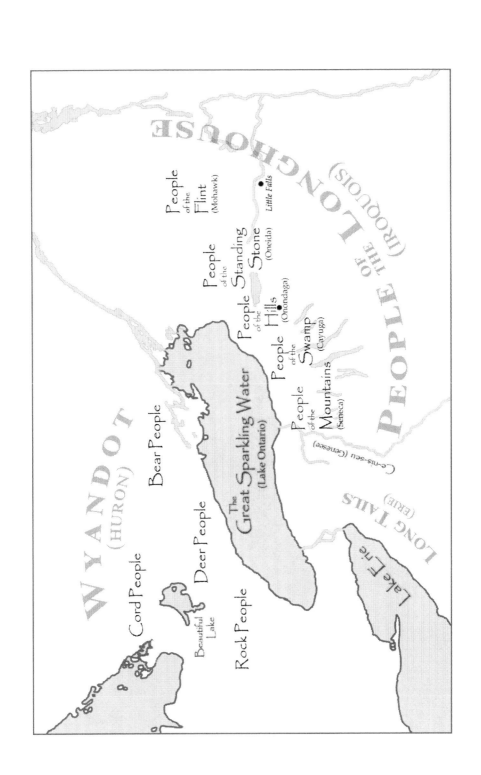

CHAPTER 1

"Come on, you can do it."

The War Chief's outstretched hands shook as he held them up, not touching the balancing figure but ready to catch it should the adventurous climber lose his grip on the ladder's rung and fall. A slim chance, as the child was hanging on to his precarious perch with an obvious desperation, taking no chances by freeing one of his hands in order to reach for the next challenge, opting for staying where he was, gripping it for dear life.

No adventurer, this one, reflected Ogteah, amused. A perfect opposite to the wild thing that was already hopping up there on the upper shelf, forcing his way through the clacking pottery, happy and unconcerned, having scaled this same ladder with an indecent ease before the watching grandfather managed to discern his intentions and rush closer, just in case. A fierce addition to the War Chief's family, unlike his twin brother, a perfect opposite.

"Go ahead," prompted the War Chief. "You won't fall, but I'm here to make sure of that. See how close?"

The older man's voice rang hoarsely in the dimness of the compartment, even though in this part of the day and the season the interior of the longhouse was well aired, with all venting holes opened along the long corridor, and both entrances gaping into the crispiness of the high noon. No stinging smoke to make one fight for breath like in the earlier time in this season. Still the old man's cough was rocking the air with alarming frequency, the result of a prolonged illness acquired through the Cold Moons, or so Ogteah was told, worried to hear this particular news.

Having arrived in High Springs only this morning, he didn't

fail to notice the prominent leader's pallor and the haggardness of his features, the way the man's bones were protruding sharply, in no encouraging manner. Oh, yes, it was easy to see the cough in the thinly pressed lips and the lightly convulsing throat, the way it was held back, with typical stubbornness.

Straightening up, he glanced at the standing man, ready to spring to his feet in case of a need.

"Come on, little one." One of the large palms moved closer, touching the child's back, supporting, giving it of its strength. "You can reach your troublemaking brother, lend him some support, can't you now?" The mischievous glance shot at Ogteah, accompanied with a light wink. "No use trying to get him down now either, once he has made up his mind. A stubborn little thing."

Ogteah grinned, then got to his feet anyway. The resumed conversation offered a good pretext. "I would have worried about the other rascal."

A glance at the upper shelf confirmed his claim. The wilder twin was busy plundering, stumbling between baskets and items of wear, spilling some of it as he roamed about, high spirited and unafraid but clumsy, having the restrictions of his still developing walking skills to deal with. They had seen not much more than one or maybe one and a half summers of their lives, remembered Ogteah, not truly interested in babies that weren't his own. The Wolf Man's woman was staggering about with this or that baby tied to her back or snuggled on her breast on his last visit in this town, more than two seasons earlier, way before the Cold Moons. So maybe they didn't see more than one span of seasons, after all.

"What did you find up there, Takoskowa?" called the old leader, shifting on his toes while still maintaining the same pose, keeping the more timid twin safe. "Don't make a mess out of it or your grandmother will have my skin for this."

A tumbling down basket with remnants of dry cookies was his answer. His favorite ones, with nuts and berries, discovered Ogteah, catching the flying object, balancing it so as to not let more of its spilled contents fall on the floor.

The perfectly round face peeked from above, puckered in too

obvious of a manner. The flood of tears was imminent.

"You wild thing." The War Chief's voice trembled with laughter, dripping warmth. "Why did you do that?"

"He didn't. I don't think he anticipated the unruly basket jumping off that shelf after a simple tossing and throwing it around," suggested Ogteah, amused yet wishing that someone would come already and take the children away. The opportunities to talk to the prominent man alone and undisturbed were few and far between, unless he asked for a private conversation specifically. Which he didn't. There was no need for that. He hadn't come to High Springs on his own initiative, not this time. The invitation of their unofficial warriors' leader was the one to bring him here; a word sent through a casual third party, nothing alarming or even formal. Still, it had him started on his journey here at once. The Wolf Man wasn't in a habit of summoning people, especially those he trusted with responsibilities, for the simple pleasures of good company or to pass time. Not this man!

Knowing that it was unseemly to demand the talk he was summoned here for immediately upon his arrival, Ogteah had wandered off, greeting many friends he had all around this town, getting filled with food offerings at every place he had visited until his stomach threatened to burst. It was unheard of to see a guest off before he sampled the tastiest of the local treats, and of course no visitor would claim his full belly as an excuse, a terrible impoliteness. So now, a quarter of a day later and enjoying the company of the renowned old leader, he could barely breathe, let alone think of anything edible nearing his mouth for the duration of the next moon at the very least.

He didn't count on the powerful leader to be idle and alone, intending to go out in search of the man's powerful elder son next, the Wolf Man's influential brother, a very important dignitary these days, en route to all sorts of positions of power, the representative of his town in the Great Council being one of the proposed speculations. However, the War Chief was at home and alone, visibly aged, thin and haggard, weakened by the winter sickness that he was still recovering from, something no one outside the town had heard about. Why? wondered Ogteah. Was it a matter of pride on the War Chief or his family's part, or were deeper political motivations involved?

"Oh well, intentionally or not," the old man's eyes twinkled, turning back toward the more timid counterpart of the wild whirlwind that was again sweeping through the upper shelf, "we are done for as it is, the three of us, so just go up there and help your brother make the new order out of things, will you? Come on, little one. You can do it for your brother's sake, can't you?" A following outburst of soft laughter ended with what sounded like a suppressed cough, the old man's face twisting, losing some of its recently gained color that the activities with the energetic pair of toddlers must have brought. "And it will... will be safer up there... when your grandmother comes back..."

As Ogteah rushed to the older man's side, his eyes scanning the interior of the lower shelves, seeking a bowl of water, or better yet, a container with medicine, the War Chief shook his head, holding the rest of his cough between the tightly pursed lips, his eyes glittering with wetness that the effort must have brought but determined, as forceful as always, ordering him to leave it at that. But of course. What man of pride and dignity would concede to being treated like a sick person unless truly unable to help himself? Still Ogteah fumed at the womenfolk of this family for leaving the old man unattended, with no better company than lively toddlers to watch after.

"There is water in the bin," he said as noncommittally as he could. "I'll get you some."

The nod of the old leader was accompanied by an apologetic smile, while the large hands pushed their charge up gently if somewhat forcefully now, uncompromising. The boy on the ladder screwed up his face in the exact imitation of his brother's before, amusing and puzzling Ogteah once again at the fact that two human beings could look that much alike, just a replica of each other, one person presented twice. Afraid to retrace his steps back toward the safety of the earthen floor, the little thing evidently opted for the wisest solution of trusting his grandfather, letting the old hands guide him up the treacherous path, keeping him safe until reaching a more stable ground.

"Thank you." The older man accepted Ogteah's water with gratitude, draining its contents quickly, in almost one gulp. "The annoying cough!" Another spasm was conquered more successfully this time. "It will pass eventually, but does it make one's life difficult sometimes, especially when the worried women spot you doing this." A chuckle ended with more alarmingly barking sounds. "I swear I'm tempted to do what sick animals do, crawl away and let the illness pass by itself, in peace and no fussing around."

"I can understand that." Ogteah grinned, not truly relating. When sick or wounded, he liked being attended and kept company with. Well, as far as it was Gayeri who did that, of course. His woman certainly knew how to spoil a person and make him feel better and fast, unlike her fussing aunt or various female friends and relatives. So maybe the War Chief just lacked proper company. Or maybe he was a different person, striving to be at his best, hating being caught in a weakness, the likelier of assumptions. A great leader of countless summers, oh yes, the old man must have been needing to feel powerful and of use.

"Every man would." Breathing with more ease now, even though the colorlessness of his face was still alarming, the old man positioned himself to the left of the ladder, ready to catch falling toddlers should they begin tumbling down the upper shelf. Judging by the noise both boys were now making, not able to converse as yet due to their young ages but communicating by calls and grunts and excited exclamations, it was the most prudent course to pursue. "So what have the Lone Hill's people been up to? That village of yours *is* busy expending, turning into a large settlement with all their growing population, eh? Something you've been contributing mightily to, or so one hears."

As always it was easy to join in the great man's laughter, the impressive leader's ability to put his conversers at ease remarkable, something to wonder about.

"This sort of news travels fast, doesn't it?" He tried to suppress the familiar glow, knowing that the old man didn't care, not the way he, Ogteah, did. "She doesn't mind having another child. I thought she might wish to avoid that, with her aspirations to join our longhouse's women council, but she says it won't interfere."

He brought his arms forward, palms up, an accepting gesture that reflected none of his real excitement, real elation concerning this particular matter. Oh, but how he had rejoiced when she had told him, the moment she knew, just a few dawns after her blood didn't come. So different from the first time, when she had waited for him to come home from his first war, with him being wounded, exhausted, shaken, not excited in the least by the prospect of turning into a father yet again, the first time back in his lands being such a failure. And yet, how little did he know back then, having no clue, not the slightest.

The girl Gayeri had brought to this world only a few seasons later and after much fear, on his part more than on hers, come to think of it, with the shadow of his missing mother looming in the background, reminding of childbearing dangers, was an enchanting, flawless creature, the most perfect human being, exciting beyond measure, a true fruit of love. Having known his daughter for close to three summers by now, he was still amazed at how his excitement with her never faded, blossoming and growing with every passing day, enhanced by every development, every new skill she had learned so fast and with such eagerness, having a mind of her own on many matters by now, freely expressed, and great deal of cheek into the bargain.

He had spoiled the girl rotten, Gayeri kept complaining, powerless against their daughter's charm as much as he was, something the little beast possessed in abundance, just like her mother before her, he suspected. Gayeri said that many of her problems arose out of her being atrociously spoiled, never disciplined, a claim confirmed by her aged aunt's attitude. Still he would grin and take no notice. His daughter deserved everything she wanted, the prettiest pelts and the shiniest purple shells straight away from the far east. His venturing into the Flint People's lands and their warfare beyond the Great River had both his women looking as decorated as a ceremonial ground before an important ceremony.

"It will interfere, of course it will. Another child will slow her down, but not for good. Women know how to deal with it." The older man moved sideways, following the creaking of the planks right above their heads. "How is her father? I heard the Honorable Representative has not been well through the Cold Moons."

"No, he wasn't, but he is well now." Deciding that it was his duty to tell the details the old leader might not learn until fit to travel, Ogteah positioned himself next to the ladder, ready to join the hunt after falling toddlers as well. "The False Face Society healers have found right foods for the Honorable Elder to eat along with the foods he was to avoid. It changed his health for the best ever since." He hesitated. "He will be attending the Great Gathering of the next moon."

"Good." The War Chief nodded thoughtfully. "I should love to meet him there. There are matters I would need to hear his opinion on before those are brought before the august assembly's official consideration."

He hated the knot that was tightening in his stomach, undesirable and unwelcome. It could be anything that the renowned leader might have wished to discuss, anything and everything. It didn't have to be his, Ogteah's, former people or their growing impudence, with the talks of peace abandoned some summers ago, on that same span of seasons when they had received the word of Father's death, the summer the Long Tails were defeated so soundly. Since then, the resumed war was a looming possibility, but it was something he had managed to push out of his mind with a measure of success. There was no need to agonize over possibilities until they happened, no need to toss on his longhouse's bunk sleepless, thinking of what he would do should the war break out. It was a waste of time. When it happened, he would have enough time to feel bad, trapped, torn, undecided. But until then there was no need to lose his inner peace, or his presence of mind for that matter. Enough that he had gone to fight the Flint People's traditional enemies last summer because of that, to be away in case the Wolf Man decided to start gathering warriors for the raids that were to be sent across the Great Sparkling Water. A plan that worked nicely, his private scheme of getting away, as a few raids were, indeed, sent across, with some of his former charges from the Standing Stone People's lands joining in, to tell him all about it later on. There was not much success in those ventures, with the glaring lack of knowledge as to the location of more important towns than a few scattering villages to assault, or even the enemy's actual war readiness. There was not enough information to be had, and the only encouragement was in the fact, or at least the assumption, that the enemy had been facing an equal disadvantage. A small comfort.

"What was wrong with the representative's health, anyway?" The War Chief's voice tore him from his unhappy reverie, brought him back to the dimness of the compartment and the agitated blabbering that was pouring from its upper parts. "The usual winter sickness?"

"No, it wasn't that. The Honorable Elder was losing his strength very rapidly, turning as thin as a stick, wandering into the dream worlds too often. The healers didn't know what to do, until the man of False Face Society from Onondaga Town came. He made the elder cut fat foods out of his eating habits, made him eat only greens and fruit and drink water sweetened with honey. Then the Representative got better and better, until most traces of illness were gone." Moving closer just in case, Ogteah watched the older man taking a hold of the balancing ladder that was pushed from above, in a clear effort to mount it. "He is satisfactorily fit these days, not needing attendance apart from his special foods being prepared." He grinned. "Gayeri took that responsibility upon herself, otherwise her father would have had a harder time to survive, with the rest of his womenfolk being quite an unorganized lot, prone to hysterics and not much usefulness otherwise."

The War Chief's laughter was merry, even though inhibited by a new bout of coughing, as he stretched his arms, trying to reach for one of the descending toddlers. The adventurous one, judging by the deftness and the self-assurance of his movements. No need for help there. "If you are not careful, you'll end up living with a clan mother."

Ogteah didn't try to stifle a chuckle. "I'm careful."

The sound of rapid footsteps made him glance toward the stretching corridor, his other senses still tuned to the elder man and the growing commotion upon the upper bunk. The remaining twin, left behind, was beginning to howl lustily, with much gusto.

"Father!" The Wolf Man burst upon them, skirting over the glowing embers of the nearest hearth in one forceful leap. "You should be resting. Not running after two wild rascals. You promised!"

"That's not what you think," pleaded the powerful War Leader, smirking without shame. "I'm not running after anyone. Those two wild things were running after me. Before deciding to raid the upper bunk, that is." Moving away, he let the indignant father scale the ladder in order to retrieve one of his howling treasures, the other twin already down, exploring the space under the lower pallet with zest. "I'm telling you, this pair is unstoppable."

"You should be resting, Father," insisted the Wolf Man, not amused. "Mother would kill us both if she knew. Have you drunk your medicine yet?"

"Not yet," admitted the War Chief, giving Ogteah conspiratorial look. "But I will. You can put your worries to rest, honorable clan mother."

The Wolf Man snorted with a flicker of his old mischievousness. "I'm nagging with good reason," he muttered, giving Ogteah a look of his own. "He made us seriously worried through the last of the Cold Moons, you know. And still I keep catching him messing about with the twins." Bending to retrieve the more spirited part of the pair from under the bunk, dragging the culprit out with little consideration to the protesting toddler's will, the timid boy already nestled snugly under his father's free arm, the man shook his head. "I'll dispose of these two and will be back quickly."

His footsteps echoed firmly, typically determined, as though no protesting or howling toddlers hindered his step.

"They are challenging, this pair," said the War Chief, sinking onto the lower bunk with a sigh of relief, his smile wide, holding no shadows, the sunken eyes crinkling. "I never knew how challenging a pair of twins could be."

"I can only imagine," nodded Ogteah, secure in the knowledge that his daughter didn't have to share her parental attention with anyone as yet. "And they are so different even though they look exactly the same."

"Twins always are." The older man's smile was surprisingly wistful, holding sadness. "People expect from twins to be as alike inside as they are outside, but they are not one person, such children. Being a pair, they are completing each other, complementing one another's differences, you see? They are one, and two different things at the same time."

"Like the celestial pair, the Great Spirits, the Right-Handed and the Left-Handed Twins."

"Oh yes, something like that. But not in the good as opposed to the evil sense." The eyes peering at Ogteah twinkled, even though the man's face contorted, dealing with a new bout of dry coughing. "It would be too easy if people were to be divided in such a way, wouldn't it?"

Ogteah nodded, rushing toward the bowl of water once again.

"I was born to be a part of such pair." The water gulped down to its last, the man reclined back, obviously tired. "We were about the same, my brother and I. And when he might have looked as timid as our little Tsitsho does now and I was as wild as that unstoppable Takoskowa the Mountain Lion, my brother was always the drive, the thinker, the mind behind our adventures. It might have not looked this way on the outside, but it was I who followed him or his ideas and not the other way around." The intensity of the gaze lessened, blurred, wandering through the mists of the past. Not a happy place, reflected Ogteah, surprised, his heart twisting at the sight of the sagging shoulders, at the deep voice that all of a sudden lost its storytelling quality, dropped to mere whisper. "They said I had sapped his strength when still back in our mother's belly, and maybe it was the truth. He was always sickly, not as robust as I was, not as forceful in disposition." The eyes focused, rose, peering at their converser, challenging. "Still he was the drive behind our adventures, the originator, always."

What happened to him? Ogteah wanted to ask, but couldn't bring himself to do this. Whatever made this man's brother go away, it wasn't good, or pleasant, or timely. The War Chief had lost his brother, his other half, and it must have been bad, the anguish of the lined, grief-stricken face told him that. So much sadness! Outside himself, he put a comforting palm on the weathered shoulder, relaying it all in one simple gesture.

It helped. The eyes focused, cleared. The smile that blossomed was brief, showing an open gratitude.

"Such long-forgotten memories." Shaking his head as if trying to be rid of those, the man sighed. "How did we get onto this subject, when all I wanted was to quiz you about your recent adventures in the land beyond the Great River of my people? It must have been interesting out there. Aside from my son, I know very few Onondagas who went to fight as far the lands of the River People. What made you join those particular raids?"

"Well, it was an interesting journey, yes." Grinning lightly, Ogteah shrugged. "I suppose I wanted to get to know my mother's people better. To go and fight alongside them seemed like a good start. What with some of my friends from the Standing Stone lands being eager to talk me into it." He felt his grin widening. "Some of these folk can be forcefully convincing, and the stories regarding the lands of the savages your son provided while loitering over this or that campfire didn't help to put any of us off the projected raid to help our Eastern Door Keepers." He smirked. "Not that I would dare to use the word 'savages' in your son's presence."

"You better not, yes." The old man's laughter shook the air, ending with a new bout of coughing. "Unless you wish to... to end up... being lectured on the River People and their merits and integrity, enemies or not." The old eyes looked him over shrewdly. "Also it kept you away from the developments in our areas; away from encounters with your former people, their raiding parties or our retaliating efforts."

His sense of wellbeing evaporated all at once. "That was not my intention at all."

But the older man's smile held no reproach. "I didn't mean it as an accusation." The pale lips stretched in a kind way. "You are a wise man and I approve of the manner in which you conduct yourself under the strangeness of your circumstances. You proceed wisely along your chosen path, and your loyalty is not doubted, not by the people who matter. Your loyalty to both your former and current people." The wide shoulders lifted in a shrug. "I wish we could help you with that by keeping the peace between both sides of our Great Sparkling Water, the way the Great Peacemaker wanted us to do, the way your father and I, and some others, strove to achieve."

The warm coziness was returning, banishing the chill. "If only Father had not begun his travels to the Sky World so soon."

"Oh yes, if only." The older man sighed, fending off another outburst of coughing. "But when it comes to this particular undertaking, the peace between our peoples, it seems that the Evil Left-Handed Twin himself takes a special interest, thwarting all our efforts and plans."

"Father was trying so hard—"

The echoing footsteps heralded the return of their forceful company, with the Wolf Man bearing down on them, unhindered by protesting children this time.

"Dumped them on their cousins," he reported, panting. Dropping on the vacant mat near the fire, he let his breath out loudly. "My brother's daughters are old enough to watch after toddling babies, and if they stay in their longhouse while their entire clan went out preparing the fields, then they have only themselves to blame, lazy skunks that they are."

"Hanowa is still recovering from the winter sickness," protested the girls' grandfather, reproachful.

"And her cheeky fox of a sister?"

The older man raised his hands in the air, palms up, defeated. "Yes, this one must have stayed behind to laze around." A wide grin. "So yes, she got what she deserved. But she'll actually deal with your wild pair, you just wait and see. Even with little Takoskowa. She is a match for him. She'll manage."

"We'll hear her carrying on about it for moons, either boasting or complaining." Obviously somewhat less enamored, the girl's uncle rolled his eyes. "Why do they always have to be away and swamped with work just when we need them, those women?" His chuckle rolled down the corridor, deserted but for faint snores coming from one of the farther compartments. Then the lightness evaporated. "I'll be off with the first light."

The War Chief narrowed his eyes, the good-natured expression leaving his taut face as well. "Where to?"

"First Onondaga Town, of course."

"Thought so." The older man nodded. "Then a swift stroll westwards?"

"No, it's too soon for that." The younger man hesitated, eyes resting on his father but lacking in focus, wandering through some inner worlds. "Or maybe yes, but not seeking an actual volunteering, not yet. Just preparing the ground. Clearing the field, one might say." The contemplative eyes focused, shifted, came to rest on Ogteah. "That's why I asked you to come here this time. I need to talk to you."

The memory of the unauthorized recruiting three summers ago made Ogteah's stomach flutter with anticipation.

"Will we receive official permission this time?" he asked, pushing the possible destination of those future recruitments aside. One thing at the time, and gathering warriors' forces, officially or less so, was the most pleasing activity, as satisfying as it was rewarding. His mind rushed through possibilities. Okwahli, the oldest Standing Stone brother and his various cousins would be involved, and some other of his former charges, the troublemaking elements of the Long Tails War he had kept close in touch with ever since.

"It depends," drawled the Wolf Man slowly, his smile one of the widest, an openly conspiratorial grin, full with as pleasant memories. "When the time comes to the actual recruitment, I believe we will have the permission to do that." The smile disappeared as quickly as it came. "But for now some of us will just travel around, sound people out. No need to bother the councils with any of that." The dark eyes narrowed, measuring Ogteah quite openly. "Yet I would rather have you busy with a different sort of a mission."

"What?" For some reason he didn't like this gaze, the strange glee in it, the excited anticipation. "What would you rather have me doing?"

The man sprang to his feet with a startling suddenness. "How about we go for a walk, breathe some fresh air? This corridor is barely visible from all the smoke." A businesslike gaze leapt toward the older man. "Father? Are you up to a walk out there with us?"

The War Chief's smile flickered weakly. "Your mother would have me thrown out of our longhouse if I left without drinking that medicine she is sure to send here at the high noon. So you two go for a walk, and maybe I will join you later, toward the afternoon."

The younger man nodded thoughtfully, flashing an affectionate smile toward his sire. "We will be back before it happens."

Watching the old man recline on his bunk with obvious relief, Ogteah fought down a bad feeling. Somehow he didn't want to be involved in secret side missions. Not now that he had proven his worth and his ability to lead people. Why did he suspect it was something the Wolf Man wasn't sure about, something shady maybe, worthy of the old Ogteah from the other side and not the new man he had become?

"It would be refreshing to lead a huge force again, but one we were entrusted officially with," he said, as the thatched roof of the façade swept above their heads, giving way to the pleasantly soft rays of sun, satisfactorily strong for this time of the seasons, just before the summer moons hit.

"We won't get there that fast." Absently, his companion kicked at a thrown log, his gaze again wandering, busy with his inner thoughts. "But I do want to be prepared in advance, so when the need arises I'll be there, gathering our formidable force of warriors with no troubles and no delays." Another kick at the hapless log. "It was a near miss back at the Mountain People. Our lack of knowledge about the Long Tails and their war readiness was appalling. We could have been caught napping under the trees, or worse, not there at all, wandering with our monster of a force in the places we weren't even needed. Or not there in the first place, sending no help to our Western Door Keepers at all. Think about it." The dark gaze focused, flew at Ogteah. "We knew something was going on, but the real extent of it was nowhere near to what I was expecting, and but for a few lucky developments, this first great victory of ours could have turned into our first great defeat. And then even the Great Spirits wouldn't have helped us, because certain elements among our enemies would have pounced on us without a second thought, regardless of their own war readiness. Wouldn't they?" The suggestively arched eyebrows were accompanied by a fleeting, somewhat mischievous grin. A difficult combination to resist. "Our lovely neighbors from across the Great Lake wouldn't think twice before plunging into their war canoes, would they?"

"No, they would not." Somehow, when this forceful warriors' leader dwelled on the subject of his former people, an often enough occurrence these days, Ogteah didn't feel threatened or pressed to be carefully noncommittal as with some others, even the War Chief himself. "But we were prepared and ready, and with a little help from the Great Spirits we did achieve a great victory instead of a sound defeat. So why would you fret about it now?"

His companion made a face. "I'm not fretting. Just not happy with the need to tread in the dark when it comes to our enemies and their dealings. We know painfully little and sometimes it's a real hindrance." Slowing his step in order to skirt around a row of extinguished fires, the man blew the air through his nostrils. "Take that much-lauded Long Tails' adventure of ours. Had we only known in advance that they were gathering warriors and in such numbers, planning to head here in force, we wouldn't have to go around the Great Council to gather our own forces. We would have their keen and eager blessing instead, and more help and encouragement than we would have known what to do with. It would have been easier and more pleasant, and we wouldn't have had to gamble and guess, chancing a great failure instead of a great victory." The man's prettily embroidered moccasins made a screeching sound as he stopped abruptly, facing Ogteah, forcing him to do the same. "Do you see what I mean? The simple knowledge of their intensive warriors gathering would have been enough. I wouldn't have asked for their war plans and exact numbers of their fighting forces, even though it could have been helpful to have those as well. But that would be too much to ask. What I would have settled for happily was the most basic information, the mere knowledge of the fact that they were going around, enlisting unusual amount of people or trying to do so, planning to cross that Ge-ne-see River. That's all." Another snort. "That limping leader of their, the enterprising grass-eater that he was and probably still is, bore watching. But we didn't watch him. We didn't even know of his existence, let alone his enterprising activities."

Agreeing in general with what had been said but at a loss as to where his companion was trying to get, Ogteah found it safer to shrug. It was not like the businesslike Wolf Man to reminisce about the past, glorious or doubtful or anything in between.

"How do you propose we should have gone about it, learning of this man's activities?" he asked, rolling a pebble with the tip of his moccasin, watching the half circle it drew in the dry earth.

"Through you. Or people like you, if there were more of your type around."

"What?" That got his attention off rolling pebbles and back toward his companion's smirking face in an instant. "Me? What's that has to do with me? I'm no Long Tail! I've never been to their lands and my knowledge of their minds or politics is no better than yours."

"No. But you are what you are, the perfect person for just that sort of a mission, and you know it as well as I do." The now-amused gaze flickered, challenging, mocking but in a friendly, genuinely appreciative way. "No one can blend into unfamiliar surroundings the way you do, strike easy friendships and be everyone's acquaintance in one single lousy evening, embraced and admitted by the locals as though you were one of them. I swear I kicked myself hard for not thinking about it back then, when we were milling around Tsonontowan, making its residents angry. I kept complaining about the uselessness of our scouts and the untrustworthiness of former adoptees from among the Long Tails until my brother said that if anyone could have gone into the enemy lands, sniffing around, it should have been you, the restless adventurous spirit that you are. That's when I kicked myself viciously for not thinking of that in time."

He couldn't help the chuckle that threatened to erupt into real laughter, imagining his formidable companion reaching to tear his prettily done warrior's lock out in frustration, spitting muttered curses along the way. He knew the man too well by now.

"I hope it hurt, that kick."

"You would." A hearty laughter was his answer. "But smirk and make jokes as you might, he was right, that brother of mine, the wise person that he is. You are made for such missions, and we should have asked you to do that back then."

"Instead of gathering warriors or fighting? Not sure I would have chosen to do that."

"No, not instead! Before, way before, brother. What use would your information have been to us if you told us about it when we were already milling around the Mountain People's lands? None, none whatsoever." The raised eyebrows made Ogteah feel stupid. "But if you went sniffing around there before, a whole season before or even more, when I had my inkling but nothing else to base my assumptions on, oh, then it would have made a great difference. Then your information would have saved us plenty of headache and unlawful actions. Not to mention that the fighting would have happened on the other side of that Genesee River, the *correct* side of it!"

"I see." Squinting against the sudden gust of wind, Ogteah nodded, unable not to appreciate the wisdom in such an innovative approach. "Yes, it could have been done, I suppose. But well, you didn't even know me back then. We have met much later, if you remember. I could barely speak your tongue in an understandable manner in those times, so I say, you missed nothing by not sending me straight away into your favorite enemy's claws. And you did achieve your great victory later on, so there is no point in kicking yourself about any of it anymore." He winked. "The post-deed wisdom is always the deepest. Didn't you know that?"

"And the most useless, yes, I know." The Wolf Man made a face, then shrugged. "Unless one learns from it, and this is what I've been doing, Lone Hill's man of wisdom. Not reminiscing about the past for the sake of musing about it. Do you know me so little?"

Ogteah grinned back, unabashed. "Who knows?"

His companion's snort dissolved in the crispy air. "Cheeky grass-eater, that's what you are and always were." Then the grin came back. "It's never too late, they say, and not all our enemies lay as low as the filthy Long Tails do now, licking their wounds. Other people were active as you know, their alliances growing stronger, implacably inimical, set on the warpath since the sad event of four summers ago. The same event that must have pushed the Long Tails into their imprudent adventure."

He stopped listening, his stomach tightening in a hundred little knots. "I won't be spying on my former people!" It surprised him, the way his voice sounded, calm and firm, albeit with a strained tone to it. "Don't even think of suggesting something like that."

His companion's face hardened. "Why ever not?"

"Plenty of reasons and I won't go into any of them."

Their gazes locked and for a while the staring contest professed enough danger to make the air around them thickened.

Then the younger man shrugged and turned away. "Do as you please." The dark gaze retuned to Ogteah, considerably colder, holding just the slightest amount of disdain. "You may find it hard to reconcile your loyalties if that's the way you feel, now that your former countryfolk deem it wise to profess their warlike intentions. You will not be able to escape being involved, one way or another."

Ogteah drew a breath through his nostrils, his lips pursed too tightly to use them in this way as yet. "I'll manage."

"I wish you luck with that." A snort and the wide back was upon him, drawing away resolutely, the decorations on the broad shoulders jumping with every firm step.

Ogteah stared at it until it disappeared behind the next building's wall.

CHAPTER 2

To skin a deer all by herself was the challenge Ononta did not look forward to. She was not that adept with her father's long-bladed, viciously ragged flint knife, preferring not to touch such dangerous-looking weaponry at all. Still with her various newfound aunts and cousins spending their day in the fields, preparing for the hectic activities of the planting, and her father sleeping in relative comfort after drinking yet another draft the medicine man had prepared for him only this morning, she had no choice, had she?

"Yes, well, I'll come. Of course." Shooting another hopeful glance at the heavily breathing figure that sprawled upon the lower bunk, willing it to move, to wake up maybe – it was not a good thing to wish on her sick father, but she was desperate enough, wasn't she? – Ononta sighed. "Where is the carcass? Is it far? I dare not leave my father unattended for too long."

An impatient grimace was her answer. "Just get on with it, girl, before that deer begins to rot. If enterprising forest predator doesn't make its way toward it, then this enterprising town's dwellers will. Don't be so useless. It's just a short walk off the trail and down the river."

Reconciled to her fate, Ononta dropped to her knees, fishing a pot and other necessary utensils from under the nearest bunk, her father's knife being among those, a cherished, valued possession she wouldn't dare to touch but for her own lack of appropriate cutting tools. She was just a girl of barely seventeen summers, and she didn't plan on spending almost a whole season so far away from home. She should have been prepared, yes, every respectable woman in her place would have traveled with an arsenal of her personal belongings, tools and ware and not only pretty dresses; still with her mother usually around and ready to spoil and pamper and her sisters doing the same, she somehow suspected the useful items would always be there, appearing out of thin air when one needed them. How silly!

Rolling her eyes, she hurried down the corridor, not pleased with its emptiness. The annoying man didn't even have the courtesy to wait for her, rushing her out and about to do his bidding, as though she owed him something. An alleged uncle of hers, the husband of her father's cousin. As though those people were her real family! They may have been members of the same clan and Father's relatives, yes, but her real people were not these Rock People from the far west. Her people were Bear People, out there in the east, at the shores of the Great Sparkling Water, on the wind-stricken bays and deeper inland, her town being the coziest of them all, situated in the protection of the forest, no coldness and no cutting winds there. If only they could start traveling back home with no delays!

The thought of the cozy, nicely warm and prettily decorated longhouse with the symbol of a carved porcupine adorning its façade made her heart fall as it always did. Oh how she longed to be back home, surrounded by people she knew well, people she loved and cherished, people she trusted, her true family and not these strangely-speaking neighbors that didn't even deign to honor the Wyandot Union by joining it, and this after so many talks and deliberations.

The firm agreements of unwavering help and true brotherhood existed between her Bear People and the dwellers of another Great Water out there in the northwest for enough summers to take it seriously by now, to trust the whole thing. Atuye's father, such a great man and the most prominent leader her Bear People ever had, worked hard to make it happen. Everyone knew it, but her friend never tired of repeating that, over and over. He was so proud of his father! Every time they talked about the prominent man, his deeply set eyes would shine beautifully, with an unconcealed adoration. When it came to his father, Atuye forgot to be serious and reserved, striving to look older and more important upon regular occasions. He was so proud of his father, almost as proud as she had been of him, the youngest son of the prominent man, and his living image. But how happy he was when she would comment on that remarkable likeness, even though everyone stressed this fact, to Atuye's mother's imminent pleasure. Still, she, Ononta, had known him better than everyone, hadn't she?

The longing was back, the painful twinge in her stomach. His father never got far in his attempts to draw the other two nations into the newborn Wyandot Union. He died still trying to make the stubborn neighbors, Deer People and not even these western dwellers, listen, but desolate Atuye did not hold a grudge against this indecisive nation. Stoically, he maintained that his father's work could not go unraveling because of something no one but the Great Spirits might have control of. He said that the Deer People would become the part of the union now, and then the Rock People too, because this is how his father wanted it to be.

He was determined to dedicate his life to this end, to make his great father proud now that he was in the Sky World, among the brightest of stars, watching, wishing his sons well. Most of his sons, but not all, not the one who was responsible for his father's failing health, or so Atuye's elder brother, Sondakwa, had claimed, because the blame had lain there, not among outside nations, friends or enemies or just neutral neighbors, but at the door of one of his own family, Ogteah, their oldest sibling.

Not a real brother, they were careful to point out, but a half-brother. Or maybe an adoptive one. He could not be a true relative, not such a worthless person, Atuye's other brother would claim, and this time the man's eyes would cloud over, his pleasantly broad face twist unpleasantly. The scum their father had chosen to rise as his own for this or that reason was no brother of theirs, and he wasn't their mother's son either.

Vaguely, she remembered this object of so much resentment. Of course she did. Everyone knew, or at least heard about the prominent leader's eldest son, a troublemaker, a gambler, a good-for-nothing person who did all the wrong things, played, gambled, lazed around, seduced women – to think of something like that! – finally fathering a child, only to leave shortly thereafter, driven out of the town by the enraged community who had just had enough. Yahounk, the woman of the same clan as her but not the same longhouse, made a huge scene while throwing the useless man out.

Being barely twelve summers old back then, Ononta remembered it well, the fuss and the scandal. Already inseparable with Atuye, her best friend and playmate, she had heard this story many times and from eye-witness account. Atuye's mother had plenty to say on the matter, even after her unwanted stepson had left promptly after what happened. Naturally the disgraced man did not wish to return to his original longhouse, to face his real family and the wrath of their disappointment, but Atuye's mother claimed that the worthless good-for-nothing didn't feel even thoroughly chastened. No shame, no remorse. All he did was grin cheekily, stating that if any offended relative felt like challenging him to a fight they knew where to find him before he left for good, then indeed, leaving after a short while, never to return. Good riddance!

But not that good. Apparently a few summers later and just as the First Gathering of the two nations was held in the faraway northern lands, Atuye's father had to face his disgrace of a son again, in more dubious circumstances than ever. The rumors that flooded their town later on were plentiful, each more colorful than the next.

Enjoying as much time with her childhood friend as ever, even though they were not such small children anymore, aware of their uneasiness and the awkwardness of some situations but unwilling to drift apart all the same, Ononta had spent enough afternoons in Atuye's family compartment, helping his mother and other women of his longhouse, involved in their affairs more than in those of her own clan and family. So the rumors about what happened at the huge northern settlement called Ossossane reached her ears with enough frequency. Fights and murders, seduced women and theft, shameful flights and whatnot, were just the start of it all.

The great leader refused to talk about any of it upon his return, even though Atuye's mother pressed unashamedly, in front of their guests sometimes even. Still the dignified old man wouldn't budge. This matter had nothing to do with the Great Gathering and the unification of the Wyandot People, he would say curtly, and those were the only things that mattered. The rest was just filthy gossip with no truth to it and no real knowledge. As always, the old man stood up for his failure of the eldest son, and that drove Atuye's mother and her other sons positively mad.

Clutching her cumbersome cargo clumsily – she should have brought a bag, shouldn't she? – she rushed through the cluttered space of the storage room, emerging into the world of the blazing sun, blinking against its fierce greeting. If only there was a way to travel home now, with no delays. Take their canoe, put her ailing father into it, some provisions to last them the journey and sail, just sail. Oh Mighty Spirits, but was she to stay here, in this Rock People's settlement for the rest of her life now? Why did she agree to come in the first place?

She frowned, seeking the man who demanded her help with her gaze. But for him leaving for good, finding another female relative's help! Not much chance of that, with everyone who could walk and wasn't needed around the town being in the fields, clearing and preparing the earth. If not her father's worsening condition, she would have been required to attend the field work as well, every pair of hands valuable, even if those hands were foreign and soft, uselessly helpless – oh, but they all thought her to be pampered and spoiled. Back home she was used to receiving gentler tasks, sewing clothes and weaving baskets, commended on the neatness of her work, not frowned upon because she was too delicate or soft. They all praised her elegance and her craft, her skill at producing wonderful patterns and beautiful items to make use of, from corn-husk shoes, mats and dolls to blankets and clothes no one felt ashamed to wear for ceremonies and rites. But all people seemed to praise here was strength and resilience.

She swallowed the tears. What made her volunteer to accompany Father when he decided to travel to Onentisati, this Rock People's town, in order to visit his family, after so many summers living with his wife's clan and people? She didn't have to come along. He had asked her, yes, wishing to boast about this exquisitely special daughter of his, she surmised, knowing full well how her entire community, not only her clan and her family, took pride in her, liking the feeling. So that was that, her prideful attitude was what made her go. How stupid, how unworthy!

"Come, girl, hurry. We don't have the entire day to loiter in the sun." The man waved at her impatiently, his frown rivaling that of the evening sky. "It's not far, but we want to reach it before Father Sun goes to sleep this night."

Unable not to, even though it was not proper or polite, Ononta rolled her eyes. Father Sun had hardly enough leisure to wake properly as yet. He had some time to spend in the sky, enough to see her toil with an uncooperative carcass, gathering frowns and remarks on her uselessness as she worked.

Another curt wave had her following duly, still seething. What if Father woke up in a fit of that frightful coughing, with no one to give him water or rush to fetch those who understood the secrets of healing? And was she supposed to cut that deer all alone, carrying it back to the town with no help whatsoever? Somehow, she knew that it was exactly what was expected of her. The annoying man wouldn't linger to see if she needed help. The most he would do was to send help in a form of another available woman of their longhouse if he happened to run into such, a slim chance, as the women were all in the fields, working hard.

Why did this man have to wander out there, shooting a deer all for himself and not as a part of a hunting party? For that was what had surely happened, a sole hunt, resulting in the need to fetch a woman, any women, in order to carry the meat back, as only in this way such sole hunter didn't have to share his private catch with the entire community. That was the law. If the man had brought the silly deer all by himself, then he had to share. But if a woman did it, then there was no need. Women's hunts were their own, an old way of evading the law. Everyone knew it and everyone did it, still at such times she felt like taking a moral stance. If only she had enough power in this community to do that, a foreign girl of not enough years to say anything, let alone argue with respectable hunters.

The wind pounced on them as they finished their walk along the tortuous corridor and emerged in the world of the rustling trees and the gashing light clouds. Such a fine day! She watched the silhouetted figure hurrying toward them, coming up from the river and the shore where people were leaving their canoes without much care. These Rock People seemed to face no enemies since the birth of the Wyandot Union, even if they didn't deign to join the proposed alliance as yet.

Ononta shielded her eyes, curious to see better. There was something about the newcomer's gait, something awkward. Her companion's coarse palm came up as well, creating a sort of a screen above his squinting eyes.

The foreigner didn't squint. With the sun being directly behind his back he didn't have to, reflected Ononta, hard put not to stare. He was a formidable looking man, strongly built and weathered in a way that suggested a rough life, his eyes large and nicely spaced but cold, reserved to the point of hostility, the thinly pursed lips matching.

His face might have looked pleasant but for a long scar that slipped from somewhere under his long, loosely tied hair, twisting down the high cheekbone, deforming it in an almost imperceptible way, impossible not to notice. It gave him an aloof, dangerous look, and such was the expression in the cold eyes that slipped past Ononta, resting on her companion, thawing a little.

Fascinated, she watched the visitor's head moving in a reserved greeting, her own eyes finding it safer to rest on the child that was nestled in the curve of the man's arm, a little boy as it seemed, all angular, childishly plump limbs and disheveled hair, with his face hidden safely in his father's wide chest.

"Greetings, Southerner. It's been a while since your last arrival here." There was a light, strangely reserved amusement in her companion's voice, which puzzled Ononta to a degree. Did this man know the fearsome foreigner? "I trust all is well with you and yours. Whoever they are." The town man's gaze brushed past the child, displaying a measure of open surprise

The visitor grinned with one side of his mouth, a smile that did not reach his eyes, which remained cold and aloof, apprehensive somehow. Shifting to change his position, doing this again in some imperceptivity awkward way, he bounced the child higher up in the curve of his arm, making the little one more comfortable.

"Greetings, Onentisati man," he said finally, with a matching light yet wary familiarity. "I'm delighted to set foot inside your town once again. It's always a pleasure to warm beside your fires."

"The pleasure and honor are ours, oh mysterious man from the south. In such turbulent times… "

More polite platitudes. Amused for a change, Ononta listened to their fencing with words, both men calm and unperturbed, matching each other, pitting their wits and their subtlety one against another, saying nothing and yet much. The man from the south? she wondered. What south? As far as she was concerned, the Rock People resided at the western edge of the Turtle Island, with nothing to stretch beyond their forests but the endless waters of the eternal sea, the same sea that had been there before water birds and animals created the world. What people resided to the south of here? Fearsome foreigners with scarred faces and a strange way of walking, carrying children that didn't seem to belong there?

The boy in the curve of the foreigner's arm squirmed, peeking out of his hiding place like a small animal, gathering every morsel of courage that he had. Yes, a cute little thing, all hair and dimples and eyes. She winked at him, safe in doing so with both men's attention on each other and away from her.

"Onentisati townsfolk's hospitality is well known and one hears that their medicine men have no peers in treating sick and wounded. Their names go ahead of them, or so one hears." The foreigner narrowed his eyes, his attention growing.

"Indeed our healers, both men and women, know their trade, their knowledge encompassing, peerless in its depth," confirmed Ononta's companion, standing there as though having the whole day to do that. As though he hadn't hurried her out, worried about that hunted deer, tearing her from her father's sickbed. Speaking of healers… She measured the sun with a quick glance.

The foreigner shifted a large leather bag he had had attached to his free arm. "I remember your clan's medicine man as a person of deep wisdom. I hope my humble offerings will please him."

Oh, so the foreigner wasn't well and he was seeking a healer's help, concluded Ononta, mildly interested again. The healer who had taken care of her father was, indeed, a renowned medicine man, but there was even a nicer healer woman in the neighboring longhouse, the one she preferred to ask for help when given a choice.

A ventured glance at the foreigner puzzled her again. He didn't look sick or unwell, but maybe it was someone else, someone of his family, that needed help? Were the medicine men of his own settlement that useless?

The child was staring at her openly now, his eyes wide and unblinking, full of fascination. She smiled at him fleetingly, then noticed the crude leather bandage that encircled the small arm, wrapping it up to the elbow. The simple-looking, unadorned shirt the boy was wearing concealed it but only partly. So maybe it was this little thing who needed treatment.

"If you wait just a little while, I will be happy to escort you in, Attiwandaronk man." The impatient glance her own escort shot at Ononta made her angry again. It wasn't her idea to head out and into the nearby woods, in search of an independently shot deer. She didn't do any unauthorized hunting and as far as she was concerned that dubiously gained meat could rot or be eaten by someone else. There was no famine in those lands and no need to hunt outside the properly organized hunting parties.

"The price of waiting will be made up by a freshly broiled stew and juicy meat cuts you might wish to partake at along with our longhouse's dwellers." Apparently, the town's man deemed it necessary to echo her thoughts.

The foreigner pursed his lips, evidently not pleased with the proposed delay even at the prospect of a feast offered as compensation. "Do not rush yourself on my account," he said with his previously polite coldness. "This matter can wait like any other."

But it couldn't, she knew, watching him clasping his child

tightly, protectively. The boy was in a need of help if his father had traveled so far in order to see a certain healer that didn't even belong to his own countryfolk. *Attiwandaronk man? Who were those people, those distant southerners?*

"I just need to show this girl to a carcass of a deer." The town's man seemed to understand the urgency of the situation as well. "It won't take long to do that. While she works on it, I will escort you back into the town." She didn't like the slightly amused derisiveness of her escort's grin. "It will give us enough time to do that. My cousin's daughter is not the most efficient worker when it comes to important tasks."

Ononta gasped, hard put not to burst into tears at such open words of criticism, such casual mention of her deficiencies and in front of a total stranger. However, the foreigner's eyes brushed past her again, displaying no more interest than before.

"I'll wait as long as need be," he repeated, shrugging with his free shoulder.

Readjusting the crook of his arm that provided the child with his comfortable perch, he moved out of their way, his limp more pronounced than before. Such a strange gait. Still upset by the received critique, Ononta stared at it absently, until the man's glare made her drop her gaze, aghast at her own impoliteness.

"He is after something," muttered her companion as they began making their way down the forested hill, glimpsing the view of the river that was flowing strongly at this time of the seasons. "Not his usual unperturbed self, our mysterious foreigner. Not today."

Pressing her lips, Ononta said nothing, refusing to engage in a conversation, not about to forget the previous insult. She wasn't useless, or inefficient. She wasn't!

"A strange bird, this Attiwandaronk man. Appears out of nowhere, says little, listens much." The man's sudden chattiness made Ononta puzzle. What had come over this one? "Limping into Onentisati every now and then, bringing things to trade, usually furs, rare stuff, mountain lions and bears, not your regular pelts or skins."

"What does he want in exchange?" Her curiosity was getting

the better of her, despite her resolution not to engage in any sort of conversation, not after the implied uselessness.

"Foodstuff. Corn, dried squash, seeds, or so the women say." The trail twisted atrociously, taking them yet closer to the low river bank. "Rarely something else." A shrug. "He gave a good winter wolf's pelt for a pair of female moccasins last time. A very pretty pair, my woman said, with plenty of quill and beading." Another shrug came accompanied with a chuckle. "And now he turns up with a child in his arms. So maybe our mysterious foreigner is not as alone as he seemed in the beginning, a wandering spirit that he is."

"If he has a woman, then he has her longhouse and her family to live with." Grabbing a protruding branch to make the steep descent easier, Ononta made a face. "He wouldn't need to exchange things for foodstuff like dried squash. He would have it all back at home."

"Well, he obviously doesn't." Her companion was losing his inclination for good-natured chattiness again, and fast. The impatient look that was shot at her told her that. Not that she cared at this point. All she wanted was to be rid of his company, and of the task he was about to charge her with. Fancy skinning deer, with no help and no worthwhile companionship, all alone in the woods. She contemplated kicking at the nearby log, not sparing her lavishly decorated moccasins, not this time.

The river shimmered to their right, taunting, offering better pastimes than wallowing in meat juices in the heart of the woods. As the man besides her beckoned her to circumvent the shallow shore that peeked at them through the thinning vegetation, she glimpsed a lonely canoe drawn up on the pebbled bank, a woman crouching next to it, clutching a baby in her arms, her pose that of a startled animal, ready to spring back to her feet and probably flee. She looked very young, just a girl really, strangely wild, frightened in an exaggerated way, like a forest dweller, a slight winter fox with a cub, ready to fight or run, or maybe do both. Against her will, Ononta flashed what she hoped would appear a reassuring smile. This girl was really too frightened.

Her companion didn't spend his time on staring. "Maybe we

better take that carcass as it is, have you work on it back in the town," he muttered, diving back into the unwelcomed shade of the woods. "Too many foreigners sniffing around this morning."

"Who is this girl?"

He just shrugged. "No local fox, this one. Her men must be somewhere around." His lips twisted with an obvious doubt. "Probably someone from one of the villages. On their way to Onentisati, I presume. Or toward the Great Sparkling Water." More charged silence. "Yes, better take that deer with us."

However, when they reached the pile of stones he had hidden his treasure under, the annoying man changed his mind again.

"Start working on it, little one. Skin as much as you can until I come back. I'll be as quick as I can." A wink. "Can't have mysterious visitors with rare presents wait, can we?"

"My father will need to take his medicine soon," pleaded Ononta, desperate at the size of the hunted deer. Such a large specimen, with so much meat and fat lining its bleeding ribs, where the arrows stuck deeply, cutting the long-legged creature's life in an instant, or so it seemed. "He can't be left unattended for too long."

"I'll check on your father on my way out." He was already turning away, his greedy excitement at the possibility of a good trade getting the better of his misgivings about the hunted treasure he didn't wish to share with anyone but his family. What a skinflint! But for his stinginess, she wouldn't be here, she knew.

On the other hand, Father might benefit from a freshly prepared stew. He would manage to keep something like that down, even if he didn't manage to do so with the rest of the foods he had attempted to consume. Not even the medicine, sometimes.

She bit her lips until they hurt. Why did he have to become so alarmingly sick? And why here, in these foreign lands of his people that were not her people at all. Oh, but she missed home so very badly. It had been already more than a moon. They had arrived here when the snow was barely melted, when the rivers were still so dangerously high.

Fighting with the slippery hide, struggling to make the large hunter's knife do its work, she suppressed a sob, but the tears kept gathering, blurring her vision, making the task of skinning into an impossible affair, as though her lack of expertise in this sort of work wasn't enough.

When the razor-sharp flint slid over the solid piece of the hide, cutting it unnecessarily while nicking her finger in the process, she could not hold it in any longer. It was useless, hopeless, futile, beyond her. Everything! Her mere existence and this hide and everything in between, Father's health and her wellbeing, and the life she was leading.

The knife clanked dimly, hitting the nearby stone, bouncing off it, landing on the carpet of moss-covered earth as she threw it away. She didn't care. If it broke or got damaged it would be just one more thing that got broken, along with her life.

Careless of her prettily embroidered dress, inappropriate wear for the task of the skinning, she sank onto the soft earth, sobbing her heart into her pressed palms, praying that no one would come to see her so shamefully weak and out of control. They wouldn't understand. They would only make faces and roll their eyes. Even the girls who were friendly with her. There were many such men and women around, but not like back home. Here she was just a burden, a silly little thing, clumsy and easily upset, laughed at behind her back most probably, mimicked for sure. Oh, but she didn't want to be here and if Father was to die now…

The hesitant creak of a branch made her hide behind the protective screen of her fingers with yet more determination, even though it sent her heart into frantic pounding. Let whoever was there laugh at her or grimace with disdain, or comment on her uselessness once again. Maybe her father's cousin was back already, having run his foreigner all the way to the town, planting him in their longhouse with instructions not to move a muscle, racing all the way back, expecting to find the neatly spread hide and the suitably carved meat, all prettily arranged and packed, waiting to be picked in ease and comfort. The annoying man, could he not have done the carving himself the way many hunters would do?

The silence hung, wearing on her nerves. No more creaking, but she knew someone was there, watching her patiently, maybe curious, maybe frightened. A hungry forest dweller, some predator out of the woods? It was not the right season for the forest dwellers to be hungry or protective of their litters, but one could never be sure.

Shifting her head slowly, afraid to let the movement show, she peeked through the screen of her fingers, finding it difficult to make out a slender silhouette at first. It was outlined sharply against the glow of the midday sun, not made to shimmer by the sparse vegetation of the clearing. The girl from the shore?

Oh yes, it must have been her, standing there warily, thin and angular, but fit, not looking helpless despite her unimpressive size. The baby in her arms seemed to be fast asleep, tucked in the pocket of a loosely tied blanket around the girl's torso. Randomly, Ononta wondered how the little thing managed to fall asleep with all the wailing and howling that must have been rolling down this clearing.

"I'm sorry," she muttered, taking a deep breath, hating how it shook, closer to a sob than a sigh. "I didn't, didn't mean to disturb you."

The girl didn't react, frozen in her previous pose, although her eyes narrowed slightly, the only thing that moved in the otherwise stony figurine. Ononta felt the warm wave washing over her face, making it burn. Was her hysterical sobbing that embarrassing?

"I'm sorry," she repeated. "I... I was just... it was just a moment of sadness..."

Still no reaction. This time, she felt the budding of rising anger. Mere politeness dictated that the girl should answer her, reassuring her that, of course, she wasn't disturbed in the least. It was very rude to just stand there all accusing and she, Ononta, wasn't going to justify herself any longer. The foreigner had no right to complain. They weren't inside the town or someone's longhouse for that matter.

Resolutely, she reached for the thrown knife that had luckily landed nearby, not forcing her into the further humiliation of getting to her feet and walking to fetch it, admitting her previous lack of control. She could feel the annoying fox still there, staring at her arching back. Focusing her eyes on the brutally butchered side of the carcass, she forced her thoughts to concentrate on that, wondering where to start cutting this time. At the shoulder blades, surely.

"You are doing it wrong." The voice behind her back made her jump, the suddenness of it and the unexpected loudness, the strange unharmonious stridency to it.

Whirling so abruptly the knife slid from her greasy fingers once again, Ononta stared at her unwelcomed company, blinking. "What? What do you mean?"

The girl seemed as though preparing to bolt away and into the woods, the way she stood there, her body tilting, legs planted at the right angle, eyes unblinking, their alertness enhanced. The best of solutions, reflected Ononta, as far as she was concerned.

"You are cutting this thing wrong," repeated the girl, her voice somewhat quieter, but still strange, oddly unmelodious. "You should have started from its neck, and worked your way down its back and sides." Her accent was distinct but not dreadful, like that of the man with the child, the familiar words twisted in an understandable way, not hard to recognize.

"Oh, the carcass?" Incredulous, Ononta glanced at her work, a brief side glance, as her full attention was still on the intruder, wondering. Who was this girl and what did she want? And what was that strange thing about her speech? Was that the foreign accent to blame? "I... well, yes, it is not easy, this thing. It is so large, you see? Cumbersome..."

Her new company listened to that with her eyes narrow, resting upon Ononta's mouth rather than her eyes, as though listening to her own thoughts.

"You just do it wrong," she repeated, eyeing the bloody mess thoughtfully, with a fair amount of doubt. "It has to be skinned in a consistent way, from upwards on. *Because* of its size." A brief pause. "Otherwise it gets messy and the fair amount of meat gets lost." One slender eyebrow raised. "Not to mention the hide. You ruin it the way you cut it."

"Can you do any better?" asked Ononta, wishing nothing more than to yell at her uninvited company to shut up and be gone.

The girl contemplated the question, again avoiding Ononta's eyes, watching the lower part of her face, instead. Such a strange woman.

"Yes, I can. If you hold my baby, I'll do it for you. But you go and wash your hands first." The thin lips pressed tighter. "And arms, too. I don't want him smeared with all these meat juices."

Incredulous, Ononta kept staring. "You'll cut this deer for me?"

This time, her companion's eyes deigned to meet her gaze, reinforcing a matter-of-fact nod. Wary, measuring, openly on guard, pleasantly large in the gentle smallness of the delicate face, those eyes dominated it, rivaling the mass of the surrounding hair, untied and uncared for, so much of it. This girl was all hair and eyes, reflected Ononta randomly. Certainly too young to cradle a baby in her arms. Or to teach someone how to carve a deer.

"You know how to do those things?"

The girl nodded impatiently, a frown just a natural extension of her previous expression, clearly not an uncommon occurrence. All the same, it didn't sit well with the gentleness of the small features. Her eyes again slipped toward Ononta's mouth.

"If you want me to do this you will have to wash yourself before you hold the baby." The pursed lips squeezed. "And you will have to hurry. I can't spend here the whole day. My man will be back soon." Matter-of-fact, she came closer, thrusting the edge of the blanket into Ononta's hands with little consideration. "Just wipe them with this. I'll wash it later on."

Taken aback by so much efficiency, Ononta did as she was told, finding herself clasping the swaddled bundle soon thereafter, holding it close to her chest, pleased with the warmth it radiated.

Her companion was already on her knees, having taken a possession of the knife, holding it expertly, ready to plunge. Mesmerized, she watched the slender arms attacking the bloody mess, their movements competent, decisive, practical, confident in the extreme. It was as though this girl did nothing but carve meat all her life. When not busy making babies, that is, reflected Ononta numbly, taking refuge in amused thoughts. There was only so much wondering one could do in one day, and the strange girl gave more cause to puzzle over than anyone she had meet recently, if at all.

And she didn't even bother to answer occasional comments, the attempts to make conversation on Ononta's part, uncomfortable with just standing there, with nothing to do but hold the swaddled blanket with a warm little creature in it. Bored, she studied the smooth little face, all rolls of fat and roundness, the eyes closed, the budding lips moving from time to time, sucking on an imaginary breast. What else would such mysterious creature dream about?

She touched the round cheek with her finger. A mistake. The small face puckered and the calmness left it all at once. The low grunts that erupted boded no good, that much Ononta knew, having been always around helping raising her brother, ten summers younger than she was, an adorable little thing.

She tried to pacify her charge with a gentle rocking, but the adamant creature wouldn't have it. The grunts grew in frequency and strength.

"I'm sorry. I think he wants to have his meal again."

Hesitantly, she came closer, astounded to see the industrious mother still at work, as indifferent to the growing protests of her baby as she was to Ononta's earlier attempts at making a conversation. Didn't this girl care?

She rocked the baby some more, at a loss. The wailing grew in frequency.

"I... I think he really wants his mother now."

Still no reaction. The slender arms worked diligently, the dim glittering of the greasy flint flashing every now and then, the pile of cleanly cut pieces of meat growing along the neatly folded hide, salvaged but for a few torn places where Ononta's previous ministrations had ruined the leather for good. The butchered carcass was miraculously turning into the most neatly carved meat she had ever seen.

Rocking the baby as best as she could, on the verge of tears herself at the desperate crying of the poor creature, Ononta stood next to the crouching figure, leaning forward as much as the baby allowed her. "Please... you must..."

That generated reaction, at last. The girl whirled around with the same forceful resolve she kept displaying through their entire encounter, eyes flashing with suspicion, her entire pose radiating readiness to act.

Ononta fought the urge to take a hasty step back, still clutching the howling baby, afraid. The intensity of the fury in the dark, wide open eyes was unsettling. In the next heartbeat the howling bundle was snatched from her hands so violently, she found herself wavering, struggling to maintain her balance.

The girl was murmuring something inaudible, rocking the baby in the crook of one arm, trying to wipe the other from the dripping meat juices. The moment she was done the screams faded into sobs, then just pitiful hiccups, with the small mouth busy sucking on the offered breast, its obviously favorite source of food and reassurance.

Ononta just stared, but as the busy gaze brushed past her, resting on her for a moment, holding a grudge, she stood it, glaring back, enraged. It was not her fault the baby had got to such a hysterical stage. His mother was the one who paid no attention to the poor thing's crying before.

"Why didn't you tell me?" Again too loud of an exclamation.

"What? I told you, I did! I kept telling you, but you paid no attention." She put her hands on her hips, a sharp movement that drew her accuser's gaze back toward her, its wariness increasing. "*Both of us* were trying to tell you, but you didn't listen!"

Suddenly the girl's eyes widened, losing a great deal of her aggressively practical self-assurance. A strangely frightened expression flooded in, reflected in a gaping mouth, in the round terrified eyes.

Another heartbeat of staring and Ononta's unexpected company was gone, fleeing down the river bank, her worn, probably once upon a time prettily decorated moccasins making much noise, her baby bursting into a new bout of howling.

Blinking, Ononta just stared.

CHAPTER 3

The breeze was annoying in its insistence, blowing mildly but adamantly, not about to stop. The scent of the Great Lake it brought might have been welcomed under different circumstances, but for their being on the wrong side of it.

Ashamed at yet another spasm twisting in his stomach, Atuye clenched his teeth, his hands clutching the club sweaty and slippery, clinging to the weapon he didn't happen to use as yet.

With a conscious effort he made his fingers relax their grip. Would he panic when the time to wield it came? *Oh, all the great and small uki, those who inhabit this enemy forest and those who remain back home, please, don't let it happen!*

To concentrate his gaze on the valley they were observing helped. It took his thoughts off the impending test of courage. Their leader did not wish to sneak up upon the women working these recently cleared patches of land, the reclaimed old fields and the new ones. His plan was better, more daring and intricate, a plan worthy of the veteran warrior that this man was.

Involuntarily, Atuye's gaze strayed, seeking the shaved pate adorned with the proud lock, braided tightly and decorated with colorful threads and a feather among the heads popping all over the thick vegetation. It was easy to decipher those sights, but not from the valley below, with the sun shining strongly from behind their hills, shielding and assisting.

Not a coincidence, that. Their leader was careful to explain his plan beforehand, including Father Sun's helpful location. Still, many things could go wrong, like clouds crawling to obscure the sky. Or a wandering local lucky to spot them and get away. But then, this was the part of their plan. Their leader did not wish to kill or kidnap enemy women. This time it was all about bringing the club down upon the unsuspecting enemy, killing the men who rushed out to defend their womenfolk, pell-mell and ill prepared. That was the plan. A good one, a well thought out strategy.

Atuye stifled a yawn, disregarding the mild pounding in his head. It was tiring, all this waiting. Even though he wasn't sure he had been ready for the next stage of the plan to develop. Fighting the enemy was one thing. He wished to do it, eager to prove his worth, to others and to himself. He was young but not that young. At eighteen summers he could have joined a few raids but for his traveling all over their people's lands, accompanying this or that delegation his father's most ardent follower and closest of companions, Honorable Tsineka, insisted on carrying out, despite Father's death. Or maybe because of it. The man was Father's sternest of supporters, as firm as a rock and as formidable, a good man, saddened by Father's death greatly but not broken into retirement. The great leader's work should be continued, maintained the old man, and it was their duty to make it happen, to excel in their efforts and make the vision of the Wyandot Union come true.

The claim Atuye agreed with wholeheartedly. Of course Father, now residing in the Sky World among the greatest of spirits, must be still anxious to see his lifetime desire come to exist, pursued as eagerly as by himself, with as much effort and keenness. His spirit would be happy then, satisfied, fulfilled, watching their people's union blossoming and bearing fruit.

Oh yes, it was a worthwhile ambition. It helped him, Atuye, to cope with Father's death too. Always busy, traveling, involved, no more than a youth of little years could have expected, but still involved. Honorable Tsineka came to rely on him and his good judgment, his readily extended assistance. The closed-mouthed man even got into the habit of airing his inner thoughts aloud when they were alone and in relative privacy, around this or that campfire, tired of their travels but not daunted, not defeated into admitting failure, never that. This is how Father always was, maintained the old man, steadfast, undaunted, dedicated, believing in hard work and no idleness.

Well, on that score Atuye could have testified as earnestly, having an example of his eldest half-brother dangling before his eyes when he was younger, a mere boy, surrounded by too many brothers, one half and one full, two violent things of almost the same age and temperament, wild in their disposition. No, Father tolerated no laziness, no inactivity, no leisure pastime, a standard not easy to live up to, but in this he had managed better than all his siblings put together, he knew, greatly pleased.

The verdict that was supported by everyone, sounded freely, from his doting mother, always around and swelling with pride, to the entire community of their town; to even Father himself on this last summer before his death, when this remarkable man had returned from the Great Gathering that had seen their towns and villages reaching good, firm agreements with the Cord People from the far north, the first bark sheet stuck between the first poles of the future union of all their people, all Wyandot nations, just as Father had desired.

Through the last span of Cold Moons that the Great Man had spent back in the town, they had talked about it ceaselessly, often deep into the nights, often while plodding through the snow, tracking a deer, or checking their winter snares, many, many trips that saw Father going out with only his youngest son for an escort, willing to talk, willing to listen. Such an unusual pleasure, but since his return from the Cord People's land the Great Man had changed oh so very greatly. Thinner and paler – had he been sick already back then? – but happier somehow, content in an unusual way, as though fulfilled, smiling more readily, as reserved as always but now approachable, the sadness in his eyes lurking then going away, replaced with a satisfied smile. Was he pleased by the achieved agreements to that extent? Was he afraid it wouldn't have happened?

No, it had to be something else, something different that changed Father, contributed to his calm and serenity, to his inner peace; something different that made the Great Leader wish to spend time with his family instead in endless conferring and councils. He was attending important meetings too, in their town and all around, but now he was taking him, Atuye, his youngest and most promising, along on his travels to those important meetings as well. This is why he had been present on that fateful meeting at the Deer People's main town.

He shuddered, then pushed the dreadful memory away. This and the nagging worry that while trying to do everything the way Father would have, he was now displeasing his spirit greatly. By sailing across the Great Sparkling Water and not as a part of a peaceful delegation, he was treading on one of Father's desires, the one to see the people from both sides of the Great Lake living in peace. Not a popular ambition, but Father deemed it important to insist upon while arguing against many.

Why?

The question nagged, but not overly so, and there was never a good time to ask that, even through the winter that was spent in such delightfully close proximity of Father and an atmosphere of true closeness with plenty of opportunities to talk. There were just too many more important, more relevant issues, and now it was too late, too late to find out why Father was adamantly against the war on the savages from the other side.

He pushed another wave of longing away. He was here now and that was that. And it's not that he might have felt strongly about the implacable enemy from the other side, like so many of his countryfolk did. He didn't care one way or another, but there was no one to raid these days, with the Deer People finally joining the union, the fence sitters that they were, still not so firm in their commitments, and the Rock People, the last of the Wyandot, beginning to send tentative messages with suggestions.

Even the Long Tails, weakened by their terrible defeat too greatly to be considered a threat, were not an enemy these days, so more and more warring parties sailed across the Great Lake, and there came a time when a young man was to prove his worth as a man and a warrior. He wasn't a coward, or timid, or indifferent, but people might decide that he was if he didn't raid this or that enemy, occasionally. He had seen enough summers, had been to enough hunting parties, had served as an escort for traveling elders as those visited all kind of towns and villages, located often in their former enemy's lands. Having been to his share of boyish mischief and violent exchanges, he never shied away from a brawl, never tried to avoid getting into one, even though he did not seek such confrontations actively, like some of his friends and peers did. There were boys and men who were on the constant look out for violent exchanges, like Sondakwa, the oldest of his full siblings, a close friend and protector, pleasant enough company but for his tendency to needle and his spectacular outbursts of temper, frequent enough to make people frown.

And there was that other son of their father, the eldest, the one who was not really their brother, or so Mother would claim; a son Father might have had by another woman some long, long time ago, before Mother, or maybe a boy he had just found and adopted once upon a time. No one knew a thing about this dubious half or step-brother's history or roots, with even the man in question being in the dark about any of it. A puzzling situation, but Father was just not the sort of a man to accost with idle questions on someone else's identity. He had three sons and a daughter, not all sired by the same woman he had shared his life with, and that was that. End of story. Even Ogteah, that same dubious first son himself, didn't dare to ask about any of that. A notorious lightweight, a drifter and a gambler, the troublesome man just didn't seem to care, shaming their family with wilder and wilder escapades. When he had finally left, unable to embarrass their town any further, it was a relief for all of them, the problematic man himself more than anyone, or so Atuye suspected. Mother certainly was happier when it happened. Sometimes he thought that she might have a special reason to resent the man so, reasons rooted in more than a personal experience at raising an unsatisfactory stepson.

A nudge in his ribs woke Atuye to the sunlit reality and his fellow warriors, crouching beside him, spreading along the forested hill. *Watch carefully,* the brief gesturing told him, the curt nod inviting him to concentrate on their target.

In the strengthening breeze the foliage shifted, revealing a better sight of rows upon rows of conical mounds, spreading as far as the eye could reach, spilling downhill. Fields, ready for planting. Or maybe already planted. It was difficult to tell. Just like back home.

He felt his stomach twisting uneasily. Father wished to live in peace with these people. He had worked hard to achieve this end, to have the projected Wyandot union maintaining a friendly relationship with the mighty league of the notorious neighbors from across the Great Lake. Not many agreed with him on this, but his strength and determination alone warranted attention, and people were in the habit of accepting his views anyway. But now Father was no more.

He pushed the new wave of misgivings away, turning to watch the renewed gesturing of the men responsible for their group, those who had volunteered or were assigned to their small unit of shooters, five men all in all, adept with their bows. He wanted to join the actual fighters, wishing to prove his worth with the club, in a good hand-to-hand skirmish, but his skill with the bow made his leader decide otherwise. They didn't listen to the wishes of a youth who had seen less than twenty summers as yet, a son of an important but dead leader or not.

Why did Father have to die so suddenly, so untimely? he had asked himself time after time, refusing to let the pain go. With no one remained to take his place, to wield enough power or clout to stop the escalating hostilities. After the downfall of the Long Tails, after the terrible battle when those brave warriors had perished by thousands and skies and rivers cried blood, oh after those terrible happenings, no one could remain neutral or indifferent. The Longhouse League must be stopped, must be brought down or back to what it has been. It was growing into a monster, a stone giant, and such a thing could not be allowed to happen.

And not that he disagreed with all those opinions, with people who were eager to wage war on the notorious league, still when invited to join this raid – a small, not very important sortie – he hesitated. It was a good opportunity to show himself and his valor, to learn and earn people's respect. Still, the doubts were there, nagging. Was he betraying Father's memory by doing this? There was so much yet to accomplish, so much to achieve, the agreements with the pushy Cord People still fresh, not rooted deeply enough, still needing nourishment and support, the agreements with the Deer tentative, with the Rock as yet non-existent. Father was working so hard to draw the Deer into the union, and then he just died, dropped cold and breathless, like a person that has been shot. But he wasn't. No arrow pierced his chest, no blow of a club cracked his skull, no poison brought his life powers to a halt. Honorable Tsineka, Father's closest of followers and friends, said it had something to do with his heart. The formidable warrior admitted that Father was having difficulties with it for some time, after strenuous efforts and travels, or when he was truly upset.

Oh, but he still remembered the shock, the stupefied bewilderment with which they all stared at them when they had brought the news back home, together with Father's body. How could it be? Mother had broken down and cried for so long they thought she might follow her husband on his Sky Journey, willingly and with her eyes open. She loved Father greatly, everyone knew it, even though she was angry with him many times, their years-long arguments saturated with strain and old grudges, short and vicious, because Father never bothered to prolong these. He would just say his piece and go out, unwilling to stay and face his enraged wife's passionate complaints, leaving him, Atuye, his youngest son and the favorite of his mother to be the recipient of her tirades and loudly expressed grievances.

Her husband never loved her, never appreciated her, she would sob; he was too busy for that, his work, his lifetime ambition left him no room for simple comforts, but at least he could have talked to her, could have asked for advice. Even the greatest leaders did this, listened to their women and talked to them. But not him. He had more important things to do than to love his woman or enjoy the family life she gave him. Stubbornness should have been his name, or at least a part of it, stubbornness and obtuseness. No wonder he was dead now, a man in his prime as yet, an elder but not truly an old man. If only he had listened to her more, had rested and paid more attention to his meals, enjoyed his family and let them take care of him.

Anxious to escape all those litanies, Atuye would caress his mother's arm, would say a few non-committal platitudes, would beat a hasty retreat whenever he could, leaving Ononta to comfort the desolate woman in the ways known only to females.

Ononta was the best girl ever, his friend since he could remember himself, a shadow of his, cute, funny, and always there. Until the end of the last Cold Moons, when her father had taken her along while visiting his relatives at the other side of the world, on the far end of the Great Sparkling Water.

What had gotten into the old man was anybody's guess, but the sudden itch to travel to the Rock People's towns had his, Atuye's, best friend taken from him, and at the worst of timing. Had Ononta been around, maybe she would have managed to talk him out of joining this raid. She would have used all the right arguments, he knew. She would have told him that Father's memory demanded his avoidance of such an enterprise, even if at the cost of a few raised eyebrows. They all knew he was no coward. He didn't have to prove it, even if his brother teased him on the matter of his lacking warring experience. Mother cried and said it was Sondakwa's fault that her youngest had joined the War Dance less than half a moon ago, against the tearfulness of her protestations.

"Something is wrong." The whisper brushed past his ear, just a gust of warm air.

He felt his heart coming to a halt. "What?"

His companion, a hardened, impressively scarred man from the Turtle Clan neighboring longhouse, motioned with his head, suggesting watching the fields.

"There is barely anyone out there."

Squinting against the glow of the strong morning sun, Atuye scanned the spreading hillside again. In this time of the seasons it was easy to see it all, without the high stalks of maize concealing the view of the conical fields and the women wandering around them, toiling to free the earth of unwanted growth.

Free to roam, his gaze caught quite a few pliant figures moving along, carrying baskets or flasks, wearing dresses or skirts, their hair piled high. An ordinary picture; like back home. But now, after his companion's remark, he noticed that indeed there were too few women down there, too little activity for this time of the planting season.

"What is happening?"

The man besides him just shrugged.

Stay here. The motion of their group's leader was unmistakable, his hand instructing them to keep quiet, his silhouette disappearing in the nearby bushes, twisting like a snake upon the wet ground.

Will they have to change their plans now? wondered Atuye, his skin crawling, covering with bumps, as though he was cold. Would they try to attack the village itself?

It was a fortified settlement, the leader of their expedition had explained before they had set off, crowding around their boats, impatient and ready, eager to plunge into the blue vastness. No small village and no wandering parties of hunters or women gathering forest fruit were their destination, not this time. This raid would be different, remarkable, outstanding, a blow that would harm the enemy more than simple incursions would. Their destination was an important enough settlement called Lone Hill in one of their foul-sounding tongues and it would suffer even if they didn't have enough warriors to try and storm its palisade walls. To lure its denizens out would be more than enough, all these men who were not busy out there, hunting or fishing, half a settlement at least in this part of the seasons, with only the women wandering about, planting their crops, unaware and unguarded.

"Why don't we just kidnap the women?" someone had asked, a young warrior, too impatient to wait for this aspect to be aired in its proper time.

A good-natured chuckling was the readily offered answer, but their leader chose not to explore the opportunity of making his wit known at the expense of youthful hotheads with no finesse.

"Because we are warring on men, not women. Kidnap your own bride in your free time." More smirking all around made the young man blush so deeply even the skin of his neck turned darker. "When their men will be running out, pell-mell, unorganized and ill-prepared, that's when we will achieve the results worthy of our traveling efforts."

A good plan, indeed, but for the unexpectedly small amount of women in the fields. Where did they all go? Were the enemy foxes that lazy as to not be in the fields in the middle of the day, and at the pressing planting time at that?

Squinting against the fierceness of the midday sun, he scanned the opposite hillside once again. Nothing. Or was there a movement, somewhere between the densely growing trees? Nearer to the top, yes. People were certainly moving there, between the thick vegetation. Quite a few, judging by the swaying of the foliage. Hunters? No, not likely. He would have never detected those on a hunting path, not so easily and from such distance.

He swallowed, his throat dry, hurting. Would this group be spoiling their surprise, or enhancing it? Carefully, he nudged the nearest man with his elbow, indicating the suspected hillside with a wave of his head. His companion narrowed his eyes, then signaled the others. In a short while another silent figure crawled away, aiming to reach the other part of their group.

What would Father have done now? wondered Atuye, his mouth dry, heart fluttering. He would have surely known what to do, wouldn't he? Even though Father did not lead warriors since before he could remember himself; still, before turning to the peaceful path of unification, he must have been leading raiding parties. He must. A man of Father's stature could not but do this. But Father did not want them warring with the people from the other side of the Great Lake, so maybe it wasn't wise to think about this great man just now.

The man who had gotten away before came back, bubbling with excitement. They would proceed according to the plan, his vigorous gesturing confirmed, the lack of women in the fields or the people spotted on the other side of the hill notwithstanding.

"Remember to scare them off and make them fuss and get away, some of them," he whispered, addressing everyone, breaking the silence for the first time. "Let some of them run back and bring the best of their men out. Those young foxes over there."

CHAPTER 4

"Help! Help! The warriors!"

The cries tore the crispiness of the high noon, making people stop in midstride, freeze with dreaded surprise.

"Down by the fields. Please! Please, hurry. Do something!"

Ogteah felt his heart coming to a halt, then throwing itself painfully against his ribcage, with much force. As he rushed toward the screams, oblivious of reason, the hurried steps of the Standing Stone man followed him, racing alongside, heavy and determined. It reassured him, made his head clear a little.

"Where?"

A small crowd was already pressing all around the panting girl, her face glowing red, glistening with a thick coat of perspiration, scratched and smeared with mud, her hair askew, eyes wide, terrified.

"Where?"

Before he knew it he was inside the crowding villagers, pushing his way in with little consideration, heedless of politeness. *No, not a raid, not on their fields!* His heart was thumping inside his chest, leaping insanely, as though trying to jump out for good. *Not, not that. Anything but that!*

Catching her sweaty shoulders in a supportive grip, or so he hoped, he turned the girl forcefully, making her face him.

"Tell me exactly what you saw!" He tried to soften his bark with as reasonable an expression as he could achieve, hard put not to shake her in order to make her information come out and fast.

"By the fields!" She was gasping for breath, having clearly raced all the way back to the town, her braids sticking wildly, eyes lacking in sanity. "Please, please, hurry! You need to hurry!"

More people came running, pressing from all sides. Ogteah used his shoulder to shove the most impatient away, sheltering her with his body, sensing her dread.

"Where exactly? Tell me!"

"The other, other side," she gasped. "The east. The lakeside. Quick. You must hurry. You must…"

"How many?" This came from his Standing Stone friend, a reassuring presence. The man's voice was encouragingly calm, as though talking about regular matters. "Quick. Go fetch your weapons and tell everyone you meet to do the same." These words addressed the surrounding people. "Be back here in a matter of heartbeats."

"I'll get everyone ready." Ogteah tried to force his mind into working, pushing the splashing wave of dread aside, eyes following the men who were already charging toward the fence, panicked beyond reasonable thinking, not even stopping to fetch their weaponry, let alone pausing to consult their fellow defenders, to coordinate their action. Everyone had a wife, a sister, a mother or a daughter out there, vulnerable, frightened, defenseless, under attack.

Oh Mighty Sprits, but for the gossiping neighbor from his own longhouse, eager to relate the story of yesterday's quarrel; *but for the knowledge that she was nowhere near the fields, not this morning…*

He drew such a long breath it made him dizzy. How to organize their men, those who didn't rush out on their own? How to make them calm down and listen? There were so many shouts and outcries all around, so many voices talking at once, yelling and screeching, such terrible clamor.

The girl, still clutched between his palms, was trembling badly, her eyes darting wildly, like those of a cornered animal. There was no way to release her without risking her falling. He pushed her toward the nearest man without any further questioning. She probably didn't even know, didn't stop to count. Not this one.

"Help her to the nearest woman you see."

Turning abruptly, he took in the surrounding faces, not a few pairs of eyes glancing at him with a measure of wild expectation.

Not an uncommon occurrence these days.

He tried to jolt his mind into working, the only coherent thought circling around his skull, surpassing any other – *she was in the woods, gathering berries, making her point against those of their clan council's members who were opposed to the Strawberry Ceremony being held earlier than usual. Oh all the great and small spirits, thank you for that!* And yet the woods were as exposed, as vulnerable for the raiding parties of enemies to attack.

"Get your weapons! Fetch anything you can lay your lands on in the next few heartbeats. We'll be off before a hundred of those could be counted."

In Lone Hill his reputation of a warrior with close connection to the leaders of High Springs and Onondaga Town went ahead of him since the Long Tails War, with his last summer's exploits at the Flint People's borders doing nothing to dispel it. His numerous friends and adherents from among the Flint and the Standing Stone People were very vocal, prone to traveling, visiting Lone Hill often, to remain there for days, enjoying pleasant evenings full of light bantering and games of luck he would organize and supervise, his name going ahead of him in this department as always.

The stories of exploits in the lands of either the rising or the setting sun were bountifully entertaining, with much laughter being made out of his way of leading people, of taking wildly unusual missions and making worthwhile undertakings out of those. Told by the night fire, his audience replete with food and tired of tossing stones or beans, such storytelling provided wonderful entertainment. On those nights even his fellow villagers would opt for sleeping in the open alongside their guests, ignoring the comforts of their own longhouses, to the direful frowns of their womenfolk. But not his woman. Burrowing her way into her longhouse's leading circles, now a busy mother and about to become a mother again, a member of many smaller councils, Gayeri tended to forget her duties at such times, joining his gatherings and enjoying them greatly.

Gayeri!

His chest squeezed in a new strangling grip. But no, she was not in the fields. They said there had been an argument; they said she had been among those who went to collect strawberries, against the better judgment of their clan's leading elements. Still out there, outside the safety of the village's palisade, dangerously exposed.

He remember passing it by only this morning, arriving in Lone Hill after a strenuous journey, a little more than a day to cover the distance between High Springs and his village, in indecent haste.

Angered by the altercation with the Wolf Man, by the unreasonable, unseemly demand and the open hostility at his, Ogteah's, refusal, he had left on the same noon, telling no one, boiling inside. It wasn't the wisest course of action, and not the politest one. He didn't say his farewells to the War Chief, let alone other important men, old friends and acquaintances that he didn't have a chance even to greet on the day of his arrival. A puzzling behavior, but he was out of patience, furious at the unreasonable request of the man he considered a friend and an ally.

To spy on his own people, former or not? Beyond acceptable. Even Father, who had sent him on a somewhat similar mission into this lands once upon a time, did not ask for something like that. Not outright spying. What a dishonorable demand!

So he had made his way back home, walking for the most part of the day and the night, boiling inside, his rage helped by the physical effort. There was nothing to think about and nothing to consider. He would not be pushed into this sort of shady acting. Not even by the people he liked and respected, good friends and talented leaders.

Awash with the strong high-morning sun, Lone Hill had greeted him with its usual liveliness, not as deserted as one would have expected the village to be at this time of the day and the season. Children darted all around, yelling at the top of their voices or laughing, popping onto pathways between the longhouses, then bolting away, free of discipline or clothes. Men who should be out there hunting or fishing strolled between the sprawling buildings, not in a hurry to be on their way.

"What's all the excitement?"

Narrowing his eyes against the group of rushing by

youngsters, Ogteah searched for the familiar mane of flowing hair and flying garments, easy to spot and pick out, his daughter's weakness for pretty clothing setting her apart in any flock of unclothed boys and girls.

"The faith-keepers began talking about having the Strawberry Ceremony earlier than ever this span of seasons." One of his fellow longhouse dwellers grinned, not hiding his own enthusiasm. "That set the fox among the waterfowl. Or rather fox among our local foxes. The various clan representatives' meetings spilled deep into the night."

"What were they arguing about?" Himself not opposed to one of his favorite ceremonies to be held earlier than usual, Ogteah grinned, feeling the warmth spreading, overcoming his tiredness. It was good to be home, away from duties, away from politics.

"Well, some claimed that the fields should be finished first. They had been late with the planting, even without hordes of our women storming out and into the forest, pillaging it of its fruit before finishing ensuring our village's future wellbeing."

"I see. So what did the faith-keepers say to that?"

His companion waved his hands in the air. "They kept out of the Clans Councils' squabbling, wise elders that they are."

He could not suppress a chuckle. "Wise men, indeed. I wonder what made them consider something like that in the first place. In High Springs no one talked of interrupting the field activities, not as far as I have heard. The Strawberry Moon's festivities don't require Grandmother Moon being at her roundest, do they?"

A shrug was his answer. "Who knows? If you keep asking such questions, you'll end up a faith-keeper yourself, brother." A pensive side glance measured Ogteah briefly. "Your visit in High Springs seemed to be rather short. It's been only a few dawns since you left."

This time, the shrug came with a certain effort. "If I had stayed I would have missed all the action here," he said lightly, narrowing his eyes in the direction of yet another babbling wave of squealing children that was spilling from behind the nearest longhouse's corner, threatening to turn into their direction. Older rascals, no three-summers-old lovers of pretty clothing among them.

"Our old War Chief isn't well, they say." The worried gaze was upon him, heavy with concern.

"Well, he hasn't been well some time after the Cold Moons, but he is recovering his strength now. There is no need to worry. This man will not be leaving us, not soon."

His companion nodded gravely. "This is, indeed, good news, brother. The War Chief has been with us since our Great League was born or maybe even before. It would be a sad day when the old leader decides to embark on his Sky Journey, sad for all our people."

"Yes, it would." The thought of the old man made Ogteah uneasy. It was a pleasure to spend his time in this remarkable person's company, the only pleasant time he had had on this last shortest visit of his. Oh, but it wasn't proper to leave in the way he did, with such abruptness, such speed.

"One of your Standing Stone fellow warriors arrived on the day before this one." His companion's voice came as a welcome distraction. "Or maybe it was on the day before that."

He didn't try to conceal his excitement. "Who was it? Ohkwali from Great Rapids?"

"Think so, yes. One of the Standing Stone toughs." The man's grin held all the mischief. "There are too many of them coming visiting you, claiming Great Rapids for their hometown. All those brothers and cousins."

"Oh yes, there are plenty of this family's representatives in our warrior forces. Last span of seasons, when we went to fight with the Flint in the east, third of the force I've been a part of seemed to be comprised of this or that Great Rapids cousin of the Wolf Clan. Well, not a third but fairly close to it and we were a group of three times ten warriors. Not just a few brutes." His smile widened. "He is still here, I trust."

A shrug was his answer. "Not sure about that. We didn't expect you to be back so soon and he was on his way to High Springs himself."

As his longhouse stood in the close proximity to the Wolf Clan's one, there was no need to change his direction. Trust the

Standing Stone leading brother not to turn around and scamper off the moment he heard of his, Ogteah's, absence. He would stay with his own clan members among the Onondagas, that one.

Ogteah grinned. Oh, but this man had turned out to be the best of companions, the most loyal of friends. They had learned to appreciate each other back through the Long Tails War, growing closer and closer ever since. The last raid against the Flint People's enemies had the Standing Stone horde of Great Rapids participating mainly because of this man. They didn't even make a secret out of it, all these Standing Stone toughs, because Ohkwali rarely accepted anyone's leadership, and when he did, so did the rest of this family, hot-tempered beasts and great warriors that they were.

"So the half-planted fields got neglected, did they?"

"Well, they can't do this, but yes, the Clans Councils held urgent meetings, each in its own fashion. With plenty of other females around and listening, contributing to the shrill arguments and claims." A smirk. "Well, I can attest for our longhouse personally. One couldn't help but hear all those raised voices and the semi-polite 'but sister, you don't understand the importance of' exclamations. You missed an entertaining evening." The conspiratorial gaze brushed past him, twinkling. "Your woman did not keep out of it, so you know. That one will end up in our Clan's Council, mark my words, man."

"Gayeri?" His smile turned impossible to suppress, the warm glow in his insides a welcome thing. "Oh yes, she'll make a good Clan Mother." The laughter erupted, regardless of his will in this matter. "And then I will be well set, brother. Better than anyone."

"That's what you think." His companion's outburst of mirth matched his in its loudness. "You think it will make your life easier, having such influential person for a woman. But I say, it will be just the other way around. A clan mother for a wife, with her eye on you constantly, expecting proper behavior? Hah! A free-spirited beast as yourself, with the trouble on the lookout for you every now and then..." An elbow thrust toward his ribs, deflected halfway. "I'm telling you, man, you will see yourself crying for mercy."

"Not me." Elbowing his companion in his turn, Ogteah squinted in the general direction of their longhouse, located not far away from the eastern edge of the double-row palisade. "So she went out there, plundering the woods this morning? Leading other rebels?"

"Not rebels, not according to them. Our Clan Mother was undecided, as was the neighboring Wolf Clan's leading woman. After all, the faith-keepers were the ones to suggest the forthcoming ceremony, earlier in the seasons or not." The man shielded his eyes against the melee around the next building's edge, with some children and women milling about, busy with preparations of food. "So before Father Sun had a chance of as much as peeking out from behind the eastern side of our palisade, a whole party of those who claimed that the ceremony should be held with the nearest full moon, even though the planting hasn't been finished as yet, spilled out and into the woods. With your pretty woman among these, yes; in the lead, one might say." The man shook his head, still chuckling. "Needless to mention, their opposition headed toward the fields, as showily or worse."

"And no one bothered to drag their children along to either location, I presume," muttered Ogteah, watching the hubbub near the covered façade as well, detecting the familiar flying garment, his heartbeat accelerating. "Who needs the little ones running all over when the war for female domination breaks out?"

"One may put it this way, yes." The man looked around, as though surprised. "And here I had been wondering what was so different this morning. The little rascals. Oh yes, they had definitely got left behind."

"Father!"

The high-pitched yell shook the air, followed by a colorful blur of movement that shot toward him, heading for an inevitable collusion. He caught the angular mess of her limbs deftly, lifting her off her feet and into the air, as light as a bird and as beautiful, the warm wave threatening to overtake him, like always when holding this most exquisite, most perfect creature, basking in her unshaken adoration, the purity of her love.

"And what you have to say for yourself, little rascal?" he

asked, holding her on one arm and away, in order to see the flushed little face better. It was covered with muddy stripes, smeared with something fresh and greenish, like war paint. "What have you been up to?"

She squirmed to make herself more comfortable, eyes glittering, darting whichever way, face shining brighter than the high morning sun. "Nothing!" More writhing of the small limbs. She was all dimples and soft curves, angular and round at the same time, an impossible combination and the one that made him melt inside. "Mother went out and she didn't take me. But she will bring me the sweetest, the juiciest berries. The strawberries! Yes, yes, she will." The small face puckered with indignation, reacting to his raised eyebrows most probably. "She promised. She said it would drip with juice and I will be all sticky."

"That you will be." He made her more comfortable in the crook of his arm. "I trust you to get as sticky as possible, smeared with juice, covered all over. Until someone may try to eat you by mistake."

The round eyes peered at him, full of suspicion. "Who?"

"I don't know. Someone who may think he just ran into an especially large strawberry. The sweetest strawberry of them all. Round and perfect, rolling all over Lone Hill. Talking in a squawky voice." He let his eyebrows arch suggestively. "Maybe me. I may be tempted to eat it. I may even do that now, even before…"

Her entire being was engaged at fighting his advance, the small palms pitted against his chin, pushing it away, her body shaking with giggles, her squeals deafening in their loudness. "No, no! You can't eat…"

He let her back away into her previous perch in the crook of his arm. "But I'm hungry. I just came home after running here all the way from High Springs."

"Great Aunt has food," she informed him, her hands still thrust forward, precluding another attack. "She was cooking just now. She made me eat porridge. She said Mother will be angry if I didn't. It didn't taste good, the porridge." The small nose wrinkled in the funniest of manners. "It wasn't sweet. Not even a little."

"No maple juice?" he asked, his own laughter impossible to conquer. "Not even a drop?"

"No!"

"Well, then we go back now and make sure to rectify the matter. How about that?"

The huge eyes stared at him blankly, lacking in understanding but trustful and expectant. He winked at her, turning toward their longhouse that was towering to their left, his obligations to see to the wellbeing of his possible guest that may be enjoying the Wolf Clan's hospitality at those very moments forgotten. She deserved a round of thoroughly sweetened porridge, didn't she? And he was not opposed to a bowl of the same delicacy as well. The journey back home was marked by no more than a few ready-to-pick treats the forest had generously offered at this time of seasons, unplanned and unexpected as it was. Consequently, his stomach was churning loudly, too loudly for his peace of mind.

"We'll make your Great Aunt fill our bowls to the brim," he promised her, helping her climb up and onto his shoulders, to perch there comfortably, at the top of the world. Which was her favorite seat to cruise around the town whenever he was within her reach. The little beast wouldn't settle for less.

"I don't want any more porridge. I ate a lot of it," she protested, clutching into his braid to stabilize herself. Refusing to shave parts of his skull like many warriors did, he conceded collecting it in a more appropriate fashion than his usually carelessly tied bun. In a battle it was a necessity, but somehow it began spilling into his regular life as well, affecting the carefree façade he was anxious to keep for reasons unknown even to himself.

"What you ate wasn't sweetened," he reasoned, turning to detour through the Wolf Clan's longhouse after all. The Standing Stone man was just the company he needed, he realized suddenly. A no-nonsense presence to discuss the general situation on both sides of the Great Lake, even if he wasn't about to share what had transpired in High Springs, maybe not even with Gayeri. She was concerned with his status among her people, ever worried that someone may nurture old suspicions of him or his loyalties, may turn against him. Was the Wolf Man now suspicious, mistrustful? He forced the new wave of irritation away.

"This time we'll make sure half of your bowl is full of maple. The same as the porridge, eh? How about that?"

The increased amount of wriggling and jumping around told him that his idea was received with enthusiasm. "Half a bowl? You'll make sure it's a full half?" He had a hard time making sure she didn't fall off. "Really, really full—"

"If you stop jumping around, trying to make us both fall flat on our behinds..." He squinted to see the people who were spilling from under the shadow of the Wolf Clan's façade.

"Father! You are going the wrong way!"

"I want to see if my friend who has been visiting here is still around." Slowing his step, he tilted his head, trying to look at her, his eyes doing no better than catching a glimpse of the dangling leg encased in a muddied moccasin, not many of its decorations still intact. "You do remember my friend, don't you? The Standing Stone man, the one with the scars and huge shoulders."

"Yes, yes," she was saying impatiently. "I remember. But you promised the bowl of maple. You promised and..." Her voice picked the tone he knew well, the one that bode no good for both of their tempers. She would always get an upper hand, using her tears as the most efficient of weaponry, better than the sharpest flint or lightest spear. Even so, such spells of indulgence gritted on his nerves.

"Stop mewling," he demanded, trying to win her goodwill back by the lightness of his amusement alone. "We'll meet my friend if he is still here, then go and get your over-sweetened porridge. We'll take him with us, eh? Do you remember if you saw him around yesterday and maybe even this morning?"

A stubborn silence was his answer, but as he lurched forward, pretending to shake her off her precarious perch, catching her at the last movement, her giggles shook the air and the pouting was gone, for good, or so he hoped.

"Did you see him around?"

She wriggled to break free from his grip, determined to reconquer her favorite seat at the top of the world.

"Did you?"

"Yes, yes. The bear man, he came, on the evening before, yes." Back on the top, she writhed some more, hurting his skull with her maneuvering, the little palms clutching his braid with merciless determination.

"The bear man?"

"Oh yes. His name means bear. Mother said so."

"Yes, it does." He shifted her to make it more comfortable for both of them. "In the Standing Stone People's tongue Ohkwali means Bear. Not so very different from our Onondaga tongue, eh?"

"Yes different," she claimed. "In our tongue it's Ohgwaih. It's different."

"Oh well."

To squeeze through the narrow opening under the sheltered façade with his proudly sitting cargo was not an easy fit, but as he began maneuvering himself in, the familiar booming voice called from behind, and in no time they were back out, strolling toward his own longhouse this time, enjoying their easy bantering, their friendship going back to the Long Tails War, to the times when he had been entrusted with leading his improvised group of troublemakers, sent on unusual missions, either disrupting the enemy movement while making sure the invading horde headed straight into the trap they had spread, or holding communication between their split forces while in the middle of the battle. He had barely made it alive out of this particular engagement, but this Standing Stone man was his main support ever since, helpful and always there, even though these days he was not under Ogteah's leadership anymore, entrusted with group of warriors of his own, his Standing Stone leading elements recognizing his potential at long last, despite the shortness of his temper and the wildness with which it sometimes would explode.

The death of his youngest of brothers back in the Long Tails War had hit this man hard, had killed something in him, damping the spectacular outbursts of temper, making them subdue. These days he, indeed, was calmer, more rational, but only on the surface. A state of mind Ogteah understood and accepted, more than this man's surviving siblings and the rest of his family and people did. Something the man in question evidently appreciated, giving back undivided friendship and loyalty, spiced with peppery advice and baiting remarks aplenty. The best of companies.

"What are you doing here in Lone Hill?" he had asked when the bulky figure eased itself beside him, acknowledging the passenger upon his shoulders with a conspiratorial wink.

"He came to eat strawberries," called out his daughter, dancing with excitement, her previous protests forgotten along with the promise of the over-sweetened porridge. "A whole basket of it. No, two baskets. Yes, that much! He said so himself!" The last words were shouted defensively, an answer to Ogteah's outburst of healthy laughter.

"The little woman is right," confirmed his companion. "I said it and I'm standing behind my words. I'm here for your Strawberry Ceremony. They say it will be held in just a few dawns from now. Because your woman wished it so."

It was difficult not to let his daughter slip off his shoulders while laughing so hard. "Is that so?"

"Oh yes. You missed a very loud evening, you wandering man." A smirk. "Your loss."

"So I keep hearing." He rolled his eyes. "Don't make me sorrier about the pointlessness of this last journey of mine than I already am. The visit to High Springs was a stupid waste of time."

The side glance he received was brief but unmistakable, the penetrating quality of it. "What happened?"

"Nothing. And that's the trouble. I traveled there for no better reason than to pass someone's time."

"Is our glorious Onondaga war leader that bored without a decent war on his hands?"

"Something like that."

Another contemplative glance. "Your neighbors from across the Sparkling Water will not let him die of boredom, not them. Or so one hears."

His daughter's dangling feet jumped with the abruptness of his shrug, a difficult business. "Maybe they will. Who knows?"

"The High Springs leaders, surely."

Ogteah just snorted, incensed at being drugged into this sort of discussion against his better judgment.

"I was on my way to High Springs myself, before I decided to detour by that lively village of yours, the one that is determined to enjoy their Strawberry Celebration earlier than anyone else in the land."

"Great Aunt!" yelled the girl as they rounded their longhouse's corner, spotting Gayeri's aunt thanks to her elevated position easily, agog with excitement. "Look, look, Father came home!"

Unsettled, Ogteah glanced at his companion in his turn, trying to read through the pretended lightness of his gaze. "What are you seeking in High Springs?"

An enigmatic grin was his answer. "Like you, I was summoned there." A light shrug. "Maybe someone up there in that hilly town needs to pass some time as well, the bored people that they are."

"Who sent for you? Okwaho?" Settling the ball of wriggling energy down, Ogteah watched his daughter absently as she shot toward the elderly woman, the rims of her decorated skirt flying high.

Why would the Wolf Man need to talk to one of the Standing Stone minor leaders, one of Ogteah's closer associates at that? What was he up to? And how was all this connected to this whole business with his former people and the trouble they were clearly about to make?

He wasn't sure he wanted to know, and yet now, facing the terrified refugee from the fields, whose hysterical howling shook the crisp high noon air, hushed away by the elderly women who came running from various longhouses as well, the growing commotion all around him threatening to burst into an unregulated mess, he had the sinking feeling that he was about to find it all out anyway. Those were his people who were attacking their fields, his former people. It could be no one but them.

"Be back here in less than a hundred heartbeats," he shouted, turning to race back toward his own longhouse in order to fetch his club, his favorite fighting weaponry these days, the Flint

People's prettily carved shaft, stored under the bunk, within an easy reach. "Just grab your weapons and run back here. We are leaving immediately, whether you come back here or not."

The stony fist clutching his stomach refused to loosen its grip as he burst through the dimly lit storage room, racing down the corridor, oblivious of fireplaces and various cooking facilities spread around many of these, not tripping over some piles by a miracle as it seemed.

"What is happening?" One of the men was sprawling in the neighboring compartment, blinking the sleep away.

"Grab your club and come," tossed out Ogteah, not bothering to even look in his direction, pushing a pile of baskets out of his way. It scattered over the floor, getting in his way worse than before. Trampling those with little care, he pulled the club out by its string, whirling to go as it dragged over the floor, crushing more baskets.

"What do you mean—"

"Just come!" This came as quite a roar that made several other people, two or three elderly women and a bunch of children, go still somewhere down the corridor. Briefly, he wondered if his daughter was still around the house, hopefully looked after by Gayeri's aunt.

Gayeri!

The sun assaulted his eyes as he burst back into the outside, pleased to see more armed people spilling out of other entrances and allies, joining his race, more than a few. Even if not in the fields, Gayeri was out there, unprotected, dangerously exposed. And what if not all the attackers were concentrated in one place? The cold wave threatened to take him, to wipe the last of his sanity away, to make him charge blindly, with no preparation or thought. No, no, she can't be allowed to fall into the enemy's hands, not again. Anything but that! She won't survive it, not her. Not another captivity. If he wasn't in time to stop that from happening, she would deal with it in the only way she could, by taking her life before it happened. She would do it, he knew. Just a mere chance of the old nightmare and its recurrence...

He heard his teeth screeching loudly, the ugliest of sounds. Oh, but he needed to be there *now*, not in another many heartbeats, too long, all this time that would take even the fastest of runners to reach the fields. No, he needed to be there now!

Ohkwali was standing by the inner palisade's opening, talking urgently, gesturing, directing people to pick their weaponry probably, the wandering newcomers. His own prettily decorated club was already there, clutched in his broad palm, belonging. Rare were the instances when it managed to leave its owner's vicinity, even when inside friendly towns or longhouses.

Ogteah gestured the people who were already there and ready. "We'll head out now, let the others catch up with us when they come." He forced his concentration back to his friend. "Stay to organize the rest of them, will you? Follow us the moment you can, when enough of the newcomers are ready. When you have, say, close to twenty or thirty men."

The narrow gaze held his. "We should go out together. It'll be wiser to do that. There is no telling what the enemy might have planned with this outright attack. Maybe they want you to rush out pell-mell, blind with fury or panicked." The flinty eyes narrowed some more. "It won't take long to wait for the rest of your people, those whom you sent to fetch their weapons in the first place. Why rush out with barely twenty men and no plan?"

Ogteah took a deep breath, then exhaled loudly, shutting his eyes for a moment, frustrated beyond reason. The Standing Stone man was right, of course he was right.

"It's better this way," he said, turning to race along the twisted corridor the double row of palisade created. The most efficient way to slow down any invader, but now it was slowing him and his men down as well, the defenders that were needed out there in the fields. "We'll fall on them with little force. That will take their attention off the fields and the women, while also serve to put them at ease, assuming that it is all that we have. Then your reinforcements will come, catching them off guard and for good." He clenched his teeth against the climbing eyebrows of his converser, against yet again narrowing eyes. "The girl said it's on the lake side of the hill. There is a shorter way to get there. Have our people guide you until you reach us."

The heavy palm arrested his progress, grabbing his elbow so suddenly it made him sway.

"Wait, brother. Just wait. It will take a little time to organize all our men. Let us go out together. They are already there, in the fields, according to the girl. But they will not get away with the women they might manage to kidnap. We'll catch them before they as much as reach the shores of the Sparkling Water. There is no need to rush blindly, straight into their trap, maybe. Think about it."

Wrenching his hand away, Ogteah heard the screeching of his teeth once again. Yes, of course it was the better way, of course. But it didn't matter how far the shores of the Great Lake were or how removed from these people's canoes, how impossible it might be for them to get away with their spoils without being apprehended.

It didn't matter, because he could not afford any kidnapping, not even for the shortest span of time, not even for a fraction of a heartbeat. By the time he would catch up with the enemy it would be too late, too late for her and her sanity.

"Just do what I asked you to do," he breathed, beginning to race along the towering poles, glad that it enabled him to avoid meeting his friend's eyes. "I need your help in this. Please!"

He didn't look back to make sure if he was followed.

CHAPTER 5

As though eager to prove their leader right, the locals didn't make them wait before beginning to pour out in quite an ill-organized horde, maybe twenty or so men, running down the hill, in no sort of an order. The cries and screams of the trapped field workers did not have enough chance to spread into the nearby forests as yet, but here they were, the frantic defenders.

His heart fluttering strangely in his chest, Atuye held his bow firm in his hands, pleased to see it poised steadily, not trembling or dancing as he was afraid it might. The effort not to move or lose his aim was challenging. For how much longer?

Not yet, signaled their group leader, his gesturing hand barely moving the air. *When they reach the open patch of the earth, behind that cluster of trees down there. Wait for the signal.*

He followed the running figures with his gaze, difficult to make out their forms in the glow of the high-noon sun. How many?

He tried to count the ones he had managed to glimpse so far. Six? Seven? Which meant that there must be twice as many men out there, probably more. Close to twenty? As frantic and disorganized as their leader wished them to be? He hoped that that was the case. Their own warriors down by the fields numbered about twenty-five men, with their ambushing bowmen group destined to joined the fighters after discharging all their arrows. Not a bad plan, but for the enemy turning out not as confused, not as ill-prepared, as expected.

The yells and screams from the fields were persistent, enhanced by the volume of noise the attackers were making, all those bloodcurdling shrieks and war-cries. Considerable attempts were made to make the defenders hurry, preferably while losing the last of their clear thinking in the process.

Atuye pushed the involuntary grin back. It was not the time to reflect on their leader's wise planning. Later, after besting the enemy, after he had proven himself a warrior and a worthy son of his great father.

"Now!"

The low hiss made him almost jump out of his skin, his hand tearing at the bowstring, reacting as though of its own volition, eyes straining to locate the target. The running figures reached the open strip of land and were rolling down the hill, obvious in their desperate hurry to reach the assaulted women. He could see their lack of proper attire, their loosely tied, flowing hair, their clubs, bows or spears – bows for such a fights? – running in spectacular disarray. No warrior force. Good!

It was hard to tell if his first shot took anyone down, or if the other arrows did this. He didn't spend more than a heartbeat on the attempt to determine that. The next arrow found its way into his shooting device with an admirable swiftness. Another hiss, a light recoil. He groped for the next pair of missiles, then allowed himself a quick look.

The running men were still there, still running. Or maybe just milling around. A likelier possibility. He could see them darting whichever way, with no visible purpose, waving their hands and shouting. Oh yes, it must have been their yelling that joined the cacophony down below. Was it time for his group to join the fighting as well?

He discharged the next two arrows, their feathering a brilliant blue intermingled with yellow, catching his eye momentarily, pleasing it. He had invested much in his weaponry just before leaving, between the War Dance and while the preparations for the raid were at their highest. Even on the way here, between endless rowing and pitching camps, there was plenty of time to improve, polish and groom whatever needed to be improved or attended to. How much of the brilliant blue and yellow would be adorning the enemy's bodies? He hoped much.

"Keep shooting!" The leader didn't bother to keep his voice low, not anymore. "We'll be charging soon, but not before all your arrows are down there, fluttering at the enemy."

Of course! Atuye groped for the next pair.

Upon the clearing the enemy was doing not as badly as one might have wished them to. Even his inexperienced eye could see the way the darting silhouettes were regrouping, in no desirable disorder, diving under the coverage of the available shrubbery, running low and in zigzags, making difficult targets.

A tall man was waving his club, pointing whichever way, clearly using his weapon to direct people. Shouting too, most probably. Protected by the foliage of a wide-branched tree and the way he darted everywhere, without halting for more than a heartbeat, this one made a challenging target. Still the man's way of straightened up racing, waving his club to get the attention of the people he was directing, singled him out, made the arrows draw toward him, more than a few.

Atuye let his quiver drop with the last pair of arrows out and ready. To take the leader this time. Oh yes, it would be a worthwhile shot. The man with the club would bring him fame, or at least enough respect of his townsfolk for the young aspiring warrior that he was. A worthy son of his father. By taking the prominent enemy down, he would make the rest of this group lose their presence of mind, something the leaders like the man with the club were clearly determined not to let happen; and just as their warriors in the fields were about to fall upon the defenders now, to finish what the arrows had started, to add to the confusion, to disorient the enemy for good, to take captives and not only their lives. Their return home would be spectacular, adorned with achievements.

Taking his time, he followed the reappearing figure with his gaze, the man running low, balancing his weaponry. His destination was obvious, a group of silhouettes crouching behind the long row of bushes. The abrupt gesturing of the club made some of the shadows melt away. Only a few stayed, taking care of the wounded maybe. Oh yes, not everyone down there crouched or squatted. There were some who sprawled or moved strangely, jerking with their limbs.

Atuye pulled the bowstring to its fullest, ignoring the opportunity to shoot one of the shadows as it slunk straight into his aim. Not this one. The man with the club, where was he?

"Come!" Even the voice of their leader, rasping with impatience, had no power to make him move. "All of you, run down there. It's time!"

No, it wasn't. He held his breath, watching the club-wielding man leaving the bushes and the remaining silhouettes still crouching behind those, rushing into the open again, heading for the opposite cluster of trees.

There must be more people huddling there, judging by his urgent gesturing, decided Atuye, forcing his eyes off his prey momentarily, to make a quick calculation. Even if running low and in zigzags, the man's destination was obvious. And so was his path.

He released the first arrow at once, aiming a few paces ahead of the running figure, the hurried footsteps of his fellow ambushers rushing past him, distracting him. The silhouette of the club wavered, tossed sideways. Did the man dart aside, or had he been thrown this way because he might have been hit? His second, last, arrow pounced toward the actual target this time and not its projected destination, but the figure was moving again, throwing himself in the opposite direction, half rolling half scampering into the cover of the meager vegetation a few paces away, not his original destination. Oh, but for another pair of arrows!

The sounds of his companions' retreat were already dying away, even though they didn't bother to keep quiet. Not anymore. Their charge down the hill needn't be a concealed affair; not after the effectiveness of their ambush. The enemy would be disrupted enough now, disoriented, at a loss.

Tucking the bow behind his back, Atuye picked up his quiver, regretting again his lack of additional ammunition. The man with the club might not have gotten away that easily but for another pair of arrows. Or maybe he didn't get away, maybe he was wounded after all, at least that.

The last glance at the clearing told him that it was abandoned now, with the wounded safely hiding and the defenders spilling down and into the fields, more confused than before, or so he hoped.

Time to catch up with his peers. Hastening his step, he hurried in the direction their voices disappeared a short time ago, resenting the idea of being alone and left behind. These woods were not his woods, and the Longhouse People were fierce enterprising enemies. Father always—

The suspicious movement caught his eye when he momentarily emerged from the thickest of the grove, running low, perturbed by the brilliance of the sunlight pouring over this more exposed part of the descent. A passing glance at the opposite hill had him stopping dead on his tracks. Dropping behind the meager protection of thinly spread bushes, he peered at the curve of the forested shelf, desperate to see again, to catch the movement.

Oh, yes, it was there. Just a fleeting blurry motion but there. One more, then another. People were rushing down the opposite hill, passing the exposed side of it hurriedly, running low.

He counted the muffled forms. Five, six. No, close to ten, probably more. A group of warriors, unmistakably, heading in the direction of the fighting. Doing it carefully, by stealth. Straining his eyes, he watched them for another heartbeat, waiting for more blurry silhouettes to reappear from behind the swaying foliage.

The next thing he knew, he was racing, oblivious of the hurdles and obstacles, roots and stones and moss-covered rocks, leaping over those, risking a fall, indifferent to this possibility.

His people, they needed to be warned! The enemy at the fields was to be reinforced, and by a new force of warriors, men who knew what they were doing, bent on surprising the attackers this time, on trapping them maybe...

Oh, but his people needed to be warned!

CHAPTER 6

"What do you want me to do in the lands of my former people?"

The last of the light was lurking upon the ground, slinking playfully, seeping through the dense foliage, coloring it in a spotted pattern. In this time of the seasons, the evenings already turned into most pleasant affairs, warm and temperate, the soft touch of the breeze brushing against one's skin, caressing it.

Ogteah felt none of it, too tired, his senses numb. Even the obviously cold, reserved demeanor of the Wolf Man, who now walked beside him in his usual wide, forceful stride, sure of himself but lacking the easy friendliness that had characterized their relationship so far, did nothing to alleviate his apathy. He just didn't care. It didn't matter if this man, already an important leading warrior despite his relatively young age, such an influential person since the Long Tails War, suspected him, Ogteah, of divided loyalties, or any other possible sin; it didn't matter that so far he had cherished this man's and his family's friendship, prizing it very high, flattered by it. Even the fact that he was about to comply with the shameful request of outright spying on his former people didn't mean a thing anymore.

What mattered was what had happened three dawns ago. No, four dawns by now. The disaster, the debacle that should never be allowed to happen again, never, not with his woman, his daughter and his yet-unborn child living so close to the Great Sparkling Water. By whatever means, such an attack should be prevented long before it actually started to happen. That's what had brought him here to High Springs, just a few dawns following the assault, traveling on foot and with barely any rest, nearly running most of the way.

Even his Standing Stone companion was made to complain on this account, difficult to keep up. They had been tired, exhausted really, sustaining various flesh wounds, bruises and cuts. They deserved a good rest and caring attention the distraught, grief-stricken village was eager to inflict on the heroes who had fought so fiercely, with no regard to their own lives, saving many. But not everyone. Two women were lost, probably kidnapped; two more got killed along with four defenders and three others dying from their wounds later through that terrible day, with the rest hurt to a greater or lesser degree, injured, shocked. An attack of such magnitude hadn't happened for a long time, even to a borderland settlement like Lone Hill. Not since the Great Peace was created. Small incursions, yes, occasional raids, like the one when Gayeri was kidnapped, but not an outright, well organized assault that was obviously planned to have the remaining men lured out into an uneven battle, ill-organized and ill-prepared.

Something that the enemy had no difficulty achieving, reflected Ogteah darkly, rethinking the happenings over and over when back in the village or upon his journey to High Springs, unable to concentrate on anything else. Neither the chanting by various funeral platforms, nor the agitated chatter of distraught, grieving people, not even his own cuts and bruises, taken care of by Gayeri who had to almost force him into accepting the treatment, helped; not even the fact that she was all right, physically unharmed, unscathed, having, indeed, missed the whole thing by being away with the other women, those who insisted on gathering strawberries for the ceremonies.

It didn't help. She *could* have been there, killed, hurt, kidnapped, reliving the nightmare. *It could have happened*.

And it could happen again, any time the enemy embarked on another crossing, another raid, another attempt to harm and kill and kidnap and lay waste. And then he would again make all the mistakes, lead people out with no plan and no strategy, blind with worry for her and her safety, or that of his daughter, not thinking as a leading man should. But for Ohkwali and his presence of mind, his lucid thinking, his collected behavior and ability to organize the rest of the villagers, to hurry them out in a proper way, with no panicked fits and no rushed decisions, oh but for the Standing Stone man's helpfulness, it would have been bad. His, Ogteah's, frenzied lashing out did little save adding to the chaos, even though after being ambushed by the arrows on that stupid first clearing, he did manage to organize his men, to retreat carefully and withstand the attack of the remaining invaders before launching an offensive of their own, having received a word of the approaching Ohkwali by then.

Something that his fellow villagers of Lone Hill appreciated and admired, with the Town Council commending his way of organizing their people so quickly, of leading the first wave of the defenders out and saving the women in the fields from the worst of fates. People kept praising him and thanking him, but it didn't matter. He didn't want to talk about any of it, or listen to their words of gratitude and appreciation. He knew they were wrong.

Grinding his teeth, he pushed the choking wave of frustration away. He would solve this problem, but differently. The Wolf Man was right. They needed to know the enemy's plans and moves before making their own.

"What do you mean?" His companion slowed his step and was staring at him, genially surprised, or so it seemed.

"Just what I said." Not amused as he might have been under different circumstances, succumbing to no temptation of making smart remarks, Ogteah stood the incredulous gaze, his own unblinking. "You wanted me to go and spy on my former people. I will do it, but I need to know more. What exactly do you want of me out there? In detail. What precisely do you want me to learn about? From what places? They are scattered quite far and wide, as you must know, from the Long Tails or their Attiwandaronk neighbors all the way to the Freshwater Sea in the north, not to mention the other side of the Sparkling Water, the one that faces us." He pressed his lips. "Due to my past, I can't show my face in quite a few places. Actually the important towns and people will be out of my reach."

With the startled surprise gone, the large eyes of his companion narrowed, measuring him in a businesslike manner.

"What's about those important towns or peoples? What places you can't visit?"

"The Cord People, for one." He knew his gaze might be radiating an outright hostility, but he couldn't help it. It was just too much. The culmination of the terrible strain of the last few dawns, this conversation brought memories he didn't wish to remember or face. "I can't go to any of their major settlements unless you don't want me to report back." Taking a deep breath, he tried to force his anger away. "Then, of course there are the towns of my actual former people, the Bear People. I can't stroll into most of those as well, surely not the town where my father lived." His shoulders proved somewhat heavy to lift, a shrug coming with difficulty. "It actually leaves two of the most important peoples out of your spy's reach. But that's the most I can offer."

His companion's eyes were as narrow as slits in the broadness of his face. "The Cord People are the ones who live up there in the north, besides another Great Water?"

"Yes, they are. They inhabit the northern forests, beyond Beautiful Lake, all the way up to the Freshwater Sea. Which is a huge chunk of water, larger than our Sparkling Lake, or so they say." This time, a shrug proved easier. "In case you haven't heard, I've left a lasting impression all around these places, not a favorable one."

"I've heard about that." A hint of a grin tagged at the corners of the pressed mouth, bringing life into the stony intensity. "My brother returned home full of stories on that particular summer."

Ogteah felt his own lips quivering, if only a little. "I'm sure he did."

The silence prevailed, interrupted by the sounds of the forest busy preparing for the night.

"I understand why you are suddenly willing to do this, and I'm sorry it came to pass through such a terrible event. The people of your village, those who died at the attack, their spirits will not dwell in the Sky World restless and unavenged." The Wolf Man resumed his walk, heading for the nearby clearing apparently, the stumps of cut-down old trees dotting it aplenty, offering comfortable seats. "I wish that this filthy raid hadn't happened. I wish there was a way to avoid us warring with your former people. A son of my father, I honestly would do much to avoid that." He shook his head. "The trouble is that the other side seems to be determined to have it their way, the warring way. Your father did everything in his power to prevent that, but he is not with us now. Regretfully so." The eyes resting on Ogteah were not distant or sealed, not anymore. "I understand your misgivings and I respect you for that even more. You have much courage, Wyandot man, much conviction. I'm sorry that you found yourself in such a situation, but I must admit that I'm glad that the Great Spirits made you settle on our side of the Great Sparkling Water. Your former people are poorer now, not having you among their warriors and leaders."

To take his gaze away became a necessity. He watched the deepening shadows the trees around were turning into. "They may not have been sharing this sentiment of yours."

"More foolish of them." This time, the pause was comfortable, encouragingly light. "They make many mistakes, those people from across the Great Lake. Too many for their own good, sometimes. Mistakes of strategy, mistakes of judgment; mistakes of underestimating people or alliances. They made even the Great Peacemaker leave, move to our side of the Great Lake, speak to our people. You are not in such a bad company on that score, come to think of it, eh? Following the Great Messenger's example, why would you be complaining?"

This time, he couldn't help it. "The Great Peacemaker, eh? You *are* desperate to have my cooperation."

"I can use you, yes," agreed the man, unabashed. "You are an asset, when used correctly. That was the trouble with your former people. They didn't use you in the right way, if at all."

"Don't push it."

A good-natured chuckle was his answer. Then the smirking expression disappeared all at once.

"I want to know how would you go about it, learning of your former people's situation, their intentions, their plans. You said you can't show your face in certain places and towns. Well, where do you think you can show up without arousing suspicion? Among what peoples?"

"Rock People would be the surest location to have no one asking questions. But I'm not certain as to their usefulness. They may not be even a part of the Wyandot alliance at all." Perching upon another vacant seat, a stump comfortably wide, padded with plenty of moss and fallen leafs, Ogteah sighed, letting the air out loudly, clasping his lips. "The Deer People would be the next choice. Those were always closer to the happenings, more involved. They even sent a delegation, a small group to sniff around that Great Gathering my father had organized among the Bear and the Cord People." He pushed the new wave of unwelcome memories away, irritated but not deeply. The Deer People weren't that bad, fishing Gayeri and him out of the river, bringing them to their destination in relative comfort. This was not such a bad recollection but for the events that followed. "I suppose it would be more logical to start with the Deer, yes. They must be a solid part of that union by now. Father made tremendous efforts to make them join."

The Wolf Man pursed his lips. "Actually, it's the Rock People that interest me. They are the ones who took to our defeated enemy, or so one hears."

"What do you mean?"

The rugged, decidedly handsome face was again nothing but a mask chiseled out of hard wood. "They are extending their support to the Long Tails quite openly these days. Keeping close contacts after taking their refugees during the last summer's raids. They had been supporting both Long Tails and Attiwandaronk in various ways, making no secret out of it." The pursed lips pressed tighter. "And what I want to know is this – are they doing this on their own and for their private purposes, stirring trouble, declaring themselves? Or do they act as a part of the Wyandot union, with their entire alliance standing behind this outright provocation, sanctioning it?"

"I see."

Now it was Ogteah's turn to stare. Oh, but he didn't expect this. Again the Wolf Man was displaying more grasp, more understanding than one would expect from such a spectacular looking warrior. Or was it he who was thinking too simply? While asking for clarifications, demanding to specify his mission, to define it more precisely, he didn't count on such detailing. To spy on the enemy in order to learn of their inner dealings; yes, it made sense. But the Wolf Man was better prepared than this, gathering information of evidently various sources, not about to rely on a lonely spy among those, keeping an eye on the Long Tails, the defeated enemy, wishing to know who kept aiding them and why; who had the interest to see them recovering.

Oh, yes, if the Rock People supported the Great League's enemies, openly at that, then it was essential to learn if they did so on their own or as a part of a bigger menace. Quite essential, one might say.

"You have your spies all around, I see," he said lightly, taking his eyes away. "Well, yes, I do see what you mean. If I spent some time among these people I might be able to answer those questions." He began warming to the idea. Rock People were so removed from everyone, so apart and aloof. It would be easy to travel through their towns without arousing even a ripple of suspicion. He would be back home before he knew it.

"Yes, we need to know if they are acting on their own or with the official consent of the Wyandot union, if they are about to become a part of it."

"Well, it shouldn't be difficult to find out. A moon of wandering around their settlements should supply us with all the knowledge we need." Unable to keep still, Ogteah jumped to his feet, suddenly excited by the prospect. "I'll pose as a Bear People's man, but a respectable person this time, a man who has traveled to trade some goods, not a gambler or drifter, or just someone out to have a good time. The bean games worked with the youngsters we wanted to enlist for our Long Tails War, but this time I'd better mix with more respectable folk, those who love to rub their shoulders with dignitaries and elders." Picking a pinecone, he hurled it into the deepening shadows, watching it disappearing, swallowed by the darkness. "Yes, someone out to trade nice-looking things. A perfect excuse for traveling far without committing the crime of wandering, angering watchful clan mothers and such. Will you give me a few pretty trinkets, clothing or jewelry to take along? I'll say I got those from this or that raid on you, the savages."

"You can have every trinket you desire. I'll make sure to load you with every silly object that catches your eye." The Wolf Man's eyes were crinkling, but their expression held a healthy amount of wondering doubt. "You are getting all excited, brother. Too excited, if you ask me. It won't be as simple as our unauthorized gathering of warriors. Or as harmless." The narrowed eyes held his, unusually open, sincere, relaying a message. "You'll be putting yourself in grave danger. Should something go wrong, should someone recognize you or divulge your true purpose, you will be as good as dead before you manage to say 'great sparkling water.' Your life won't be worth a piece of a broken pottery kettle. You realize that, don't you?"

A gust of wind came from the nearby hill, rustling in the dark treetops, grim and foreboding. Ogteah swallowed, aware of the knot that was tightening in his stomach, pressing with sudden force, the sheen of perspiration covering his back, not helping against the wind.

His companion straightened abruptly, before that nothing but relaxed upon his perch, knees wide apart, elbows propped upon those, chin resting on the folded fists. But not anymore. Now the spectacular warrior's pose reminded Ogteah of the animal tattooed upon the man's cheek, a wolf, a dangerous, mature, unarguably lethal specimen, listening alertly, ready to pounce, to attack the danger if not to avoid it.

"Did you feel it too?"

He pushed the new wave of fear away. "No," he said firmly, aware that his jaw might crack from the force with which he was clenching it. "I feel nothing and there is no special danger in what I propose, *what you want me to do.* Any raid, even the smallest one, holds more danger. These days I'm in the position to attest to it, am I not?"

The Wolf Man rolled his eyes, getting to his feet in one forceful movement, beyond any bad feelings or in similar denial.

"Just be careful. Don't turn too confident or smug wandering out there. Engage in bowl games, ask questions. Enjoy yourself. But not too much. Before another full moon has thinned, I want you back here, ready to do work for me. Like that new warriors' gathering, eh? No one does it better than you, especially now that you made yourself quite a name out there in the east." A broad palm landed upon Ogteah's shoulder with a resounding thud, relating much affection. "Your exploits among the Flint People did not go unnoticed here, so you know. And they say that in that shameless attack on your village you organized and led the men out in a blink of an eye, quick enough to prevent the enemy from kidnapping your women or hurting them otherwise. The Standing Stone man was full of praise, spreading the stories about you all over High Springs, since you both arrived here."

This time his mood did not deteriorate as quickly or as determinedly. "Ohkwali is exaggerating. He was the one to save the situation from turning into an absolute disaster." Surprised with the lack of this previously frustrated anger of his, he shrugged. "I rushed them out without much thought. Presumed the enemy was busy assaulting the women, trying to kidnap them before we came. Which turned out to be nothing but a ruse. They wanted us to think that, and what I did, played into their hands." The familiar splash of anger hovered near now. He let the air out through his nose. "Ohkwali was the one to approach the enemy with a measure of reasonable thinking, taking his time to check their whereabouts before rushing out." He shrugged again. "They weren't as surprised as expected, he said, but at least it gave us the opportunity to foil their plans."

The Wolf Man was watching him closely. "Your woman, she didn't get hurt, did she?"

"No."

"Good." The man nodded, eyes still on Ogteah, studying him thoughtfully. "You had a good reason to rush out. The Standing Stone man was in a different position. He could afford the luxury of thinking before charging. He had no family members out there, under attack and in danger."

His jaw tightened so painfully, he thought his facial muscles would get cramped. "My reasons did not help the man who got impaled by the arrow in the ambush I led our people into. His wife, mother, his sons, they are mourning and lamenting, and my reasons to rush out do not lessen their pain. Nor does it help the other wounded, those who absorbed more arrows."

"No, it doesn't." The young leader's lips were pressed very tightly, an invisible line, his eyes resting on Ogteah, dark with intensity. "But neither does your beating yourself up over this or that hastily taken decision. I've led plenty of raids over the Mountain People's Genesee River the last spans of seasons, let alone through the summers since I became a warrior. We warred together in their great battle three summers ago. Do you think I never regretted taking this or that decision? Do you think I never felt bad over people who died under my leadership? Think about Akweks, for all great and small spirits' sake! I should have been there for both of you, but I wasn't. Do you think I never wanted to beat myself up over this? My brother was there to save your life, while you did everything to save Akweks'. And where was I? Busy elsewhere." The forceful gaze was burning fiercely, violent, agonizing. "Do you think it doesn't pain me, doesn't make me wish to scream and curse, to do something wild? *To hold myself accountable!* Oh, how bad this feeling gets sometimes." He watched the wide shoulders lifting in a shrug, the pursed lips twisting slightly, in a resemblance of a crooked mirthless grin. "Where do you think I would be if I let such thoughts enter my mind? Not leading our people, surely; not helping to keep our Great League powerful and safe. The quivering ball of nerves and frustration I would turn into would be of no help to any of that."

A resolute shake of the proud head seemed to make the unwelcome thoughts go away. The eyes peering at Ogteah were still dark, but calmer now, determined and serene.

"Take it out of your mind as well. It's not helping, this line of thought. If you think you acted recklessly, heed it as a lesson. Do it better next time, plan your moves more wisely. That is all there is to it. No need to beat yourself up over the things you can't change. People think you did well in this last fighting and that is what should matter to you now." This time, the generous lips were twisting into an inverted sort of a grin. "I know how your mind is working. You like finding fault with yourself. You do it a lot. My brother noticed that about you. But it isn't helping, neither you nor any of us, or your family, or your current people. So get rid of this tendency. Do what needs to be done and stop mulling over things that could have been done better. You kept your clan, your village, your woman and child safe, and that is all that matters. You did well."

Ogteah watched the powerful shoulders lifting again, the corners of the full mouth going downwards, widening the inverted grin, flickering with an unapologetic admittance, taking the awkwardness of the unasked-for advice away. *Stop being such a whiny coyote*, the twisting lips suggested. *We've got more important things to attend to.*

And that was that, he decided, shaking his head as tellingly, his own grin sneaking out, as crooked and as poignant. No need to argue, justify or explain, to claim that it was not what he felt or thought, that this man, his junior in years but not in status, didn't see through him in most embarrassing of manners.

Oh yes, he did, apparently quite clearly. Understanding him, Ogteah, maybe better than he himself did. And yet, it didn't hurt his pride for some reason, didn't make him wish to argue, to tell the tender of the unasked-for advice to go and jump off the nearest cliff.

Why? He didn't quite know as yet, but it didn't matter. The fact remained that the man might have been right, that his inner qualms and misgivings were immaterial, irrelevant, unimportant, that they *did* have more important matters to attend to.

"Fine faith-keeper you will make, with all this insight into people's minds," he said lightly, turning to follow his companion who was already on his feet, charging into the deepening dusk. "Something to do in your old days, when you are tired of warring."

"Oh yes, wise man." The unconcerned chuckle floated in the air, taking the last of the awkwardness away. "I will make sure to come to you for guidance when that happens. An advice for an advice."

For some time they proceeded in silence, picking their way carefully, having brought no torch to lighten their way.

"How long will it take you to get organized?" The Wolf Man was back in his businesslike mood.

"If you get me a good canoe and some things to take on the road, I will be on my way tomorrow at dawn."

The man's moccasins made a plopping sound, enhancing the abruptness of his halt. "Tomorrow at dawn? How so?"

Ogteah slowed his step, refusing to halt. "Why would I wish to loiter in your silly town for longer than that? If I get a canoe and supplies, I can start battling the current of that Great River of yours, reaching the Mountain People's watershed in less than two dawns." Grinning against the open puzzlement of the wide eyes, he shrugged. "What did you think I was planning to do here in High Springs? Chase pretty foxes?"

The man exhaled loudly, snorting as he did. "I wouldn't put it past you, wild man." Then he shook his head resolutely. "Yes, I see the merit in starting your journey from here. It will save you quite a few dawns of delay, will get you on your way nicely, with appropriate swiftness. Still," the pointed eyebrows were climbing high, questioning, "wouldn't one wish to pass through one's home first, take farewells and all that? This is no pleasure trip you are embarking on. Don't you want to talk to your woman first, hug your child before going to face all this danger the other side of the Great Lake is willing to offer you?"

The lightness of his mood evaporated with no trace. "I did this already, before coming here. She knows about it all."

The thought of Gayeri's tear-stained, twisted, agonized face, the depth of her worry and desolation, made his stomach tighten in such painful way he wondered if he had eaten something bad or been punched. She didn't want to let him go, wasn't ready to agree to his desperate plan. Her protests were fierce, loud, atypically inconsiderate. She, who had made it her business to support him in any enterprise or new undertaking, backing him up always, smiling, cheerful, approving, fiercely loyal, not letting her worries or misgivings stand in their way. Such a novelty after decades of being frowned upon and disapproved of.

A luxury he had grown used to, he discovered, as the fierceness of her objection had taken him by surprise. Didn't she see how necessary it was, how crucial and important? Only he could do what the leaders of their nation, if not the entire Great League, wished him to do? It was not even his personal idea at the first place. Didn't she trust the decisions of the War Chief's son?

The arguments she proved deaf to, unaffected, unmoved, adamant in her refusal to see a reason. The other side of the Great Lake was no place for a person to sneak around, spying and doing only Great Spirits knew what. The leaders of their great union had no right to ask him to endanger his life in this way. It was different than warring, and no amount of reasonable arguments had the power to stir her into more reasonable thinking. She wasn't prepared to listen. There must be other ways of ensuring her people's safety, regular, accepted ways; his past was of no consequence, his unique ability to blend among the enemy and gather information notwithstanding. If he hadn't been around they would have found another way, wouldn't they? So why couldn't they pretend it was actually the case?

A solid female logic that left him with no arguments besides words of rage and exasperation, her tears angering him even more, the unreasonableness of those. He had faced more dangers in the Long Tails War or beyond the Great River of the Flint. Didn't she see that?

Yet another argument she didn't appreciate in the least, claiming that it was different, not the same, sniffing and hiccupping as she tried to make her case, determined to say her piece. When fighting or warring or just traveling to gather warriors' forces, he wasn't alone, not left to face the enemy unaided and unattended. He had friends and associates, men put under his responsibility or just peers, people who were on his side, people who didn't wish him harm. He had his back *watched*. While crossing the Great Lake on a dubious spying mission would put him into a terrible danger, with no one to trust, no one to help if he needed help. What if he had been challenged, recognized, asked for his purpose? What if he was provoked into violent deeds like back in Arontaen? His former homeland was sure to bring the worst out of him, even if his real purpose was not exposed, and then what would he do, how would he escape?

Refused to be comforted or reassured, she skulked through the remnants of this day, making his last evening at home into an unpleasant affair, not helped by their daughter's agitated chattering and insistent demands for attention. He would rather have the girl going to sleep at Gayeri's aunt's compartment, a place the little thing always enjoyed, yet his wish of spending this last night with his wife alone did not come to pass. Sensing that something was amiss, the clever little fox was not about to be palmed off and away from the happenings. And with no opportunity to talk about what preyed on their minds, with Gayeri's thundering silence and accusingly turned back, he had eventually fled into the night, in search of lighter, more reasonably inclined company. Ohkwali was still around, enjoying Lone Hill's hospitality, accepting his unexpected companion with flickering smile and no questioning. Speaking of friends, he wished he could have taken the Standing Stone man along. That would have put some of Gayeri's fears to rest.

Impossible, of course. Familiar with not a word of any tongue but this of his own people, the Standing Stone man could pose no more than a miserable captive on the other side of the Great Lake. Still, when offered to travel to High Springs first thing in the morning, the man didn't even hesitate.

"Oh, your woman does know about your destination?" The Wolf Man's voice brought Ogteah back from his unhappy reverie in time, before the longing and the remorse took over. He shouldn't have left without another try at putting her fears to rest, of mending the things between them.

"Yes, she does. Of course she does. What did you expect me to do, sneak out without telling her that I won't be back for a moon or two?"

"You didn't have to tell her precisely everything." His companion's lips tightened, relating displeasure. "The statement that you are going away on yet another important mission on behalf of our Great League should be more enough, if you ask me. There was no need to elaborate on any of it."

Well, I didn't ask you, he wanted to say, but held his tongue, this time succumbing to no temptation of taking his anger on the first person at hand. For obvious reasons the Wolf Man wished to keep their unusual enterprise a secret, and it was a good decision, too. He, Ogteah, certainly didn't need every dweller on this side of the Great Lake aware of his projected tour around his former homelands. This might make some busy minds jump to all sort of wrong conclusions.

Enough that he did confine in Ohkwali on their way here, unable to keep it all to himself, hurt with Gayeri's lack of support. She was being difficult out of love and worry, still her anger was offensive, somehow. Didn't she trust him to come out of even such a difficult adventure successful and unhurt? Or was she afraid he might choose not to come back for this or that reason? A thought that left him rigid with anger. Didn't she trust him after so many summers together?

"I shared it with her, because she is involved and trustworthy," he said, rubbing his face tiredly, wishing to finish this conversation for good. "She won't be running around, sharing this story with every dweller of Lone Hill and beyond it. You can trust her on that." Shrugging, he forced a semblance of a grin. "And she won't be sending warnings to the Crooked Tongues across the Great Lake as well. She hasn't got that tired of me."

Or so I hope, he thought grimly, remembering the coldness of her expression when her back was not turned on him. She had made such a show of talking to their daughter pointedly, about her father and how he would not wish to leave her alone, fatherless, every word innocent for the girl's sake, carrying a clear message for him. The devious fox.

"Well, don't talk to any more people about it while you are around. The Standing Stone man got involved, so he will be sailing up to the Genesee River with you." Again the man paused, forcing Ogteah into slowing his step as well. "No one else is to know where you are going. I'll explain to everyone, people of your village as well, that I sent you to do something important. My brother will help us with inventing a good story." The large eyes bored into him, their gaze again fierce and intense, penetrating the darkness. "I asked you to do this not because you came from the other side and can speak their tongue. We have other people, who are as fluent with the Crooked Tongues way of speaking, my brother included, even though he is such an important dignitary these days. I asked you to do it because you are the best man I can think of to make the most out of it and to come back full of news and unharmed. So don't disappoint me on this score. Come back swiftly and in one piece. Over here we value enterprising, strong-willed, courageous people. Don't make me regret my sending you there, which I would if something happens to you."

Grateful for the merciful cover of the darkness, Ogteah felt his face washing with a warm wave, as though splashed by hot water. Swallowing hard, he made sure the crookedness of his grin matched that of his companion.

"That mission, well, yes, it is not something I would have chosen to do. But life can be strange at times. I don't want to spy on my former people, but I won't let them harm my family." He took a deep breath. "All my family and not only my woman and child."

The Wolf Man's smile was wonderful in its openness, his teeth flashing bright out of the darkness. "Then all is well. Together we will keep *all* our people safe."

CHAPTER 7

The shadows were lengthening as Ononta emerged from the semidarkness of the storage room, blinking at the brightness of the outside, too worried to reflect on the miserable state of affairs that made her spend yet another day inside the crammed dimness of the airless compartment.

Father was not getting better, still coughing as viciously, even though the fever was gone. Which was a good thing, everyone reassured her. Long burning was what made people hurry on an untimely Sky Journey, the mere exhaustion that it brought to a sick person, healing potions or not. But Father's fever had been gone on its own now, so his spirit must have been winning the battle against the bad *uki*. A consolation, but she was too spent and exhausted to rejoice at the thought.

"How is he?" called out an elderly woman, who had crouched next to the border stones of an outside fire, busy fixing a clay kettle above the lustily raging flames.

Ononta did her best to produce a smile. "He is asleep."

"Oh." The elderly face crinkled in a frown. "Has he eaten since the morning meal?"

"No, not much. But what he did eat he managed to keep down." Pushing the fluttering tendril away from her sweaty face, Ononta wished nothing more than to wander off, to enjoy peace and quiet, or better yet – a good, thorough, luxuriously long washing in the company of her friends back at home. "He didn't vomit, not even once today."

The frown didn't clear. "Good, good." Then the old eyes concentrated, resting upon her, assessing. "Go and rest a little, girl. Take a stroll out there, enjoy the fresh air. You need it. A good, thorough wash, eh?"

Ononta tried not to roll her eyes. "Yes, but…" She hesitated, her gaze following a group of girls who swept by the far end of the alley, their hair askew, limbs muddied from the day in the fields, their laughter rolling, reaching this side of the longhouse, uninhibited, unheeded. Lucky foxes. "He coughs badly. I don't want to leave him alone."

"Go and fetch Second Niece, then." The woman nodded briskly, turning back to her cooking. "Her mother went to our other Deer Clan's longhouse not long ago, to see how that little boy of the foreigner is doing. Ask her to send her girl here, to keep an eye on your father." The wooden spoon got back to work, moving in monotonous circles, stirring the heating stew. "Maybe she can send him another of her brews as well. It worked miracles last night, didn't it? Ask her."

Not relishing the prospect of running all over yet another alien longhouse full of people she didn't know, Ononta nodded her thanks. That second niece was a cute little girl, cheerful, helpful. Good enough company, considering the circumstances.

While she neared her destination, another loudly animated group passed her by, giving her curious looks. Not mean or hostile, they still made her feel bad, an outsider that she was, not belonging. She glanced after them, wistful, then almost tripped over a little boy who spilled out of the entrance with the symbolic deer engraved upon it, struggling to bypass her, failing on that count. As she caught the little thing with her arms, trying to soften the collusion, none other than this same second niece rushed out as well, hot on the running boy's heels, squealing happily, laughing hard.

"The little rascal!"

By this time, the boy had broken free from Ononta's grip, his struggle fierce and uncompromising. In the next heartbeat he was pressing against his pursuer, not laughing anymore. The sight of the quivering lips and the unnaturally rounded eyes made Ononta feel bad.

"Don't cry!" She brought her hands up, imploring, one of her palms surprisingly sticky, glistening with ointment.

"Yes, little one." The girl, herself barely ten summers old, pressed the boy closer. "It's Ononta, she is our guest. She is nice. Don't cry."

But the little face refused to come up from its hiding in the folds of the colorful sash, and now Ononta remembered where she had seen the child before. In the arms of the foreign man, a few dawns ago, when one of her father's cousins made her go out and cut that deer.

The foreigner was still around, apparently, even though she didn't encounter him anymore. No wonder of course, with her spending her time packed in the airless compartment, perched on her father's sickbed. The visitor may have performed miracles or run naked all over the town and she wouldn't have known about it but through the network of rumors and talks.

"What's wrong with him?" she asked, eyeing her own palm, smeared with sticky mixture.

"Oh, it's his arm," said the girl importantly, while the subject of their conversation tore free from yet another embrace, shooting back through the gaping opening, disappearing in the depths of the storage room, set on his course. "It's wounded and the cut is not healing well. Mother says it needs much care, ointments and medicine."

"Oh." Ononta shifted her weight from one foot to another. "We need some of your mother's medicine as well. The Great Aunt sent me to fetch you, and your mother."

The girl frowned, looking again inappropriately thoughtful for her age, too serious. "Tegshee? The Great Aunt?"

"Yes." Forcing a smile, Ononta tried to contain the familiar wave of impatience. It was splashing near, threatening to burst out in some silly display of more tears. She didn't want to be here. Her falling upon these people and their benevolence was not of her choosing. "My father, his blood is not boiling anymore, but his cough is just getting worse. He can't rest, can't sleep. He can't even eat properly." She bit her lower lip against its annoying trembling. "Great Aunt wanted your mother to prepare something for him to drink. And she wanted you to watch over him until I come back to do that." Another attempt at a winning smile. "It's just for a little while. I won't be long, I promise."

Her converser's face was crinkling in an attempt to decide. A funny sight that might have amused Ononta but for her predicament.

"I'll ask Mother," said the girl finally, turning around and disappearing in the same direction, matching the speed the little boy had displayed earlier. It was as though this particular opening was sucking youngsters in. Determined and ever so lightly put out, Ononta followed. A ten-summers-old could have had better manners. Not to invite the visitor in was a true impoliteness.

Even though it was as dimly lit as any other longhouse's corridor, she found it easy to locate the compartment in question, as the little boy was howling, his noisy protests overcoming the voices of other speakers, quite a few if her ears were to be believed, females mainly.

"You have to drink this, you must." This voice sounded somewhat familiar, the strangely pitched quality of it, the exaggerated loudness.

The girl from the riverbank, Ononta's eyes told her, putting the voice with the face the moment she neared the commotion. The strange fox was huddling the boy in her arms, protective as though shielding him from the rest of the adults rather than trying to make him do something they all wanted him to do. Like back in the woods near the river, she looked out of place, too thin and too nervous, ill at ease, belonging anywhere but here. Who was she?

The question that was answered most readily by the culprit himself, whose face was buried firmly in his protector's chest, the small fists clutching his rescuer's clothing, not about to let go.

"No, no, no," he wailed. "I will not drink, not drink. It's awful, bitter, yuck!" A more vigorous burrowing into the folds of the undecorated dress. "Motherrrrr!"

The girl looked at the rest of them, her gaze pleading. A mother? But it couldn't be? She was too young and she had another child back there on the riverbank, a mere baby —

"He must drink it," repeated the woman, whom Ononta recognized as the one she had come to fetch, standing next to the huddling couple, her eyes reflecting little compassion. "This and the ointments, he must keep it on until his wound dries up."

"Tsamihui." The tall man she remembered from that same other day, the foreign visitor, stepped forward, pushing himself through the circle of females, his voice strong, dominant, commanding, overcoming the others. "You will drink your medicine, boy, and you will do it now. Come here!"

The little thing responded by pushing his face deeper into his mother's chest, but when the man's hand rested upon his shoulder, he didn't wince or try to resist.

"Come. We'll do it quickly and get it over with."

A mild struggle resulted in the puffy face peeking out, to hesitate, then dive back into the safety of the girl's embrace.

"Tsutahi, help me." Another curt order. "Get him here."

The Second Niece slunk closer to Ononta, evidently having forgotten her mission of asking her mother on their new visitor's behalf. Ononta didn't mind, as immersed in the unfolding drama. What a strange family, with the impressive foreigner being too prominent and important-looking, displaying scars and other ravages of war and hard living, not to mention his limp, impossible to miss something like that, to have this slip of a girl for a wife, a mother of his children. Only now she noticed the baby, tucked in a basket upon one of the pallets, sleeping snugly, indifferent to the noisy scene.

"He refuses to drink the medicine," whispered her new companion, pushing close to Ononta, a pleasantly warm presence.

"Why?"

"It's dreadfully bitter. Bad smelling, too." The girl huddled yet nearer, full of importance, enjoying herself. "Mother says it has to be this way. She can't sweeten it with maple or honey. It would spoil the medicine. And the ointment, it stings when you put it on. So Tsami makes trouble every time they want to put it. He fights so!" The girl's voice warmed with affection. "He is a wild beast, that one."

Fascinated, Ononta watched the boy losing his battle, hauled to his feet gently but firmly, with no misgivings, having no chance against his powerful father.

"This man, he looks scary," she related in a whisper. "I don't like him."

"Oh no, he is a good man!" cried out her converser, before remembering to lower her voice back to whispering. Luckily in the general hum and with everyone's attention on the howling child, no one seemed to listen to their exchange. "Mother likes him. She says he is a good man." The girl giggled. "If it wasn't for him having a family, she might have liked him to come and live in our compartment, I think." This observation was breathed straight into Ononta's ear.

Ononta frowned, watching the girl from the riverbank openly, safe in doing so as the poor woman's attention was on her screaming child, her face full of changing expressions, relaying a whole gamut of those, from anguished distress all the way to a quite open anger, a clear resolution to pounce forward in order to save her child from his tormenters.

"Poor thing," she whispered.

"Tsamihui?" The girl clearly enjoyed the show, having watched it before, for the last two dawns probably. "He'll forget all about it the moment it's over. Until the time to put on the new ointment comes."

"No, his mother. I pity her."

"Oh, this one." Her companion made a face. "She is strange. Never smiles or speaks nicely. Huddling with her baby, barely talks to anyone but her man. An odd fowl." Snorting, the girl rolled her eyes. "I don't know what he sees in her. She can't hear, Mother says. But then suddenly she says something and you just know she has been listening. So maybe she just pretends and speaks strangely on purpose." Another snort. "I don't like her at all."

All eyes now, Ononta peered at the object of so much dislike, remembering the young woman's strange behavior back in the woods, so brisk and helpful, and bossy, then suddenly turning frightened, not noticing her own child's screams, but somehow blaming it on her, Ononta, as though she should have let her know. Oh, yes, she worked with her back on them, carving that carcass, and if she couldn't hear like this Second Niece and her mother claimed, well, that would explain the strangeness of this situation, wouldn't it?

The child, gurgling and kicking, but not daring to defy his father by spitting out the medicine openly, grasped tightly in the protective arms of the formidable man, buried his face in yet another familiar chest, rocked gently, soothingly, as his mother, her slender arms trembling visibly, leaned toward the basket, rocking it lightly in her turn. The healer woman wiped the sweat off her face.

"Good. Until the next time." There was a smile in her voice, a light shimmering amusement. Then her eyes rested on Ononta. "Yes, young one? You came to ask me to attend to your father, didn't you?"

Ononta just nodded, uncomfortable at turning into the center of their attention. Even the foreigner, still busy comforting his child, glanced up, giving her a cold, indifferent look.

"How is he? The fever didn't return, did it?"

"No, but—"

"He is coughing badly," burst out the Second Niece importantly, apparently set on gaining as much attention as she could. "Ononta says he can't keep his food down."

"No, he can. He didn't vomit for the entire day." She took a deep breath, wishing to turn around and leave. Why couldn't they discuss it on their way out? "It's just that he is coughing so badly, and the Great Aunt, she says, she told me to come here, ask you to help. To make another medicine, maybe? And I need to go wash, and the Second Niece…"

Oh, but she hated to stumble over her words as she did. They were all staring at her, even the girl with the baby and the unruly boy. This one narrowed her eyes and was studying her, or rather her lips, with much concentration.

"I'll come," said the woman, her smile motherly, not making Ononta feel any better. It was not as amusing as some of them clearly thought it was. Rather it was highly embarrassing. "Let us go."

It was already near dusk when she managed to slip away, hurrying toward the opening in the palisade, running along the twisting path. Back home she would never had been forced to do something like that, to go and wash at the creek's shores all alone, with no company and no protection from possible prying eyes. It was daunting and boring, this lack of friendly attention. If nothing else, it reminded her of her lack of belonging. But for the opportunity to go home!

Had she only been a man, like Atuye, she would have taken Father and made her way back all by herself. Surrounded by people who loved and cherished him, truly loved and cherished, his health would improve right away. Oh, but for the ability to do that!

As expected, the shore that girls and women frequented in order to seal yet another day in the fields was abandoned, with everyone busy up there in the town, finishing their meals, preparing for various evening activities, such a pleasurable pastime at this span of the seasons, mildly chilly and warm at the same time.

Still, it wasn't completely deserted. The voices from beyond the bushes adorning the river's bend were distinct, impossible to miss. Or maybe it was just one voice, familiar in its uninhibited liveliness, its lack of restraint, whether rejoicing or protesting, and probably, everything in between. Sure enough the boy was there, hopping above a tiny stream that was draining itself into the river, glimmering in the last of the light.

Watching small pebbles shooting from under the bare, muddied feet, making their owner laugh and stomp on yet another obstacle harder, Ononta could not fight her smile. Such wild, unrestrained spirit. No wonder it was next to impossible to make him drink the medicine.

"Feeling better, little one?" she asked, stepping forward, herself enjoying the touch of the wet gravel upon her bare feet, her moccasins and the blanket she brought clutched safely under her armpit. To plod in the shallow ripples was a real pleasure.

He didn't look startled, not favoring her with even the briefest of glances. The lift of the small shoulders related it all. He didn't care, not anymore. The unpleasant occasion was in the past, forgotten until the next time.

"Where is your mother?"

There, pointed the small finger, indicating the general direction of the river.

"Washing?"

He shrugged again, his eyes large and widely open, full of cautious fascination.

"The baby brother," he related finally, gesturing vigorously to reinforce his words. "*Nnen* says he needs washing." The small face puckered in mocking disgust. "She says he stinks. She made faces like that." More vigorous grimacing made Ononta chuckle again. He was so impossibly cute, talking with his hands rather than his mouth. "He is pooped all over. His cloths, and *annen*'s dress, too." The round arms swung widely, in a demonstrating way, describing the incident. "All over. He made them both smell bad. But not me. He didn't poop on me." A victorious wave. "He does it all the time. But I'm careful."

It was harder and harder to keep her face serious. "She is your mother, your *nnen,* isn't she?"

He considered it for a heartbeat, his forehead creasing in an attempt to decide. "Yes, mother is careful. But not always. Little brother poops all the time." He giggled. "She says I did it too. When I was little."

"And now you are big?"

"Oh yes." His eyes opened wider, while he peered at her as though making sure she could see his words coming out of his mouth. "I'm big now. Really big. Father says so. He will take me hunting soon, he promised. And *annen* says I'm a big brother, she says it's important, makes me big." Again the angular arms were fluttering, relating the story better than his words did. "She knows everything. Like Father." Leaning forward, he dropped his voice, his eyes alight with enthusiasm, sharing a secret. "Father says Mother can hunt like men. He says she is a real warrior."

Oh, but she remembered the woman snatching the knife, tucking the baby into her, Ononta's, useless hands, proceeding to carve the carcass, with such expertise, such skill. It was actually easy to imagine this little slip of a girl hunting that deer, shooting it maybe, or killing it with a spear. The thought made her giggle.

"*Annen* can war like a man, Father says." The boy was fully immersed in his story now, aglow with excitement, his hands flapping in the air, the sticky bandage upon his elbow waving, loose and about to fall off. "He says she was in a battle, a huge battle, a really, really big war. He says she was like a warrior, brave, with no fear."

That was taking it too far. Ononta laughed. "What battle?"

"A huge battle." The little face creased in a funny grimace. "He told me not to tell anyone. *Annen* says he was a great leader. She says he led many, many men. More than pebbles on the creek's shores, she said. More than squirrels in the entire forest." His hands came up once again, eager to show how many those people were. "That many warriors!" The large eyes crinkled with mischief. "Mother tells me things. She says I'm big and smart and should know. She tells things Father said not to. She says she trusts. That means she can tell secrets and I won't tell," he added importantly, the frown back, making him look like a funny replica of a grown man.

Tired of squatting, Ononta attempted to spread her blanket without getting up. The boy was a sweet, chatty, lighthearted company, but if she got up he might get scared and run away, looking for his secrets-sharing mother and her protection. "So your *nnen* tells you secrets, eh?"

He just nodded, back to his hopping above the trickling spring.

"She can do many things. She can hear you even if you are not near," he related, waiting for no invitation before coming closer, standing on the edge of the spread blanket, leaving wet, muddy marks upon it. Ononta fought the urge to tell him off.

"How so?" To motion him into a sitting position seemed like the most harmless of courses, for her blanket that is. "Just sit there, on your behind. Yes, like that. Don't jump on my blanket, or I won't let you be on it." He was pondering her words carefully, his forehead furrowing in what looked like thousands of wrinkles. It made him look like a small version of a grown man again. She fought her laughter no longer. "Just sit and stay still, won't you? You can do it, I'm sure you can. At least for a little while. Good!" Nodding her approval, she watched him dropping down, folding his legs with a suddenness of a shot down deer – one moment standing, the other squatting, facing her, all eyes and expectation. "My name is Ononta. That's a short for a mountain spring, in my people's tongue. I was born near a beautiful mountain spring." Smiling gently, she smoothed the edge of the blanket, brushing off drier pieces of earth and small leaves he had brought upon it. "Now your name is Tsamehui. I heard your father call you this. And it is a mighty name. The Eagle is a name to live up to, eh?"

His small face was a study of concentration, its forehead still creased, registering no understanding.

"But you were telling me about your *nnen*. You say she can hear you from far away. How is it possible?"

His frown disappeared. "She just can," he related. "But," the small palms thrust forward, to support his shifting weight, about to leave more marks, she knew, "if you sneak up behind her, she won't hear you at all. I know she won't, I tried it. Father said never to do it, but I did." The wide-opened eyes were beaming, victorious and full of delight. "It was funny. I yelled really hard and she didn't hear."

"Oh, I see. She can't hear well."

"Yes, she can," insisted the boy. "She can hear you. But not when you are behind her. I found it out. By myself!"

"Good for you." It was again proving difficult to keep her face straight. He was such a bragger, the cutest little thing. "What else does your *nnen* tell you that your father doesn't want you to hear?"

He stared at her blankly, clearly missing the essence of the question. However, the rustling of the wet gravel made them both jump, turning in time to see this same discussed, or rather gossiped about, mother reappearing from behind the low bushes adorning the incline of the shore, ascending the trail, the baby balanced upon her hip easily, snug in the curve of her arm, supported, bubbling funny sounds.

In the contrast, the woman's expression related anything but contentment, her frown wary, mistrustful, deepening upon seeing her son's company, the large eyes narrowing into slits.

"What do you want?"

Ononta shivered. "Nothing."

The woman's lips pursed thinly. "Tsamehui, come here." A curt order made the boy hesitate before jumping to his feet, shooting in his mother's general direction.

"Is the baby-brother clean?" he demanded to know, clearly missing the accumulating tension. "I want to hold him. You promised. She," the small thumb pointed toward Ononta, fluttering in the air with each hop of its owner, "she wants to see me holding a baby. Don't you?" Now a pair of hopeful eyes were upon her as well, pleading. "You want to see me holding the baby, yes?"

Ononta shrugged helplessly, wishing nothing more than to go away, to put as much distance between herself and her current company as possible.

The woman's lips tightened, but the baby on her hip began making mewing noises, wriggling as it did, and this took its mother's attention away. Bettering her grip on the plump little thing, she pulled it into a better position, glancing at her older son. *Afraid to miss his words?* wondered Ononta numbly, remembering what the boy said. His mother heard everything but not when he was speaking from behind her. How odd.

"Listen, sister," she said, terribly uncomfortable with this whole situation. "I meant no harm. Your son talked to me, that is all. I didn't do anything wrong." The suspicious gaze was back upon her, glued to her lips, but when she brought her arms up, imploring, it followed the gesture quickly. "Your son is a very sweet boy. He wanted to talk to me."

The depth of the woman's frown rivaled that of the stormy sky. She watched the small teeth coming out, pinching the thin lower lip. The baby began crying harder, again taking its mother's attention away. She pulled it to her chest, clearly contemplating feeding possibilities.

"Here, sit on my blanket." It came out suddenly, surprising Ononta herself as much as it did her unfriendly company, the girl's gaze sneaking toward her face again, full of suspicion. "You'll be comfortable feeding him sitting." She had seen enough feeding mothers struggling to do that in all sorts of positions, while maintaining the fields or working around the town. There were plenty of babies in their particular longhouse through all spans of seasons, and she was the one who volunteered to mind many of those, hungering after a baby of her own since she knew how to walk or talk.

"I can feed him in any way I want to," said the woman firmly, evidently gathering her senses and her former unfriendliness alongside with it. "I'm comfortable now as it is."

Ononta tried not to roll her eyes. Such an annoying fox, with no basic politeness whatsoever. "Have it your way."

"Her blanket is soft. Look!" With as little consideration as before, the boy bounced back toward the folded square, landing there on all four, his fists and knees taking the impact, his feet splashing dirt, marring more of the clean leather.

"Tsamehui!" cried out his mother, her eyes widening, the crease upon her wide forehead clearing momentarily. "Step off it now."

"But, *nnen*," he protested, planting his knees and palms wide upon the conquered leather, as though readying for the attempt to dislodge him off it. "Ononta, she lets me, she lets me on her blanket. She told me I can sit on it. But not to jump."

"Sensible." The young woman shrugged, losing some of her former hostility. "Even though his feet are all over it, sitting or not." Suddenly the delicate mouth stretched into a surprisingly unguarded smile, an unexpectedly pretty sight, even if a brief one. "Your blanket won't look presentable in the end, and I will be the one forced to wash it."

"No, no, of course not." Politeness demanded that she protest vigorously, meaning it, even though it was a sound idea what the woman said. "He is a good boy and he kept me company."

"Are you here all alone?" Again the girl's voice rang in a strangely loud, disharmonious way.

Ononta sighed. "Well, yes. I was busy when the other girls came back from the fields. My father, you see…" A shrug seemed to be in order. She glanced at the boy, who was busy rolling back and forth, as though trying to smooth the blanket with his stretched limbs, himself as straight as an arrow.

"Yes, the healer woman went to see your father after taking care of Tsamehui, didn't she?"

"Yes."

"What ails your father?"

Ononta shrugged again. "He coughs and he was hot for many days."

"But not anymore? He isn't hot now?"

"No, may all the great and small spirits receive my endless gratitude for this!"

The girl was watching her lips again. "Well, it's a good sign if he is not hot anymore. Maybe he was not destined to start his Sky Journey at this time." The contemplative gaze left her, shifted to rest on the blanket and the boy upon it, now wholly immersed in the study of a colorful insect he had evidently just caught, holding it on his outstretched arm, fascinated and quiet for a change. Her gaze returned to Ononta. "You are kind to befriend him like that. I'm grateful."

Resolutely, she dropped on the fallen log, repositioning the protesting baby with a practiced ease, making it snug and comfortable in her lap and upon her breast.

Ononta made herself more comfortable as well. "It wasn't hard to befriend him. He is the friendliest little thing." A glance at the object of their conversation confirmed what she suspected, the experimenting attempts to prevent the captured bug from running away were at their highest, occupying its perpetrator's attention to the fullest. "I love children. I always took care of the babies of our longhouse, since I was very little. All women of our clan trust me with their children, and many from other longhouses as well. They are such a pleasure to care for or to mess around with, those babies. But your son, oh he is the sweetest." She laughed. "And he never stops talking, not for a heartbeat. He doesn't even pause to take a breath."

The smile flashed again, as pleasantly unguarded as the first one. And as brief.

"Yes, he does that. He talks much. There is no stopping him unless he is asleep or very, very busy. Like now." The girl's gaze followed the plump limbs as they pushed interminably, the small form shooting off, hot on the heels of his evidently escaped prey. "Otherwise it's long stories and talks, regardless of who is listening and if at all." The attentive gaze returned, concentrated and somehow searching, as though making sure nothing was said when she wasn't looking – probably the case – the woman hugged her baby absently. "He has surprised us. None of us thought he would be so open to people, so trusting and willing to make friends."

"Why ever not?" Smiling, Ononta followed the running boy with her gaze. "Most children of his age are like that. He must be the same back home. Isn't he?"

The woman just shrugged, readjusting her baby without letting his favorite source of food slip from his mouth, not taking her eyes off the running boy.

"What's wrong with his arm?"

A silence was her answer. Puzzled, Ononta repeated the question, before recalling the boy's words. Was this woman truly unable to hear unless seeing the person's expression or movement of lips? It sounded strange.

"What were you saying?" Her converser's gaze returned, clearly noting Ononta's scrutiny.

"Oh, nothing. I just…" She took a deep breath, embarrassed. "I was just asking about his arm? What happened?"

"Oh, that." The woman pursed her lips. "He got it wounded, you see. When the Cold Moons just retreated, he fell out of the tree. Restless spirit that he is, he never keeps still. It was a challenge to keep him in the house through the Cold Moons, let alone when the snows started to melt. His father was out there, hunting, and Tsame was running out every moment he could, to see if he was coming back." Pressing her baby closer, she sighed. "Apparently, he climbed a tree, to be able to see better, I suppose. Or maybe he was just bored. And well, he fell down and got his arm damaged badly. He tore it in several places, and it was swollen terribly." A forcefully drawn breath made the nostrils of the delicate, nicely shaped nose widen. "He did manage to come back all by himself, despite the pain and the bleeding. And I wasn't even in the house, but out there, clearing our field. He is such a strong, courageous boy!" The proud spark in the large eyes was gone as quickly as it appeared, replaced by the returning gloom. "I did what I could to clean his cuts, put his arm in a sling, made him feel better. But, well, I'm no healer. His father tried to clean the biggest wound again and again when it refused to dry up, to smear some mashed roots on it, but it still didn't heal properly. The rest of his cuts are nothing but scars now, with only the biggest wound, where the swelling was the worst, refusing to close properly, and it's been more than two moons already." A small half a shrug came, accompanied with an attempted smile. "So my man, he insisted we came here, to ask for the help of your local healers. He was in the habit of traveling here through the last spans of seasons; he is familiar with your local people. You must have seen him visiting."

Ononta just shook her head, trying to comprehend. Something was wrong with this story, something that didn't make sense.

"I... no, I didn't see your man, not before you two arrived here," she muttered absently. "On the day when I was out, cutting that deer, remember? That's when I saw your man first."

The widely open eyes were peering at her, somehow perturbed. "You didn't see him before?"

"No, I didn't. How could I?" It was irritating, this slightly troubled, even suspicious, expression. It made her feel guilty, as though she should have known this man and was just hiding such information. "I don't belong in this town. My father arrived here less than a moon ago. I'm a stranger here, as much as you are, and I wish I could have gone back home already. My town is nicer. With more pleasant people; friendlier, you know."

Glancing back at the topic of their original conversation, who was now attempting to jump over a fallen log without using his hands in the process, the escaped bug evidently forgotten, she suddenly realized what was wrong with her companion's story, what was missing.

"Your town," she said, turning back, not forgetting to make sure the woman's eyes were upon her, helping their owner to listen, "doesn't it have people who know about healing wounds and sickness? The other women of your longhouse, why didn't they help you with your boy? To take care of his wounds, or to watch over him for that matter, while you were out there in the fields?"

"Other women?" The puzzled expression was deepening, twisting the sharp, yet delicate features, making the woman look younger than she must have been, just a girl, really. Again it made Ononta wonder. How a young thing of her own age probably, or maybe even less, could have family and children already? "I don't know what you mean. What other women?"

"You know, women of your town, women of your longhouse." It was strange, this conversation, as strange as the women in front of her. "You must live with other people, don't you? Not just you and your man…"

The baffled expression dissolved all at once, replaced with a sealed, not overly friendly gaze, familiar from the beginning of their encounter.

"Oh well, yes, it's different, yes." This time the girl's voice dropped, difficult to hear for a change. "It's a long story. My man, you see, well, we live differently. Not like you. But it's not something he wishes me to talk about. Neither of us wants to live in a regular way, you see? We are happy the way we are." The painful frown was deepening again, making Ononta wish to reach out with a comforting pat. "Well, *I'm* happy to live the way we do. And, well, I hope he feels the same. I hope he isn't too unhappy about it. He was not used to…" The words were trailing off, now a mere muttering.

Ononta fought the urge to touch her companion's arm no longer. She was so uncertain, this girl, so out of place. Less belonging than she, Ononta, herself was, because she did have her people, her town, her family to go back to, while this woman evidently lived a strange life.

"Well, you are here now, and the woman from the Deer

longhouse, she is a good healer, as good as any men of the Medicine Men Society. She will make Tsamihui's arm heal."

"Yes, she is nice and very kind to be willing to help." Yet, there was certain coldness to the young woman's voice now, which again climbed to unpleasantly loud tones. "Aing—, my man, he brought goods, furs and skins. Good, rare furs. He made it worthwhile for the healers to help. He compensates them lavishly for their trouble." A decidedly crooked grin twisted the pursed lips, one corner of the tight mouth climbing up, the other staying where it was, turning downwards. "He promised it would take little time, maybe one dawn, maybe two. He said that I won't have to enter this town; that I will wait out there with the baby. But now," the girl sighed and looked away, following her son's progress with a practiced gaze, "now here we are, staying in this longhouse for three dawns already, not about to go back home. Instead, he is the one who is intending to leave, to go further along the Great Lake, eager to accompany some locals who are heading to visit some other locals." Blinking away what seemed like suspicious wetness, her companion looked back at Ononta. "I know he is doing what is best for us, me and Tsami and the baby. He wanted to visit these people of the east for a long time, but he didn't want to leave us alone for so long. And now, suddenly, he has this chance. Tsami needs to drink his medicine and smear some ointment on his wound for more dawns, the healer woman says. So he sees his chance, to leave us behind, cared for, not alone, until he comes back. But I don't want to be here. I don't!" The glittering eyes were upon her, imploring. "I prefer to be alone in my grandfather's cabin. With my children and my fields. I can manage to keep us well fed until he comes back. I can!"

Ononta forced a smile, her stomach knotting with compassion. Oh, but she knew how this woman felt, no one better.

"Yes, I know how it is." She sighed, watching her companion's face that the last of the light made looked softer, the most pleasant sight, not as sharply outlined or as angular as it seemed before. Or maybe it was its expression, surprisingly open, less guarded or cautious. "But he won't make you wait for too long, your man. And we can keep each other company in the meantime…"

Embarrassed, she looked away, appalled at her own straightforwardness, hating the awkwardness of the silence that prevailed. Luckily, the boy was upon them again, clearly about to jump straight onto the middle square of the blanket, regardless the state of his newly muddied feet.

Deftly, his mother caught him in mid-leap, directing the bouncing body toward her lap instead. "We don't want all this dirt smeared all over this kind woman's blanket, don't we? We'll go and wash it all off, then have you wearing your moccasins. Yes, we *will* do that." The boy seemed as though about to start arguing, but the last phrase cut his forming protests short. There was no mistaking *that* tone, the prerogative of stern mothers.

"My man will be heading there, toward the people who are living at the lands of the rising sun," she said, holding the boy tight by his good arm but looking back at Ononta again. "If you are coming from there, let him know where from, what town or village, where it can be located. He knows many Wyandot people, having visited many of their settlements once upon a time. He may know the place you are coming from." This time, the smile was shy, yet more encouraging than the widest of grins. "And if he won't be visiting it, he can forward a message, try to send word to anyone you might wish to contact. It will be closer to the places they will be traveling, easier to deliver."

"Oh." In her turn, Ononta got to her feet, trying not to let the wave of sudden anticipation wash over her, coloring her cheeks into glaringly autumnal colors. "Thank you. You are so kind. Yes, oh yes. Maybe I can forward a word. Do you know where he will be traveling?"

The girl shrugged with her free shoulder. "I'll ask him."

Ononta wanted to hug her. "Oh, thank you, thank you! I can't believe we didn't get along at first." She giggled at the memory. "You were cutting that deer so expertly. You did all the work for me."

Several expressions chased each other across the small slender face, from wary amusement to open hilarity. In the end the girl actually giggled, a strange, not very natural sound. "You were killing this poor carcass. I couldn't watch it."

"I don't like carving meat." She glanced at the boy, who was pulling at his mother's arm now, impatient to have the washing he was protesting against just a few heartbeats before. "I'll come with you. I need to wash, too. That's why I came here in the first place." She made a face. "The women of the longhouse we are staying at won't be happy about me taking so long. But I deserve to have a rest too, do I not?" Kneeling, she picked up the baby, careful not to wake him up. "I'll watch him until you are through with Tsami. I'll handle him better this time, I promise. He won't be screaming his head off like the last time. I'll let you know before it happens."

The widest of smiles was her answer.

"She made the baby-brother cry?" the boy was asking, his eyes huge and as round as a pair of wooden bowls.

Their rolling eyes and stifled giggles did not help to allay his confusion.

CHAPTER 8

The sight of the sleek, healthily padded whitetail interrupted Ogteah's concentration, making his stomach growl. It had been three days since he had eaten anything better than slices of boring dry meat, this morning improved by fresh berries he had bothered to plunder from the clearing next to the grove he had hidden his canoe in. Blended with ground maize powder mixed in warm water, they improved his monotonous diet but not like a roasted cut of a good juicy meat would. No need to go hungry on account of lacking supplies, not yet, but he was careful with the way he was spending his treasures.

Three dawns since the crossing had seen him deep in his former people's lands. Not precisely his people, as of course the towns of the Bear Nation remained in the east, facing the Onondagas and the Swamp People and some of the Mountain folk across the Great Sparkling Water. Another unsettling thought. Were those his *actual* former people who had raided Lone Hill this time?

The speculation that had his stomach tightening in a painful knot every time it visited itself upon him, on quite a few occasions since his canoe had plunged into the vastness of the Great Lake, when nothing but the splash of his paddles and the cries of occasional water bird remained to keep him company.

Never fond of solitude, he didn't welcome this additional layer of loneliness, not having even the solid land and its liveliness to brighten his journey. The only time he had crossed the great water obstacle was all those summers ago, when his life had changed so dramatically. But back then, Gayeri was by his side, chattering away, enlivening his journey in the best of ways, as trustful and as loyal as ever, fiercely supportive, believing in him. Oh, but for the opportunity to have her in his canoe again! Or at least out there on the shore, waving and promising to wait, expressing her belief clearly, certain that he would be coming back and soon, successful and unharmed. It would be easier to believe that if she declared her faith in no uncertain terms.

However, she wasn't there on the shore. She was back in Lone Hill now, angry, disappointed, upset. She didn't believe in his and the Wolf Man's solution. She wanted her man at home, keeping her and her child and her people safe. But to do that properly, to wage war on his former people most effectively, to better them as thoroughly as required, they needed to know what was happening on the colder side of the Sparkling Water, what was going on – what agreements were made, what understandings reached. It was the logical, wisest, most sensible of solutions, something only he could achieve. In order to ensure her safety he had to do that. But she didn't see it this way and she didn't come to wave him off.

To take his thoughts off such unhappy directions he would force his mind back to his mission, reminiscing in the details of his plans. Having never traveled as far as Deer People's forests, let alone the towns of the slightly mysterious, always aloof and distant Rocks, he had no certain idea where to start. Each destination would be helpful in learning something, even though the Wolf Man was interested in the Long Tails' neighbors alone.

Well, on this Ogteah did not agree with their aspiring warriors' leader, not entirely. To discover general intentions of the Wyandot Union was important, with or without their possible connections with the defeated Long Tails. This was a side issue, an additional thing to sniff out. The main goal was to learn of this people's union and its plans, its leaders, its strategies, its future designs.

Not something terribly difficult to do if he played his beans wisely, did nothing to give his true identity away. They must have been keeping close contact with the Bear and the Cord People, those other two nations, especially the Deer, the possible new members of the alliance, but they couldn't possibly know a thing about him, his past family connections, or even his old crimes. There was no reason anyone would surmise, or even suspect him of being anyone he claimed he wasn't. All he had to do was to approach this or that settlement and get invited in, welcomed cordially. Not a difficult task if he was confident and had goods to offer in trading. No more wandering like in his younger days. This time he needed to make a good impression.

They had discussed his back story with Ohkwali while rowing against the current of the Great River that connected the Onondagas with their western neighbors all the way to the Genesee River of the Mountain People. Scowling at the memories, their private losses still fresh, their grief never going away – Ohkwali's younger brother had embarked on his Sky Journey together with Akweks – they crossed the accursed river and, more careful now, headed deeper into the former enemy's lands. In the valleys and forests between the Genesee River and the Thundering Waters of the Long Tails, the presence of the Great League was felt more acutely these days, with the Mountain People behaving as though already at home, wandering local woods, hunting and fishing, getting acquainted with the lay of the land.

The remaining Long Tails, those who did not retreat behind their Thundering Waters, endured this pushiness with relative forbearance, attacking some of the travelers or hunters but on a small scale. One has to be careful while sailing these streams, but not overly so. As it was, neither Ogteah nor his Standing Stone companion were opposed to a possible confrontation, their mood being one of vengeance, their sense of wellbeing and success left behind in their homes. It would be so infinitely better to wage war on the Long Tails instead of on his actual former people, so much simpler and clearer, with no nagging worries and qualms.

The wonder as to the identity of the Lone Hill's assailants would return, a nagging unwelcome thought. Were the perpetrators his actual people? His former family members? His childhood friends? Oh, but what if he was forced to fight, and kill, his own blood relatives one day? What he would do then?

Forcing his attention back to the present, he watched the

dancing tail of the deer darting between nearby trees, its behind sleek, skin quivering against the bites of the forest insects, ears poised high. But for the presence of people further down the slope, the people he had been staking since high morning, he wouldn't have hesitated to shoot it and have a good feast. Or maybe that was exactly what he was to do, because of their presence and not in spite of it?

He took his eyes off his prey and scanned the thick greenery again, counting the distant figures. Five all in all, but there might be more around. The way these men squatted there, relaxed and unhurried, conversing loudly, not trying to conceal their presence, suggested a sense of security on their part. Very sure of themselves, indeed, on their home ground, probably, or at least in the place they knew well, not feeling threatened.

Fragments of their conversation would reach him with rare gusts of strong wind, yet not enough to decipher what tongue they were speaking. Deer or Rock? It was supposed to be the Rock People's forest. Or so he had assumed. The Attiwandaronk Long Tails from the other side faced the Wyandot Rock, didn't they?

Or were those just travelers, mere visitors like him? What was their direction? The rising or the setting sun? Would they turn with this or that river's flow, sailing northwards, heading for Beautiful Lake and the Cord People's towns? Arontaen or Ossossane? Oh Mighty Spirits, but he didn't need any of that!

Another scrutiny of the clearing in question. To hunt or not to hunt? The small herd of whitetails was still there, drinking thirstily.

Well, his presence in these woods was supposed to be an open affair, nothing clandestine about it. If he was to sneak between the trees, peeking at groups of passing travelers while hiding, he would come back with nothing but the realization that he might have saved himself much of unnecessary rowing around.

A fat doe moved into a perfect range, her swollen side facing the flint tip of his arrow, her clumsiness self-proclaimed. He shifted his bow ever so slightly. Not this one. In the late spring moons males were the targets, not the females swollen with progeny.

The people at the river bend were talking louder, their words reaching him, clearer now. He tried to listen, eyes on the skinny buck that had pushed its way closer to the water's edge, shaking the velvet stubs of his early antlers, desperate to impress his peers. Indifferent, the nearby does didn't even move.

Not a worthy catch, not if he was about to share it with his prospective fellow travelers. He raced through his back story again, just in case. A Bear People's man, he was traveling westwards now, to visit his mother's distant relatives; and to trade some goods. A respectable enough undertaking, something he shouldn't feel uncomfortable or uneasy with. People did travel for such purposes, visiting relatives, exchanging goods and gossip. Although, they usually did so in groups, accompanied by friends or family members. No man liked to travel alone. It was unsafe, and also boring. Still one wasn't committing a crime by sailing these rivers unescorted. Wandering in the lands of the Cord People all those summers ago he had more occasions to feel uncomfortable, running away from his people and his responsibilities, drifting with no purpose. And yet, he was bursting with confidence back then, and there was no reason to feel edgy or hesitant now as well. Breezy self-assurance and a carefree attitude were the best of his weapons, always. The Wolf Man was right to point out that it was not his origins and his command of the local tongues that made him into a perfect man for the mission.

His arrow swished, spooking the entire herd into a wild run. Pebbles flew from under many hoofed feet, shattered branches creaked, trampled-upon bushes groaned and gave way.

He had his second arrow planted safely in his prey's backside before rushing out and into the open. There would be enough time to track the injured buck and come back in time to greet his prospective companions. The noise the running herd created was sure to bring these people here, sniffing around. Good.

Indeed, by the time he staggered back, swaying under his heavy burden, not doing the sensible thing of stopping to skin his whitetail at the place he had found it fallen, three faces stared at him, suspicious, their frowns deep.

His nonchalant nod did not lighten their scowls, but as he dropped his cargo and knelt beside it, pretending a keen interest in nothing but his work, as though his stomach wasn't as tight as a wooden ball and as heavy, one of the men came closer, hovering not far away, watching intently. As did the others, their gazes burning his back.

"Greetings, stranger." The closest man's voice was deep, his words pronounced in an unfamiliar way.

Ogteah nodded again, wholly immersed. Or so he hoped it appeared. The ragged flint of his knife was cutting the deer in a wrong place, far to the left of the shoulder bones. "Greetings, brothers."

Another spell of uncomfortable silence. He could hear the voices of the people who had probably chosen to stay in their camp. So yes, they must be more than the original five he had seen.

"A good catch," observed the first speaker, when no one else ventured a word.

Ogteah nodded again, busy separating the hide from the muscle, aiming to reach the spinal sinew, precious for its length and durability.

"I'd be honored to share it with my brother travelers," he said, glancing up briefly, his gaze lingering for long enough to catch that of his converser's. "There is more than enough meat for all of us to enjoy."

The atmosphere cleared in an almost perceptible way. He could feel their nods, their open approval.

"It's always a pleasure to share a good meal around the fire after the hardships of a long journey." This time another man spoke, his words twisted as strangely as those of his companion. Rock People, now for sure. "You must have spent many days traveling."

"Indeed, I have." Ogteah hid his smile at their probing, concentrating on extracting the sinew without damaging the precious material. They knew where he came from. His speech had already given him away. Well, why wouldn't it? He didn't mean to pose as anyone but a Bear People's man. "It's been a long journey."

"Why don't we take it to our camp, brother; work on it all together. That will make our mutual feast arrive faster."

He stifled a huge sigh of relief. "Yes, why don't we?"

An invitation to join them in their camp and so soon? Oh, but what could be better than this? And what was he so uncertain about? A Wyandot man, from relatively distant Bear People's towns or not, he had every right to travel this far, visiting whomever he liked. Of course, they would accept his reasons and wouldn't question him on any of that. And so would the people of the towns he was about to accost. These Rock People were no different from their neighbors in the north and the west. There was no reason they should turn inhospitable or hostile.

"Do you camp somewhere around?"

Nodding, Ogteah straightened up, yet not before cleaning his hands and his flint blade in the helpfully trickling stream. Sheathing his knife, he wiped his forehead. "I left my canoe in the small inlet down by the river. It should be safe there." Now it felt proper to grin lightly, more openly. "Unless you are traveling in the same direction I'm heading, there is no need to interrupt this boat's well-deserved rest."

Their chuckles were reserved but not unfriendly. Wary, cautious; gauging his reactions.

He picked the hind legs of the partly cut carcass, glancing at the nearest man, a tall person of an impressive girth. Nodding solemnly, the man hurried to pick the other pair of the hoofed limbs.

"We are coming from Onentisati, but if you are heading back home, Bear People's man, then we are traveling in the same direction." One of the others came to prop the carcass from its side, rendering much needed support.

Ogteah shook his head lightly. "My current destination lies near Beautiful Lake and beyond it. In the Cord People's lands I have family members I'm eager to visit."

Oh, yes, that should do. What did these people have in common with the co-founders of the Wyandot Union, the alliance they didn't even bother to join as yet? Or did they? He straightened, reminding himself to be careful with his tongue, concentrating on more listening and less talking, an unfamiliar trait.

They exchanged glances. "A long way to travel."

"Oh, yes, much sailing, and through the high grounds, most of it."

He tried to recollect his previous travels, five, no six summers ago. Was it a difficult journey? He couldn't remember. Drifting without purpose, in the most leisurely of manners, as he did back then, had its upsides; no urgency to get anywhere, no pressing duties or commitments. No real friendships or real warmth as well. He pushed the wave of longing away.

"At least it's not a dangerous journey these days," he said lightly, bettering his grip on his slippery burden. "It wasn't safe to travel northwards until not very long ago."

"It's not such a pleasure to sail against all those raging currents and streams as well nowadays." The man who had addressed him first fell into their step easily, not attempting to offer his help in carrying their prospective meal. "I traveled to visit one of their towns before the Cold Moons, me and two of my cousins. We came back carrying interesting items, pretty pottery adorned with copper and other interesting trinkets, but it was a rough journey. Not worthy of repeating, unless traveling in greater state." A side glance brushed past Ogteah, measuring him with an open doubt. "Alone as you are, you'll arrive there exhausted." A chuckle. "Or rather out of breath, for the northern savages to do as they please with you."

Struggling to stabilize his cargo, Ogteah shrugged in pretended indifference. "We are all brothers now, not at war anymore."

"Or so they try to convince us." The man grinned, his walk enviably light, breath even as opposed to the panting of the rest of them, toiling uphill, crowding the narrow trail. "The leaders of that union, especially your pushy Bears and the Cord."

"Well, the People of the Deer joined in," drawled the man who was supporting Ogteah's offering from the other side. "And well, we might consider something like that, if you ask me. Some members of our Town Council certainly agree with those who think this might be not such a bad idea."

"The alliance of our nations is not a bad thing," contributed Ogteah, wishing to keep his thoughts on something that had nothing to do with his uncomfortable burden, so awkward, so cumbersome to carry. They should have carved it back near the spring after all. "With all that is going on with the other side, or the Long Tails and such, well, our people are better off united and prepared."

He shifted his grip once again, longing to let go of the carcass. Why did he volunteer to feed these people in the first place?

"Prepared for what?" The man who was supporting their cargo from its other side evidently did not have a hard time doing it, joining the musings about alliances and politics with a satisfied beam. "Our towns are not suffering from anyone, neither Long Tails nor the savages from across your shores of the Great Sparkling Water. They just keep pestering us, messengers from your lands and those of the Cord People. Not to mention our Deer neighbors, the most insistent of late, like hungry mosquitoes, as though in themselves they didn't take their time to join the notorious union, resisting their pressure and besieging."

The trail forked, and Ogteah found himself too busy struggling with the narrowed path to roll his eyes or say something sharp at all this flood of silly nonsense. Also why should he care, he reminded himself. This side of the Great Lake was not his business, not anymore. Still it was saddening to think of Father battling so much prejudice and indifference. As though the union of his creation needed these people more than they needed it. What nonsense! No wonder Father was so busy and tired-looking back in Ossossane.

He pushed another wave of memories away. What if someone of the present back there was traveling any of these lands, visiting their newly acquired partners in the alliance, making sure they were in for good? Someone of the Cord or the Bear People, someone who might have remembered him? The stony fist was back, squeezing his insides. How to sniff out such danger before it happened? How to avoid it?

"Almost there." The man who was walking ahead motioned

toward the sounds of the cracking fire, the people's voices reaching them freely now, carrying from the thick vegetation.

"The Attiwandaronk will welcome the prospective change in our meal," another muttered, a chuckle in his voice, his head turned back, addressing his peers. "He was looking down that prominent nose of his when they started fishing maize powder and berries out of our bags. An arrogant southerner that he is."

"If he was so fed up with eating porridge he should have limped away and hunted something." The man who had shared the burden of the uncooperative carcass with Ogteah contributed to the conversation through his panting breath. "If he was so hungry for a fresh meat."

"Well, our honorable visitor took care of the problem." The man beside Ogteah grinned at him in a surprisingly friendly manner. "Your offering could not have come with better timing."

Ogteah forced a grin, blinking the sweat out of his eyes. It was accumulating in his eyebrows, threatening to obscure his vision for good. Politeness demanded an answer. "Have you been traveling for a long time?"

"A few dawns." The man hastened his step, moving forward, pushing the poking branches out of the way, helpful for a change. "We've been visiting one of our neighboring towns, and our current destination is lying in the lands of the Deer. We have still a long way ahead of us."

"That we have," murmured the panting man from behind.

The last of the sun burst upon them from behind the receding trees, allowing a glimpse of a lovely shore, spacious and comfortably flat, bordered by thick vegetation on one side and several canoes on the other, the longish vessels pulled out of the water and piled in a neat row, creating a border.

Ogteah squinted, seeking the nearest fire. To get rid of their cumbersome cargo was the first priority, to place it somewhere, anywhere, before the damn thing slipped from his grip, dropping to the ground, embarrassing him even before the introductions were made. The hastening step of his fellow carrier told him that the man shared the same sentiment. Oh, but this deer better yield plenty of meat, enough to feed them all to bursting. This camp contained quite a few squatting or moving figures, more than he have expected, or have liked, to see.

Free of his burden at last, he straightened up, wiping his brow, deliberating as to the advisability of waiting for the introductions rather than proceeding with the cutting of the deer's legs with no delay, before anyone else volunteered to do this. He might have invited these people to partake in the freshness of his prospective meal, but he wasn't about to let anyone get away with such priceless treasures as sinew and hide.

Two more fires raged inside the encircling stones, large pottery kettles hanging above each, spreading the inviting aroma of something cooking and babbling. Exaggeratedly straight-backed, the people squatting nearby turned to stare. He returned their gazes through the brief introduction, nodding solemnly, impatient now, not sure of this course. What was he to gain from passing his time in such a large company, knowing not a thing about these people besides their belonging to the nations he was intending to accost?

"Now if we will all give a hand in taking this carcass apart," the man who had led them here was saying, again taking charge, briskly at that. With no intention of doing more than direct everyone and engage in an idle talk, surmised Ogteah. "Our prospective meal will be ready before Father Sun goes to sleep tonight. Thanks to our unexpected visitor this fresh meat will sustain us as nothing else will."

Still worried about the legs and their sinew, Ogteah took his knife out, kneeling next to the backside of the creature, exuding detachment he didn't feel. How to make his intentions concerning this carcass's treasures clear without looking petty, cheap, narrow-minded? They should have understood that themselves, they should—

In the next heartbeat all such thoughts froze in his head, losing power, coming to an abrupt halt. Eyes glued to the uneven gait of one of the nearing men, he felt his heart doing a silly dance, slowing dramatically, then jumping high, as though intending to slide up his throat, interrupting with his ability to breathe. Not that his emptying chest was craving any of that. *Just like back then, under the scowling afternoon sky, with the wind and the smothering dampness, and the stench of the valley below, with the dead scattered everywhere, all those crushed, broken bodies...*

Well, this time there was no stench stronger than the odor of the butchered carcass, and the fragrant aroma of the surrounding forest mixed with the smell of fires and cooking meals. But his chest felt smothered just the same, as though his ribs had been cracked anew in this vicious inhuman blow, and the voices of the milling around people floated above, not touching him, not for real. Nothing did, but the reality of his knife, grasped tightly in his sweat palm, and his mind frantic, calculating, readying to throw his body sideways, to avoid the initial attack, to gain a precious heartbeat or two in order to regroup, to find a way of rendering the enemy harmless, or better yet dead. He had to—

"You will keep the hide and the sinew, of course?"

Someone was kneeling beside him, talking, addressing him as it seemed. More people squatted around the carcass, their knives already at work. They were trying to tell him something, to receive an answer, unaware of the danger, probably, or indifferent to it.

He tried to process this information as well; however, his eyes were glued to the silhouette that was still standing at some distance, talking to someone, presenting Ogteah with the well-defined profile that was carved in his memory, the prominent nose and the forcefully protruding chin, the long unshaved hair collected in a loose braid, not glistening with oil and sweat, not sticking out in the remnants of the elaborate warrior's hairdo, *not like back then.* Standing there calmly, in control, putting more weight on his good leg in an obvious manner but holding the other one naturally. *Not like back then. Not desperate, dangerous, cornered, fighting the last fight.*

"Are you well, brother?" The face of the man who had led them here swam into his view, puzzled, strangely worried.

Ogteah paid him no attention, not daring to take his eyes off the enemy, seeing the cold gaze concentrating, turning alert, apprehensive, as though sensing the inimical scrutiny, narrowing even before coming to rest on him.

For a heartbeat that felt like an eternity their gazes locked, and he felt the hilt of his knife cutting into his palm, the familiar protrusions in the polished wood reassuring, promising help. The ground under his moccasins was firm, supporting, even though he didn't remember himself springing up and into an upright position. It didn't matter. Only the Long Tails man mattered, the ghost from the past, the reminder. He pushed the terrible memories away. Not now, not when he needed his senses alert and ready, not when…

The foreigner's eyes bored at him, narrowing, emanating cold suspicion. The obvious question in them threw Ogteah off balance again. No recognition in the wondering depths, no recollection. It was as though the man didn't know who the newcomer was, or who he might be. Ready to fight, oh yes – the man couldn't *not* sense the agitation, the hostility of the incredulous staring – yet seemingly unaware of the reasons behind those. How so? Had he mistaken this man for someone else? No, no, it couldn't be. There could be no mistaking this face and this bearing; neither could such a limp be a common occurrence. He had watched this man for long enough back upon the accursed cliff, wielding his club, fighting Akweks— *there could be no mistake.*

"This is our guest from Attiwandaronk forests." The man beside him was still talking, apparently. "Have you two met before?"

The need to tear his eyes off the Long Tails left him drained off strength, almost trembling.

"No, no…" He blinked, licked his lips, wishing the world was more stable, having no swaying quality to it. It was as though he had been hit on his head. Not an unfamiliar feeling. "I… I must have mistaken…"

The Long Tails was studying him with an utmost coldness, with a light but pronounced suspicion. Not about to attack, most surely not, but not intending to turn his back on the strange newcomer either. Must be typical of such a man, with a trail of hurt people and enemies thirsty for revenge that must stretch to long distances…

No, there could be no mistake! This man *was* the leader of the

Long Tails, the man who had led hordes of enemy warriors into the fertile valleys of Genesee River, the man who had almost managed to catch the Great League unprepared; the man who had fought Akweks and who had almost killed him, Ogteah, with one beautifully directed blow of the sturdy club adorned with a terrible spike.

The effort of turning his head in order to face his converser left him breathless, nearly trembling. "We'd better carve this deer before nightfall, hadn't we?"

"Well yes, we should."

The silence around him became lighter. *How many people noticed his untoward agitation?*

He forced his gaze to meet theirs. "I'll keep the sinew, yes. The rest is yours, including the hide."

A generous offering. Their nods confirmed their approval. Not as reserved as before, even if still puzzled and questioning.

He knelt beside his rightful catch, his nerves as tensed as an overstretched bowstring, his back feeling the gaze of the other man, most acutely. It wasn't wise to turn one's back on such a bad enemy. But what choice did he have?

CHAPTER 9

"They are going to hold a gathering of all our people out there at the shores of the Freshwater Sea again."

In the process of stretching in order to get up and sneak away as unobtrusively as he could, Atuye froze, all ears. The Freshwater Sea! The place where Father had held the first gathering, the place he had told him, Atuye, so much about. Father had planned to hold another meeting, this time including the Deer and maybe even the Rock People, but not out there at that large presumptuous main town of the Cord People. Oh no! This time the important gathering was planned to be held among their own, on the shores of the Great Sparkling Water or somewhere inland. Maybe even here, in the valley next to their very own settlement. And why not? Their town was large and influential. With Father living here, how could it not be?

"Another Great Gathering out there in the north?"

The question brought Atuye back from his musings and into the sunlit reality of the first summer moon, safely home and for quite a few days, a warrior now, bloodied in a war expedition, approved by his leaders, having not shamed himself, even though the raid was anything but a true success. The enemy from across the Great Lake proved, indeed, fierce and not easy to shatter, not prone to falling into traps and able to extricate itself if it happened.

He shivered, then forced his mind to concentrate on the present, his current company lively and loud, various men of all ages idling in the alley between their and another longhouse, enjoying the softer afternoon sun.

"Yes, but of all people this time, or so they wish it to be."

"The word 'wish' being quite essential, if you ask me." Atuye's oldest brother, Sondakwa, grimaced as though he had bitten into a green strawberry, rolling his eyes as he did. "All people? I wish them luck with the elusive Deer or the arrogant Rock. They can't be made to commit even when faced with the challenge in their own stinking towns. And whoever wishes to try and drag their representatives into the Cord People's cold vastness, all the way to that main town of theirs, makes a good joke." He snorted, grimacing against the most indignant of glares, not everyone in their company taking his words well. "What is that silly settlement called, anyway?"

"Ossossane," said Atuye, unable to stop himself. Still too young to sound his voice even in such an unofficial gathering, the last thing he wanted was to draw attention to himself.

"Oh, thank you, young buck." His brother's eyes flickered at him, teasing and amused but encouraging. "See, you all? This boy is the son of his father, knows more than many of us, remembers it all." The provocative twinkle grew, sparkling against gathering frowns. "What? Who of you remembered the name of that place where the First Gathering happened? A few, in the best of cases. And let's face it, without my father's work, the second gathering would not be a possibility, let alone contain more than us and the annoyingly opinionated Cord again."

"This is not so, Sondakwa," cried out the man who was standing next to Atuye, a tall well-developed youth, older than himself by only a few summers. "My uncle was your father's most devoted friend and supporter and he worked as hard to make the First Gathering happen. He did!" he added hotly, stepping forward, but whether to reinforce his claim or to start a fight was difficult to tell. "I was there. Unlike you, I bothered to travel with them and be of help to my uncle *and* to your father. Not everyone here is as indifferent as you are. The opposite is true!"

That, of course, wiped the provocation off Sondakwa's face at once, replacing the idle amusement with the expression of well familiar flash rage.

"What are you trying to say?" he growled, but the others

stepped forward, pushed themselves between the two men, knowing the signs. Sondakwa was liked in this circle of younger warriors, as much as in other circles throughout the town. He was a good man, despite his spells of hot temper that never lasted past the first stage unless developing into a serious confrontation. He was a real hothead, this brother of his, but being a son of their great father helped in the matter of townsfolk's readily offered forgiveness, reflected Atuye, not moving to join the volunteers in stopping the possible brawl.

Glancing at the sun, he considered sneaking away as originally intended. There were friends he wanted to find, and Ononta's longhouse to visit. It'd been close to two moons since she had left, trailing after her father on some strange homesick quest that the old man suddenly conceived. Why she would do this he couldn't fathom, but as certain as the Strawberry Festival that was to be held through this blissful first summer moon, they should have already returned by now. He had expected to find her back in town upon his return from the raid – his first raid! – all excitement and admiring eyes, beaming with pride at his prowess as a warrior. It was annoying not to have her around, her presence being always a part of his life, since he could remember himself. He didn't think he would miss her acutely, but he did, sometimes, a little. Food for thought? They were not children anymore, and she was a good-looking girl, as attractive as any, and if the annoying Rock People did something to her or her father…

"They will be sending a delegation to the Rock People's towns," one of the men was saying, interrupting Atuye's thoughts in a timely manner. Rock People? His attention snapped back, to notice that the discussion, apparently, had been progressing as though nothing happened, unruffled by the near-fight, with both antagonists chatting as lively as before, their possible irritation with each other either forgotten or well hidden. "And this time it would be composed of both our nations; or maybe even all three. It won't be easy to get rid of them with the elusive 'maybe' and 'we will be thinking of you, brothers.'"

"Oh yes, it would make them stop making light of our proposals," cried out several voices at once.

"Who is to lead the delegation?"

"My uncle, naturally." The old leader's nephew was oozing smugness again, matching Atuye's brother's arrogant probing quite well. These two had had a history. "He will make the stubborn Rock listen."

"And if he won't?" Sondakwa was not about to be outdone. "What would your much-admired uncle do should the intractable westerners persist in their polite 'we wish you well, brothers'?" The goading eyes flickered, provoking again, bright with their challenging contempt. "Will he lose his temper and declare war, lead our united three nations against the stubborn Rocks? His patience seems to be growing thin of late, one can't help but to notice that."

"And so is mine with *you*," breathed the younger man, two spots glowing upon his normally pale cheeks, his effort of holding into his temper showing in a pair of clenched fists.

"Stop that, Sondakwa," admonished one of the elder warriors. "Stop goading people for no better reason than your own disinterest or boredom."

Atuye watched his brother grinning broadly in response, unabashed by even such an open reprimand. Sometimes he envied his older sibling this ability to tread the thin line, to balance light cheekiness and an open disrespect, an attitude that could have landed him in serious trouble but seldom did. Somehow people tended to forgive Sondakwa his playful impudence, although since Father's death his brother had become more brazen and less playful, pushed into violence more easily, with less provocation. Through the past two summers he was a part of enough brawls and even serious fights. Mother kept complaining about it, and so did Sondakwa's woman.

He would end up like that other son of their father did, Mother would rant, sobs interrupting her harangues, waving her clenched fists at her firstborn, choking on tears – thrown out of his wife's longhouse, shamed before the entire town. Just like that good-for-nothing Ogteah. The mere mention of which was enough to lift Sondakwa out of his contemptuous arrogance and make him behave for some time. There was nothing in common between the two situations, he would mutter, eyes gleaming with fire. The actions of their universally despised half-brother being so much worse, from gambling to laying with women to general unwillingness to do something constructive and worthy of the community's trust. He, Sondakwa, was nothing like that, a respectable hunter and warrior that he was, a man who did not neglect his work and his duties.

Still the similarities were there, not according to their mother, but according to everyone else. Both men had a great deal of charm to cause people forget many of their smaller transgressions, both had violent tempers that rendered that same charm and generally good nature useless from time to time. Still, his brother was no purposeless drifter like Ogteah, concluded Atuye, forcing his concentration back on the Rock People's argument. Sondakwa was a good man.

"Will you join that delegation?" he asked later on, after the meeting had broken up and he glimpsed Sondakwa's broad figure drifting away, unaccompanied for a change, heading in the general direction of their mother's longhouse in the typical, springy, light pace, surprising in the heavyset man that he was these days. "Should they actually get organized and do it for real, send that delegation?"

The light snort was his answer.

"They won't, Little Brother." He watched the full lips twisting into a decidedly crooked sort of a grin. "And if they do, they won't get any results. The Rock People are not one of us. They are like Long Tails, more related to those westerners, witness the close contacts they are maintaining. Nothing like us or the Deer, or even the Cord bastards from out there in the north." This time, the wide shoulders lifted in a brief shrug. "There is no need to force them into our union, or even to accept them if they ask. Father said nothing about Rock People. Well, yes he did, he wanted to have all our nations united." For a moment the man hesitated, as though rethinking the matter. "Yes, he wanted them in our union, but notice that he never did something to actually make it happen. He traveled the Cord People's lands until those arrogant pieces of meat agreed to meet and talk, sending enough representatives to satisfy his wish." Halting his step, Sondakwa shook his head. "He traveled to visit the Deep People's towns at least twice, to my recollection, maybe more, until some of their representation did arrive at his cherished gathering. Remember how proudly he talked about it, with what satisfaction?" The gaze resting on Atuye was gleaming with atypical openness, soft and earnest, surprisingly sincere. "He was set on having these people in our union, and he did everything, sacrificing his life, working himself into premature death even, to make it happen."

The wide shoulders sagged all of sudden as the broad face turned away, abruptly at that. For some time they proceeded in silence, both needing brief privacy to cope with their grief. Not so fresh anymore, after more than three summers, but still there. Neither of his elder siblings was as close to Father, not as he, Atuye, was. Still they all grieved at their loss most acutely.

"I will ask Honorable Tsineka to take me along among his escorting warriors," he said finally, when the silence turned calmer, more comfortable to bear.

"Why would you do that?" Sondakwa didn't slow his step, heading for their family's longhouse, it seemed, and not the one he lived at. "It will be boring and futile, Little Brother. Dragging along the Sparkling Water's shores, all the way to its farthest edge, listening to frustrated elders complaining? You will be bored out of your senses. Especially now," the flickering gaze measured him openly, from head to toe, making Atuye feel naked, "that you have turned into a warrior at long last. And not a bad warrior at that. I talked to the leader of the group you went with, he is an old acquaintance of mine. That raid was not a huge success, yes, but for yourself you did well, shooting accurately, spotting these other circumventing warriors in time. You made me proud, Little Brother. Not so little anymore, come to think of it, eh?" The mischievous wink flickered, accompanied by a playful shove of an elbow. "Time to have more out of life, warrior, and I have in mind taking you along when we go up there to the north, to that Freshwater Sea and around. Now, out there in the Cord People's forests it will be more interesting. Bound to be."

He tried to contain his elation at so much praise, or even a mere interest from his much admired elder sibling who didn't bother to notice his very existence at times. To keep out of politics and serious dealings aside from sounding his mind, his frequently saucy, derisively offhanded remarks and observations that didn't spare people's feelings, was Sondakwa's rule in life. No one liked to be an object of his comments when Sondakwa was in the mood, but having so many summers apart Atuye was usually safe from those, unless doing something glaringly stupid. Mother always scolded her firstborn for that. And yet, now this formidable man was praising him, wishing to take him along to the Cord People's lands.

"I… yes, I will come, of course. It must be interesting out there in Ossossane. I wish Father had taken me along when he went there at first." He swallowed, desperate not to let thoughts of Father unman him, not in front of his brother who had seem to take him seriously, at long last. "But they won't start proceeding with meetings before people like Honorable Tsineka and other important dignitaries arrive. So this journey to the Rock People's towns should not prevent me from joining you later on."

A flock of girls sprung from the entrance of the nearby longhouse, their laughter preceding them like a shimmering cloud. He followed them with his gaze, then took it away as one of the girls glanced at him, her eyes flickering with amusement. She was tall and prettily built, with her hair flowing free, unrestrained by strings or combs.

"The delegation that would go to the Rock People," he hurried to say, hastening his steps when his brother wouldn't. "After they are done I'm sure they would head straight toward this Freshwater Sea and that town of Ossossane. With or without the stubborn Rock accompanying them, that is."

"Probably, yes." His brother was still trailing behind, admiring the view of so many temptingly swaying hips. At this time of the seasons some girls didn't bother to wear more than a skirt and a sash tied around their waists, in the typical field working fashion.

The girl with the free hair turned her head briefly, bestowing on Atuye another mischievous glance.

"I, well, yes… so there is no harm in me traveling with this delegation. I'll, I'll still be in time to join you out there in Ossossane."

Sondakwa's laughter was mercilessly loud, attracting the attention of everyone, not only the drifting away pretties. Even the older women who were working next to another façade, building a fire or sorting strawberries, looked up.

"You, well, yes, there might be no harm; you, yes, you will be in time." The mimicking speech came out well, making Atuye wish to cover his burning face and run away in a hurry. "Maybe you better stay and enjoy some local treats, eh, Little Brother? You are certainly old enough for this pastime, and, come to think of it, I didn't see you strutting around with pretty foxes aside from that little thing that was around you since anyone could remember you two. Why is that?"

Clenching his teeth, Atuye willed the hot wave off his face, taking a deep breath, instead. "I'm not in a hurry. To take a woman, I mean. You know, there is time for all that..." He hated the way his voice trailed off, in such helpless manner.

More laughter greeted this statement. "No one pushes you to move into this or that fox's longhouse, Little Brother. But there are plenty of pretty things out there who don't expect you, or even wish you, to commit that badly." A wink. "Like this nice-looking fowl that has been staring at you just now. Why not go after her, find out what she has in mind? Maybe it is something you wouldn't mind giving her, eh? You are not too shy to do that, young buck, do you?"

Grateful that they were still in the open, with no readily listening ears the houses were always full with, Atuye clenched his fists.

"Forget it, just forget it! I don't want to talk about it. I'm fine." Hating a new outburst of laughter, he glared at his brother, wishing he had the means to wipe all traits of amusement out of the prominently broad face, at least this once. "Just leave it alone!"

"I will, I will, oh perfectly chaste, well-behaved youth." More guffawing. "But you do need to look around, Brother. Take that advice from me." The narrowed eyes scrutinized him again, with friendly curiosity this time. "Or maybe you are waiting for that cute little shadow of yours to come back. Do you?"

Atuye just shrugged, not sure he wished to share such private thoughts with that particular brother of his. Or anyone else for that matter.

"Weren't she and her father supposed to come back already?" Sondakwa's musings followed them through the façade of their longhouse, with a turtle engraved upon it in bold lines. "How long has it been since they left?"

"Close to two moons." He slowed his step, not about to discuss any of his private affairs inside the house or in the vicinity of their mother. Not with as inconsiderate a person as Sondakwa.

"Too long to stay out there, I say." This time, his brother's voice rang with sincerity, not amused or baiting, thanks all the great and small *uki* for that. "Where did they go?"

"Onentisati."

"Where is that?"

He exhaled loudly, trapped. "Rock People. One of their towns. On the shores of our Sparkling Water."

"Rock People? Oh, I see." Of course there was no stopping Sondakwa's tongue again. "So this is why you wish to join that delegation, to go and look for your girl..."

"No, I'm not!" If he could shove his brother into the mud and come out of such an attempt unharmed and with his dignity still intact he would have. Too much to hope for, of course. Sondakwa was terribly strong, even if his temper didn't flare with violence at smallest of provocations. Though in most cases he would regret the damage he caused when blind with rage – fairly fast in his case – it didn't help the ones he would hurt while still angry and not thinking with clarity.

When Atuye was small, their longhouse would rock from monumental fights his older siblings would have, Sondakwa and Ogteah, two hot-headed boys, and then adolescents, with too easily ignited tempers. Being a summer or so older, their half-brother would usually get the upper hand, which drove Sondakwa into depths of real madness, forcing the older boy into desperate means to restrain his kicking, mad-with-anger sibling from doing silly things like trying to hurt for real, with anything handy from sticks to hoes to knives, to even a real club sometimes.

He smirked, seeing a sure way of diverting his brother's unwelcomed attention to more harmless paths.

"Do you think Ogteah is living somewhere there, among the Rock or the Deer People?"

The mention of the detested name worked miracles, as always. "I don't care where this good-for-nothing piece of meat is living. Hopefully nowhere near here."

"Well, he has to live somewhere." The storage room of their longhouse greeted them, dimly lit and relatively cool, a welcome change. "He can't live among the Cord People. They are after him, the Ossossane dwellers, or so one hears. People say he caused some big trouble there." Skirting around the first fireplace, the compartment it belonged to deserted at this time of the day, he breathed with relief. Oh, yes, now his brother's attention was anywhere but on his infatuation or possible love interest. "And he isn't anywhere here, among our people, evidently. So maybe Deer or Rock. I would say Rock. The furthest from here and from anywhere."

Sondakwa's snort could be heard on the other side of the corridor, of that Atuye was certain. "He can be living in the underworld of the Evil Twin as far as I'm concerned. As long as he doesn't come back here. Which he wouldn't. Even the unprincipled and immoral man that he is!" Another snort. "I saw his boy the other day, throwing sticks with other children out there on the ceremonial ground, playing at spear throwing. A living image of his. Disgusting!"

"Do you know what he did out there in Ossossane?" Nodding his greetings at some of their neighbors, who stretched on the bunks of their compartments, resting or talking, or squatting on the floor, busy with various tasks, Atuye headed for the fireplace belonging to their mother. "Father refused to talk about it, but I know he met him there and that something happened. Tsineka's face was taking on the color of an especially dark storm cloud every time anyone mentioned the Great Gathering and our half-brother in the same breath."

His full brother's shoulders lifted in a shrug. "Maybe we'll learn something about it out there in Ossossane." The broad face cleared with typical suddenness, over his spell of anger and as always breathtakingly fast. "Forget the stubborn Rock and come with me. We'll satisfy your curiosity in this matter and then you'll stop missing various family members that shouldn't be missed."

CHAPTER 10

"In Onentisati you will have no difficulty finding worthwhile items to exchange your goods for."

The man who said that stretched casually, covering a yawn. His name was Entiron, and being one of the prominent denizens of this same settlement called Onentisati – or so the man claimed – his pretended indifference fooled no one, lest of all Ogteah himself.

He would have been amused, replete with food and at ease, bursting with wellbeing and a sense of achievement, making the first contact and so soon, accepted readily, asked no difficult questions. Oh, yes, this mission promised to prove, indeed, an easy one, as easy as he had assured the Wolf Man it would be – some wandering about, a few days of loitering in several towns and villages, listening, asking questions, enjoying himself; then back home, full of useful information and maybe even suggestions and plans, ensuring his woman's and daughter's safety. An easy, pleasurable task, but for the Long Tails leader, the ghost, the apparition from the past. And what apparition!

He glanced at the man once again, unable not to. An unsettling vision in the flickering light of the dimming flames, or just a man, like any other silhouette around that fire, tired, relaxed, idle in a good way, a man on a journey? Not the leader of the invading enemy hordes that their warriors had made such desperate efforts to hunt down once upon a time.

According to the High Springs man many groups of eager, highly motivated warriors were sent to find this man or his body, hungering for revenge, determined and relentless, their blood boiling for the kill. They had combed every space of the shallow shores and the bushes surrounding it, finding nothing. No body, no captured warrior fitting the description. Even though it might have been still there, on the bottom of the lake, of course. The man had been wounded, unconscious most probably, spiraling down that cliff, hit by the High Springs man's club that he had hurled with such accuracy, so timely, saving his, Ogteah's, life. What a way to use a wielding weapon. But it saved him from a certain death and this was one debt he didn't mind owing. There were people one didn't feel bad being indebted to.

Again, he glanced at the Long Tail, this time meeting the impartial gaze, averting his own quickly. It was unseemly, out of place. He needed to stop this silly staring.

"I would be honored to visit your settlement, yes," he said, nodding at the man who suggested that, a friendly local who had been a tremendous help while carving and skinning his deer, leaving barely any remnants to bury in the crouch of a tree as customary. "It shouldn't be much of a detour from my original route."

"Onentisati is an important settlement," claimed another man, a broadly built type with a twisted scar crossing his right cheek all the way to the man's ear. "You will enjoy its hospitality and wouldn't wish to leave in a hurry."

Aware of the Long Tail's continued scrutiny, Ogteah forced a grin. "I have little doubts as to the hospitality of your people. So far I found no cause to complain."

Their murmurs of agreement filled the night, making it warmer, cozy and more intimate to enjoy.

"How long have you been traveling?"

He reached for another piece of charred rib. "Some dawns, less than a third of a moon. I'm not in a hurry." His shrug accompanied by a light grin was suggestive enough, he knew, meant to put them at ease. "Nagging women tend to turn more malleable when missing their men, presented with presents upon their return."

"Oh." Their grins and chuckles warmed the night. "Wise thinking, brother, wise thinking."

"Where are you heading?" Now it was appropriate to ask that, the atmosphere of easy comradeship established and firm.

"Here and there." The noncommittal answer was irritating in its lack of helpfulness.

"My people's settlements?"

"The Bear People?" The man with the scar chuckled. "No, we are not as adventurous as you are, Traveler. Your Bear People are not our enemies these days, but our brothers they aren't either."

Did this mean to confirm that the Rock People were not a part of their union? The temptation to explore the subject was difficult to battle.

"The union of all our people is not such a bad idea." He inspected the rib he was nibbling on for anything edible that might have been left there. "All our Wyandot people are brothers, aren't they?"

"Well, naturally you would say that." This time, the silence was longer, less comfortable to bear. "Your people have been pushing this union from the very beginning. Quite forcefully, one might say."

"But with a good reason." He shrugged lightly, on his guard but trying to conceal his misgivings. Was it the right time to start fishing? Or to argue about it, for that matter, making statements on behalf of his former people, backing them up on a stance he didn't even know they were holding. Even though, judging by his current company's reactions, his people were still involved in the unification process, as heavily as under Father's leadership, maybe. An interesting observation. Who was leading them these days?

"That depends." One of the men across the fire drawled his words slowly, rolling them in his mouth before letting them out. "With the firm leadership your and the Cord People are offering, so very generously at that, some might feel like avoiding joining that newly concocted extended family of yours."

So there was some pressure to have these people in. Not a mild pressure, judging by their evidently deep rooted resentment.

"What town you are coming from, what settlement?" Another cool inquiry.

He met another reserved gaze.

"My village is of no importance to anyone." Shrugging, he threw the bone into the fire, then regretted the gesture, having been left nothing to fiddle with. "Five longhouses and no worthwhile location to put us in important dignitaries' paths or concerns." He grinned, picking another roasted slice. "But I say, I like it this way. Staying away from politics and various councils kept me out of trouble so far, I can tell you that much."

The softness of their chuckling warmed the darkness again. "The best way to go about it."

"And yet you think these people should join in the Wyandot Union." The Long Tails' voice did not raise, still it overran the hum of several conversations that began breaking quietly, separating from the general talk. "For a person who claims to keep away from politics and trouble, you do have solid opinions and views, or so it seems. Well," the man shifted into a straighter pose, pulling his good leg up, resting his elbow on the comfortably bent knee, "why do you think these people should join your people and the rest of the Wyandot? And in what capacity? To straighten the non-warring agreements? To participate in your Bear People's wars? How do you envision this alliance your people seem to be eager to draw everyone into?"

Ogteah felt his stomach going rigid, turning into a solid rock, squeezed in a familiar stony grip. No possibility of relaxing or drawing a deep breath, not with this man around. He forced his limbs to remain in their semi-sprawling position, even though his entire body was like a coiled sinew, ready to recoil, to spring up and face a possible assault.

"I envision nothing," he said, marveling at the sound of his voice, calm, aloof, only mildly irritated. "Like I said, I don't associate with influential people, neither in my village nor in any other. The matter of our people's union is up to our councils, elders and clan mothers to decide on, to insist or persuade or make others join in." With an effort he unclenched his palm from the remnants of the juicy meat, forcing what was left into his mouth, his jaw numb and tingling, needing to be coerced into chewing with a conscious effort. "My lot as a simple hunter satisfies me."

"And yet you do have goods to trade."

Again, to go on chewing required an effort. "Yes, I do."

"What do they seek to offer in exchange for our goods up there in the north?" The Onentisati man shifted easily, the lightness of his voice alone bringing the level of the tension down, or so it seemed. "Do they miss something we do have in abundance?"

Ogteah forced his mind to concentrate. What did he remember from his stay in Arontaen? Did this town's people possess things that his own people didn't? He couldn't recollect. Time to gamble, then.

"Oh, they do have different things. Pretty jewelry, for one. Beautiful bands of quill and shells, spectacular necklaces." He let his imagination wander. To prove him wrong the man would have to travel all the way to that Beautiful Lake or the Freshwater Sea even, and by that time he, Ogteah, would be safely back home, with the entire Great Lake separating him from the people he was deceiving now. "Their strings of white and purplish shells are incredible, very pretty. Sometimes they symbolize important agreements with those."

He remembered the *wampum* belts he had seen commemorated, or given, or exchanged at the Onondaga Town's valley. Beautiful items with deepest of meanings. It felt that he could study those for days, if allowed, enjoying just holding them in his hands. Not an option, of course. Only certain faith-keepers and the representatives who held important positions received these tokens of the entire union's trust. Even the War Chief hasn't been offered a *wampum* upon receiving the burden of responsibility.

He shook the memories off. "Some of their utensils, pottery and ware are different, too. And the pipes, those are beautiful, very invested, alluringly carved."

"Oh, I didn't think..." The Onentisati man's eyes sparkled greedily, full of attention. "And what do you bring to offer them in return?"

Ogteah stretched, relaxing gradually. The Long Tails was still watching him – he could feel the scrutinizing gaze most acutely, measuring him, hiding neither dislike nor suspicion – still it felt better to talk to someone gullible, eager to listen.

"My goods are mostly the spoils from the other side of the Great Lake," he said lightly, reminding himself to stick to the truth now, any lie easy to discover the moment he went to fetch his canoe. "Weaponry, decorated clothing. Tools. A birds' trap. Practical items," he added with a grin. "They like practicality, those northerners."

"*Wampum* belts too?" Again the mere voice of the Long Tails served to disperse the comfortable feeling. There was such an obvious note of pronounced contempt to it, such aloof self-assurance. It was as though the man knew that he, Ogteah, was lying, spinning a web of tales and half-truths. But how? Did he remember him after all and just pretended that he didn't?

"What belts?"

"The white and purplish strings of shells, the ones you mentioned in connection with the northern people." A light pause. "The savages are commemorating their events and agreements in much the same way. An interesting similarity."

Was that a purposeful statement? Ogteah's back covered with cold sweat. What had come over him to lie in such silly way, with no necessity to do that at all? Why did he let his tongue loose while sinking into nostalgic recollection?

"Yes, the savages do that," he said calmly, then wanted to bite his tongue off once again. How was he supposed to know what 'the savages' did if he wasn't supposed to cross the Great Lake but as a part of a raiding party? Stupid, stupid, stupid! "I heard people saying something to that effect." He forced his shoulders to lift in demonstrated indifference. "A strange custom."

"Not so strange." The Long Tails shifted closer to the fire, passing one of his palms above it as though trying to feel it. "This is one of the customs that I would imagine your alliance should be adopting. They are not such mindless brutes, those savage enemies of yours. Sometimes they can be quite sensible in their ways." The narrow face twisted. "In certain rare instances."

Pondering his answer with extra care now, Ogteah heard one of the men snorting. "They are your enemies too, Attiwandaronk man. Your people have been defeated by the Great League soundly, and not so very long ago."

The darkness thickened. Even though the Long Tails man didn't change his position, didn't stir or moved for that matter, his dark silhouette emanated a momentary danger, an almost tangible threat. A mountain lion one might have disturbed without thinking. But what did these people's name mean if not exactly that – the long tail mountain lion.

"They are our enemies, yes." The voice of the foreigner was just a little too stony. "We have fought the Great League, and we put everything we had into the attempt to curb the stone giant, to arrest its progress and stop their gobbling more valleys and forests and hunting grounds." The air hissed, drawn in forcefully through the boldly carved nostrils. "We have lost but not through lack of determination, bravery or skill. Hundreds of our fallen warriors testify to that matter. They had fought until not a grain of strength was left in their bodies. The enemy has to work hard to better them, and their own fallen littered the ground worse than the colorful leaves of the Hunting and Fishing Moons."

Another spell of silence prevailed, interrupted by the wailing of the wind, the strong gusts coming from the lakeside, as though eager to contribute, to create a background. He remembered the dead, yes, littering the ground, their and the enemy's warriors, strong, worthy, unyielding, the best of their nations, all dying for what? He didn't know, didn't ask these questions, not anymore.

Clenching his teeth, he pushed the memories away, dominating them with a practiced skill, a possible feat these days. After the fighting in the Flint People's lands it was easier to put such things in the right perspective. People fought because they couldn't not do so, because if you wanted peace you had to be strong enough to maintain it and make your neighbors understand and respect, by force if necessary – a circle with no way out. Was the Great Peacemaker troubled by such dilemmas? Did he see a better way out?

"Have you participated in this battle?" The voice of one of the men rang out eerily, mesmerized by the story as they all were.

The Long Tail shuddered, as though awakening from a dream.

"No," he said slowly, eyes still on the fire, wandering far, far away. "The elders of my village did not believe in this war and they didn't let us, the warriors, join." A shrug. "We are located nowhere near the troubled areas, nowhere near the hideous enemy or the Great Lake of the western Long Tails."

"Oh." The people nodded, satisfied, breaking into another bout of smaller conversations. Everyone but the greedy local of Onentisati noticed Ogteah, who was studying the Long Tail with his eyes narrowed into slits, highly attentive. As did Ogteah himself, his thoughts swirling wildly, trying to grasp the meaning of what had been said.

Did this man just lie about his lack of participation in the Long Tails War? He was out there, most certainly he was, and not just participating but leading, huge contingents of warriors if not all of them. Was he really Attiwandaronk rather than the western Long Tail? Maybe. They still didn't know nearly enough about these people, even after besting them on the battlefield and in such spectacular manner. Questioning captives helped, let them learn a great deal about those dwellers of the Thundering Water River falls and beyond them. Not nearly enough to comprise a worthwhile picture, but something, more than they had known before. The Wolf Man was prowling these areas for the last three summers, sniffing around, making it safe for their own people to wander, hunt and fish, if not to build towns as yet. He had far-reaching plans, this younger son of the Onondaga War Chief, such spectacular warrior, a born leader.

Oh, but the Wolf Man would welcome the tales of the fugitive Long Tails or Attiwandaronk leaders, surviving the war but hiding their identities. For wasn't it what this man across the fire was doing now, lying about his past, posing as someone he clearly was not? Much like him, Ogteah, come to think of it. But for what purpose? Why was this one sniffing around the Wyandot and their prospective alliances, and why disguised?

Putting his attention back to the greedy local, who seemed eager to inspect the new visitor's goods, Ogteah forced his mind into calmness. He had an entire night to spend with these people, to wheedle all sorts of invitations, whether to accompany his newfound companions on their way back home to this same

Onentisati town, or to any other possible destination, which would serve his purpose as long as their exotic Long Tail company came along. Oh, but this was an unexpected bonus, the best way of going about his business, learning their plans. Didn't the Wolf Man express this particular concern, the Rock People's obstinate support of their fierce but defeated western neighbors?

Well, running into the former leader of these same people they didn't even dream to learn about was a rare stroke of good fortune. Especially when this same leader had evidently gone to some lengths hiding his real identity. Not an opportunity a wise person would let go by. And he was wise enough, wasn't he?

Elated for the first time since the unnerving encounter, he eyed his adversary across the fire, sitting there calm and unperturbed once again, at ease, his liabilities like the bad leg not on display. A formidable man, a dangerous presence. What was his game? And why was he hiding who he truly was while traveling among these people, people who had nothing to do with the Long Tails War, people who cherished no soft spots for the Great League or its members, no eager volunteers to hunt down the prominent leader of the defeated nation, on the run or not?

"The war of the Long Tails and the Longhouse People was vicious, or so one hears," he said casually, eyeing the prettily carved pipe that was making its way toward him, passed to their side of the fire. "Some say there were hundreds of warriors fighting each other. Many hundreds." He shrugged. "I suppose it must be a wild exaggeration."

"It is not." The Long Tails voice rang out stonily, its irritation open. "This was the greatest battle our people, *any of our people*, even the savages from across, ever saw or participated at." He gave Ogteah a dark look. "And the time of keeping away or being careful and neutral is gone. One day, not so far removed from now, your people will also learn all about the Longhouse League's might and viciousness. And you'd better be ready, united and prepared, more than we were. Otherwise, you will face as terrible a defeat as ours was."

In spite of himself Ogteah shivered, the detached, almost dispassionate voice making the words sound more ominous and portentous, more real. Oh, but how it must have felt, to be defeated like that and after making such a tremendous effort, gathering so many warriors and making such daring plans. Had they lost the battle of Honeoye Lake they might have spoken like this man now, gloomy and accepting yet somehow not dispirited, not defeated as yet.

"The enemy from across the Great Lake is not a threat to our people or settlements," said the man to whom Ogteah had passed the pipe in his turn, his voice as calm and detached, but lacking the undercurrents. "We do not need to join their alliance to fight our neighbors' and brothers' battles."

The Long Tail didn't stir. "The enemy will start sniffing around your settlements soon enough. As soon as they begin feeling at home around the Thundering Water of Oniagara River and these shores of the Great Sparkling Lake that are facing your forests from across."

"They will never venture so far," cried out several voices.

The Long Tails' chuckle held not a flicker of mirth or lightness. "You had better prepare for this to happen and in the near future, too. A few more summers and they will feel at home at the forests and valleys they have pushed us from, with the villages of the Mountain People, your prospective neighbors, popping out like mushrooms after a good rain."

You are well informed, thought Ogteah, holding his breath, afraid to miss a word. *Where do you get your information from?*

"Why do you assume that?" he asked, anxious to keep his voice as casual as he could. "We warred on these people for summers, for longer than anyone could remember, aside from some brief attempts at peace that never held. It is an old tradition with us. Still you don't see their, or ours for that matter, settlements popping out anywhere outside our own forests and clearings."

This time, the pause looked as though it would last forever. Then the Long Tails man shook his head.

"You compare two different situations, Bear People's traveler. The Great Lake is separating you from your most ancient enemy, while nothing of the sort stands between my people and the savage league of their neighbors to the east." The air hissed loudly as the man drew a deep breath, the boldly carved nostrils of his impressively prominent nose widening. "Once they crossed their Ge-ne-see River and spread around unopposed, as they did through the last summer and sometime before that, there is nothing to stop them from claiming these forests for their own, and from doing so with confidence, backed by the knowledge that there is no one to prevent them from doing this. It is not the same with the obstacle the Great Sparkling Water provides you. The enemy won't be spreading around your side of it unless as a raiding party, no matter what defeats they may be inflicting upon you."

Good thinking, reflected Ogteah, hard put not to admire the man's grasp and understanding. *We are spreading to the west of the defeated Long Tails – how does this man know all about it? – and we are spreading to the east behind the Eastern Door Keepers as well.* Even in the south, where there was nothing but scattered villages of some people he never bothered to learn about, not yet, his new Onondaga countryfolk started to send an occasional raid. He has been too busy fighting with the Flint last summer, learning upon his return of those southern incursions. Some people lived there along another great river, a watershed with muddy waters, or so one might have assumed. People of the Muddy River they were called. An amusing name, but then Crooked Tongues or Rontaks – Tree Eaters, as the Flint were calling the neighbors they had fought against – were not better aliases, either.

"I see the strength of your argument," he said, not willing to appear suspiciously obtuse, or worse yet, probing. How did this man come by so much knowledge of what was going on behind that Thundering Waters of theirs? Was he still the leader of the Long Tails, and only this time traveling in disguise? "And I appreciate the wisdom of your words. However, even if not facing an immediate danger of being thrown out of our own towns and forests, we still need to confront the enemy with more efficiency than we did until now. Strong and allied to our brothers, we stand a better chance."

It came out well. Unsettled, he listened to himself, not liking the way he was thinking now, *like they did*. But he was not one of them, not anymore. Father was dead and these people were not his people. Strangers, enemies, they threatened his family, his woman and child, and the rest of his countryfolk, his true people. Convincing the stubborn fence sitters of the Rock to join the Wyandot alliance was not his mission. Anything but!

"Yes, united you do stand a better chance," the Long Tails man was saying, less hostile than before as well. Did he too sense a change? Ogteah pressed his lips tight.

For some time he listened to the others speaking, quietly, at peace, envious of their lack of concern. These Rock People truly had it unfairly easy, situated between the grudgingly friendly Deer and Cord, who wanted them and wooed them to join in an alliance, and the defeated Long Tails, who could do little save offering amiability and peace. Were these people helping their southern neighbors actively, supporting and aiding the Great League's enemies, maybe even encouraging them to rise again? The Wolf Man wanted to know that and judging by the presence of the Long Tails former, or maybe not so former, leader on the first casually traveling party he had met, these people, indeed, might be keeping very close contacts. And no, not as a part of the Wyandot Union they hadn't even bothered to join as yet.

"We did hear of the Longhouse People's intrusions somewhere there in the south or the west," he said later, when the conversations broke and the people began drifting away, most into a restful sleep, curling in their blankets. Some wandered off down the shore. To do their needs, he presumed, eyeing the remaining silhouettes, five all in all, with both the Long Tails and the local interested in Ogteah's goods still there, squatting comfortably, talking quietly or just staring into the fire, the case with the foreigner, as expected.

"What did you hear about that?" The formidable man didn't change his position, eyes glued to the dancing flames.

Ogteah shrugged, his own gaze on the glowing embers. "Rumors, stories of strange places, rivers with difficult names, an unheard of amount of warriors. We didn't hear about your war with these people until it happened. But then the stories that reached us were wild. Not many believed those." He shrugged again. "That's why I'm curious."

"There was no exaggeration in the stories that reached you." The man paused, closing his eyes for a moment, as though recollecting his thoughts. "I wasn't a part of it, but I know many people who were there, fighting bravely, giving it all in their desperate effort to stop the enemy." His sigh was deep, holding a measure of acceptance. "There were many hundreds of warriors fighting on either side. The enemy was twice as numerous, and better prepared." The silhouetted head shook forcefully. "No, we were as prepared and as determined, but our leadership was divided, in disagreement. We listened to too many war chiefs, with each claiming better knowledge, a better planning than the rest, unwilling to *actually* listen, sometimes too hesitant, sometimes too eager and battle-hungry, behaving like simple warriors and no leaders." The man shook his head again, then looked up, his eyes coming to rest on Ogteah, alive with passion. "The mistake you will have to remember to avoid when your time comes. Your people must be led by wise men, united in their thinking. They will have to remember to listen to each other and let the best leading man among them decide. Your enemy is too devious and too well prepared to contain them with a raid or two, or with a horde of too many warriors charging at once. That won't work. They think quickly, these people. They listen to their leaders who are in enough agreement between each other, and they change their plans when they see advantages of the situation. You will have to be all that and more to best this menace." The wide shoulders lifted slowly, as though too tired for even this simple gesture. "Or you will go down in as terrible defeat as ours was."

Hopefully yes, thought Ogteah, making sure his face reflected nothing but an appropriate attentiveness mixed with light interest, a noncommittal curiosity.

The man was wise and perceptive, full of knowledge and deep thoughts, a formidable enemy, indeed. No wonder he was still alive, still involved, still trusted by his people, despite the defeat. Was he leading them, Attiwandaronk or any other Long Tail that he might be? Was he stirring trouble once again?

Most certainly he was, but to what extent and among whom? The Rock People or the other Wyandot who were prepared to listen, like he, Ogteah, now seemingly did? Oh, but just a little spark of interest, a lightly expressed curiosity, made the man talk readily, with less care than before. Was he doing it a lot, going among local towns and villages, teaching them how to fight against the Great League, how to try to best it using its own tactics?

Oh Mighty Spirits, but this man was dangerous, a bad influence, his evaluation of the situation and the past mistakes astute, disturbingly correct. That was exactly what some of their captives, those who consented to talk, had told them back after the battle. The Long Tails and their Attiwandaronk allies had no concord, no mutual understanding as to the way of conducting their war; they didn't wish to listen to each other, and some of their leaders thought they knew better than the ones who planned this entire campaign.

But how did you know about us changing our plans on a spur of a moment? he wondered, trying to remember, to find a clue, a possible explanation. How would this man know of their original plans, that the Honeoye Lake's trap was an improvisation, a grab of an opportunity, with the fleeing woman informing them of the nearing invasion and the treacherous little snake of a girl tricked into conveying their message back. The girl! These days his stomach did not convulse as violently as before, in a wave of a terrible rage the moment he thought of her. Still, he remembered. Akweks' spirit deserved it, if nothing else did.

"Do you know people who were in leading positions while conducting this war?" he asked innocently, enjoying the measure of superiority his knowledge gave him over his opponent. Even though he couldn't help but feel strange sympathy toward the man. An impressive person and not shabby or evil, or treacherous, something one would wish to believe of one's enemy. Especially this one, responsible for so many deaths and destruction. "Do they share your opinion on the mistakes that you believe they made?"

"Some of them." The man nodded gravely, as reserved as before, again on guard. "Not many leaders survived that battle, to make it back home and busy themselves with trying to understand what they had done wrong." He snorted bitterly. "But those who did certainly know what their blunders or errors of judgment were. One has to be blind to miss that. Or make an effort not to see." The prominent features froze again, set into a stony mask. "Or sometimes to refuse acknowledge the truth."

"Enough of your people must have made it back home," prompted Ogteah when the pause turned too long, promising no more revelations. "Even though it must not have been easy. Didn't the enemy chase you?"

But this was taking it too far. The stony mask hardened even further.

"How should I know? Like you, I heard it all from various sources, often contradicting stories and tales." The eyes measuring Ogteah grew colder. "You are curious about that war, Bear People man. One may start wondering why? You are not anywhere near my people's forests, now any more than when in your homelands."

He didn't take his gaze away, answering the flinty challenge with a freezing stare of his own, refusing to be intimidated.

"I'm curious, yes," he said coldly, aware of the listening ears, the nosy local and some of the others. "The enemy you fought was my people's enemy long before your people became aware of its viciousness. I appreciate your people's bravery and daring and I want to learn about it from more than mere rumors. That is my only reason."

Slightly raised eyebrows were his answer. Accompanied with a cold nod, they made him wish to breathe with relief only when the man turned away, back to his flame-staring, probably.

What was that about the annoying piece of meat? he wondered. Why did this man keep putting him, Ogteah, on the defensive? Because he had almost killed him once? But it happened a long time ago, and not in a fair hand-to-hand. He might manage to overcome such a rival these days, or at least to put up a good fight. What happened on the cliff above Honeoye Lake did not represent him as a warrior or a man. And neither did it represent the Long Tail.

"The Strawberry Ceremony would be held through the first part of this moon," the Rock People man was saying, interrupting the tension, inadvertently, or so it seemed. "A spectacular celebration in as large a settlement as ours. You should not miss it, Bear People man. Onentisati is such a short way from here. Just a few dawns of a journey."

Nodding, Ogteah transferred his attention to the greedy local, knowing too well what the man wanted. His goods, or some of them. He would have to be careful while dealing with this type. The possibility of sailing away poorer was a fair one, and no, not through violence or theft. This man must be a shrewd trader.

"I will be honored to attend the celebration of your people," he said, all courtesy and goodwill, his smile not wavering, even though his skin felt the glance of his Long Tails converser once again, a prolonged inquiring stare. "But I wouldn't wish to be the cause of you interrupting your original journey."

And I would rather join you and your foreign company, he thought, desperate to find the excuse to suggest that. Something, anything.

"Oh, it would be my pleasure to escort you back to Onentisati. Our people's hospitality knows neither limits nor boundaries. You will find nothing to reproach us with, Bear People's man."

Ogteah stopped his eyes from rolling. Fat chance! But to enter one of the Rock People's settlements, invited and escorted, eagerly at that, had its merits. These people would yield enough information, about their relationship with the Long Tails as well. Oh yes, this direction was as good as any.

CHAPTER 11

"You can't be serious."

Blinking, Ononta watched her companion maneuvering the compact dugout canoe she and her father had arrived at Onentisati more than two moons ago, navigating it deeper into the water, disregarding the currents that were ready to pounce on it. This part of the river invited anything but a leisurely sail, the high banks towering all around, aloof and unfriendly. Not a place people were coming to wash, or even to fish, for that matter.

"What are you doing?"

As expected, her companion ignored the anxious questioning, too busy with her paddle, standing in the middle of the boat, maintaining her balance with an enviable ease. When her eyes were not busy estimating the obstacles and the currents, they shot at the boy, who was leaning over his side of the vessel, dipping his palms into the current, unconcerned. Even the baby in Ononta's lap was napping. Out of all four, she seemed to be the only one worried.

"Here." Finally, the concentrated glance brushed past Ononta, businesslike and oblivious of her continues protests. "Now give me the baby and take the paddle."

"No, I can't!" Backing away as much as the crowded vessel allowed her, Ononta pressed the warm bundle tighter to her chest. "We'll sweep into the rapids."

"No, we won't." The smile flashed, one of the rare ones, an encouraging, somewhat mischievous grin that she came to recognize from the recent days spent in the company of this strange woman. Half a moon to be precise, but what a half moon!

"We are far from the rapids, very far and the current isn't strong here. Come, we've been through it already. You know what to do. You rowed this boat before."

"I rowed it on that other shore, with calm waters. I didn't—"

But the paddle thrust into her hands uncompromisingly, as the girl snatched the baby, deftly enough not to cause him even to stir, snug in his blankets, not minding changing hands.

"Come, start rowing. We are drifting toward the cliffs. See those shoals. We don't want to have our canoe tossed between them." Another encouraging smile. "Get us back to the deep water."

Clutching the boat's side with her free hand, Ononta pushed herself up, causing their vessel to waver, precariously at that. Or so she felt.

"I can't… I won't be in time!"

As her guide's eyes were on the river again, estimating their changing course, no answer came. She clenched her teeth and half crawled, half stumbled toward the middle of the boat, not helped by the boy's giggling, his laughter ringing merrily in the clarity of the high morning air. Angered, she stabilized herself by spreading her legs wide between the rough wooden borders.

"Good." Apparently, their guide's eyes were back upon her. "Now start rowing. Push against our right side until we reach deeper water. Then do as I did. No, not like this!" This time, the unmelodious voice raised a little, and the canoe wavered again as she felt the young woman's presence beside her, one hand free of the baby, gripping Ononta's paddle, directing it. "Like this. Put more effort. Dip it deeper, much deeper. After the boat is back and steady, you can relax. But make sure you sink your paddle equally, like I told you before. Sink it into the water, don't just caress it."

Encouraged by the realization that she was not completely on her own, that her friend was still able to take the lead if necessary, the baby weighing her slender arms down or not, but mainly because the boat reacted at long last, turning away from the unfriendly crags, Ononta did as she was told. It was harder to plunge the paddle up to the middle of its wider side, but there was no arguing the fact that the boat did react now, more readily than before.

"Yes, just like that."

To her further sense of security their self-appointed leader remained where she was, not attempting to take herself and the baby to a more comfortable spot, keeping her balance next to the tottering Ononta as though still on a dry land.

"Harder, dip it deeper, push with all your strength."

Ononta almost shut her eyes with an effort, as though her clenched teeth weren't enough. It seemed futile, all those attempts to best the current. It was more powerful than her. But of course it was. The river was an entity in itself, a very powerful presence. Of course it was stronger than her. That's why she never thought of trying to challenge it.

"Good. Don't stop. Go on or we'll be back drifting toward the shoals." The boat was now wavering, as though hesitating between the courses. "Pull the paddle out, don't let it linger in there. Bring it back in faster."

The relentless orders kept coming, making Ononta wish to tell its owner off. It was not her idea to challenge the mighty current. Tsutahi – by now she had learned her newfound friend's name – was the one to take them on this adventure. And it wasn't their first time.

To steer her thoughts off the unpleasant task, she recount their first encounter. Not the one with the carved deer and much embarrassing misunderstandings, but the later one, when she had played with the little son of this strange woman and they had talked.

Since that late afternoon, they had spent much time together, as much as they could manage between Ononta's ministering to her ailing father and her halfhearted attempts to be of help around the longhouse that hosted her. Father wasn't burning with fever anymore, and his coughing was hard but not as hopelessly choking as before. Which left her with more time to herself, a time the women of the longhouse that hosted her would have usurped by putting her to work in their fields but for the planting being almost over. There were not many pressing tasks for the female population of the town to undertake besides engaging in preparations for the Strawberry Ceremony, which required many groups being sent out there and into the woods to gather the wonderfully sweet, juicy forest fruit.

A chore everyone welcomed eagerly, even the woman of the foreigner. In absence of her husband and with her boy needing to be fed his medicine only a few times a day, the strange girl took to escaping the longhouse that hosted her and her children on every opportunity or even without it, grabbing quite a few baskets on her way out, coming back with plenty of fruit. A decent way of paying for one's upkeep. But hadn't she been afraid to wander out there all alone?

When asked about it, the girl laughed in her unmelodious, inappropriately loud voice, the smug expression that Ononta came to recognize smoothing her perpetual frown, making the sharp-looking face look younger again. The woods were the best place to be at, she had been informed, the best and the safest, and why didn't she come along on the next day?

The suggestion Ononta jumped on eagerly, happy to inform the women of their longhouse that she was going to do something useful, at long last. She knew what they said about her behind her back, or even into her face. Too soft, too delicate, maybe not lazy but certainly not much of a help. Oh, but how she craved the journey back home!

"And why won't you?" Her newfound friend asked her, when they had roamed through the woods, following invisible paths the strange girl was finding with an impossible ease, as though sensing where the deer would go, plenty of imperceptible tracks disappearing in seemingly impenetrable bushes until stepping right through the prickly wall, discovering a narrow corridor. A wonder! "Why won't you take your father, now that he doesn't burn anymore, and sail home?"

The boy was tagging at her hand, demanding attention in that typical, bouncy, energetic way of his. Ononta smiled at him absently.

"What do you mean? Father is not burning up, yes, but he is terribly weak. He can't even walk by himself. He doesn't leave his bunk but for making his needs out there, and he needs help to do even that, you see?"

Her companion dived into yet another trackless congregation of foliage. "Do you have a large enough boat?"

Following the bouncing silhouette of the boy that disappeared at the same impenetrable spot, Ononta discovered that if she moved a few prickly branches away, a tiny pathway was facing her, offering its guidance. "Well, yes, our boat is not tiny."

This answer, as expected, was greeted by cracking vegetation, her and the boy's progress marked by enough noise, but not that of his mother. That woman moved like a real forest creature.

"Our boat, it's not very small," she repeated, when back in the more open ground, catching their guide's gaze for a heartbeat. The girl was scanning the clearing they had reached suspiciously, as though listening to imperceptible sounds all around them. Or maybe to her inner senses, the likeliest of cases.

"You can make your father as comfortable as you can," she said, still watching the surrounding trees, as the boy broke into an excited yelping, rushing to plunder the treasure such well-hidden clearing managed to secret away. So many berries! "He will have plenty of rest while on your long journey, and the forest and its freshness would help him recover even faster." The girl's face darkened. "It always does."

Ononta found herself staring. "What do you mean?" Shifting her basket while putting the other two down, she glanced at her companion, making sure she hadn't been talking in vain. "I can't take my sick father all alone and on such a journey. How can I?"

"Why not?" Busy untying the blanket, fishing the sleeping baby out of it, the young woman made a face. "It can't be such a difficult journey. You did it before, when arriving here, didn't you? So you know how it is. How many rapids did you have to overcome by walking rather than sailing? If not many, then you have nothing to worry about." Briskly, she rearranged the blanket in one of the vacant baskets, placing the baby in there, its grunts faint, floating in the crispy air, not threatening to turn into screams. "Just follow the rivers you followed on your way here and make sure to bring plenty of dried food, in case you don't manage to hunt."

"Me? Hunt? You must be joking!" Not pacified with her companion's lack of mirth – the girl couldn't suggest what she did seriously, could she? – Ononta shook her head. "I don't find it funny, your jokes. It's not the time."

But a deepening frown was her answer. "Why would I make jokes? If you want to go home, you should go. Your father would feel better this way as well. I think you should do it. I would have."

Picking another vacant basket, her companion shrugged, proceeding toward the un-pillaged part of the clearing, with the little rascal still busy in his original spot, gorging to his heart's content, his face smeared with so much juice it turned unrecognizable, a warrior on a warpath. Ononta paid the little rascal no attention, busy with her own storm of feelings.

"I can't navigate the canoe all by myself, not through so many rivers and streams." Pushing next to her companion, she made sure her face and mainly the moving lips were visible, within her converser's view. "How can you say something like that? How can you assume I could take my ailing father and just sail away? It's insane. I don't believe you would have done it, despite what you say. It's not a sail toward the nearest village!" As though she would have attempted something like that, still she pushed on, too enraged to try to be honest. "How can you say that? Women don't do that, they don't travel by themselves. Well, decent women don't do that. They sail with their men when they need to travel. Or other male relatives. You did it too, you did!" The victorious feeling prevailed. "Why don't you take your children and sail back home where you came from, if you say it can be done? Why wait for your man to have him take you back, huh?"

The girl was glaring at her, enraged as well now. "We came in one canoe. I can't leave him with no vessel to sail home, can I?" The slender eyebrows straightened, shot to meet each other across the scowling forehead. "And anyway, I'm waiting for Tsami to finish with his medicine. The moment it's over I will be thinking over this matter again. If my man doesn't come back shortly thereafter as he promised, I may be gone, yes. And he will have to carve or trade himself a new boat!"

Ononta felt like shaking her head in frustration. "You wouldn't do that to him. And it doesn't make much sense, anyway. You can't sail all alone. Even if you don't live that far…"

"I can and I will," stated the woman firmly, turning back toward her empty container. "And so should you."

This time, the pause lingered, filled with the sounds of the hopping-around child and the rustling of his mother's basket, getting filled in a vigorous manner. Ononta studied her own empty vessel.

"We don't belong here, either of us." Again the woman was speaking too loudly, in an irritating disharmony of words. "It's good enough reason not to stay. And yes, it won't be an easy journey for you, without help from your father and with the need to care for him, but this is not a good reason to stay in the place you are clearly unhappy at." The thin shoulders lifted in a brief shrug. "If you were happy here, yes. If your father was happy and healthy. But it is not so with both of you, so you should gather your courage and leave. You'll make it. There is no reason to assume you won't."

"No, I can't. How can I?" Forgetting all about her companion's inability to listen with her back on the speaker, Ononta waved her hands in the air. "The journey back home is long and so terribly difficult. And we must bring plenty of food, and maybe medicine. And I can't row for days on end. How can I?" She pressed her palms to her burning cheeks. "And the rapids! How am I to carry our canoe and our things, and… and help Father when, when we need to detour by foot? We had plenty such crossings on our way here. And I wouldn't even recognize raging water before it would be upon us. And I…"

The sight of her companion picking her berries placidly, wholly immersed, made Ononta angry. Did this girl care at all for any of that, her plight, her troubles, besides giving an offhanded, judgmental, annoyingly condescending advice? Did she enjoy her superior knowledge and abilities here in the woods, the unfriendly, unsociable person that she was?

Then she remembered, and the burning in her face grew worse.

She was talking to herself now, addressing her passionate protests to no one but the forest itself. How stupid!

"Rapids? We have rapids at home." Apparently not the forest alone was her audience. The boy hopped above the nearest cluster of bushes, positively beaming. "Those are bad rapids. So very loud. And Father says not to sail them. But *annen* does, sometimes. When she is in a hurry to get home." He straightened his back, triumphant. "We never fell out of our canoe, never."

Ononta attempted a forced smile. "Your *nnen* can do anything, can't she?"

A series of vigorous nods was her answer.

"Listen." Whether the object of their gossiping felt the developing discussion, or maybe she just thought about what had been said before, the delicate face was peering at them from below, half squatting, half kneeling, her basket partly full already. "I know it won't be easy for you. You are not used to taking care of yourself. Not in the way of surviving out there," she added hurried, clearly sensing the forming protests. "But believe me, you can do anything, just anything, when you decide that it needs to be done. You just manage." The girl shrugged lightly, shifting her shoulders to ease the tension. "And things do work out, they do, always, when you are prepared to put in a real effort." Another shrug came accompanied with a light, surprisingly amiable smile. "You know that you will have to undertake this journey. There is no point in postponing it, or trying to hope for easier solutions."

Ononta just stared, as did the boy, surprisingly still and attentive for a change. Even the baby in his cozily padded basket stopped his muffled grunting, as though wishing to listen, too.

"No, no, my determination is not enough." But her protests were brushed aside, in a surprisingly patient manner this time, and so they finished filling the baskets they brought later than expected, spending much time on talking, instead.

There were more days like that, gathering more forest fruit for their hosting longhouses, or just wandering about. Her companion knew everything, just everything, was Ononta's dazzled conclusion. From reading the earth to picking its hidden treasures and offerings, to knowing what had to be done with those, this young girl, barely her own age if not less, was at home at any surroundings, in the forest or upon the river, climbing cliffs to get especially tasty treats such as birds' eggs, or prowling the shallow waters, picking various delicacies from the shoals for the three of them to gorge on.

Talking readily and with surprising patience, she would explain every step, then insist that Ononta and not only her eager little boy would do it all by themselves, track fresh prints in the mud or at least recognize them for what they were. Reluctant at first, Ononta found these challenges more and more of a pleasurable pastime, astounded at the ease with which some tasks could be completed if a person knew what to do. The power, the knowledge, and the occasional success thrilled her senses to no end. She wasn't as useless as they all assumed, was she?

"How did you learn to track the forest dwellers so easily?" she had asked after one day their mentor led them to a whole herd of lively grazing deer, their whitish tails up, skins twitching against the assaulting mosquitoes.

Already heading away, having done nothing with their discovery – well, obviously, what could they do about it? – the young woman shrugged, her smile fleeting but good.

"I lived in the woods since I was little. Only Grandfather and I." The smile was back, atypically open and warm. "He taught me everything. He was a great man."

There was no need to ask what happened to the old man. The fading smile told Ononta the story.

"And your man?" she prompted, anxious to divert her companion's thoughts to more cheerful paths, curious to learn all about this strange family. They did live all alone in the woods, didn't they?

"My husband is as great of a man," declared the girl firmly, the gathering sadness, indeed, leaving her eyes, replaced with a firm conviction. "I can't tell you all about his past, but just believe me when I say that he is one of the greatest men my people or their neighbors ever saw."

"What did he do?" breathed Ononta, fascinated.

"I can't tell you that. I'm sorry." But it looked as though the

young woman was sorrier for her inability to tell it all than
Ononta was for her inability to hear any of it.

"Yes, *nnen* says not to talk about Father and what a great
warrior he was," contributed Tsami, as always skipping all
around when not busy exploring. Earlier, while sneaking about
the herd the boy displayed a surprising ability to keep quiet, but
now he had had enough.

"Tsamihui!" called out his mother, apparently watching her
son's lips. There were many occasions upon which the little rascal
managed to speak freely and without receiving a well-deserved
reprimand, occasions that were no mere accidents. This boy was a
clever little thing and such a mischief! Ononta stifled a giggle.

"I won't be running around telling things about your man,"
she said, smiling broadly. After a few days spent together she felt
completely at ease in her current company, the way she never felt
with any of this town's people after living in Onentisati for more
than a full moon. "After all, I will be leaving soon too, won't I?"

That statement drew a matching smile in return. "Yes, you will.
Very soon."

They had been planning her and her father's journey for some
dawns by now, discussing the details, all possible hurdles and
difficulties and the ways of coping with those, from the amount of
provisions to take along, to Ononta's lack of experience in
navigating a floating vessel. Just on the day before, her mentor
insisted on visiting the shore where many local boats were stored,
to look up Ononta's father's canoe.

Spending no time on mincing the matters, the girl had made
the three of them enter the boat, forcing a paddle snatched from
another canoe into the protesting Ononta's hands, demanding to
be shown what her charge could do with it. Some training, a bit of
practicing and she would manage, maintained the girl in the end,
insisting that Ononta should bring the vessel to the exactly
indicated spot, uncompromising. Some rowing around and she
would be able to undertake the journey, and so here they were, a
few dawns later and in more challenging waters than Ononta felt
confident to sail.

"Strike stronger, on your right side." The orders kept coming, loud, firm, implacable. "Yes, like that. Forget the other side. Stick to this one until we straighten with the current."

Straighten with the current? But what did her tormenter mean by that? Concentrating her entire attention on the rowing, she couldn't be expected to check on their course as well, did she?

"Look ahead!"

The new demand showed that, indeed, she was expected to watch where their boat was heading. As though battling angry currents wasn't enough! There were so many of these, the river doing everything in its power to pull and push, to make sure their boat floundered everywhere but in the middle of it.

Ononta grunted through her clenched teeth, glimpsing a tip of a greasy rock that swept by, screeching against the side of their boat, making it lurch in a pitiful manner, as though pushed by a gust of a sudden wind.

"I told you to watch this thing!"

Too busy with her struggle to keep upright, the cumbersome paddle getting in her way, Ononta groped the side of the boat, clutching to it desperately, afraid to fall out. The unsettled vessel lurched again as the blurry form swept by, pouncing toward their only means of navigation, the wet paddle bumping against the hard wood, bouncing off it, skidding toward the rushing water, about to disappear in the eddy's depths.

Holding her breath, Ononta watched her companion balancing at the very edge of the titling boat, sure of herself and unafraid, the baby clutched tightly in the crook of her arm, mewing its disapproval.

In the next heartbeat it was over, with the boat still floating, still possessing its navigating device, now directed back toward the obstacles-free midstream, steadfast again. At least!

A few more mild tosses, and Ononta was able to stabilize herself as well, watching the slender figure clasping the bundled blankets with one arm while moving with her entire body in order to provide the other with enough force, stirring the stubborn vessel away from the shore's tussle. Only now, with nothing to keep her mind preoccupied on rowing alone, did she notice how truly close they were drifting, so dangerously near the massive bedrocks adorning the bottom of the towering bank.

"I'm sorry," she muttered, when the hum of the shoreline receded, allowing her to hear her own thoughts, even if not the exact words.

As expected, no response came from their determined leader. Wholly immersed in reaching the safer course, the girl's only digression came to pass in occasional glances shot at her son, who had now crawled next to Ononta, not afraid in the least, his eyes sparkling.

Aghast, she realized that she forgot all about the boy and the vulnerability of his situation. Oh, but they shouldn't have gone sailing in such waters. It was insane, irresponsible. What was her companion thinking?

"*Annen* will let me paddle, too," he informed her, huddling close, a pleasantly warm presence, his clothes soaked but not as badly as hers were. "You did it bad. Not good. We were tossed all over."

"I know that!" grunted Ononta, feeling childish. Was she to be reprimanded by a few summers old cheeky squirrel? "Your *nnen* won't let you row now. She is the only one who can do it properly."

"Yes, she will," he insisted, rearing away as though she bit him. "She promised!"

"Sure she did." Rolling her eyes, Ononta pushed herself up and forward, unwilling to unbalance their boat again, but knowing that at least she could offer her help by taking care of the baby, who had woken up from all the tossing and screeching and was already voicing his displeasure, adding to the steady hum all around.

"Take the paddle back." Instead of the baby, the wet, choppy stick was shoved into her hands by the way of a greeting as she reached the forefront of their boat again, not a difficult feat, this being a relatively small vessel. "Keep to the middle of the stream this time. Don't steer from it."

For some reason, the crisp words stopped the protests that were mushrooming rapidly, made them recede before reaching her lips. Spreading her legs to stabilize herself, Ononta gritted her teeth, determined to push the water away in the correct manner this time. No more swerving and veering, no more alternating sides. The boat jerked occasionally, as erratic as a frightened squirrel, but at least it did keep away from the shallow swirls and it was better than nothing.

"Should we try and turn around?" she shouted, not daring to take her eyes off the water in order to look at her possible audience.

"Not yet." The answer surprised her, as she expected none. How did the woman hear what she said? The explanation presented itself in the form of the boy appearing in the corner of her vision, standing upright and fearless, not large enough to unsettle the canoe's steadiness. Still she felt like hissing at him to sit down.

"*Annen* says I listen to you and tell her."

"Oh." Appreciating the suitability of this ingenuous solution, Ononta squinted against the glow of the high noon sun. "Well, tell your *nnen* that when she thinks it's time to go back, we should do it. No, wait!" Striking the water to her right, time after time, she remembered the woman's advice, and dunked the wide shaft deeper, receiving immediate results. "Tell her that I think we should go back, and well, I'd probably better take care of the baby."

"Just put your attention on the river and nothing else," was the laconic answer that came shortly thereafter, uttered in the usual commanding tones, crisp and inflexible. "Just do what you are doing now, then turn to our right when I tell you to."

Ononta ground her teeth, but soon her misgivings gave way to a delighted stare. The river widened, and just as their self-appointed leader was commanding her to steer to their right, the prettiest of pools opened itself up, sparkling invitingly, sheltered by towering cliffs, a fitting protection.

"Oh, it's beautiful!" she exclaimed when their improvised interpreter forgot his duties, rushing back to his *nnen*, upsetting the boat once again.

"We go there, yes? Please, please!" he yelled at the top of his voice, making even his mother hear, let alone every creature and *uki* inhabiting these woods. "Can I jump in? Can I?"

"Not until we reach the shore," said the uncompromising mother. "Now turn the boat, but slowly. Slowly!" These words clearly meant her. Ononta returned her attention back to her paddle. "Yes, like this. No, no more. Stay like that, half with the current, half outside of it. Yes." Another pause. "Now slip out of it gently. Yes, like that. Now paddle on. Alternate sides."

When finally the relative dimness of the towering cliffs admitted them in its shadowy haven, Ononta's back was soaked with sweat, her limbs trembling, drained of strength. Yet, her spirit floated, oh so very elated. She had brought their canoe here, she had! All by herself too, receiving no more than some occasional advice and direction, with only one actual intervention. Oh, but it was not such a bad achievement. For a person who was held to be hopeless when it came to tasks rougher than sewing and decorating, she had done surprisingly well, hadn't she?

The boy was already splashing in the shallow water, oblivious of their presence.

"Pretty, isn't it?" His mother looked him up briskly, adjusting the baby's blanket, the smile tagging at the corner of the pursed mouth, lurking at the gaze turned to Ononta. "Drag the boat up and into that cove." The toss of her head indicated a dark opening, a crack between oblique cliffs. "Remember to put it upside down when there."

Ononta's sense of wellbeing began to evaporate. Why couldn't they leave the boat where it was? She was too tired to drag anything anywhere, let alone a heavy canoe she was too happy to escape by now.

A glance at her companion made her bent to pick the edge of the boat.

"No, no, don't drag it now that it's reached the shore." The new outburst of uncompromising directing made her jump. "You don't want to leave too many traces of your traveling around, no matter how safe the camping here is."

What? No!

Before she could open her mouth – but she couldn't be expected to lift the heavy boat all by herself, could she? Was she to haul it upon her shoulders the way she saw the men doing? No, it was ridiculous! – the girl's grin cut her budding protests short.

"I'll help you this time. We'll carry it up there together." The smile widened, came to life with an atypically mischievous glint. "But you will have to do it by yourself when you travel, or you won't get truly far." A light toss of the head indicated the back of the boat. "Grab your edge."

Shifting the baby higher in the crook of her arm, the girl lifted her side of the vessel, tilting her body deftly, adjusting to the additional burden.

"Come, it's just a few paces away. Let us hurry."

As though she needed that reminder. Ononta wished to curl up right there on the wet gravel and cry. Through the haze of her misery the words of her mentor kept coming, unpleasantly strident, bothering.

"You must always make sure of that, first thing after each landing. Without your boat you are stuck. So take care of it first thing. Before you as much as start thinking about making fire or looking for an appropriate place to do that."

The renewed howling of the baby interrupted the harangue, for good, or so Ononta hoped. Would her relentless teacher be forced now into halting, putting their burden down for a heartbeat. Oh, but for such a chance! This boat was heavy and revoltingly slippery, its rugged surface tearing at the flesh of her palms, hurting them.

"This is most important. First you take care of your vessel, then of the things it carries, including you and anyone else who is in it." Rocking her protesting baby with one hand, the girl didn't show any sights of distress, any willingness to stop their progress. Only a few paces? Well, they had already made more than a few. Ten paces at least, and there seemed to be another such amount ahead of them. Some estimation of distances!

Yet, as they made their way up the nearest cliff, with the boat tucked safely in its small hideaway, concealed against prying eyes, Ononta's mood began improving by leaps and bounds. With no cumbersome burden it was such a pleasant walk, the steady wind from the riverside cooling, abating the fierceness of the sun.

The bag of her companion looked promisingly plump.

"We'll have a nice little meal up there on that cliff." Her companion grinned, catching Ononta's inquiring gaze. "To reward us for all the trouble we went to in order to arrive here. Don't we deserve it?" Shielding her eyes with her free hand, the bag now balanced on her shoulder, she peered at their destination and the dancing silhouette that was skittering near the top of the cliff. "Tsami did explore our path already, didn't he?"

Ononta grinned, then hurried to take the baby. It was wrong, the way this young woman kept doing everything all by herself, so competent and efficient, so determined to have it all done. How useless she must think her, Ononta, to be! She pursed her lips tight.

The boy had crawled to the very edge of the cliff and was peering down, all eyes and ears.

"Tsami, not so close!" Her frown light, concentrated, the woman dropped her bag with little consideration before hurrying toward her boy, determined.

"But, *nnen*, look," he cried out, protesting at the hands that wrapped around his muddied shoulders, pulling him back, uncompromising. "Look, there are boats. Canoes. Over there."

The small finger pointed toward the bend of the river, where the water was gushing with real strength. Thanks all the great and small *uki* they didn't proceed with the current, thought Ononta, shivering.

Squinting, she tried to see better, but the rocks guarding the bend revealed nothing, concealing what the boy might have spotted, not willing to share. She put her attention back to the bag.

"Come, Tsami," the woman was saying, steering her reluctant charge toward the safer ground. "We'll see these boats as well from that perch over there. Sit!" This time it was an order.

"Who would be going fishing in a place like that?" asked Ononta, mildly curious now that she could actually see the vessels. One, then another two, they appeared from behind the bend, materializing out of the angry foam, as nimble as trout and as sure of themselves. No spinning around or lost paddles, not with these people. She wanted to groan in frustration. No, she wouldn't be able to undertake the journey home, not until Father got better.

Her companion was studying the approaching vessels with even more eagerness. "They are returning from the east," she muttered. "Maybe—"

"Yes, yes, yes!" squealed the boy, bouncing back to his feet, his excitement spilling. "Father is coming back! He does, he does. He promised!"

With his mother's eyes still glued to the river and the darker forms that were challenging it, it was left to Ononta to address the excited tirade. "You think it's your father?"

"Yes, yes, it's him!" yelled the boy, proving that his voice could go higher as yet. "He is coming back!"

She touched her companion's shoulder. "Do you think it's them?"

A sigh and a brief glance were her answer. "I hope so, yes."

Ononta sighed, pushing her own disappointment away. The return of the foreigner would leave her all alone again, deprived of her friend, the only company she wished to spend her time at.

"He promised this journey would not be too long," the woman was saying, turning to take the baby, who was again beginning to protest, demanding his mother's warmth or maybe another round of feeding. "I didn't believe him on that. I thought he would find his travels in the east too fascinating to head back in a hurry, but I suppose I was wrong." A guilty smile flashed. "So it's good that I didn't leave on my own."

"Would he be angry if you did?"

The smile widened, turned playful. "Oh yes, he would. But he is used to me making my own decisions. I went against his wishes under far more dangerous circumstances once upon a time." The wistful gaze clouded, wandered. "He cared about me before he came to love me as a woman. He tried to protect me, tried to make me live a normal life. He tried to convince me to go and live with my people, my family." The fragile shoulders lifted in a shrug. "It didn't work out. I didn't want to live with other people. I wanted to be with him."

"Why couldn't he come and live with you in the longhouse of

your family?"

Fascinated, Ononta watched the sadness banishing the smile, making the pleasant face harden.

"It wasn't possible. He had his important mission, his people to take care of. He wasn't seeking to settle with a woman. His destiny was greater than this."

"What was it?"

For a heartbeat the silence prevailed, as the girl's eyes went back toward the river, the canoes better visible now, cutting the water in a decisive manner, three vessels only, following each other, hurrying to complete their journey.

Resolutely, Ononta's companion shook her head. "It's all in the past now. Forgotten past." Another toss of the tight braid seemed as though intent on banishing the last of the memories. "He made me his woman in the end. I insisted."

"You?" This time, Ononta did not try to suppress her laughter. "Isn't it the other way around usually. The boys, they are supposed to court us, ask their mothers to make marriage cookies."

The smile of her companion did not reflect any matched mirth. "It was different with us. There was no one to ask to bake those cookies, no one to send them to." Another lift of the thin shoulders made Ononta reflect again how inappropriately young her friend was, a mother of two children when most girls were still flirting around, thrilled at the prospect of those special curving cookies being sent their way. "There were only us and my grandfather's cabin, and the clearing around it, and the woods. Nothing else." The sadness was there again, tagging at the corners of the pressed lips, pulling them up into a wistful smile. "That winter was harsh and we had not enough supplies to withstand it. He was recovering from his wounds, and I, I did all I could, so we weren't starving, but comfortable we were not. Still we survived. And," another pause had the girl's eyes back upon the river, narrowed but not seeing any of it, wandering the mists of the past, "I loved him, always. From the moment I saw him first. I didn't know it back then, but later on I understood. While he?" Another shrug. "I don't know if he loved me before I insisted that he made love to me." Her frown deepened. "Yes, he did. He did love me, but it wasn't the way men love women. He loved me like Grandfather before. He cared about me." The large eyes focused, flickered with little playfulness. "But I made him love me as a woman."

Taken with the story, Ononta tried to imagine that lonely place, the clearing, the cabin, the encroaching woods, surrounded by bare rocks maybe, drowning in the roaring of the nearby rapids – oh yes, such strange place should have this menacing quality, should relate foreboding sensation, deter petty humans from coming closer. Still those two did. Why? It took the impressive foreigner a whole winter to recover from his wounds, the girl claimed. How did he come to be harmed in such a way? And why?

She glanced at her companion, the narrow eyes attentive, glued to the approaching canoes, one arm wrapped around her boy's shoulders, the baby on her breast forgotten. There was no point in asking questions, in expecting more revelations. No answers would be forthcoming, not from this one. Close to ten dawns spent in her friend's company had taught her that.

"Like grandfather?" she said, wishing to lighten the atmosphere and thus stay on the subject. Maybe the girl would say more. "That's a strange way of putting it. He is not that old, your man." The pair of widening eyes was back upon her, clearly wavering between outburst of indignation and healthy amusement. "Maybe like father, but not like grandfather. Grandfathers are old and wrinkled. They don't make love to women."

This time the amusement won, for certain. The unmelodious laughter erupted unrestrained. Not such a rare occasion, it still startled them, even the boy.

"*Nnen!*" he cried out, making a face.

His mother shook her head, still snickering. "It's her fault. She says silly things." Shifting the snoring baby higher into the crook of her arm, she returned her gaze to the boats, her mouth still quivering.

The first canoe was passing their cliff, no more than thirty, maybe forty paces away, keeping to the middle of the river. Wisely so, reflected Ononta, remembering her own earlier experience with the same current, her stomach heavy with disappointment. The foreigner would be taking away the only company she came to love here. How very unfair! The girl threatened to leave on her own, oh yes, she did, but it was not as certain and she did keep lingering, staying in this town despite it all. Tsami's arm was healing for good now, with barely a remainder left but a glowing crust, perfectly dry these days, with no oozing liquids. They didn't need to smear ointments on it anymore, and the medicine he was still made to drink was less bitter, not as strong and as concentrated as the earlier brews, judging by the boy's milder protests.

Oh yes, his mother could have left already, had she wished to do so. If at first Ononta was tempted to treat the declarations of independent traveling, or living for that matter, lightly, ten dawns in this woman's company taught her a different story. Her newfound friend knew everything, absolutely everything, and there was nothing in the forest she wouldn't find and use, to survive comfortably and arrive home with herself and her children well and lacking in nothing.

And yet, she didn't leave. An encouraging development that reassured Ononta, pleasing her enormously. It was due to her, she knew, to their friendship and the time spent together. But now her friend would have to leave all the same.

The other two boats were speeding past their cliff now, passing it by. She watched one of the figures in the longer canoe gesturing at the smaller vessel that was navigated by only one rower. This one stood at the prow of his boat quite proudly, with no visible effort, an impressive figure, his hair long and fluttering, not cut or shaved or even tied adequately. The third vessel was closing the procession and even though it was difficult to tell from such distance and with all this haze in the air, she thought she recognized the familiar features of Entiron, the man of the longhouse they had resided in, her father's cousin by marriage or something. Oh yes, the man had scampered off happily upon the arrival of the foreigner, sniffing the possibilities he feared his peers might manage to snatch for themselves. A greedy man. Even Father had said something to this effect, when they had first arrived here.

She sighed. The foreigner was certain to be back now, and… A glance at her companion made her ashamed of her selfish thoughts. They had waited for him so, the boy and his mother.

To her astonishment, her companion's eyes were fixed on the middle canoe carrying the lone traveler. It was still near enough to see the man relatively clearly, standing upright, relaxed, shielding his face with one hand, rowing steadily with another, more likely just holding his paddle, preventing the boat from changing its direction, his attention on the gesturing local. There was something strangely familiar about this man, something blurry, a forgotten memory, vague and somehow not especially pleasant. But why? Ononta strained her eyes, trying to decipher his features despite the distance.

"Who is this man?" The girl's voice broke into her thoughts, echoing them, apparently.

"The one in the smaller canoe?" Receiving no answer, she glanced at her friend, surprised to see an unfamiliar expression twisting the pleasant features, making the gently pointed face look… frightened? Dismayed? In disbelief, she saw the slender throat moving jerkily, swallowing hard.

"Are you all right, sister?" she asked, putting a reassuring hand on the girl's shoulder, so painfully thin, sporting a bruise from their recent boat-carrying activities.

"*Nnen*, where is Father?" The boy was asking, his voice taking on the unmistakable note. He was readying to burst into tears upon an unsatisfactory answer, so much was obvious. "He is not… I didn't see him…"

Shuddering against Ononta's touch, the young woman blinked, her gaze brushing past them both, lacking in focus, her face not frightened anymore but still upset, still unsettled, her frown deep, unappealing. Another glance shot at the speeding canoes, the smaller one already away, hurried to keep up with its peers.

"Mother," insisted Tsami, his voice trembling openly, about to break. "Where is Father? Where?"

The girl shook her head, as though ridding herself of unpleasant vision. "What did you say, little one?" she asked, the lightness of her voice forced.

"Father! I didn't see him. Where is he?"

"Oh, oh!" She ran her palm through the fluttering fringes of her disheveled hair. "I think maybe he wasn't there. But maybe we just didn't see him. Maybe he will come later…"

CHAPTER 12

The loudness of Sondakwa's yawn embarrassed Atuye to no end.

Admittedly, the meeting was boring and not truly important, after their dignitaries and the leading people of the town that hosted them finished their witty fencing of high-flown words and hidden messages, moving to the less official part of the gathering, retiring toward the babbling pots and the mats spread all around those. To produce more figurative speeches in between the mouthfuls, assumed Atuye, amused, trading a glance with one of their fellow escorting warriors.

Not especially hungry after being fed to bursting since their arrival more than two dawns ago, with plenty of snacks and sessions of cracking nuts in between, none of the comfortably squatting escorts hurried to join the elders. Instead, they had stayed where they were, some slipping into lighter conversations among themselves and their less dignified hosts, some letting their eyes wander toward the colorfully adorned skirts swirling near the fires, some yawning like Sondakwa, but not as openly bored, respecting their company.

Here, in the Deer People's large hilly town, they were to part their ways, those who were to travel to the Cord People's lands, Sondakwa and his fellow escorts, and those who were to detour through the Rock People settlements, Atuye's designated group. They would have done it already, set on their way, but for the group of those same Rock travelers that had descended upon the town they were staying at only this morning.

One good turn, or so Honorable Tsineka, the leading man of their delegation, seemed to be thinking. It was good to know what the Rocks were up to before heading there, unheeded and uninvited. The residents of Onentisati, an important enough settlement situated not far away from the shores of the Great Lake, those people could provide mines of useful information, could serve as an indication as to the advisability of the projected journey at all.

"We've been traveling for some time, yes," one of the newcomers was saying, an impressive looking man, an owner of such broad shoulders his entire torso looked square, an array of beaded bands covering his arms to their elbows. "The end of the fields clearing season gave our men freedom to do that."

"Are your females that demanding?" inquired Sondakwa, eyes twinkling. He was on his best behavior so far, facing the important hosts and their more prominent visitors, however now, surrounded by less formal company, Atuye feared his brother would slip the leash.

"Of course, they are." The decorated man glanced at the inquirer warily, uncertain as to how to respond. "Do your women clean the fields all by themselves?"

"Sometimes," drawled Sondakwa, stifling another showy yawn.

"No wonder those Bear People are roaming around, nagging on ours with all sorts of wild ideas," chuckled one of the locals, a man at whose company they had spent a pleasant evening of a bowl game on the night before. "They have time for that. Their foxes must be all affability and good grace toward their lazy males."

That drew much smirking and outright guffawing from everyone present, their own Bear People escorts no less than the rest, reflected Atuye, hard put to suppress his own chuckling. The youngest among this crowd, he couldn't afford that, lest they would be tempted to remember him with inevitable teasing and good natured jokes.

Eyes traveling, taking in their glimmering faces, everyone relaxed and at ease, he caught a sight of another man who didn't join the general outburst of mirth, an undeniably formidable type, not fitting in this particular crowd any more than he, Atuye, did, but for an opposite reason. Clearly the man had seen well over thirty summers in his life, enough hunting seasons, not all of them peaceful, far from it. With such a face, how could he not? So ragged and weathered, so set, the square jaw protruding strongly, the eyes cold and clouded, attentive but in a measuring manner, giving nothing away, the scar running down the sharpness of the cheekbone, starting under the hairline, adding to the foreboding impression, deterring. No lightness behind those eyes, and no warmth. Atuye took his gaze away hurriedly. Such men were not to be stared at or even just studied openly. One of the Rock visitors, he remembered, the man's limp impossible to miss or forget.

"Our women wouldn't let you step around without demanding that you did something useful." To the continued merriment of their growing company, Sondakwa carried on, his grin good-natured but taunting, challenging them to dare an answer. "But one always has ways to deal with the wild foxes, to avoid being kept under their pretty moccasin's sole. If one is a man enough, that is."

The decorated Rock who has spoken first stiffened dangerously once again. "What are you implying?"

But Sondakwa's grin didn't waver, flashing with his typical winning lightness. "Why so touchy, brother? We didn't come to wage war on you, or our hospitable hosts here for that matter. Relax and enjoy this free-of-clearing-fields time of yours." Twisting, he tried to reach for a bowl of nuts without straightening into a sitting position. It was already half empty, largely due to his own mighty efforts. "Have you traveled here to trade goods or just to pass time?"

"We brought some goods, yes." This time it was another of the visitors speaking, reaching for the bowl Sondakwa was still hunting after, grabbing a handful of nuts before pushing it in Atuye's brother's direction. "We were more people heading out initially, more canoes, but your Bear People kept getting in our way. There are plenty of you traveling all around these days."

"In these lands?"

More of the visitors nodded readily, even the decorated man.

"A delegation?" It felt uncomfortable to find himself in the center of their attention, but he couldn't help it. The implications of another traveling party that originated in other than their own leading settlement, were startling, odd. Of old, none of their countryfolk were in the habit of traveling these western lands, and even these days not many had done this having no particular purpose, no pressing need. And why weren't they told about a delegation being sent to talk to the Rock or Deer People? Or were they? Their elders should know about such undertakings, should be able to express their opinions, to coordinate their actions.

"A delegation of one man." Two of the newcomers chuckled, exchanging glances with none other than the silent man with the scar.

This time, even Sondakwa straightened up. "One man?"

"Oh yes, one chatty foreigner in a lonely canoe. Loaded with goods, too. He said he came to trade things. Was on his way up north, but ended up heading for our Onentisati."

Onentisati! He caught his brother's quick glance. Wasn't that the name of the town Ononta's father went visiting?

"Had some rare goods from across the other side of our Sparkling Water, that man," went on the Rock visitor, sprawling in full comfort now, with the bowl of nuts within easy reach. "So we assumed not all of your Bear People were lazy skunks who do nothing but talk politics."

Sondakwa was fishing fragments of nuts from between his front teeth. "Look who is talking. The people who never bother with alliances or wars, preferring to keep their lazy behinds in the safety of their home fences." Grimacing, he studied his fingertips with decided interest, as though fascinated by their findings. "But just so you know, that young warrior over there," to Atuye's growing embarrassment, the light nod indicated none other but him, "came back from across our Great Lake not very long ago. And a good foray into the heart of the enemy lands it was." The glimmering eyes rested on him, sparking with an obvious pride. "Wasn't it, young buck?"

Atuye found himself nodding stiffly, hard put not to shrink under the scrutiny of so many pairs of eyes. Even the closemouthed man with the scar was studying him, his eyes narrowing slightly.

"Oh, when did that happen?"

"How many were you?"

"Where did you go?"

The questions shot at him from all around, coming mainly from their hosts, the Deer People being in a habit of an occasional crossing, oh yes. He tried to keep his answers crisp, matter-of-fact, as though there was nothing more natural than to raid the heartlands of the fiercest of enemies; as though the memory of that sunlit hill and the glimpse of the locals busy circumventing their own attacking forces, about to surprise them and fall on them from behind, did not make his stomach flutter and his chest tighten with fear, just like back then, close to half a moon but as though happening only this morning.

"We managed to surprise them, yes," he said, wishing to lick his lips, making a conscious effort not to do this. "But they reorganized quickly enough. After the first onslaught of arrows, they retreated and were ready for our attack at the fields." A shrug came easier than he thought it would. "Still we killed quite a few of their men and captured two women. It was not a bad raid."

"Good." Their open approval restored his confidence. That and the way they were eyeing him, with a keen interest and respect, not condescending like older warriors would.

"You made a mistake of underestimating the enemy." The man with the scar did not raise his voice or change his position, but all heads turned in his direction, their gazes leaping at the speaker, attentive as though against their will. "The raid you described represents your mistaken thinking well."

"How so?" This time the silence was broken by Sondakwa, his voice lacking its usual needling amusement, ringing with cold politeness that relayed danger. Atuye didn't waste his time looking at his brother.

"The enemy from across your Great Lake is more devious and better prepared than you obviously credit them with." The man didn't shrug, sitting there like a figurine carved out of stone, face lacking expression, eyes impenetrable, just two dark pools. "My people made this mistake and they paid with everything they had." Another heavy pause. "You might think you know your lifelong enemy well, but your people, allied or not, should spend more time learning about the Longhouse League, its merits and its faults, its intentions, its thinking. Only then you should decide on the ways of fighting it. In an organized manner; all your four nations. Not occasional raids, every time this or that settlement, this or that group of warriors, feel like stretching their muscles, proving their valor and strength."

Another spell of silence prevailed, interrupted by lively chattering from across nearby fires, by typical afternoon sounds of a settlement calming down after a busy day.

"You are a Long Tail," muttered one of the local men.

"Our guest from Attiwandaronk forests keeps us abreast of the developments in their parts of the world," interrupted one of the visitors smoothly, not perturbed in the least. "We value his words and his continued visits."

Attiwandaronk? Atuye strained his mind, trying to remember. The word sounded familiar but only slightly, distantly. Who were those people? The accent of the stranger was distinct, but not to a serious degree. It was easy to understand the man.

"Attiwandaronk are the Long Tails, aren't they?" Again Sondakwa was the one to sound the question preying on everyone's mind, caring little for politeness or proprieties.

The foreigner nodded curtly, a mirthless grin tagging at the corner of the pursed mouth, lifting it slightly. "One might put it this way." A shrug. "We are not the same people, but we are related."

Atuye tried not to stare, relieved at being forgotten, not the center of their attention, not anymore. That raid was not something to boast about, no matter how they might have tried to put it in this way; nothing to be proud of aside from the fact that he was there and fighting. But it wasn't like the others didn't lift their clubs on other occasions. Especially the formidable foreigner. A Long Tail! Just to think of it.

"You, people, fought quite an impressive war on the

Longhouse beasts, or so one hears," went on his brother, unabashed. But sometimes he envied Sondakwa his straightforwardness, his lack of concern with convention or polite way of speaking. "Were you a part of that great battle?"

"No, I wasn't privileged to participate in this battle." The foreigner's voice didn't change, yet there was something different about it, a certain strained note, an underground current. "Still I'm in the position to tell you about the mistakes my people made, about the lessons you should learn from what happened." The dark eyes narrowed, holding their gazes, burning with cold fire. "Your lifelong enemy is better organized, better prepared these days. Better informed about you and your intentions as well. Do not underestimate them as you did on this last raid of yours." Another light shrug did not reflect the intensity of the man's gaze. "Your enemy is quick and always ready to pounce, to reorganize into attacking like they did back in the village you approached. They are ready to change their plans on the spur of a moment, as soon as they learn about yours." The man leaned forward, as though afraid that his words would be missed or not interpreted correctly. "And they do bother to learn about you and your movement. They do! They gather information and they don't dismiss the importance of it. Instead, they act upon it."

The intensified chattering by the glimmering fires interrupted the passionate speech, made it die away as abruptly as it began. The foreigner's eyes lost their glow. Fascinated, Atuye watched the weathered face closing again, returning to its previous impassiveness, the effort to do so manifested in the rigidness with which the firm jaw was protruding, as stiff as an image chiseled out of stone.

For a heartbeat silence prevailed.

"Well, if your people made these mistakes it's too bad," said Sondakwa in the end, his voice unusually quiet, lacking its typical spiciness. "We do know our enemies and we are aware of their viciousness and the savageness of their nature. As for the knowledge," he shrugged, twisting his lips in an indifferent grin, "well, we do know where some of their villages are located. The raid my brother participated in wasn't a failure even if it did not achieve all the results. Those warriors knew where they were heading, and they weren't hesitant, indecisive or afraid. They punished the enemy, killed men, captured women. They acted upon the knowledge they had and they did so bravely, with no hesitation and no fear."

The foreigner raised his hand quickly, as though warding off an unwarranted accusation.

"I did not accuse your men of indecision or fear," he said, straightening up with surprising awkwardness of movement. "I said that their plan was good but it lacked a basic knowledge of the enemy. A mistake that is important not to repeat, not when dealing with the Longhouse League." The air hissed, drawn forcefully through the widening nostrils. "I didn't talk about the location of their villages, basic information every raiding party should have. I talked about the knowledge of the enemy's war preparedness, their numbers, their possible plans, even the people who are leading them, their quality, their stamina and merits and strengths."

"And how would you go about learning something like that?" cried out Sondakwa, straightening up in his turn. "Our scouts can't roam about the enemy's forests unhindered. You know it as well as we do." He flapped his arms in the air, imitating his opponent in an unconscious gesture, of that Atuye was sure. His brother was not the person to imitate anyone, not him. "If we knew half of what you demand, we wouldn't have to work hard besting the enemy. We would destroy them in one single raid, one single crossing, brother. But how would you go about leaning all this useful information? Your people are not the only ones lacking the details of the enemy's plans and schemes."

Another spell of heavy silence enveloped them, interrupted by the even hum, the town lively and boiling but for their spot of barely visible flames.

The foreigner pursed his lips. "It doesn't take much to let the enemy know of your battle preparedness. A homesick adoptee, a runaway captive, maybe, one of your people falling into captivity when the other side is enterprising and in control, not losing its senses in order to have an immediate revenge. It doesn't take more than that to let the enemy know about you and your forces and plans." The man was staring into the flickering flames, eyes wide open and not truly focused, as though daydreaming. "When you think about it, you realize that maybe there is a way to do it intentionally, to acquire this sort of knowledge in a conscious effort. Through a former captive you can trust, if there is such a thing, or maybe through a local man who can speak the enemy's tongue and is courageous enough to pose as such a runaway adoptee." Shrugging, he shook his head, his concentration returning, gaze leaving the flames, traveling their faces. "You need to strengthen your alliance. You need to unite like the enemy did, in an unbreakable coalition of all Wyandot nations. Anything less than that won't be enough."

The foliage rustled with the renewed whispering of the breeze, interrupting the ensuing silence.

"We are working to make it happen, man. We do." Sondakwa stretched showily, displaying the renewed lack of interest, his typical attitude. "But sending our people to roam the forests across is taking it too far, I say. Who would dare to do that, wander about pretending to be one of the enemy? Only an insane person curious to find out in what ways one can die if not willing to take the usual route." A light shrug. "Our people are not that unstable."

"You may be surprised," muttered the foreigner, his eyes drifting back to the transparent flames.

"No man in his right mind would do that," insisted Sondakwa, back in argumentative mood again. "As for the need to strengthen our union, go tell them that at the Great Gathering that is about to be held up there in on the shores of that other Great Lake. And take your Rock friends along with you." The familiar unabashed grin flashed, leaving the foreigner, encircling the rest of their audience, instead. "Some of our elders are on their way to visit your settlements, anyway; to try to talk the stubborn westerners into doing what your Attiwandaronk visitor is suggesting, the obvious thing."

"It's not that simple, Bear People's man," said the decorated Rock, straightening up, incensed all over again. "Our people might join your union, yes, but on our terms. You won't be running our towns and villages or telling them what to do."

We'll see about that, said Sondakwa's gaze, but to Atuye's imminent sense of relief his brother didn't utter these words aloud. Instead, another of their men interrupted, talking about the equality of the brotherhood between the Bear and Cord People, lauding Father's work to the skies. Atuye smiled inside, warmed, then again caught the piercing gaze of the foreigner, resting on the speaker, listening avidly. *Who was this man?*

"Onentisati is the town your girl went to, didn't she?" asked Sondakwa somewhat later, when their party broke, with some people drifting toward the more lively activity of the bubbling town.

"Yes, she did." He watched the foreigner standing not far away, speaking with one of the elders, or rather listening again, his pose relaxed but awkward, not hiding the way his bad leg was held.

"But your delegation is heading deeper inland, aren't they?"

"Yes, the elders are wishing to visit Cahiague and Ekiodatsaan, the largest of their inland settlements." He shrugged with pretended indifference, not pleased with yet another attempt at peeking into his private affairs. Enough that it had taken him some days to reconcile himself to the bitter disappointment, the effort of convincing himself that his motives at joining this particular delegation originated in something other than a private reason not coming easily, not this time. "From there they may decide to head straight away for Ossossane. Both settlements are removed only four, five days from their Freshwater Sea." He forced a grin. "So I may arrive at Ossossane not much later than you."

"Without finding out what happened to your girl." Sondakwa was not about to be sidetracked.

Atuye sighed. "I didn't join for that reason. No more than you have joined your delegation of elders heading straight for Ossossane for this or that private purpose. I didn't accuse you of something like that. Why would you do this to me?"

"I'm not accusing you, Little Brother." There was unusual

warmth in Sondakwa's voice, the atypical sincerity. "But I say, you deserve to reach both goals. This Onentisati where our newfound friends headed from," a casual nod indicated their now deserted fire, "is barely a day and a half away, an easy sail. How about we detour, you and I? Three, four dawns and we are back, meeting our leaders in this same Cahiague, for one, reaching that town alongside with them." This time the swaying patch of the decorated hair pointed at the squatting elders carefully, an imperceptive nod. "Want us to stray away on a little side mission?"

"We can't do that!" breathed Atuye, aghast. How could they? Two escorting warriors wandering off in the middle of their missions, halfway to their destinations and more. Inconceivable!

"Of course we can." Sondakwa's laughter shook the air, attracting the attention of the people who were squatting along the wall of the nearest longhouse besides which most of the cooking was done. "You are such a stickler, Little Brother, afraid to put a foot wrong. But there is more to life than doing one's duty and little else. So make up your mind. If you want to go and look your girl up, or find out what happened to her, here is your chance." A smirk. "My offer is good till the first light. By then our people, those who are heading for Ossossane, might be off, so make up your mind and fast." The wide shoulders lifted casually. "I will have to talk to some of my friends, make sure they cover our backs if you decide to be a man after all. Eh, Little Brother?"

The openly taunting glimmer and the challenge in the familiar eyes made Atuye wish to strike his brother, or better yet, turn around and flee. He couldn't do something like that, he just couldn't. What would his superiors, Honorable Tsineka in particular, think about him if he did?

CHAPTER 13

The girl was staring at him, stealing glances whenever appearing from under the thatched roof of the façade, on her way in or out of the building, her gaze shy but insistent, studying him with a painful concentration. Why?

Shifting to make himself more comfortable, leaning his back against the warm bark of the longhouse's wall, Ogteah forced his attention back to his companions, puzzled. There were plenty of people walking all around, coming and going, stopping to talk to those who had squatted next to the fire, or more often to just listen. In the strong afternoon light the flames were transparent, invisible but there, dancing merrily, providing unasked-for warmth. The day was truly too hot for that, but the custom of arranging themselves around the fire whenever settling for a talk was apparently stronger than common sense. Amusing, really. Ogteah hid his grin, well satisfied.

This Onentisati town had turned out to be quite a large settlement, fairly well off, just like the man who was after his goods had promised. Which was a good thing. In a town as large and as important as this one he could learn much about his hosts' stance in the Wyandot alliance, their political inclinations and developments, their possible plans for the future, their actual involvement. And maybe about the traveling Long Tail, as well.

Even though what he had learned so far was enough in itself, the tale of the surviving leader, wandering about, hiding his true identity, oh, but this tale of his would be received with an ardent welcome. The Wolf Man would be surprised to hear that. Not by the fact that the enemy had managed to survive somehow – the

War Chief had warned them about such a possibility, claiming that the enterprising leader could very well be alive and about, given the lack of the body to prove them wrong, presenting a possible new challenge in the future – but by the fact that he had recovered his spirits, or maybe his stance among his people, and so quickly. Less than four summers later and here this man was, scheming with the Wyandot, stirring them, warning against the strengths and the dangers of the Great League, giving useful advice. What a lowlife! And yet, not such a lowlife at all. The man had his people to care for, to advance and help to recover from the terrible defeat. Of course he would seek allies and aid. Who wouldn't? Was the Wolf Man correct in his suspicion that the Rock People were extending more than a friendly hand toward their neighbors in trouble? Were they truly recovering, those fierce, dangerous Long Tails and their neighboring cousins Attiwandaronk? That man said he was Attiwandaronk, didn't he? Well, he very well might be, and yet why did even this claim sound fake, not real, no more than the man's assertion of living in a small village, having nothing to do with the Great War he evidently knew so much about, eager to talk and sound his mind.

An offered pipe brought his thoughts back into the present and the hospitable dwellers of Onentisati, squatting or crowding, talking all at once.

"Our tobacco is of the best quality," commented his neighbor, a man of about the same age, his cheekbones wide and well-defined, his features large, crowned with the fiercest nose Ogteah ever saw attached to a human face. "You will never enjoy a pipe after you leave this town."

Grinning, Ogteah took the offered object, putting the polished edge into his mouth, inhaling deeply. Indeed, the fragrant aroma had a delicate quality, more refined than the tobacco he was used to back in Lone Hill or even High Springs and Onondaga Town.

"It *is* a very good tobacco," he said, nodding, studying the prettily carved pipe before passing it on, so as to not to appear hurried or unappreciative, never fond of smoking for the pleasure of it. "Our people definitely can learn from yours when it comes to growing such fragrant tasting things."

"Your people can learn from ours, oh yes," grunted another man, a middle-aged, generously scarred individual that kept staring gloomily into the fire, not engaging in the general conversation except when complaints were in order. It wasn't his first time, even though they had arrived here only half a day earlier. "They hold Onentisati to be nothing but a village, a small settlement with no importance." A grudging glance brushed past Ogteah, not lingering but relaying the message nevertheless. "Since the Deer joined that much praised union of yours, our neighbors to the east treat us like the last of the unimportant settlements, a village with two longhouses and no fence."

"Oh, you are exaggerating, brother." The man who had brought Ogteah in hurried to interrupt the angry speech, leaning forward, peering across the fire as though trying to stop the words by the sheer power of his gaze. "There is no need to complain. Our brothers from the shores of the Sparkling Water where the sun rises each dawn do want us in, and they never tired of telling us that." A crooked, one-sided smile quivered, directed at Ogteah this time. "They are not the type to give up easily, are they?"

"No, they aren't."

He grinned back, more amused than unsettled. Was he to defend his former people's good name, to promote their policies and deeds, to convince their stubborn neighbors into joining? What if it did happen and because of him? He struggled not to snicker. Would they reward him for such a service? It was not just, not fair, that he should advocate the Wyandot union from the shadows and without any recognition. The thought made the fight against his laughter more difficult.

"Our people's union is the most sensible solution to the problem our united neighbors from across the Great Lake are presenting," he went on, shrugging inside. It was essential that he played his part and that he did it well. For now he was the Bear People's man, a villager traveling to exchange some goods, curious to see new places, to meet new people. And that was that! His loyalty to his current countryfolk would be restored the moment his canoe plunged back into the Great Sparkling Water, not a heartbeat before. "I believe all our Wyandot nations should join in. The enemy did it, so why couldn't we?"

"The savages did it with the help of the messenger the Left-Handed Twin sent their way." The grumpy man wasn't about to be quieted or pacified easily. "It is not the same."

"The Great Spirits help us, too," volunteered someone, a young man with a pleasantly round face. "The good benevolent spirits. The Right-Handed Twin watches over us and keeps us safe."

Ogteah watched the pipe making its way slowly, completing the circle. There were many people squatting around that fire. His eyes lifted toward the cluster of girls that appeared at the further edge of the alley, their giggling preceding them, heralding their approach.

"Your people's leader, the one who made your union happen, traveled aplenty. From your towns and the Deer ones all the way to the north and that other Great Lake of theirs." The complainer was addressing him again, not about to keep quiet, not even for basic politeness's sake. "That man traveled everywhere. For summers upon summers he had talked to leaders of towns and villages, convincing them to join in his union, but did he ever visit any of our settlements?" The angry eyes glared at him, burning with fire of their own. "No, he did not, Bear People's man. He never deemed our people important or necessary to approach, to sit beside our fires and share a pipe and a talk."

"Come now, brother—" one of the man reached out, but the pacifying palm was shaken off impatiently, the blazing eyes not steering off Ogteah's face, challenging.

"So now tell me, Bear People's traveler, why should we join your union at the present, when we know that at the time even your most renowned leaders did not deem us worthy or important enough?"

He fought the urge to respond with an equal anger, telling the frustrated local off and with matching impoliteness. Didn't they know how hard Father had worked to make it happen, traveling for so many summers, just like this man admitted, talking to so many settlements and nations, all divided, all busy trying to get more concessions than the others? The High Springs man had told him in detail about the Ossossane elders' shameless scheming, their attempts to gain ascendancy at all costs. What filthy snakes these people were! And now these petty complainers. How pathetic this man sounded, how worthless and insignificant, indeed.

"I'm not the person to answer any of that," he said coldly, gazing back with matching hostility, not caring in the least. "I speak for no important leaders. No elders delegated me to come here. I believe this union to be a good thing, and the leader who organized it all was the greatest man our people were privileged to be led by. If he never arrived in your people's lands, well, it might have happened due to lack of invitation. Ever thought of this? Maybe your people didn't go out of their way to invite him here. Back then, neither you nor the Deer were eager to be more than non-warring neighbors, not wishing to pledge for anything more committing than that."

He knew it wasn't prudent or wise to throw such open accusations at his hosts, the people he came to mingle with and not to anger them into throwing him out. He had learned not a little from an evening spent in their camp and on the two days' stretch of a journey. Still, there was so much more he needed to discover before trying to get away, preferably unharmed and unsuspected. How did it come to him growing angry over a mere conversation and on his first day of arrival at that?

His opponent's eyes sparkled victoriously. "How typical!" he cried out, waving his hands in a wide half circle. "To blame us for the renowned leader's negligence. But you do represent your arrogant countryfolk well, visitor. Despite your claims and protestations."

The others were stirring uneasily now, and more hands reached for the angry man's back, patting it, relating their message.

"Let us not mar the pleasantness of this day with anger and an unnecessary enmity," one of the elderly men was saying. "On the evening of the Strawberry Ceremony, let us talk of peaceful matters."

The angry local nodded grudgingly, his gaze leaving Ogteah, his pursed lips relating the depth of his animosity. What a rat!

"I cherish your words, Honorable Elder," said Ogteah as lightly as he could, himself rigid with anger as yet. What lousy hosts these people were, some of them, to attack their guests, formally brought and invited in. Unheard of. "The hospitality of your people and their generosity is above reproach."

Again his eyes caught the sight of the girl, lingering at the edge of the longhouse, her eyes boring into him, their curiosity unconcealed. What had come over everyone?

"It's good that you arrived in time to participate in our festivities," the man who had brought him here was saying. "The Strawberry Ceremony is one of the merriest, and our women make it the tastiest, as well."

As do ours, he thought bitterly, forcing out the friendliest of smiles. *But our ceremony was held already, earlier this span of seasons, with Gayeri in the midst of it.* Was that a good festival? Not with the spirits of the missing villagers, the men who were killed and the women who were kidnapped. Thanks to these people, their ceremony wasn't good or merry, of that he was sure. And she wasn't enjoying it, she wasn't. Not with her husband missing, away on a dubious mission she did not believe at or agreed on.

What was she doing now, in these very moments? Back from the fields and wondering, longing? Had they finished planting their longhouse's fields? Oh, but for the opportunity to head out and back toward the Great Lake, to sail it with no delays, to plunge into the sparkling mass of water and row for the entire night, to arrive back home with the dawn break. Impossible, but he would have tried. Hadn't he learned enough as it was?

"It would be an honor to participate in one of your ceremonies." Was it he who was speaking, lightly, breezily, in this calm, matter-of-fact voice? He wondered about it briefly. "I trust that the Great Spirits blessed you with plenty of forest fruit this span of seasons."

"They did." The pipe was thrust into his hands again, welcomed in its distraction. Something to fiddle with. Good. "You will enjoy our celebration, brother." The young man with the round face was smiling with what seemed like a genuine liking. It made him feel better. "Our girls know how to cook a good meal."

Their eyes drifted toward another passing group of foxes, their chatter pleasing the ear, soothing his nerves, encouraging. The gazes they bestowed on them flickered with lively interest, with a fair measure of mischief.

Then he felt the eyes of the staring girl, still lingering by the poles of the entrance, alone and troubled, unlike her passing colleagues. That served to dampen his mood once again. Why, why was this one staring at him as though she knew who he was?

He returned her gaze, his eyebrows raised high.

.

CHAPTER 14

"This is for you!"

The strawberry drink was dark and foamy, spilling over the edges of the pottery cup, marring its painted sides. Smiling, Ononta beamed at its bringer. "Oh, little one!"

The Second Niece – why were they calling the healer's young daughter by such strange alliance? – laughed, keeping close to the boy, making sure he didn't drop his offering. "He insisted on bringing it here to you all by himself."

"Oh!"

She took the cup reverently, forgetting to wipe her oily hands. They were so greasy, so slippery, the plates she was required to fill scourging hot. Yet, feeling like complaining though she might, it still gave her something to do, brought the goodwill of the women of their longhouse, no mean achievement.

The boy's round face beamed at her, all expectancy.

"You are the sweetest thing ever! I can't believe you carried this drink all the way here for me."

"He insisted." The Second Niece was another beaming with pride at the boy's achievements, her cheeks flushed, animated by all the commotion. There were so many people crowding the ceremonial grounds, men, women, children, milling around, stoking the fires under the boiling pots of stew, gesturing widely, their feet tapping the refrain the drums and the rattles maintained, even if inadvertently.

"They said I should bring it to you," related Tsami gravely, bursting with self-importance.

"We told him to offer the sacred strawberry drink to anyone he wanted to," said the girl as earnestly, her frown serene, laced with self-importance. "He didn't know children are to distribute the strawberry drink. I had to explain it all to him. Isn't it odd? His mother could have bothered to teach him that, couldn't she? He couldn't be such a baby a span of seasons ago, on the last Strawberry Celebration."

"He is very young yet," interrupted Ononta, not about to let anyone, even the sweet Second Niece, badmouth this boy's mother's skills and virtues. "You were really small on the previous Strawberry Ceremony, weren't you, Tsami?"

The boy's face screwed into a puzzled grimace. "What ceremony?"

The expression on the girl's face was unmistakable and it angered Ononta even further. Why did they have to find fault with their guest all the time, this girl and her mother?

The boy's eyes followed the cup as she raised it to her lips, enjoying the rich mixture with the thicker islands of mashed fragments of fruit floating in it. Ononta shook her head, hard put not to laugh. "I'll drink just a little. You'll help me with the rest of it. Good?"

He nodded so eagerly his yet-uncut hair jumped into his face, not obscuring his bubbling excitement.

"No, no, let Ononta drink her beverage, you little troublemaker." Taking the toddler's arm in hers, purposeful and bossy, the Second Niece pulled with clear resolution. "We'll go and see the dancing now."

"I'll come with you." Tossing a glance at the women who toiled above one of the fires, where she was helping with distribution of food, Ononta shrugged resolutely. They could do without her, if they had to. She was tired and needed a break. "We'll go and see the dances now, yes?"

The boy, about to argue or maybe free his captured hand, brightened visibly. "Yes, yes, the dances," he cried out, pulling his capturer now, his former resistance forgotten. "I want to see it. They dance funny. Father doesn't dance in this way. He makes a fire and he talks to the smoke. And he makes rattle shake. But not like them."

The brief exchange of their glances above the boy's head reconciled Ononta to her company, the amiable amusement in it. The Second Niece did love this boy, even though his parents did things differently, in a strange way.

"Where is your *nnen*?" she asked him, when the cup was thrust back into her hands, having been inspected for the last drop of the drink, its rims licked from the inside, leaving the boy's face smeared with pinkish remnants.

"There." The noncommittal wave of the small arm indicated the general direction somewhere behind the ceremonial grounds.

"She went to wash her baby," clarified the girl, her giggle dissolving in the commotion all around them. "He soiled himself again. He is such an eater! Wouldn't leave her breast ever, sucking and sucking. No wonder he does his needs all the time as well."

Against her will, Ononta snickered, knowing that the girl was right. On many occasions she had seen the proof of that baby, indeed, being a greedy little fox.

"*Annen* keeps the baby-brother clean."

The drums rolled strongly, echoed by the rattles and an occasional trill of the flute, the dancers swirling in a colorful wave, everyone who wished to do so joining in by that stage. As the girl attempted to burrow her way into the outer circle, Ononta hesitated, not having the privilege of such a young age to enjoy. It was impolite to just push in and anyway there was no one in there she wanted to spend her time with. If anything, she wished to clear her way out and toward the spring, where her only friend was likely to linger, using her baby as an excuse to keep away. A wise decision.

"If you can arrange for us to have a set of marked stones and a pile of beans to mark the winnings..." Some men were propelling themselves away from the commotion as well, their faces flushed, replete with food and entertainment. Her breath caught again, she watched the speaker turning to one of his companions, his grin light, indifferent, unconcerned. "We can set ourselves out there, under that pine. Plenty of shadow, plenty of privacy, as well. How many of you wish to play?"

Atuye's brother looked different from the way she remembered him, much different. How many spans of seasons had passed? Had she seen close to twelve summers at the time when he had left? Had Atuye? They were of the nearly same age, so that must have been that. Atuye must have been a little past twelve when his disgrace of the eldest brother scampered away, leaving the town with no opportunity to throw him out of it or worse. Such a shameless, troublemaking, good-for-nothing person. No one missed him back home. Still, the rumors kept flooding from time to time, circulating. Like they did after the Great Gathering in that distant Cord People's main town. Atuye's brother had certainly showed up there, according to rumors, to stir up more trouble, but his father refused to discuss the matter, not even with his immediate family members, so again they were left with nothing but rumors.

Fascinated against her will, she paused to study him now, his filled-out, still well-defined face, energetic and lively, exuding easy confidence, a light-hearted self-assurance. Oh yes, the man had changed but not enough not to recognize him, the pleasantly prominent features, the strangely tilted eyes. He was a good-looking man, she remembered, glanced upon by many women, fooling around with plenty. That was the main reason his wife had thrown him out of her longhouse, creating deliciously juicy scandal. His child, not such a small boy these days and the living image of his father, was the reminder for them all, even though his mother made sure to provide a new father and a new sibling for the boy.

Well, now, looking at the man, Ononta found it more difficult to think about him in any such context. He didn't look the gambler and the lazy good-for-nothing, certainly not when she had seen him yesterday for the first time, startled into a pure gaping, her heart beating fast. Atuye's brother! And what if… The wild hope had died away quickly. Atuye's brother maintained no connections with his family. He wouldn't know a thing about the past two moons, wouldn't be able to bring her news or pass on hers upon his departure, wherever he was coming from or wherever he was going. Still, his blood connection and a certain likeness kept bringing her out, to sneak around and watch the squatting group under every possible pretext, to study the man, to catch his gaze, maybe. What she would tell him if he recognized her, she didn't know, but it was better than to have no connection to Atuye at all.

Consumed with curiosity and unreasonable hope, she kept staring, wondering. What was this man doing here, in the Rock People's town, so far away from home? Did he live among these western people now, in some other settlement, maybe? He certainly seemed to be welcomed here, spending a whole afternoon in the company of respectable locals, invited to attend the ceremony, moving around with confidence and ease. A different man than she remembered but at the same time absolutely the same. Matured, filled out, aged but in a good way. One couldn't confuse him for the lightheaded young buck like back at home, even though even back then he was not such a youth to behave in the way he did.

"I'll bring the stones." One of the younger men rushed away, attracting attention of the other crowding people. "It won't take me more than a few heartbeats."

"Don't run too fast," someone chuckled. "Or you might trip."

"He won't." Atuye's brother's laughter shook the air, ringing with easy familiarity. Was he a frequent guest in this town, visiting every now and then, like the Attiwandaronk foreigner, Tsutahi's man?

Wincing, she met the man's gaze, not quick enough to avert hers. His smile dissipated all at once, replaced by a frown, then a resolute scowl. However, as he made a move as though about to charge toward her, someone spoke to him and he turned away, his frown deepening, mouth nothing but a thinly pressed line.

Aware of acute sense of relief, Ononta turned to follow her long vanished companions, then hesitated again. Even though dangerous looking, not as approachable and as easygoing as she remembered this man being in the past, he was still Atuye's brother. What if he knew something or could have helped her to send the message, somehow? Taking a deep breath helped, but only a little. It made her legs feel firmer, not as wobbly as before, but her thoughts refused to organize, rushing around in silly circles, like frightened forest mice. What would she say to this man? What could she?

He was folding a short undecorated blanket, nothing but a roughly cut hide, smoothing its surface, creating a neatly looking square. For the stones to roll with no interruptions, she presumed, having watched such games from time to time. Women frowned when men wasted their time over games of luck, but it was still entertaining to watch, especially when the players were good or gambled on high stakes. The usual occurrence when it came to Atuye's brother. In this aspect the man evidently didn't change.

"Where will you get enough beans on such a short notice?" someone was asking, pushing his way in. More and more men crowded the shadowed space, eager to watch if not to play, tired of dancing.

"I have a good set of throwing stones. Want me to bring them here?"

"How will we all manage to play? So many people!"

Suggestions and comments flew all around, the men as agitated and as expectant as small boys eager not to miss out on a play. She hesitated again.

"Maybe we should make it a Peach Stone game." Done with his blanket, Atuye's brother straightened up, his eyes lively and free of shadows again. Until they rested on her. Then the suspicion flooded back, the cold wariness and the open distrust.

"Why are you staring at me, girl?" he demanded, not wasting his time on empty platitudes or even the basic politeness, yet shooting a quick glance around. To make sure no indignant companions would hurry to take offense on her behalf, she surmised randomly, dazed. "What do you want from me?"

Ononta gasped, unprepared for such welcoming. People were still talking between themselves, but the nearest men fell quiet, startled by his outburst as well, as it seemed.

His frown deepened, then softened. "I'm sorry," he said, forcing a smile out of the depths of his scowl. "It was quite impolite of me." The smile turned more natural, filling with the old easy charm she remembered about this man. He got away with half of his smaller crimes and transgression using that smile, admitting his guilt but in an irresistible way. Atuye's mother always complained about that, herself immune to this same berated charm. "It's just that I'm not used to so much admiration, expressed so openly. Our girls do tend to be more circumspect with their gaze."

The outburst of laughter all around made her wish to run away and hide more than his words did. Pressing her palms to her cheeks, feeling them burning, probably glowing red, she fought to suppress her tears, to blink them back where they came from. Oh yes, now she would become laughingstock of the entire town, the story sure to make its way everywhere, just everywhere – the funny foreigner making a fool of herself, throwing herself at the guest of the town. Oh, but it was too much!

"I'm sorry, girl. I didn't mean to make jokes at your expense." His face was blurry, swimming in the crispiness of the afternoon air, its expression softer, less forced than before. Or maybe she just deemed it to be so. "It was inconsiderate of me. I'm sorry about that." He made a movement as though about to bring his hands forward, to touch her maybe, or to take hold of hers. For some reason it made her feel better.

"She is Yanionra's daughter," volunteered Entiron, the man of the neighboring longhouse, the one who had made her cut that deer not so many dawns ago. As though it explained it all. "A cute little thing." The distant eyes rested on her with utter indifference. "Go away, girl. Go help the women. Make yourself useful."

But Atuye's brother still peered at her with the previous hint of compassion. "Did you want to ask me something, young one? Do you know me from somewhere?"

She just nodded, bereft of words. In the corner of her eyes she saw the youth who had rushed off earlier heading back, half walking half running, his fists clenched, locked around his treasures most probably. Who cared about silly marked stones? Still her gaze concentrated back on the subject of her alleged staring in time to see Atuye's brother's face settling in a strange mold, his eyes narrowing with suspicion in a somehow panicked way, his lips nothing but a thin line, pressed too tightly to separate. Then the illusion was gone. The self-assured visitor was back, the man who was not as abashed as to shy away from initiating a round of a gambling game on the ceremony of a town he was nothing but a guest at.

"She and her father came from your lands, brother. They are Bear People like you are."

Another light spasm made the good natured mask slip for a moment, revealing more wariness. "Oh, I see. Well, if I can do anything for you, girl, just let me know."

"Have… have you happened to visit our town in the recent moons?" It was now or never. Another heartbeat of hesitation would see her fleeing without asking.

His gaze flew at her, cornered again. "What town?"

"Umm… err… our town." She felt like taking a step back, the people nearest to them growing quieter, listening with unconcealed curiosity. "You know, Teguenondahi, our town. Where your family lives," she added helplessly, stumbling over her words. "Your brothers, and your mother… your adoptive mother… and, well, I haven't been home for nearly two moons, and I thought… maybe… maybe you've been there, maybe can tell…" This time her words trailed off for good, quailing under the incredulousness of his gaze.

"You… you are coming from Teguenondahi?" Now it was his turn to stumble over his words. "How so? Who are you?" There was an almost touching bewilderment to his stare now, the way he was gaping at her, searching and helpless, as though expecting more revelations.

"Don't you recognize your own town's people, brother?" someone asked to the open merriment of the others.

This seemed to bring Atuye's brother from his unbecoming state of confusion. The gaping eyes narrowed, mouth closed, jaw tightened back to its previous watchful determination. "I haven't been to the town of my childhood for many summers." The uneven grin twisted, one corner of the mouth climbing up faster than the other, completing the picture, again a man in control, confident and almost at ease, *almost*. "But well," a smile directed at Ononta was more obviously forced than its predecessor, "I'm surprised you remembered me at all, girl. It's been a long time."

So he hadn't been to her town. Oh, but she should have expected that, still the tears were back, blurring her vision.

"Why did you leave?" The young man with the stones dropped next to the folded blanket, spreading his treasures on its unevenly surface.

Atuye's brother leaned forward, inspecting the evenly carved wooden chips with too much interest and concentration. "It's a long story, and not very entertaining." He looked up fleetingly, his gaze resting on Ononta again, wary and apprehensive, yet compassionate too, sensing her desperation. "I'm sorry. I know nothing about the happenings in Teguenondahi. I wish I was able to help, but I know nothing of the people you wish to hear about."

"Let us start organizing the game." Her father's cousin's glances were direful, signaling with his eyes. *Go away, girl* – the clearest of messages. "The bets, what's everyone betting? Do you all have it here with you?" A sly glance shot at Atuye's brother. "Will you be offering something from your canoe's cargo?"

Numbly, Ononta wriggled her way out and away from the crowding men, her gaze fixed on the ground, concentrating on her steps. There was so much grass sprouting all around, still fresh, brilliantly green, unmarred by the strength of the summer sun. The Hot Moons would be upon them now that the Strawberry Ceremony was held. How had it come to her celebrating one of the sweetest celebrations – her favorite one! – away from home and among strangers, with even her father spending only a little time by her side. He had managed to get up and be helped to head out there, to enjoy the first stages of the ceremony, but long before the customary fruity beverage was distributed, he had to be escorted back to their longhouse, which wasn't theirs to begin with, to lie down, drink his medicine and sleep. Oh Mighty Spirits, but how was she to take such an ailing man and on such a long difficult journey? Even Tsutahi had agreed that no matter how she believed Ononta could do, could row and navigate a loaded canoe all by herself – wishful thinking on her friend's part, she knew, a blind loyalty, a belief grounded in no reality – it wasn't wise to take the older man along before he grew stronger, depended on no medicine.

Tsutahi! So strong, so sure of herself, so efficient and brisk. Not needing friends, or companions, or just people to help her along. Not even a man, not even her man, the father of her children. Loving him, yes, but not needing him in the regular sense, intending to go home without him, if need be. Especially now, that he hadn't returned with the people who had come back on the day before, the father's annoying cousin among them. It was better that Tsutahi's formidable husband had come instead, even at the price of taking her and Tsami away. His absence made her friend and the little boy so miserable!

Gaze glued to her feet, she made her way toward the trees lining the western edge of the ceremonial grounds, where the elevated land allowed the spring waters to gush down the incline, restricted by the carefully laid row of stones. The earth was studded with islands of green, sprayed with pinecones and needles aplenty, muddy despite the recent lack of rain. It was blurring too, and she blinked the tears away stubbornly, not daring to look up. Her frustrations were none of the other people's business, and the only person she could bear to talk to was out there, washing her baby in the town's spring.

If she found Tsutahi she would feel better, she knew, would see what happened in a brighter light of an unimportant incident. Yes, she made a fool of herself yet again, approaching the almost foreign man, a guest of this town, and in such an inarticulate, naively spontaneous manner, and for nothing at all. The man didn't even remember who she was. He didn't know a thing about what was happening in their hometown, and why would he? Welcomed in Teguenondahi he wasn't, anything but.

As expected, the slender figure was there, standing near the slick stones, clearly lingering. Tsutahi, unmistakable. Who else would be anxious to miss as much of the town's merry activity as she could? Hastening her step, Ononta rushed forward, feeling better by the moment, the tears drying on their own now. As long as her friend was here, she wasn't alone, not truly. And what did it matter if that man, Atuye's brother, didn't know a thing about his family or his former town? He couldn't have helped her even if he did, unless intending to head back there, not minding the need to drag a sick man and a girl along. Slim chance!

"What's wrong?" Tsutahi's eyes narrowed with suspicion, traveling between Ononta's eyes and her mouth, frowning in too obvious a way.

"Nothing. I just..." She shrugged, then stretched her arms toward the baby, who was perching comfortably, propped on his mother's hip, fully awake and bubbling with his mouth, all eyes and softly inviting plumpness. Ononta could not fight the temptation. "Come to me, little one. Give your *nnen* a little break, won't you?"

"Thank you." The familiar shyer smile flashed, holding all the warmth. "We have to go back anyway, see what the little rascal of his brother was up to."

The softness of the chubby bundle restored Ononta's cheerfulness for good, the feel of him and that sweetish musky scent belonging to babies alone. He was such an adorable thing!

"You must find a truly good name for him before the next Green Corn Ceremony," she said, snuggling the baby closer, sniffing him to her heart's contents. "Something as powerful as Tsamihui, or maybe even better."

Tsutahi was flexing her shoulders, clearly enjoying the rare sense of freedom with no baby weighing her down.

"We will." A surprisingly guilty grin lightened her face, transforming it as always, making it look irresistibly attractive. "I didn't know we were supposed to wait for the Green Corn or the Midwinter ceremonies to do that, you see? When Tsami was born, I knew he was Tsamihui, the Eagle and nothing else, but my man, he said I can call him whatever I like, yet before certain time of midwinter it won't be his real name." The slender arms were busy, rearranging the sprinkled sash. "So this time I'm not in a hurry. Until Green Corn is ripe, this little one won't be named, not for certain."

"How so?" By now Ononta knew that her friend's life was strange beyond anything she could imagine, still the tale of such lack of knowledge when it came to something as basic as naming children was too outlandish to accept just like that.

Receiving no answer, as the girl was busy with the soaked rims of her dress, she concentrated on the babbling baby with no name. "Tsami brought me the strawberry drink at the end of the ceremony," she related, forgetting to make sure her converser's gaze was back upon her, herself addressing the baby, making faces at him. "He likes it here, you know? I think he doesn't mind waiting for his father's return, even if it takes long. He gets along with the healer's daughter so well. And I saw him running around with other children as well."

Done squeezing her clothing, Tsutahi straightened up. "What?"

Ononta adjusted the baby in the curve of her hip. "Tsami, he gets along well with the local children. I think he doesn't mind waiting for his father to return."

The delicate face closed with abruptness. "I mind."

"Yes, I know." With her free hand she reached for her friend's arm, so painfully slender but muscular, pleasantly hard under her palm's touch. "But I truly believe he will be back soon. He said half a moon, yes? And it's been only a little more than that, hasn't it?"

"Every day spent in this place is too much." Tsutahi's steps rang angrily against the wet gravel, but as the softer ground of the muddy earth swallowed these sounds, Ononta felt the hesitant brush of the slender palm against her own shoulder. "I'm sorry. I know you mean well. And I know that I have no choice but to wait, with us having only one boat. And what would a few more downs change? Still it is annoying, most inconsiderate of him, and, well…"

The rest of the tirade died away as they neared the ceremonial grounds and the clamor upon it, the drums and the flutes intervening with people's voices, footsteps, clamoring utensils, shouts and laughter and children's yells. On the nearest edge the crowd encircling the players grew considerably, many men standing around the squatting group, throwing advice and good-humored insults.

"That foreigner who came here was once a man of my town," related Ononta, catching her friend's eyes momentarily as they brushed past the players and their audience, moving toward the booming drums. "It was so strange to see him here, after all those summers. He is Atuye's brother. Not full brother, but half one. They share the same father, you see?"

Her companion was eyeing her lips, frowning with barely hidden impatience, obviously anxious to return her searching gaze back to the celebration and the possibility of spotting her boy in it. "He was the one to make you upset earlier?"

"Well, yes. It was so very strange to meet him here. And he didn't even remember me. So odd! It was as though he didn't want to hear anything about his family or his hometown at all, as though he didn't want the people around here to know that he came from there." The baby was beginning to make grunting noises and she rocked him gently, trying to convince him to stay in her arms for a little longer. He was so pleasantly warm, such a soft, welcoming presence. "I hoped maybe he knew something about Atuye. So silly. I made such a fool of myself yet again." Speaking into the plump little face helped. Her friend wouldn't hear any of this, anyway. A safe confession. "Maybe he lives somewhere around here now."

It was easy to see the players despite the surrounding people as they made their way closer, listening to the drums that were rolling down the trampled grass. Atuye's brother was crouching above the midsized pottery bowl, evidently counting its contents. As his palm reached for it, it came out holding a considerable amount of dry beans judging by the way it was cupped, and what he said made people laugh, obviously light, fetching words. Oh yes, that was the man, playing games of luck, making people laugh, doing nothing constructive, according to Atuye's mother, enjoying an unjustified amount of people's good will.

Ononta touched her friend's arm. "You see, this is him. Atuye's brother. I recognize him most easily. I'm not mistaken. Still he behaves as though he never saw me before. Isn't it strange?"

Glancing at her companion, to make sure her words were heard or understood, she pointed toward the players discreetly, unwilling to draw any more attention to herself, not from this particular group. The wide back of Entiron was turned toward her, thanks to all the great and small spirits for their mercy. She had had enough of this man complaining of her silliness.

Her companion turned her head obediently, following the
direction of the non-committal wave, squinting to see against the
mild glow of the afternoon sun. With her hair wet, plastered
around the gentleness of her small, pointed face she looked again
so very young, just a child really, not a wife to a formidable
foreigner, with a lonely household and children to take care of, to
sail alone in large canoes and hunt game for their living if need be,
if Tsami's tales were to be believed. She had such a gentle profile,
such a delicately folded mouth when it wasn't pursed into a grim
line, such...

The illusion shattered in the next heartbeat, when the girl
gasped so audibly Ononta almost jumped out of her skin with the
surprise of it, such disharmonious sound again. In the next
heartbeat the space besides her cleared of anyone's presence, with
Tsutahi leaping backwards and sideways, pressing against the
trunk of the nearest tree as though trying to disappear into it. The
pair of enormously round, terrified, gaping eyes peered at her,
reflecting no sanity, nothing but mindless terror, a fright so
tangible it made Ononta's skin cover with goose bumps.

"What..." she mumbled, her mouth dry, mind refusing to
work. "What happened?" Adjusting the baby once again, she took
a hesitant step, then another. Oh, but her friend did jump quite a
large distance to reach that tree. Why? "What happened?"

The wild gaze was not upon her at all, leaping back toward the
crowding people, the rasping of the girl's breath tearing the
crispiness of the afternoon air, marring it, somehow.

Frightened even more, Ononta followed it, from this altered
vantage point finding it difficult to see the players, the onlookers'
wide backs blocking her view. "What is it?"

The touch of her arm made her friend jump like a startled
forest cat. She had seen it happening several times when a boy
from the neighboring longhouse was allowed to keep a wild cat's
cub he had found in the woods. It was funny and cute and it
jumped truly high when one crept up on it unexpected. Well, now
Tsutahi looked exactly the same, but not like a cute, fed and
pampered cub. More like a forest thing out of her wits from fear.

"What is it?" The attempt to recapture the thin arm crowned

with little success, shaken off quite violently.

"This man..." Tsutahi was whispering, "this man... it can't... he couldn't..." The wild gaze darted at her, turning more concentrated, even if not more sane than before. "Where is Tsami? I must find him... I must..."

In the next heartbeat, the baby was torn from her hands. Disoriented, Ononta stared at the small figure as it ran uphill, toward the rolling drums, fleeing as though all the creatures of the underworld were after her. And her children as well, maybe.

CHAPTER 15

"I can't believe we missed the ceremony. What a bad turn!"

Sondakwa's whisper made Atuye frown, embarrassing in its loudness. It was bad enough to spend a day and a half in a frantic rowing, then sitting out there by the river, waiting to be noticed and invited in, pretending indifference, knowing that what they had done was bad, inappropriate, something he would never have considered but for the chance to find Ononta or her whereabouts. And for his brother's insistence.

Sondakwa was pressing, harping on his duty to find out what happened to "his girl." Bored by the continued delays that made them linger in the Deer People's main town, his brother seized on a chance. A quick side journey, to have a good time while doing the right thing. Oh, but how insistently he harped on it, the right thing, his duty to Ononta and her family, their neighbors and worried people. They owed it to their good neighbors of so many summers.

Atuye would just grunt and try to get away. His brother getting all dutiful. Oh please! Sondakwa could have saved his breath trying to convince him of that. He knew his brother, no one better. Boredom was the worst of Sondakwa's enemies. This and his tendency to reckless behavior.

He pushed the frustrated thoughts away, watching the towering fence. A proper double row palisade, but not as high as back home. And not as densely woven, neglected at places upon closer inspection. Evidently, these people feared no invasions. No wonder they were making difficulties, not in a hurry to join the union.

"If we were to hop into that canoe the moment I suggested that, we would be gorging on the strawberry drinks and the freshest of stews now, Little Brother." Sondakwa winked, evidently enjoying Atuye's embarrassment. The two men who came to invite them in walked close by, conversing between themselves. After lingering near their fire down there by the river for a considerable amount of time, fishing out as much information as to the purpose of the unexpected visitors' arrival as politeness demanded, they seemed to be disappointed now, walking ahead and talking between themselves.

What did they expect? wondered Atuye absently. A delegation of respectable people rather than two wandering warriors? Well, their dignitaries deemed this town not important enough.

"It is too bad you didn't arrive earlier," said one of their escorts, echoing Sondakwa's complaints. "Our people know how to celebrate the gift of the forest fruit."

His companion nodded in consent.

"Oh, it's a pleasure to visit your settlement and your people, no matter for what occasion." Sondakwa was again on his best behavior, the twinkle in his eyes well hidden, but there. Atuye could see it most clearly, in the folds of his brother's mouth and the glitter of his gaze. "We are honored to be invited in."

"We are honored by your presence as well," answered one of their hosts dutifully, not sounding too convincing. "Your people seem to find our settlements of interest through recent times. It is a good development. Our nations should strengthen their ties."

"Well, our elders keep inviting yours to join the alliance of the united Wyandot People. The ties between our nations would strengthen considerably if you did this."

Atuye almost gasped, appalled at the tactlessness his brother displayed. Barely invited in and he was already complaining and on such delicate, laden-with-tension matter.

"Well, your elders evidently didn't go out of their way inviting us in." The voice of the local gained a flinty edge to it. "And I still don't see any of them here, on their way to talk to ours."

"Brother." The other man's palm rested on his companion's shoulder, lingering there for only a heartbeat, conveying a message.

"We are grateful for your hospitality," Atuye hurried to add, anxious to contribute to the pacifying efforts. "Our visit is as brief as it is unofficial. We represent no one, carrying no agenda or special purpose."

Their escorts nodded stiffly, their faces closed, reflecting nothing but stony reserve. He shot his brother a direful glance, glimpsing the corridor between the high poles, longing to reach its shadowed coolness, welcomed in this first summer's moon heat. The drums reached here faintly, rolling softly, invitingly.

"I'm sure the Great Spirits are honored and pleased with your ceremonies and celebrations," went on Atuye, knowing that it was not his place to speak at all, let alone to try and smooth matters over, aware that no one else would do it for them. Should Sondakwa open his mouth under such openly expressed disapproval, it would only land them in more trouble. His brother was not the type to act prudently when challenged.

"We believe so, yes," nodded one of the men, slightly pacified. "The Great Spirits favor their children among our people. We have no cause to complain."

And neither do we, thought Atuye, hoping his brother would not sound the exact same thought aloud.

"We can say the same, yes." Sondakwa nodded solemnly, all dignity and reserve again. "Evidently we have more in common than apart, brothers," he added with a suddenly wide, winning smile. "We can't get away from it."

That pushed their hosts into returning grins, reluctantly wide as they were. Typical, reflected Atuye, amused and just a little envious again. No one could anger his audience with so much carelessness and lack of forethought, then win it back with nothing but a guilty smile.

The rest of the walk along the inner side of the fence and the sprouting plants of tobacco that dotted the vast plots aplenty, still low in this time of the seasons, proceeded in a lighter atmosphere appropriate for the sunny afternoon.

"We have guests from among your people and they didn't seem to complain," one of the men was saying. "I'm telling you, our towns turn popular with wandering Bears and such."

"There are more of our people here?" Sondakwa straightened alertly, shooting a triumphant glance back at Atuye. "A man with a young daughter, by any chance?"

"A man with a young daughter?" Both of their escorts turned their heads, their eyebrows climbing high. "No. The man who came here brought plenty of goods to trade, but no, he carried no young girls along." A snicker. "Which is a good thing. I'm not sure our people would take it well, the trading of young girls."

Their hearty laughter shook the air, enhancing Atuye's sense of disappointment. But if not here in Onentisati, then where was she?

Sondakwa seemed to be taken aback as well. "No young girls from among our people? But it can't be. The girl we are looking for came from our town. Her father was your people's man once upon a time. He had traveled to visit his family some time ago." The frowning gaze leapt at Atuye. "When did he leave? Two, three moons ago?"

"Yes, they had left well after the end of the Frozen Season. It was close to two moons ago." He glanced at the men, encouraged. Maybe they would know. Even though they claimed no young girls arrived in this town at all. How so?

"Oh, *that* man!" exclaimed one of the locals, turning toward the incline and the trickling spring, its borders restricted by carefully laid stones, as though keeping the gushing stream in place. Here the passersby were many and frequent, generating curious glances accompanied with reserved greetings. "Oh yes, old Yanionra came from the Bear People's towns, no?" A glance at his companion made the man nod. "Yes, he is the man of our Deer Clan, but he lived among your people, yes." Another thoughtful grimace, an expressed attempt to remember. "He came with the daughter, a cute little thing even if silly. She grew as thick as two beans in the porridge with another foreigner, the strangest girl you'll ever meet, her and her husband, the outlandish Attiwandaronk with plenty of rare pelts to trade."

He tried to cope with the sudden surge of information, his hope escalating.

"Where are they now, that man and the girl?" asked Sondakwa, as matter-of-fact as always.

"Here, naturally. Celebrating somewhere out there." A shrug. "Well, the old man isn't likely to celebrate anything as yet. He almost embarked on his Sky Journey a moon or so ago. Was sick for so long!" Another shrug. "And he still seems undecided about it, recovering his strength but slowly."

"Oh, so this is why they weren't coming back." Sondakwa was arriving at his conclusions fast, faster than Atuye's dazed mind could cope with. "Oh, this is good news. Our people were worried about them not coming back for so long. This young buck over here more than anyone." The wink and the nudge into his ribs made Atuye furious, too furious to think of the boiling wave washing over his face, obvious to anyone who would bother to look. Something their companions promptly did, their grins amused, flickering with know-it-all mirth.

"You'll find your girl with no trouble, brother," one of the men was saying. "Dancing on the ceremonial grounds, I presume. It is the high time for the post-ceremonial dancing, eh?" A wink. "Better hurry before someone else manages to take advantage of that."

"It is not what you think," he muttered, then cleared his throat, shamed by their open amusement and his own faltering speech. "She is a friend of many summers. I wanted to make sure that she is well, that no harm came to her on their journey forth or back."

That came out well, still their smirking didn't fade. He busied himself watching the clamor down the incline, near the edge of the ceremonial grounds. Many people congregated there, crowding and pushing, exclaiming loudly, their excitement unconcealed.

Curious, he watched them, the familiar view of men at the end of a celebration, busy with throwing games or other gambling activities, here like anywhere else. Only the unattached youths would be lingering near the fires and the dancers congregating around it, girls, boys, older women, dissatisfied with their men's gambling, many of those. Oh, but these people were just like their people, indeed. Father had been right about it, like he always was.

Don't be tempted to join in, he thought, catching his brother's gaze that lingered around the group in the shadow of a huge pine, assessing, arriving at the same conclusion as to the nature of the activities, of course.

Their escorts grinned and hastened their step, changing direction, heading toward the lively gathering. "Our other Bear People's guest has been busy contributing to the conduct of certain parts in our ceremonial procedures, as well."

"Oh yes, that he did." The second man chuckled, but there was a clear tone of complaint in his voice now. "It seems half a town have drifted here while we were wandering, collecting more guests."

Atuye fought the urge to offer apology.

"Oh yes, our people are that good," Sondakwa was saying. "Maybe we should offer them some support."

"There is only one of your people there," laughed one of the locals. "And he needs no support, judging by the way he conducts himself. Perfectly at home, full of spirit and brass."

"What are they playing at?"

"The regular throwing game, I think. When we left they were talking about making it a Peach Stone game, because too many players wanted in. Or so your countryfolk member was claiming. He seems to have plenty of experience in that sort of thing."

Suddenly, Sondakwa's gaze lost some of its flickering amusement, clouded with suspicion. "I sincerely hope it is not the worthless piece of meat..." He didn't finish his phrase, but his eyes rested on Atuye, as though demanding confirmation.

"What do you mean?"

The crowding people were very near now, paying the newcomers little attention. Sondakwa pushed his way in resolutely, following their escorts, but Atuye lingered on the outskirts of the bubbling congregation, his gaze drifting toward the rolling drums. Ononta wouldn't be spending her time watching the peach stone game players, not her. He would do better heading toward the fires and the music. Thoughtfully, he began easing away.

As though wishing to challenge him, the flatter ground spread in all directions from around the huge maple tree, dotted with many groups of people, the abandoned fires where the food was probably distributed earlier teeming with life, the elderly women successful at rounding up enough girls for the cleaning up effort.

He narrowed his eyes, trying not to be too obvious about his observations. The authoritative Clans Mothers wouldn't welcome strangers, people no one knew or recognized, staring at them or their charges, that much was certain. Still he scanned the younger girls' faces, their willowy or heavyset figures and the colorfulness of their swaying attires. Ononta would be among those, surely. She was a dutiful girl, always around and helpful. Why would she behave differently here? Was she happier in this faraway town, better content? Was that why she didn't come back? The man said something about her father's illness, but people didn't stay ill for so long. Close to two moons? No, it was truly too long to stay anywhere, unless not intending to come back.

He moved to a better vantage point, then another. Some people were glancing at him, wondering. Down the farther side of the flat ground, the circle of dancers was growing, with more people joining in.

He drifted toward it, defeated. She wasn't helping around the fires, she who was always so dutiful and involved. For some reason it made him feel betrayed. What if she changed for some reason, truly changed? What if she didn't welcome his coming here?

More glances were shot his way. He edged away from the throbbing drums and the swirling double circle, noting that like back home these people were dancing with cheerful abandon, talking and gossiping and flirting as they did, the youngsters among them. Through the last two moons, on the Thunder and Planting Ceremonies, he did his share of frivolous bouncing as well, catching gazes of pretty girls, thrilled but not knowing what to do with them. He didn't think of Ononta back then, but now the thought of her doing the same made him angry. He shouldn't have listened to his brother, coming to this town and in such an unauthorized way at that. Where was Sondakwa anyway? Throwing stones already, challenging the prideful locals?

Turning to head back toward the gambling men, he tried to listen to their commotion, recognizing what sounded like angry voices now. Was Sondakwa getting in trouble?

Hastening his step, he almost tripped over a running boy, a cute little toddler, who had jumped onto his path out of nowhere it seemed, darting aside at the last moment with an admirable agility for such a young thing. For a heartbeat the boy hesitated, then, giving Atuye a look full of suspicion, his gaze stormy, glittering with tears, he resumed his somewhat clumsy run down the incline, in the direction of the players, ridiculously determined, as purposeful as only small children could be.

"In a hurry, isn't he?" commented someone with a chuckle.

The others laughed, then moved to clear the way for the indignant mother, or rather an older sister, hot on the escaping culprit's heels. Small and painfully thin, but delightfully fit judging by the agility of her run, the girl rushed down the incline, as determined, catching the little figure very soon, holding it firmly against the fierceness of its struggle.

Amused, Atuye watched them. The little boy was so willful, so determined to break free. Too young to achieve anything, of course. The girl, even as tiny as this one, held onto her prey uncompromisingly, talking rapidly, trying to overcome the loudness of the boy's protests.

"What did the little one do this time?" mused someone, amused by the entire scene along with the rest of the onlookers.

"He is wild but not that wild," commented another, a young woman with a toddler of her own in her arms. "He listens to her. Sometimes."

More chuckling. Glancing at his fellow watchers, curious about these people in their natural surroundings – yes, just like his countryfolk, gossipy and content, at ease after the ceremonial activities, idle but in a good way – Atuye prepared to resume his walk, still afraid he might be challenged with difficult questions. It was wiser to stay with his brother and the people who had led them here, if only from the nearest shore.

Then his gaze, brushing past their faces, came to a sudden halt. Ononta was staring at him, wide eyed and as if dazed, the familiar outline of her face distorted by the gaping mouth, with the unnaturally round eyes to match.

For a heartbeat nothing happened. Gazes locked, they stayed as they were, disoriented, not daring to breathe. Her eyes were enormous in the thinner version of her familiar face, and her lips quivered but only once, as though trying to articulate something but giving up on the effort.

Then, before he managed to get hold of his own limbs' command, she emitted a funny sound, and rushed toward him, or maybe just swayed in his direction, the baby in her arms encumbering her movement. An impressively large baby, he noted absently, all bundled up in an undecorated piece of hide. It must be heavy to carry a thing like that.

"Atuye! What? How? I can't... can't believe..." she was muttering, peering at him from close up now, two spots glaring on her prettily rounded cheekbones, the glitter of her eyes bordering with insane. "How? When?"

"I..." He cleared his throat, painfully aware of the surrounding people, their attention transferred from the previous scene of the girl and the toddler and straight into the one they were making. "I came in just now. Me and my brother, we arrived only a short while ago. Missed the ceremony." What an irrelevant flood of information. He wanted to kick himself; after turning around and running as far away from here as possible, that is. "We came here looking for you. Your father, they say he was sick."

That served to bring her back to a semblance of normality as well. At least her eyes returned to normal proportions, even if they still had a wild spark to them.

"Father is better," she said, swallowing, readjusting the baby without even looking at it. "He... he was truly ill, but now, now he can sit and eat. Well, a little." Her lips quivered again. "He couldn't keep any food down before, and he was burning up for so long. They feared for his life, and I couldn't..." Her voice broke by a sob. "I was so afraid, and we couldn't go home. Even Tsutahi agreed that I can't take him until he is stronger. She said he needs to be able to support himself, because I can't carry him, not when needing to detour on foot. And, and..." More sobs interrupted her speech, but by this time the awkward sensation retreated, replaced by familiar old warmth, the responsibility to protect her. An old feeling.

"Wait, wait," he said, smiling encouragingly, trying to will her into a more spirited attitude. Another familiar sensation. "Let us make it more orderly, eh? Your father is still ill? Where is he?"

"There." A noncommittal wave indicated somewhere "there," behind the incline and the ceremonial grounds. "In the second Deer Clan longhouse."

"Well then, let us go and visit him first." To put his arm on her shoulder in an attempt to propel her in the indicated direction felt natural but for the baby in her arms. "What's with this little thing? Whose baby is it?"

"Tsutahi's," she answered readily, the smile already there, blossoming through the glittering tears. Another familiar sight. Then her gaze darted back down the incline, resting on the girl and the toddler, who was not struggling anymore, snuggling in his pursuer's arms, instead, howling lustily. "She needs to calm Tsami down. She needs to make him listen, so he won't make trouble. He doesn't want to leave, you see?" With a twinge of disappointment he watched the frown banishing the glory of her budding smile, making it disappear. "I don't understand what came over her either. She's been acting strange from the moment she saw your brother."

That got his attention off her vanishing smile. "My brother? Did you see him already? When?"

She took her eyes of the huddling pair and peered at him, puzzled a little. "Not very long ago. It was all very strange. I tried to talk to him, ask about you. I was thinking maybe he could send you word, let you know that we are stuck here and can't go home. And," her frown deepened, as her forehead furrowed into what looked like a wrinkled blanket, "He didn't even know who I am. He didn't remember me at all. Isn't it strange?"

Now it was his turn to stare at her, beyond comprehension.

"Yes, I know," she went on, breathless. "It was so odd. I recognized him so easily and he didn't recognize me at all. So strange. Even though it's been a long time, of course. But I only wanted to ask him about you, to send you word maybe."

To send him word? But how could it be? They had just arrived here and he had left his brother out there with the gambling crowd such a short while ago. How long had it taken him to wander this ceremonial ground dotted with post-cooking fires and the double circle of dancers? Not enough to let her run into his brother in the meantime, asking about him, receiving no coherent answers.

"He didn't tell you I was around here? But why? We arrived together. We came here looking for you. What you say doesn't make any sense!"

Now it was her turn to stare at him, dumfounded. It must have been funny, he reflected randomly, the way they alternated this stupid staring, one after another, reacting to each other's words. The silence around them confirmed the worst. People were listening, avidly at that.

"Come, let us go." Motioning to her, he began making his way down the incline, in the direction of the players and the girl with the toddler. This one managed to get in control of the situation as well, walking back toward them, the resisting boy's arm locked securely in her palm, uncompromising.

"You arrived here together?" Ononta was asking, trailing after him, following dully. The baby in her arms began making mewing noises. "But how? I saw him here on the day before, and even before that. Where have you been if so?"

When safely outside of people's eavesdropping presence, he halted again, turning to face her, resolved to sort out this entire misunderstanding once and for all. It was as though they were talking in different tongues. Each of them made no sense for the other.

The sight of her standing there, peering at him in this typical earnest way of hers, with no affectation or pretense, warmed his insides. She didn't change, not even a little bit! Even the expert way in which she was rocking the baby, making it calm again, was familiar. No more than ten spans of season ago she was running everywhere with her baby brother in her arms.

"Now let us start it all over, make some order out of it." Her widening smile caused the warmth inside him to spread. She was evidently remembering him just like that as well, a person in a habit of putting things right before rushing out to act upon them. "You saw my brother when?"

"Not a long time ago. When they were setting the throwing game out there." The wave of her hand confirmed the direction of the even hum that, indeed, emanated from the crowd engaged in throwing their stones; where Sondakwa was still lingering, picking no fights with the touchy locals, or so he hoped. "I talked to him then, but of course I saw him on the day before too, when he just arrived."

Again, no logic. "He couldn't have arrived here on the day before. We came here together, only a short while ago."

The girl with her toddler in tow reached them, but stopped at a respectful distance, studying him with her eyes full of suspicion, clearly ready to bolt away should he display an intention of starting toward her. He concentrated back on Ononta, whose eyes were widening again.

"I don't understand," she mumbled, then evidently noticing her friend, waved her closer. "And you are saying you two traveled together. So he was lying. Why?"

The girl neared warily, hesitantly, glancing at him with an open suspicion, still ready to act upon his reaction, friendly or less so. Despite her smallness and her obviously haunted demeanor, she was a pleasant thing to look at but for the troubled expression, the worried grimace that distorted the delicate features, made them look strange and out of place.

"This is Atuye," Ononta was saying, her excitement returning, glowing with triumph, full of pride as though introducing her friend to the most revered of heroes. "He came, he actually came! Would you believe it?"

The girl nodded absently, not even faking an interest, her eyes watching Ononta's lips, darting toward him, the intruder, every now and then. He tried not to let his puzzlement show, concentrating on the boy instead, who was peering at him with an unconcealed curiosity, his previous tantrum evidently forgotten. When he winked at him, the boy giggled.

"Tsami doesn't want to leave," said Ononta, as though trying to clarify something. "That's why he tried to run away just now."

"Leaving where?"

"Back home." This time, Ononta knelt next to the rebellious thing, having transferred the baby to the arms of the girl. Taking the boy's shoulders between her palms, squeezing them with an easy familiarity, she peered into his face, very sincere. "You can't make trouble for your mother like this, you know. You must act like a big boy. You must help her in everything until your father comes back. You must be the man of the family."

"But I don't want to go away," protested the boy, his face clouding again, lips pursing in unpromising manner. "I want to wait for Father to come back."

The girl was watching them both intently, again concentrating on the lower parts of their faces as though afraid to miss a gesture. He remembered the elderly man from one of the towns he had traveled with Father, the elder who needed to see a person's lips to hear what had been said.

"You must do what your *nnen* says," insisted Ononta, but in less forceful manner. Then she looked up. "Must you truly leave just like that?"

Her friend nodded, but said nothing, refusing to confirm Atuye's suspicion. The elder was speaking in a strangely loud, unmelodious manner and he expected the girl to sound somehow similar.

Ononta was back on her feet, squeezing the boy's palm in hers lovingly, affectionately. "This is Atuye, my best friend and the best boy ever," she declared, pushing the boy forward.

Grinning at the child, Atuye pushed his impatience away. "I think we better go and find my brother, clear up this entire misunderstanding." But again his gaze drew toward the girl with the baby, pulled to her almost against his will. There was something about this one, something unsettling but pleasing, an impossible combination. Her braids were thick and tightly woven, too long for the tiny creature that she was, framing the delicacy of her face. "Do you want us to take you somewhere? Your longhouse? Your family?"

She was busy readjusting her baby in the pocket that a blanket wrapped around her torso created, casually but prettily, enhancing the slenderness of her hips.

"She wants to leave, take her children and leave without waiting for her man to return," said Ononta when no answer seemed to be forthcoming. "She saw your brother and it scared her so. I never saw someone as panicked in my entire life. Since then she did nothing but look for Tsami and now that she's found him she wants to take their things and go at once, with not even decent preparations for a long journey ahead of them."

He shifted uncomfortably, not liking the way she was talking as though the girl wasn't there. Busy with her blanket or not, it wasn't proper to talk about someone like that, as though a person had no ears. Then more pieces of the puzzle fell in place.

"Your friend can't hear properly?"

"Oh yes, yes!" Ononta frowned too, troubled now. "I forgot to tell you. When you ask her something you need to make sure she sees your lips."

"*Annen* can hear you even from very far." The boy was evidently busy listening, having no problems of impaired hearing or the concept of good manners as yet. "But not when you stand behind her. Then you can yell and scream and *annen* will do nothing at all." His eyes sparkled with naked triumph. "I tried!"

"How does she know my brother?" Acknowledging the boy's contribution to the conversation with a fleeting smile, Atuye frowned, watching the efficiency with which the object of their discussion was tucking in her baby, with brisk, no-nonsense movements, touching in her absorbed sincerity, glancing at her boy every now and then. How strange it must be, to depend on one's vision to hear anyone, let alone a child.

"I don't know. She didn't want to tell me." Ononta's face was falling again, in her usual quick-to-cry fashion. "We were so close, the best of friends, but since she saw your brother, it's as though she became a stranger. I... I don't know what to think..."

The girl was watching them now, and for a heartbeat her face twisted with what looked like a genuine sympathy. Her free hand came out, brushed past Ononta's shoulder, caressing it briefly.

"I'm sorry," she said in a quiet delicate voice that fitted with her general appearance. No harsh stridency to it, nothing that he expected. "I'm sorry. It is not something..." Glancing at her boy once again, she fell silent, then shrugged. "I can't stay. That is all." This time, her voice rose to less pleasant tones, gaining the dissonant, jarring element he anticipated before. "That man, he is a spirit, a bad *uki* that came back to our world. I don't know how; I didn't think..." The gushing flow of words ceased abruptly, swallowed back by a convulsion of the gentle throat.

"But, sister!" Eyes huge and glittering with tears as opposed to the dry closeness of her friend's, Ononta grabbed the slender arm, pressing it in her turn. "What did this man do to you? He can't be that bad. Yes, I know, he is a gambler and no-good. He did some crimes yes, but how... What did he do to you?"

The haunted eyes were staring at her converser's face without seeing it, or so it seemed. "He is not a man, but a spirit, a ghost, a wandering *uki*. He died. I saw him dying. He was dead for more than three summers. He is not a regular man now."

Spoken in a blank, expressionless voice, so lacking in emotion it sounded dead, those words made Atuye shiver. Even though it was nonsense, pure nonsense. His brother was anything but a wandering spirit of a dead man. How ridiculous was such a claim! Still, he felt like taking a step back, or better yet, quitting the strange town alongside with this strange girl that was so anxious to get away, collecting nothing but her children for the journey, not even supplies, according to Ononta.

He saw his childhood friend swaying back, frightened. To put his arm around her shoulders felt natural, despite the openness of their location. Poor thing.

"Sondakwa is no wandering spirit," he said, addressing them both, careful to let the deaf girl see the movement of his lips. "He is just a man, and I'm afraid you are mistaking him for someone else, anyway. He has never been to these places. This is the first time either of us has traveled so far westwards. He could have done nothing wild, or bad, or crazy around here." He drew a deep breath. "And he couldn't have died around here, either!"

The deaf girl was frowning direfully, following his lips with painful concentration. But it was Ononta's puzzled frown that made him feel out of place. Again she evidently couldn't place or comprehend his words. Would they go on misunderstanding each other?

Before he found something to say, Ononta flapped her hands in the air. "Who said anything about *this* brother of yours? What has Sondakwa to do with any of it?" Her eyebrows kept climbing, in an expression of pure bewilderment. "Is he here too? Your brother? How odd! Did he come with you? Where is he?"

Refusing to sink into even deeper bewilderment, he just stared. What was she talking about? Didn't he tell her that in so many different words and ways, about his brother and how they traveled, while she claimed...

And then it dawned on him all at once, and he gasped, staring at her in his turn, blinking. She wasn't talking about Sondakwa at all. All this time, and she wasn't taking about any of his full siblings.

"Ogteah? Is he here?"

It came out in a strangled squeak, such a stupid sound. He felt the deaf girl's gaze upon him, staring pensively, with this same singular absorption he had noticed about her before, thinking, analyzing. She must be deeming him the oddest person alive. Annoyed, he drew a deep breath.

"Did you mean my half-brother? Is he here?"

Ononta was nodding vigorously, glowing with excitement again. "I told you. He arrived yesterday, and he didn't even remember me. And he said he didn't visit Teguenondahi for a long time. And, well, he didn't feel good about me asking him all these questions. I could see that. But, well, I was only trying to find out if he knew the way of sending you word."

Amidst the pieces of puzzle that kept falling together, comprising a picture he didn't like, he stopped listening. Oh, yes, that local telling them about the Bear People visitor, the one who was setting up games of luck, and then Sondakwa, growing indignant all of sudden, talking about worthless pieces of human beings, pushing his way into the circle of players. Oh Mighty Spirits, but they didn't need this sort of trouble.

He shook his head, meeting their gazes, both sets of eyes glued to him, even those of the little boy, still pressing into his mother's skirt, all expectancy now. The deaf girl looked like an alert animal, all eyes and senses. It was easy to imagine her having a pair of pointed quivering ears.

"I need to find both of my brothers. Come with me!"

CHAPTER 16

"What is this? A family gathering?"

Beyond the stage of surprise, indignation or worry, Ogteah stared at his youngest half-brother's face, well defined and nicely featured but now set into a stony mask, the unpleasantness of the surprise written across it most clearly.

Reciprocated most heartily, too, he reflected, not even starting to think of the implications. It actually fitted the young buck to look this way, solemn and serious and oh so very father-like. Did he try to imitate Father on purpose, enhancing what natural likeness was there? He wouldn't put it behind the crafty little skunk. Not so little anymore, too. Even though it wasn't easy to recognize this one, unlike the other annoying reminder, the elder of Father's second woman's brood, Sondakwa.

Having seen none of them for a considerably long period of time, five summers or maybe even more, he had no difficulty recalling his closest of siblings, the old-time rival. No, this one hadn't changed beyond filling out, growing in all sort of directions, a fat piece of meat, a family man. Were the women of his longhouse busy cooking all the time?

"Maybe it is, family man. Maybe it is." Just like expected, Sondakwa's tone alone had the power to send his irritation soaring to the skies. So much annoying mockery and scorn, all this challenging derisiveness, what a dirty skunk.

He glanced at the stony defiance of the broad face, making sure his own eyes held nothing but cold hostility, a perfectly matching superiority and derision. What a nuisance! Was his entire former town about to accost him here, in this faraway Rock People's settlement?

First, the silly girl pestering him with irrelevant questions, disturbing with her implied knowledge of him and his family. What if she put his web of lies and half-truths to the test, somehow, making the locals doubt his story, challenge him with difficult questions? After all, he had indicated an uncertain place of living, counting on these people's lack of knowledge of their Bear neighbors' affairs. Who cared what village he came from? They didn't even inquire as to its name, and he didn't bother to think of one. But now this unplanned-for girl was meandering all around, ready to supply answers to the people who might be asking questions about him. What were the chances of someone from his former town appearing in the exact spot he had wandered to? None whatsoever, and yet here they all were, not only some random girl, but his entire collection of half-siblings as well. Only his silly bothersome half-sister was missing.

He suppressed a snort, turning his attention back to the game. Somehow he was conducting it again. At first, he had just organized a few men to play a bean game as one of the locals claimed to have specially painted throwing stones. A natural behavior at the end of the ceremonial activities and the progressing celebrations, he had reasoned with himself, bored by the talks of the previous evening, with all those barely concealed hints and sometimes even outright attacks against his presumed countryfolk. It was tiring, to do it for so long, to fake personal interest and concern. These people were talkative, and as though in a need to pour it all out on the first representative of their forceful, pushy neighbors, eager to sound their resentful arguments and offended claims.

Well, he did his best listening and making them talk, and the result was quite satisfying. A few more such evenings, and he would be ready to head back home, sparing himself the rest of the journey through those lands. What he had learned was more than enough.

Still, when the next day's ceremony presented a pleasant diversion, he breathed with relief, even though to conduct a betting game of many participants might be taking it too far, stepping away from the person he was presuming to be, a respectable hunter out to trade some goods? Only a second day in this settlement and he was organizing games of chance, engaging with zeal. Was Gayeri right about his former people and lands having a bad influence on him?

When the girl had accosted him with her tearful questioning, he had to fight the urge to sneak away, climb over the fence, rush down the shore and onto his canoe and be gone. As fast as he could do that, too. She didn't present much danger in herself, still his senses urged caution. In as delicate a mission as his, one couldn't be too careful. It was better to meet no people who might have known him, no people at all.

Still he had pushed the warning tingling away. It was unseemly to just get up and leave, or even to do this later with untoward abruptness. Succumbing to panicked retreat, he might make the matters worse, raise an unnecessary suspicion. There was no point in getting nervous over nothing, no point whatsoever.

Yet, the worry kept nagging, even after he had won the first round of the game, coming out of it an owner of a beautiful necklace and a pair of good arrows and a knife. Such rich winnings. But these people did not hold back on betting. He had offered some pricy things too, to match the others' offerings, of course, still it surprised him, the readiness of the locals to part with such treasures. The necklace alone was a work of art and much investment, an intricate pattern of colorful shells dotted by porcupine quill painted in many colors. It would look beautiful on the slenderness of Gayeri's neck, he reflected, warming inside at such stroke of luck. She would love to have a present from the other side, a worthwhile peace offering, to make it up for the days of worry and neglect.

Warming to the image of her face transformed with a childish delight when presented with such treasure, he smiled inside, proceeding to organize the next round of the game out of habit, reorganizing the sitting arrangements for the new players, inspecting the offered goods, comparing their worth. Brisk, efficient, in his element. But he had vast experience at that, hadn't he? And they were accepting his authority, those generous hosts of his. Good. Why shouldn't they all enjoy a pleasant afternoon on the day of the ceremony?

"You seem to have some experience at organizing games of luck, mysterious visitor." One of the women, a tall curvy fox of about the same age as he, edged her way inside the circle of watchers, leaving the other women who had stopped to watch behind. "Have you done that often back in your lands?"

He answered her scrutinizing gaze with a matching grin, not opposed to such bantering, always a pleasant pastime. It wasn't wise to get into anything, to fool around an unfamiliar town he was a mere guest in, a temporary visitor. Still one could enjoy the bantering, couldn't he?

"I have my share of playing around, yes." Her playfully arching eyebrows made him smile. Such an uplifting sight.

"Do you always come out loaded with pretty things?" Her gaze brushed past his winnings, the necklace glittering atop of the pile.

Greedy fox, he thought, still amused. To what lengths would one such go in a hope to lay her hands on this treasure? A question that wouldn't be answered. The pendant belonged on Gayeri's neck. Still the excitement was there, climbing up in a warming wave. It'd been a lonely wandering so far.

"How about we change it to a Peach Stone game?" he suggested in general, flashing a knowing grin at the woman, an encouragement he knew he should not be indicating. "This way the next players won't have to wait for long rounds of a game to end."

"A Peach Stone game is not the same as the bean game," protested someone, but many others were nodding eagerly, seeing the merit of his suggestion without the need to explain.

"All we need is to reduce the amount of throwing stones, while sending a courageous person to pinch a flat-bottomed vessel from one of the fires back there." Their chuckles warmed the afternoon, restoring his confidence for good. Oh, yes, he could handle these people. He was good at just this sort of thing. Another day or two, and he would be off, bursting with useful information, the silly girl from Teguenondahi notwithstanding. "We'll restrict it to three tosses each pair." The woman was still there, eyeing him from the back of the crowd now, her eyes flickering with a familiar challenge. He grinned to himself. "This way no player will have to wait for too long."

Voices of people descending the trail from the direction opposite to the rolling drums made some of the heads turn. Why would the celebrating townsfolk wander out there, away from the festivities?

Ogteah motioned to the owner of the stones to hand him over his treasures. "How many of us will be playing?"

"You have thought it all out, haven't you?" One of the men rubbed his hands with an open anticipation.

Ogteah just grinned, glancing at the newcomers who were pushing their way inside the tightening circle.

"There is no need—" The rest of the phrase froze, dying upon his lips as his eyes took in the familiar broad face, the decisively protruding cheekbones, the prominent eagle-like nose that would have dominated it but for the rest of the boldly outlined features.

Once upon a time Sondakwa was nothing but a lanky boy, skinny and not that difficult to dominate, to restrain if necessary, when the crazy piece of meat was throwing his tantrums and trying to hurt for real. He was such an unruly beast when pushed. But what one was to do with the cheeky bastard out to prove his strength day and night, caring for little else? It was never peaceful around their compartment of the longhouse or out there in the open. It took them time to understand that distance did nothing but good for both of them. When pressed to spend time together at home, it was an outright war, with winters being the worst.

Their other siblings, a sister and later on little Atuye, were nothing, not even figurines to manipulate in the relentlessness of their war on each other – both were above using any such means. It was about them and nothing else. And did it make Father's woman mad, stupid, fat doe that she was, ever moaning about her stepson's unworthiness, unruliness, his laziness and bad temper. Should have looked no further than her own son to find all that and more.

He shook his head to get rid of the memories, staring at the unwelcome bringer of those, receiving a fiercely burning glare as an answer. The people were staring at him as well, puzzled.

"You were saying…"

He took his eyes off his sibling, the effort of doing so coming with difficulty. "Have anyone gone to fetch a flat-bottomed bowl yet?" It came out curtly, too curtly. He moderated his tone. "We can play a Peach Stone without actual pits, to replace those with marked stones. But no flat-bottomed vessel to toss them in would be pushing it too far, would it not?"

The hum of the chuckles and arguing voices rose again. Unable to fight the temptation, he let his eyes draw back toward the unwelcome presence, still towering there darkly, nodding at the people he had been introduced to. Quite a few. Where did the annoying skunk come from and by whose invitation? Alone or a part of this or that delegation? Oh, but it wasn't good, this development. Authoritative elders of his former town were the very last people he needed to face!

"Another guest from the Bear People's lands," one of the newcomers was telling. "But aren't we popular with our distant neighbors these days?"

More lightly amused agreements. People were talking all around, animated and bright, bursting into frequent fits of laughter. It let them glare at each other with no interruptions this time.

"What are you doing here?" The question hung in the air, openly challenging. He didn't mean to ask that, or do so in such an openly hostile manner, but here it was, ringing with animosity worthy of adversaries or enemies at the very least.

"I would say, it's none of your business, Brother." Sondakwa's dark eyes narrowed into slits, his full mouth disappearing into an invisible line, curving with derision. "You haven't changed, eh? Wandering about, playing games of luck. Ready to be thrown out of this town upon the first scandal, eh? Not far away from now, I predict."

"None of it is of your business as well." His own voice had a freezing quality from the dead of the Cold Moons, and it pleased him, the crystal frostiness of it. He made sure his face reflected nothing but cold indifference, always the best of weapons against the filthy skunk. To be dismissed as nothing but a chirping bird drove the unruly piece of meat positively mad, heralded of his lack of importance. Another who hadn't changed besides growing fat.

Pleased, if ever so slightly, Ogteah turned to the owner of the throwing stones. "We can make a quick round of throwing, determine who will be the one to risk his life out there by the fires, begging or stealing from the Clans Mothers."

"Not a bad idea." The young man laughed, turning to the others, knowing himself to be out of danger, having run the previous errand, bringing the marked stones. "Marked or unmarked?"

"Marked!" cried out several voices.

"Whoever gets the most marked sides goes to fetch the basket. Those who don't throw now won't be playing at all." One of the locals, a hardened man of enough summers and inarguably dignified bearing, was taking initiative, to Ogteah's imminent relief. It was time to draw away from the center of their attention, to slip off the moment it became possible and think about all this, consider the implications. Did his brother's unexpected appearance change things? What did the filthy skunk know about him?

Enough, judging by the allegation of towns throwing him out and fast. Did they all hear about Arontaen? Probably. But what else?

Father surely hadn't told a word about his son's new life. Even Tsineka, Father's closest of friends and his right hand in everything, the man who had surely been involved in the night escape out of Ossossane, even this man didn't know about his, Ogteah's, true destination.

No, his brother couldn't know a thing. And yet, his presence was messing it all up, complicating the already complicated situation, regardless. Why did he have to appear here, of all places, and at the just "right" timing? What were his people doing wandering those distant rocky shores? Another piece of useful information to think about and reflect. At this rate of friendly mingling the Wyandot would end up united and faster than expected, surpassing their own expectations, maybe.

He glanced at his sibling once again, seeing the man shaking his head in refusal, not about to join the game his despised half-brother was conducting. Annoying piece of rotten meat!

"Where is your companion?" The man who had brought the guest in was looking around, frowning in puzzlement.

A companion? Only one? So maybe not that many more of his former countryfolk were roaming around, no delegation of respectable elders. Good!

Sondakwa's broad shoulders lifted in a shrug, his face still close and stormy, concentrating on Ogteah, burning him with the nakedness of his animosity. He made sure the coldness of his expression didn't change, fighting the urge to spring to his feet, if for no other reason than to face the filthy skunk from the same height, to exude no implied inferiority. Before he could decide on a passable excuse to do so, Sondakwa's heavy frame dropped in the vacant space of the circle, doing so with the ease and agility fitting a smaller person.

"That's better, Brother?" Apparently the annoying skunk retained the ability to follow his hated sibling's inner thoughts. "Makes you feel less threatened?"

"When I ever felt threatened it was never by you." To shift his attention to the man who was pushing his way in, a shallow basket clasped tightly in his hands, seemed like the best of courses. He wished his hands would stop trembling from all this accumulating rage. "This thing should do. The best of solutions."

The man with the basket beamed, pleased with himself. "We'll pad it with the blanket, fold it in."

Amidst the growing excitement full of back-patting activities, the owner of the stones leaned toward Ogteah.

"Do you two know each other?" he breathed carefully, barely speaking the words.

Ogteah just shrugged, rolling his eyes in a demonstrative way. The clearest of messages.

The young man snickered. "No lost love, eh?"

He listened to the argument as to the agreed amount of throws, with everyone speaking at once, overriding each other. Who cared how many times one would be allowed to shake the stupid basket, an unfitting vessel to get worthwhile results anyway. Fancy supplementing a solid, appropriately heavy clay or wooden bowl with the lightness and unsteadiness of a woven container. As though their improvised stones weren't problematic to begin with, so much heavier and more cumbersome than the dried up pits they were supposed to replace. They would not manage to cause one single stone to overturn!

"So you've been living among these people now, I presume." To be heard in all the commotion his brother had to lean closer, a natural gesture, but it had Ogteah's tension leaping higher than before. Another occurrence that the filthy skunk surely didn't miss. The glitter of the narrowing eyes told him that. "Still doing nothing, but as far away from home as you can, eh?"

"You presume wrong." He willed his limbs into a more relaxed pose, then forced his eyes to stay on the unwelcomed sight of the familiar face. Sondakwa had a small twisting scar next to his right eye and he grinned a little, remembering how he got it. "And how about you, Little Brother? Still loitering about the Deer Clan's longhouse, running small errands and doing as you are told?"

If the detested epithet didn't do the work, the implied lack of importance in his wife's longhouse's affairs wiped the smug expression, made his brother's face go stiff. Oh, yes, he still remembered the annoying skunk's weakness, every single one of them. Sometimes it paid off to grow up together.

"Something of the sort." To his disappointment, Sondakwa did not lose his presence of mind either, controlling his temper better than of yore, the smile playing upon his lips thin, unpleasant but calm enough. "No abandoned families, wives or children, to report. No competition to offer you in that aspect, *big brother*." The taunting smile widened. "And you? Any more women and children littering your way? Or just regular crimes and transgressions?"

It was becoming more difficult to keep his own sneering grin in place. With an effort he managed not to let it waver. "As I said, none of it is your business."

People were glancing at them, those who were not busy discussing the projected game's terms, their expressions varying from puzzlement to disapproval and discomfort. The owner of the throwing stones made a face.

"You people have clearly much love stored for each other," he commented, then brought his arms up in a mockingly defensive gesture. "Don't turn the united front of the Bear People on me. I'm just observing. We don't get to meet your countryfolk very often, you know." The glance he shot at his squatting neighbors was flickering, drawing quite a few laughs and chuckles. "And now we get to listen to several of you at once, all this lively interaction."

Safe on his home ground, treading on the rules of hospitality and politeness ever so lightly, the man grinned at them, unabashed. A cheeky one, reflected Ogteah, appreciating the subtle brazenness.

"We do not represent our countryfolk," he said, the grin coming easier now, at the mere change of addressing faces that did not to belong to his detested family members. "I wouldn't judge our people by the two of us. Or there would have been no unification, not even among our own towns and villages." He wished to see what Sondakwa's expression held now, but dared not to, unwilling to give filthy skunk such satisfaction. Instead he went on, grinning at the people around him. "It seems that we won't be playing this evening, eh?"

They grinned back, unreserved.

"You should have gone on conducting the bean game as before," commented the man who had kept silent so far, doing nothing but rolling his eyes every now and then. "No need to complicate things by trying to be more efficient than a nesting bird."

Good advice. But for Sondakwa's presence he would have gotten to his feet and maybe tried to suggest exactly that, taking the things under control again. It was better to play something than nothing at all.

As it was he remained seated, pondering his possibilities of escape. But he would be better off beating a hasty retreat, even if his brother's presence didn't present any particular danger. It was obvious that the presumptuous skunk knew nothing of his, Ogteah's, true situation. A relief! But of course, Father would never have told.

"It's too bad you missed the ceremony," one of the men was saying, addressing the newcomer. "It was a beautiful ceremony. The strawberry juice flowed like river."

In the corner of his eye he saw Sondakwa nodding reservedly, answering with polite platitudes, a perfect guest. For how long? He tried not to roll his eyes. Why did this annoying piece of meat have to fall on him out of nowhere, bringing too many bad memories and feelings.

"Having arrived on the day before…"

"Well, we have arrived early through the day, me and my brother?" Sondakwa was saying. "But of course, we should have known better, should have rowed faster, arrived with the dawn."

Me and my brother? But what did he mean by that?

Fearing the worst, he scanned the crowding figures, trying to see the faces of those who peeked from behind, quite a congregation. Oh, yes, it wasn't difficult to detect another pair of strained, distrustful eyes resting on him, narrowed and strangely thoughtful, wary in too obvious of a way. The young man didn't try to come any nearer, staying on the edge of the crowd. Why? wondered Ogteah absently. Why didn't he push his way in the way his older sibling did?

He hadn't seen his youngest of brothers since this one was nothing but a boy of no more than eleven, maybe twelve summers. How old was he now? Probably close to twenty. Tall, but still slender, angular in a way, padded in a satisfactory fashion, with Father's face, now more definitely, a pleasant-looking sight. But not pleasing at all. Why was his entire family accosting him now and why here?

He narrowed his eyes, hoping for a mistake. The sun was glaring from behind the next incline, not letting him see properly. Could it be someone else, someone similar looking? Was his mind playing tricks on him, making him see what he expected?

No, no chance of that. Too much likeness to the thoughtful, serious, slender boy he remembered; too much resemblance to Father as well. Not the exact likeness, but enough to shatter any assumption, any hope that it *was* a mistake.

If nothing else the youth's gaze confirmed the worst. Absorbed, concentrated, peering at him and no one else, reflecting it all – wariness, hesitation, cautious well-nurtured hostility. No mistake there. And no surprise, either. Had they known that he was on his way, hurrying to reach him, to confront him here on purpose? But to what end? What did they know about him?

He fought the urge to jump to his feet no more, to push his way out of the circle of crowding people and be gone, truly gone. Even if just a coincidence, he didn't need this encounter, not now, not ever, but this particular timing was truly bad. Somehow he needed to get away from it all, to regroup, to rethink his plans. As of now, everything was going wrong, absolutely wrong. And it would get only worse, he knew. Trust everything to go awry the moment it got bizarre. His previous life taught him that. Still, this time it was turning ludicrous.

"What is this? A family gathering?"

With the sigh of exasperation, he got to his feet, from the additionally gained height noticing that the silly girl who was plaguing him with questions before was huddling next to his brother, all eyes. Another one from Teguenondahi, oh yes. But it was a conspiracy!

"Are you all right? Where are you going?" The man with the stones was asking, peering at him from the ground.

He tried to manage a light grin. "They won't arrive at any conclusion, not soon." A shrug came relatively easily, even though the struggle not to let his eyes wander toward either of his family members proved difficult. "I'm off to see what the fires are offering. All these swirling skirts and decorations."

The young man grinned, then sprang to his feet in his turn. "They'll have to find us in order to resume the game." He tossed the basket lightly, making the stones inside them clank. "They'll need those things to play, won't they?"

"Unless they run and fetch someone else's set." Shaking his

head, Ogteah grinned with less of an effort, yet the glance shot at the elder among his siblings served to darken his mood anew. Sondakwa was watching him coldly, not interested in the game or the arguments about it. The lowly scum! Of Atuye there was no sight.

CHAPTER 17

Standing next to the fireplace, clutching a bowl full of fresh water, just in case, she watched Atuye perching on the edge of the low bunk, leaning toward her father, absorbed and attentive in this typical solemn way of him.

The unpleasant smell lingered, wafting in the thick air of the compartment, dispersing toward the corridor, disappearing there. Father was feverish again, his eyes glittering brightly, too brightly, glossing over in an unsettling way. But for Atuye's presence, she knew, the recurring fever alone would have sent her into the depths of despair. Father looked so small huddling there, so drained of life, as though emptied, his skin hanging helplessly upon the suddenly sharp angles of his body, not fitting well. She had grown used to this sight, the changes too subtle, happening over time unlike the smell, which was something to get used to anew every time one came from the outside. However now, because of Atuye, she had looked at her father with fresh eyes, the eyes of a visitor. His startle caused her to do that, the stunned, obviously frightened expression, dominated hurriedly, tacked away, but still something she couldn't miss. Father was seriously ill, wasn't he?

Clutching the bowl tightly in her sweaty palms, she listened to her friend's serene, even voice, placid, calming, inquiring with utmost politeness, in control once again. Oh, yes, Atuye would find the solution. He would know what to do. Grateful, she muttered her thanks to the spirits.

"I will come back accompanied with my brother, Honorable Elder." The young man leaned closer, not deterred by the smell or maybe hiding it well.

"Would you like to drink, Father?" she asked, hovering behind her friend's back.

"No, little one." The fatigued eyes rested on her with touching affection. "But for this wonderful little butterfly of mine," he muttered, closing his eyes, exhausted by the effort of talking.

Atuye's hand wrapped around her shoulders, giving her strength to see through the veil of tears. "Stay with him until I find my brother."

They watched the frail chest rising and falling, laboring for breath. Such a familiar sight by now.

"I'll come with you. The healer woman of the Deer Clan, she must be out there, at the ceremonial grounds, or maybe at her longhouse. It's just two buildings removed from here. It's where Tsutahi's man put her and the children. I'll ask that woman to come and see him again."

He nodded thoughtfully. "Yes, of course." The sudden frown made his high forehead wrinkle. "Tsutahi is that friend of yours, yes? The girl who can't hear well?"

"Yes." Leading their way through the empty corridor, she reflected on the peacefulness of the abandoned building, such a strange sensation. "She can't hear at all, but she doesn't let it get in her way. She does everything a woman should and much more than that. She is incredible, can do everything, just everything. From navigating one's canoe through angry waters, to walking the woods as though it was her town's alleys. She can even hunt, you know?" Halting by the last compartment and the dimness of the storage room, Ononta turned back, reinforcing her words with the most earnest expression. "I'm not making it up; I've been spending much time with her through the last half a moon. We were sent to gather berries, and I'm telling you, she is like a forest dweller, can sense her way around, see hidden deer tracks and where the best fruit is. She taught me how to do it, to see signs, and many times she would say that if we had a bow we would be shooting this or that thing. Tsami was always disappointed that we didn't. He said his *nnen* hunts like his father, and I myself saw her carving up a deer with the speed and cleanness of an old hunter." Out of breath, she peered at him, pleased with his obvious fascination. "I'm not exaggerating or making it up, none of it."

He motioned her to resume their walk, bending his head to pass through the opening and toward the façade. Again it made her reflect on how tall he had become through the last few summers.

"Where is she now?" he asked, when the last of the light poured on them, most welcome in its freshness and warmth.

"In the longhouse of the healer woman, I presume." She remembered the ceremonial grounds, and how her friend bolted away, one hand clutching the baby, the other dragging resisting Tsami, determined to skirt the commotion around the throwing game by the farthest route possible. Why was she so afraid of Atuye's brother?

"Let us detour through that Deer Clan's longhouse," he said firmly. "In case the healer woman is in there too." His frown was still deep, almost direful. "I don't want this girl to act recklessly, to rush out and into this or that canoe. She can't leave just like that on account of my brother, whatever he has done to her."

"What do you think he did?" It was so good to have him by her side, to talk or ask questions without reserve, to discuss whatever she wanted.

His shrug was brief, troubled in a way. "I don't know, but it must be something dreadful." The lines furrowing his forehead deepened. "You know Ogteah. He is not the most perfect member of society. Still, before all those rumors from Father's gathering in Ossossane, I would never have said he could do something truly bad, be guilty of actual crimes, of violence and murder. Or hurting a woman." This time his shoulders lifted heavily, in a dispirited way. "He still doesn't seem like a bad or malicious person to me, not from the look of him now. Quite a respectable sight, more than he used to be." The brief grin held no amusement. "Still, all those summers wandering only Great Spirits know where, they must have done something to him. This girl was beyond terrified and she didn't agree to even pass by his possible vicinity, not even with us by her side."

"She might have been mistaken, you know. She said he was a spirit, a bad *uki* roaming our earthly world, not a real man at all." Hoping to bring him back from his gloomy wandering, she grinned teasingly. "And you thought it was about Sondakwa, didn't you? How silly."

Indeed, the anticipated smile flashed, flickering somewhat defensively. "I didn't think. You talked about my brother. You should have said half-brother, or used his name."

"I didn't know you came here with your full brother as well. But for your sister, your entire family seems to be visiting here. What a family gathering!"

He chuckled. "My sister is busy making babies."

"Oh, is Yandata pregnant again? I can't believe it!"

He just nodded, his smile free of shadows. They both liked his sister, a warm, pleasant companion, with no malice to her and no bitterness. Not her mother's daughter. But such thoughts Ononta preferred to keep to herself. His mother was not a bad person, just bitter and sour, and he did love her, more than the rest of her children did.

The longhouse with the symbolic deer carved upon its façade greeted them with the same eerie silence, even though the drums and the occasional trill of a flute reached them here more clearly, the building situated higher up on the incline and closer to the openness of the flatter ground.

No sounds of lively toddlers' footsteps echoed along the corridor, but they could hear light shuffling somewhere deeper inside the building. There was no point in calling out, in sounding polite warning to whoever was in there. A wasted effort in her friend's case, and who else would be there, hiding from the celebration?

Not surprisingly, Atuye fell behind again, letting her lead, his footsteps ringing with less determination than before. A brief glance at him made her puzzle. He was peering straight ahead, wary like a hunter entering unknown woods, on guard but somehow expectant, all eyes and ears.

The girl knew they were approaching, greeting them with a wary glance of her own. Her taut features relaxing, she nodded softly, the smile tagging her lips. She was the sweetest sight when she smiled, reflected Ononta, rushing toward her friend; too bad she didn't do it more often.

"We thought we would find you here," she said breathless, remembering to make sure the movement of her lips was watched. "The Honorable Elder Sister, the healer, she isn't here, is she?"

Tsutahi's smile faded as she shook her head, vigorously enough to make her loose braids jump. A wandering tendril fell across her face, and she blew at it from the side of her mouth to make it go, her hands too busy to help her in that, one holding the baby attached to her bare breast, the other balancing a half folded blanket, a simple undecorated hide cut in two. More of such garments were strewn across the mat and upon the floor, the pallet that she occupied along with her children.

"You are collecting your things." Another glance confirmed the observation, with two familiar-looking bags, just crudely sewn hides, thrown next to the lower bunk, stuffed to their brim with more blankets and cooking utensils. "You are leaving!"

That brought Atuye back from his withdrawn state of mind, his frown as deep as before, lacking in usual confidence, this pleasantly sincere self-assurance of a person who knew why most things should be done and how. Instead, he seemed to be looking everywhere but at the temporary dweller of this place, seeming more uncomfortable with every passing heartbeat.

"You can't leave," he said, forcing his eyes upward and toward the girl's face, concentrating there painfully, as though afraid to let his eyes wander toward the baby upon her breast. "It will be night soon."

Surprisingly, Tsutahi reacted, even though her eyes were not on the speaker at all. Frowning as direfully, she nodded, her lips pursed. "I wasn't going to leave at night." The words came out jarringly loud, worse than her regular speech was. "I will be sailing with dawn."

Resolutely, she turned toward one of the bags, tucking the blanket in neatly, as though working with both hands free. The baby on her breast grunted, then fought to get back to his favorite source of food. For a heartbeat they all watched him struggling, making smacking sounds.

"You can't go away all alone." Atuye tore his eyes off the baby, or the roundness of the breast it was sucking on – for a wild moment Ononta wasn't sure about that – and was peering at the girl, back to his efficient self again. "Ononta says your man promised to return soon. And even if it wasn't for him, we can't let you travel all alone. You can't jump into someone's canoe and just plunge into the river. "

Tsutahi was watching him with her eyes narrowed and her face setting into the mold Ononta knew too well by now. For a thousandth time she wondered if even the formidable Attiwandaronk, Tsutahi's man, managed to tell her what to do.

"I don't have to jump into people's canoes," she stated, glaring at Atuye quite darkly. "I have my own boat and I don't need anyone's permission to sail it. You came to help Ononta. Good for you. She could have sailed all by herself too but for her father's illness." Glowing like a fire that a jar of oil was spilled onto it, she stood there, tiny and challenging, radiating power, maybe even danger. "I'll reach home, faster than you would reach yours, even if we were living at the same distance from here."

Atuye's eyes were as wide as Tsutahi's were narrow, noted Ononta, amused against her will. It was funny to see him losing his aplomb in such way. Even in as serious situation as this.

"I... I didn't say you can't sail your canoe," he managed in the end, his stammering even more amusing. She tried to strangle the threatening snicker. "I just... well, I said that you need help, that you can't sail all alone. I will, will be able to help you, maybe, if you give me some time." He stopped speaking and just stared at his unexpected adversary in curious helplessness, again a sight Ononta wasn't used to seeing.

For a heartbeat, a silence prevailed, interrupted by the baby's satisfied grunting, the drums and the monotonous singing barely reaching them here, in this abandoned privacy so far away from the celebrating townsfolk.

"I don't need your help," repeated Tsutahi firmly. "I can take care of myself and my children, and my man will not be angry.

He'll understand." A challenging toss of the proud head caused more tendrils escape the loosely tied braids. "He always does!"

Atuye looked as though unsure if it was the time to take a step back, maybe even run out and away from the unreasonableness of it all, or try to reason some more, to make sense out of it. Of course there was no logic in what Tsutahi just said. But after close to half a moon spent in this strange girl's company Ononta had come to expect all of it and more.

Oh, yes, her friend was stubborn and obtuse, not always rational when it came to reasonable behavior. But then it was she, Tsutahi, the deaf girl who lived all alone in the woods, with no family and no clan and no longhouse, no past and no clear future, no one but her man with as obscure, mysterious, well-guarded background, and her children and her small field that she took care of all by herself; her way of doing things like a man and not like a woman, whether hunting or carving meat or navigating a canoe, her independence that she was anxious to protect most fiercely, even against her own man, her insecurities that made her so aggressive at times. Oh, but what a hard life her friend must have been leading, the challenges of which could turn such a brittle young girl into something like this.

Her heart squeezing with compassion, she took a step back, put a comforting palm on the thin, fragile arm.

"Don't get that angry, sister," she said, when sure that the challenging eyes had left Atuye, concentrating on her, instead. Even though jerking away as the first reaction, the girl's gaze softened visibly and it pleased her, made her feel warmer inside. "He is trying to help you and so am I. He is not patronizing or trying to tell you what to do. If your man doesn't do it, then how could any of us?" Pleased to notice a spark of amusement lurking in the depth of the dark eyes, brief but unmistakable, she went on, encouraged. "Atuye is the best boy ever and he wants to help us both. He came to take me and my father home, yes, but he would help you too if you let him. You can trust him the way you trust me. He is that sort of a person, you see?" A glance at her friend confirmed that he was listening, as fascinated. "If you can't leave now, so close to nightfall, then why not spend your time with us, preparing your journey? We could help you with that too, you know?" She looked around, suddenly puzzled. "Where is Tsami?"

The need to repeat her question, as, forgetting herself, she uttered the last one while looking away, served to reduce the tension. While Tsutahi grimaced with desperation, relating the fact that she allowed her boy to return to the ceremony in the care of the Second Niece, Atuye relaxed his pose, daring to step inside the compartment, to lean against the pole supporting one of the bunks.

"I couldn't concentrate with all his questioning," the girl was complaining, the lightness of her tone a pleasant surprise. "He nagged and nagged, and the Second Niece just came in looking for him, so I said yes, they can go and run around the ceremonial grounds. There was no point in cooping him up here," a slightly cold, challenging glance shot at Atuye, "as I didn't intend to leave before tomorrow at dawn."

Recovered fully by now, his regular composure back at place, Atuye returned the girl's gaze with a matching amount of challenge. "You didn't behave that reasonably back there on the ceremonial grounds, talking of spirits and bad *uki* and having those panicked looks. What was I supposed to assume?"

Tsutahi's face again could put the storm cloud to shame. "I didn't talk nonsense back there on the ceremonial grounds," she exclaimed so loudly, her baby, by now deeply asleep in her arms, shuddered, then whimpered, demanding a fair amount of gentle rocking to help him back into the lands of dreams and spirits. "I did not behave unreasonably," she repeated in a moderated voice, anxious to say her piece. "I didn't lie and I didn't make it all up." Her throat moved jerkily as she swallowed, pressing her lips with touching determination. To stop them from trembling? wondered Ononta, fighting the urge to wrap her arm around the fragile shoulders again. "This man, I saw him falling dead. My man, he struck him with the club; I saw it with my own eyes! It was a terrible blow and he had fallen. Like a cut down tree. I saw it all. I did!" The huge eyes leapt between their faces, imploring. It was as though she needed them to believe her. "He can't be alive, he just can't. And if that is so, then he is just a trapped spirit, still roaming our earthly world..." Her palm was pressing into her mouth, muffling the words. "Maybe they cannot reach the Sky World, the enemies from the other side. Maybe they are not allowed...And then, well, then they are trapped and wandering, but somehow he had managed to come back..." Drawing a deep breath, the girl fell silent, her mouth still hiding behind her palm, the fingers pressing into it cruelly, about to leave a print. Her eyes glittered, silent and huge. "What if he is here to avenge, to harm me and my man? Or our children!"

Ononta fought the urge to embrace her friend no longer. To envelop her in a tight hug felt natural, the only right thing to do. Even the baby didn't protest, a snuggly warm, reassuring presence. No bad spirits would harm such a thing.

"Please, don't fret that badly," she murmured, when the girl didn't jerk away, but actually huddled a little closer. "Please. Whatever it is, no one will harm you or your children. They can't." She tried to process what had been said. "The man your husband killed, are you sure you saw him and not someone that might be just looking like him?"

Tsutahi said nothing, still frozen in Ononta's arms, reminding her that sometimes the need to have her friend reading her lips was a true hindrance. She couldn't move into a better view, not now, not with the poor girl feeling comforted, even for a short while.

"Tell us exactly what happened." Atuye's voice had a comforting quality to it too, slow, deliberated, as though measuring every word. He came closer and was leaning forward, making sure his words were seen even if not heard. Wise Atuye. "You say your man killed someone. Where did it happen? Here in this town, or somewhere around? Under what circumstances?"

His frown was deep, encouraging in its thoughtfulness. Ononta held her breath, feeling the girl tensing in her arms. Another spell of silence prevailed.

"I can't talk about it," muttered Tsutahi gruffly. "It is something I'm not allowed to talk about. But..." Slipping from Ononta's arms with a grateful smile that again made her look irresistibly pretty in her own wild but sweetish sort of a way, she bent to slide the baby into his padded basket, careful not to wake the greedy little thing up. When she straightened and faced them, her expression was resolute despite the pallor and the obvious exhaustion. "I better leave this place and fast," she said tiredly, running a weary hand over her forehead, pushing the wandering tendrils away. "My man and I, we can't talk about the past, but we did nothing dishonorable. He killed people in battle, many people, he was a great warrior. He did not kill anyone just like that. And no, it didn't happen anywhere around. That man, he was killed in a war, a fair, honorable war." A helpless shrug lifted the thin shoulders. "I don't know where the killed enemy is going. Maybe they don't reach the Sky World. Maybe they are all wandering. That might explain..." She shrugged again and fell silent, the ring of her words still there, lingering, a surprisingly calm, even sound as opposed to her usual abrupt speaking.

Atuye shifted as though awakening from a dream. "If that man that you think you recognized was killed in a war and not anywhere around here, in this or that local brawl, then you *are* mistaken. You are!" His smile was an uplifting sight in itself, surprisingly boyish, victorious grin. It was rare to see Atuye smiling so openly, with such lack of reserve. "My brother could not be killed in a war for the simple reason that he has never been to anything of the sort." He laughed happily, turning to Ononta, still shining with almost mischievous delight. "Can you imagine Ogteah going to war? What a thought. The man would think it to be too much trouble, all this lying in wait, crawling around, waiting in ambushes, doing what one is told." A new outburst of healthy laughter took him. "Oh no, Ogteah would never go to war. Anyone but him!" Over his brief spell of mirth but still smiling, he turned back toward their frowning companion. "He can be caught fighting over this or that thing, oh yes. But not in a war. So if your man killed someone in a battle, it wasn't my brother. You can be sure of that."

The girl's frown kept deepening. "I know it was the man I and Ononta saw. I know it!" The slender eyebrows turned into a single line, challenging Atuye's quivering smile. "I saw this man dying in the end of the great battle. I saw my man killing him. This was the same man who played throwing game on the ceremonial grounds of this town not very long ago. It *was* the same man!"

One of Atuye's eyebrows was climbing up faster than the other. "What war it was?" A heartbeat of stubborn silence. "You can tell me at least that. I won't be spreading that story, I promise. Even if your people did raid these local lands maybe." He shrugged. "It is none of my business anyway, not until the Rock People join our union." His frown deepened. "You are one of the Long Tails, yes? Are your people still at war with the Rocks? I thought after you were defeated by the league of the savages..." His grin was light, slightly apologetic. "I didn't mean to remind you of that. I'm sorry. I know your people fought bravely and that it was a great war. We heard much about it. I'm sure your man was a part of it."

The girl's lips were nothing but an invisible line now, pressed too tightly to part. "My man fought in this war, yes," she said in the end. "And this man that you claim is your brother was there too. He was leading the savages. He and some others. My man killed him in the end, before... before he got hit himself..." Her eyes were anywhere but on them now, boring onto the floor, her surprisingly large teeth making a mess out of the thin lower lip.

This time, Atuye didn't try to hold his laughter in. "Ogteah was leading the savages in the Long Tails War?"

But before more thundering mirth erupted, earning his being thrown out of the Deer Clan's longhouse by enraged Tsutahi's own hands at the very least, rapid footsteps rustled outside, echoing hurriedly down the corridor, ringing with urgency. They all turned to stare, even Tsutahi, who must have reacted to their changing poses rather than to her own lack of hearing.

The Second Niece stopped next to their fireplace, panting loudly, out of breath. Her eyes darted around, inspecting the crammed compartment. The result made her face fell.

"Where is Tsamihui?" cried out Tsutahi, the mother in her taking over, assessing the situation, arriving at her own conclusions and fast.

Under the intensity of the worried gaze, the girl quailed. Ononta felt her stomach tightening in a hundred little knots.

"Where is he?" Leaping toward the girl, Tsutahi caught the small shoulder, pressing it urgently, hurting it maybe, if the frightened look of its owner was anything to go by.

The girl tried to squirm free. "I don't know," she whimpered. "I thought he went here." Her eyes were anywhere but on the face of her worried assailant, and Ononta felt bad for them both.

"What happened, little one?" she asked, coming closer, ready to ensure the girl's safety. Somehow she knew that her friend could become violent, maybe even hurtful, if pushed. All of sudden, she had been sure of that, having no proof of such things from their previous relationship, not at all. "Tell us what happened." Gently, she freed the girl's shoulder, pressing her friend's arm with her free hand, trying to reassure. "Where did you think Tsami went?"

The Second Niece sniffed with her nose, pressing her quivering lips tight. "I… well, we were out there, having a good time. He danced with other children. I saw that he did!" The gaze shot at them held a fair measure of defiance, as though challenging them to prove her wrong. "It was long after the ceremonial dances, so everyone was in, having a good time. We all danced or just run around. But Tsami said it was boring. He wanted to go out, to play by the river. As though he could go do something like that, the small boy that he is." The girl's face twisted, lost its mischievous spark. "I laughed and it made him angry. He is so funny when he is angry. Other girls thought it funny too. We teased him, but in a cute sort of a way. I wouldn't have it otherwise. You know I would not!" The most earnest of looks was shot at Tsutahi, who had stood there turned into stone, only her eyes alive in the frozen dread of her face, glued to the girl's lips, waiting for every word, seizing on each.

"And then what happened?" prompted Ononta, when neither of her companions ventured a sound. Atuye's eyes were glued to Tsutahi in the same way the deaf girl's eyes were glued to the lips of the speaker, with same fascinated, alert expectation.

The girl glanced at her briefly. "Well, I said, no, we can't go out, not now, when it's nearing the dark time and we would have to ask first." A new hopeful look at the frozen mother drew no reaction whatsoever. The girl swallowed most visibly. "And then, well, he said his father is going to return soon. I don't remember what else he said, but then he turned around and ran away. And… and I thought he went here, to you. To complain maybe, or to ask when his father will be coming back." The small lips began trembling again. "I thought he went here."

The stone statue of Tsutahi didn't move, beside her eyes that shifted away from their unexpected bearer of bad news, clearly thinking of possibilities. Ononta tried to make sense of what she heard.

"How long has it been since you saw the boy last?" asked Atuye, as brisk and efficient as always.

"I, well… it hasn't been long." The girl glanced at her new interrogator briefly, then dropped her eyes, her shoulders sagging. "Not long at all."

"How many dances?" pressed Atuye, not impressed. He leaned closer, catching the girl's gaze, holding it firmly, not letting the panicked eyes to escape. "How many dances were you and your friends in until you noticed that he didn't return?" His mouth pressed tighter on the barely audible mutter. "You must tell me the truth, girl. It's a dangerous situation and if you care for that little boy you will tell me the truth, even if it puts you in a bad light." This time, his lips stretched into a hint of a reassuring grin. "After all, you did nothing wrong, besides not coming right away to inform us, didn't you? Is that why you are afraid now?"

She answered with a tiny, barely visible nod.

"How many dances?"

"Four. Maybe five." This came out in a broken whisper.

Ononta let out a held breath. So long! But where would the little boy wander off for so long and alone, the chatty, companionable little thing that he was? He didn't like being alone. Not Tsami. But then where was he and with whom?

"He went to the river, to wait for his father's return." Tsutahi's words rang emptily, devoid of emotion. She was with her back to them, wrapping a blanket around her slender torso, snatching the sleepy bundle from his basket, tucking it in the pocket the wrapped around cover created. "I hope it was not on that other faraway shore."

"Wait." Knowing by now that the mere talk was not enough, especially with their deaf audience's back toward them, Atuye caught the slender arm in his palm, holding it at arm's length, not attempting to come closer himself. "Listen."

She struggled to break free but not as fiercely as Ononta would have expected, tearing her arm from Atuye's grip yet not attempting to step away when successful. It was as though she wanted him to persuade her. To do what?

Atuye looked mighty relieved. "Listen to me. Don't run away all alone. We'll help you. We'll find your boy. Help you to sail away too, if you are that determined. Don't struggle this all alone, will you? There is no need. We'll help you, Ononta and I."

Tsutahi's face was nothing but her eyes, two enormous dark pools, dominating everything else, casting it into insignificance, their desperation on display.

Atuye was smiling encouragingly in much the same fashion he had managed to wheedle the truth out of the lying girl before.

"Here, that's better." He glanced around briskly, in control of the situation. "So first of all, we are going to the ceremonial grounds; to take a look around, see if the boy is still there." Hands light and not intruding, he began propelling his distrustful charge toward the corridor, talking as he did. "If not, we'll check other places, go outside the town. All the places you, girls, are suspecting." Another brief gaze caught Ononta's, urging her to join, to proceed along, glowing with an unspoken message. "Together we'll find him easily. He couldn't have gone too far away."

CHAPTER 18

His brother must have been still out there with the players, he realized, making his way down the hill and up another, acutely aware of the girl's presence and the echo of her hurried footsteps besides his.

Ononta and their young escort, the little rascal who had managed to let the boy slip away, not watching the toddler entrusted into her care at all, followed a little behind, and somehow it pleased him. It was as though he and his outlandish charge were walking all alone in the deepening dusk.

He glanced at her briefly, unwilling to be detected doing so. She was so tiny and thin, barely reaching his shoulder, so fragile looking and yet so determined and brisk, indisputably able, forceful, headstrong; a person with great willpower and self-assurance, if both today's encounters with her were something to judge by. An outlandish creature. And yet, he knew she needed his help.

What Sondakwa would say to all this? he wondered, taking his thoughts off her with a conscious effort. His brother wouldn't be pleased, that much was obvious. When suggesting an unauthorized detour through the neighboring Rock People's town, Sondakwa must have been counting on an easy trip, some roaming around, dispersing with boredom. However, he would have to take the consequences of their detour as well now. It was his idea after all, his prompting. Whether he liked it or not, his brother would have to help take both girls to their various destinations. Could they do it together, or would it be wiser to split up? Ononta's father could not be dragged around unnecessarily, not in his condition, and yet the venture into the Long Tails forests was not an enterprise to embark upon all alone, with nothing but an exotic girl and her unruly children for a company, and with not even them on his way back.

"He won't be here or on the ceremonial grounds." Her exclamation startled him into as abrupt a halt as her was.

"What? Wait." He peered at her, difficult to make her expression out through the thickening dusk. "What do you mean?"

"He is out there, by the river. Somewhere." Her eyes were huge and alight, dominating her slender face, glowing with strain. "There is no use in running around the town. He is not here. He is out there, trying to reach the river." She pulled away as though expecting him to try and stop her physically, by grabbing her hand maybe. "I must hurry out there before it gets dark."

"Wait!" He kept his hands glued to his sides, trying to hold her gaze by the sheer power of his will, afraid that a wrong movement would send her scampering away like a frightened forest creature. "Don't rush out there all by yourself. We will do it, together we will go out, but first we must make sure he isn't still here."

Bringing his hands up, palms forward, a careful gesturing, he listened to the voices carried by the wind. Away from the ceremonial grounds and the merry activities, sounds of which were pouring generously, men were congregating, speaking in loud tones. Not the players of throwing games, those he remembered milling on the opposite side of the flattened ground. Or maybe a different group set themselves for another game here.

"He is just a little boy, after all," he went on, concentrating on the anxious girl in front of him, now flanked by Ononta and her younger escort on both sides. A help, in a way. "He is probably back with the dancing people now, asking for his mother. He is not old enough to make all this trouble. He is really too small for that."

Eyes dark with tension and misery were his answer.

"He isn't." This time it was Ononta, another one troubled unduly. "Tsami is very able and so very fierce. Far beyond his summers." The frown did not sit well with his childhood friend's gentle features as well. "And yes, he might want to go out and look for his father. In a troublesome situation like that…" A glance she shot at her worried friend was unmistakably wary, careful, but the deaf girl's eyes were not following her lips, glued to his, Atuye's, face instead, somehow expectant. It made his stomach flutter.

"Well, what we'll do now is that," he declared, pleased for no apparent reason. "First, we pass through the ceremonial grounds, just in case. Scan it briefly. If we find nothing, then you," he glanced at Ononta, trying not to let his hesitation show, "you and the girl, you'll go around, ask people if they saw him. If you find him, calm him and keep an eye on him until we come back. In the meanwhile…" A glance at the deaf girl showed that she was listening avidly, following his words with intense, glimmering eyes. He found it necessary to take a deep breath. "In the meanwhile, we will go out and scan the river, search all the nearest shores." He scowled against the last of the light. They wouldn't have much time to scan anything, but he could not think of a better plan. "Would you trust Ononta with your baby? It would be better if we were to wander out there unhindered."

The enormous eyes blinked but only once. Through the next heartbeat both girls were already exchanging glances, their nods brief, matter-of-fact, decisive.

"Thank you," the deaf girl was saying in her unmelodious, yet strangely pleasing voice. "I will be back as fast as I can. I hope he won't make too much trouble. Maybe he won't wake up. He shouldn't be hungry, but if he is, well, then let him suck on some water. You know, from the folded edge of a blanket." Her words were gushing hurriedly, like a strong current between two narrow banks. "I hope we will be back before it happens."

Wriggling out of the multiple folds her improvised wrap created, she went on talking, as nimble and confident of movement as she was clumsy in her speech. Against his will he watched her, drinking in the serene pliancy of her arms and hips.

Then the arguing voices caught his attention again. Sondakwa?

He willed his mind into slowing its race. "I'll be back shortly. Wait for me here, both of you, or better yet, join me down there.

We'll scan the fires and the dancers before rushing out. The boy may still be out there."

Their silence held a profound amount of doubt, but he didn't stay to hear their arguments. His brother would help, having nothing better to do with himself as it was. If managed to find the boy while they were out there, combing the shores, Ononta alone wouldn't know what to do in order to keep him from running away again, but with Sondakwa involved and helping it might be easier for her. Also it would keep his brother from the unexpected and not very welcome company of their mutual half-sibling – such a strange encounter! – to glower at and try to pick a fight with. Sondakwa's energies would be better spent helping finding the boy.

What was Ogteah doing here? he asked himself, rushing down the incline and toward the nearest group that was congregating next to one of the fires, not far away from the dancing circle. Trust Sondakwa to find out by now, and then insist on not leaving it at that. The stubborn buck! But what was Ogteah up to these days? And why was the girl so afraid of him, terrified really, saying such silly things. Ogteah leading the enemy forces in the great war that rocked the entire coastline and deeper inland? Beyond ridiculous! And yet, she was so firm in her claims, so insistent.

The voices carried clearer now, overcoming the drumming and the commotion surrounding the dancers' circles, further down the incline. He knew there would be folded blanket and squatting men, tossing marked stones, or maybe hurling them toward this or that target, betting lavishly. These Rock People were no different from his own Bear People at all.

"That's the best you can do, brother?" One of the men was examining scattering stones, or rather what looked like round clay balls, picking them from a narrow trench, addressing people who lined the small incline.

"We'll see if you do any better," retorted the unsuccessful player, fingering the small necklace he had evidently put down as a bet.

Sondakwa was leaning against the nearest tree, watching the game with lively interest, talking with other onlookers, loud and unconcerned. Of their other half-brother there was no sight. At least that, thought Atuye, relieved.

Determinedly, he made his way past the players, then noticed another group hovering not far away, immersed in a quieter conversation. The broad shoulders of his controversial half-sibling stood out unmistakable in the flickering twilight, drawing people's glances, Sondakwa's included. Wholly immersed, the man didn't seem to pay attention or care, yet, upon closer inspection, the offhand stance of arms linked casually across the undecorated chest, the slightly forced grin stretching the full lips, all these related tension atypical to the man Atuye remembered, a gambler with not a care in the world. If anything, his half-brother looked the exact opposite to his old breezy self, too serious, too absorbed, weathered and noticeably aged but in a becoming sort of a way. A prominent person, not someone to discard lightly; a dangerous presence.

Father would have been satisfied to see that, he thought randomly, forcing his eyes off the man, unsettled. How could it be? Whatever they heard about their wandering no-good brother was never good, never inspiring, just like his whole previous life was. The rumored scandal in Ossossane, all those crimes and unworthy deeds. That was the real Ogteah, the one Father refused to discuss. Not the man he was watching now, an authoritative, dangerous, fascinating stranger.

"Who is the next to throw?"

The players were still at it, rolling their stones along their makeshift ditch, trying to make them land into certain holes, as it seemed. Not a game Atuye was familiar with.

"Where have you been?" Sondakwa's face lit with a flicker of well familiar, slightly goading amusement before returning to his newfound companions, the lightness of his grin forced, his gaze sneaking toward their half-sibling obviously against his will, glowering darkly.

Atuye forced his own gaze to stay where it was. They were here not to pick fights or settle family grudges. "I need your help."

"With what?"

The players' outcries burst out anew, in surprising unison.

Praising a good hit? Sondakwa's eyes didn't move, even though the people he had watched turned to look at the outpouring exclamations, Ogteah among those. He didn't change his pose, but his expression became stonier as he took in their gazes, his eyes not lingering, following the shouts of the players. When the people he had spoken to moved closer, he followed them with no visible hesitation.

"Look at that one, that hole!" carried on one of the men, hopping around the curve in the trench, waving his hands in excitement. "How many points does one get for making this one?"

Now even Sondakwa craned his neck, his curiosity aroused. The pit in the furrowed earth was tiny, dug in the inner side of the ditch's incline. The stone must be made to roll quite forcefully, halting before the curve, then changing its direction in a sort of a leap in order to land in such a crater. A difficult target. Even their inexperienced eyes could see that.

"Stop bragging." One of the newcomers, the man who had spoken to them back at the previous game, when they had just arrived at the town – had it happened less than half a day ago? – knelt to examine the freshly plowed earth. "You dug it just now, for the game," he commented, openly amused.

"No, no, it was here before," protested one of the players, bringing his hands up, as though anxious to prove his point. "We just widened it and added some new pits. But not that one."

"How about that, Bear People's man?" Getting to his feet, the man waved at his peers, singling their half-brother out, noticed Atuye. The Bear People's man. There were only the three of them representing their nation here. Or misrepresenting it. Which one?

Ogteah looked as though he would rather be elsewhere just now, he noticed, following his sibling with his gaze once again. This time everyone did this.

"Did you happen to play a Sliding Game before? Are you as good at it as at the Bean Game?" pressed the local, pleased with himself.

Ogteah grinned nonchalantly.

"Trust the bastard to admit his fondness of that particular pastime as well," muttered Sondakwa. "And for stupidly high bets, too."

"How about we pit you against the owner of that necklace you got here before?" went on the townsman, apparently echoing Sondakwa's words. "Or would you bet some of the goods that your canoe is overloaded with again?"

Ogteah's grin didn't waver. "Neither," he said lightly, in that old typically casual way of his. "Never seen any such game before."

"Time to try something new, then, eh?" The local man was not about to give up, to the cheering calls of the others. "You, Bear People, have something to learn from us as yet."

"There are more of his people around now," commented one of the players, nodding at Sondakwa. "Aren't you familiar with this game as well?"

"No," said Sondakwa curtly, then an unpleasant grin twisted his lips. "But maybe it's time we start learning from our neighbors and peers." One corner of his mouth was climbing up faster than the other. "I yield the honor of the first try to your distinguished guest."

Ogteah stiffened most visibly, his grin evaporating, swallowed into the thin line his lips were now creating. His eyes resting on Sondakwa flashed dangerously, with an unmistakably familiar, not very well hidden violence flickering in their depths.

"I don't play games I'm not familiar with," he said coldly. "The honor is all yours, Brother."

But just as Atuye suspected, Sondakwa was not seeking to avoid confrontation, welcoming the chance to vent his frustrations instead.

"Of old, there were no games you were eager to avoid playing." His lips were twisted again, this time disdainfully. "What changed?"

The nostrils of Ogteah's eagle-like nose widened with a forcefully drawn breath. "It is not the time nor the place to discuss that," he said icily, still in control but for the lightly distorted voice. "Leave it at that." This came out as an outright order, full of firm authority. Very much Father-like. Numbly, Atuye just stared.

A brief silence that prevailed was so deep they could hear the late birds' occasional chirping, the buzz of the night insects. For a heartbeat no one said a word.

"You two know each other?" The lightness of the question shattered the heavy silence, to Atuye's imminent relief. It was gritting on his nerves, that weighty stillness. "What a surprise."

To his growing embarrassment neither of his brothers ventured an answer, still immersed in their staring contest. Like old times. He gritted his teeth.

"Yes, we are." His own voice sounded as light and as noncommittal as the question of the unconcerned local. Encouraged, he didn't clear his throat as he intended to. "We are from the same community, same settlement." A brief smile. "Same longhouse, as well."

As expected a few chuckles erupted and it served to lessen the tension. Not between his siblings, he noticed with growing annoyance, but their hosts moved as though happy to return to the regular activities of the pleasant post-celebration time.

The local man who was checking the game's improvised setting strolled back toward his peers. "So you are all coming from that village out there in the cold," he commented, not phrasing it as a question. "Is that a coincidence, or is your village not as uninvolved as our first honored guest here claimed it was?"

Atuye found himself staring again, this time with pure lack of understanding.

"What do you mean?" This came from Sondakwa, displaying a fair amount of puzzlement as well.

The man frowned in light bewilderment. "You are coming from that village. What is it called?" The last question addressed their half-brother.

A glance at Ogteah confirmed the worst. If the man was tense and uneasy before, now he looked like a bowstring that was pulled to its limits.

"It doesn't matter," he said quietly, with a curiously tired, almost resigned tone. His shrug held a measure of tiredness as well. "We grew up in the same town, but I'm not living there anymore. Our ways parted a long time ago. It's an old, long, unnecessarily twisted story. It'll bore you all to tears listening to it, and you, people, deserve a better pastime while celebrating."

The locals nodded politely, already busy between themselves, even the nosy man who had been asking too many questions.

His stomach knotted into a tight wooden ball, Atuye touched his brother's arm. "Leave it at that." It was the first time he found himself telling his older sibling what to do, but Sondakwa's glittering eyes made him worried. He knew the signs. Their half-brother's obvious discomfort and evasiveness served to whet Sondakwa's appetite, like bloody prints in the snow do to a hungry wolf. "I need your help." Down the incline he came from, he could see the girls' silhouettes hurrying toward him, following his instructions. "Come with me."

But Sondakwa shook his palm off impatiently. "So where do you live now, Brother?" he asked loudly, eyes stormy, narrow with challenge. "What village has the honor of hosting you these days?"

Ogteah rolled his eyes in a familiar gesture, his taut features relaxing, but not the flintiness of his gaze. "You are like a nagging mosquito, man, buzzing and buzzing. What do I have to do or say to make you leave me alone?" His arms came up in a gesture of pointed exasperation. "We are guests in this town. Is it not our duty to behave with appropriate politeness, leaving family matters out of it?"

For a heartbeat it looked as though Sondakwa's temper might erupt into one of his spectacular outbursts of violence. Atuye stepped closer, ready to do anything in his power to prevent that, aware that there was little he could do should it come to an outright fight. Ogteah was as famous for his readiness to launch into brawls, even though he never sought those actively, preferring to breeze through confrontations if he could. But only up to a certain point, and surely not while being provoked by such outright goading. The fact that he kept holding on to his temper was startling, another aspect of this changed, difficult-to-recognize Ogteah.

"Fair talk coming from a person with a trail of crimes and bad deeds stretching behind him." Having bested his own temper as well, Sondakwa shrugged, burning their half-sibling with his gaze alone. It was, indeed, not the time nor the place, and he knew it. Atuye dared to let out a held breath.

The locals, those who were not already busy with their resumed game, looked slightly relieved as well. No one wanted strange foreigners starting a fight. Not so near the ceremonial grounds, in the sight of the sacred fire and the still-celebrating townsfolk. Out there it would be a different matter, and people kept glancing at both antagonists, but Ogteah was already turning away, his shoulders jerking upwards, in the most disdainful of ways.

"Come." About to return his arm back to his brother's shoulder, Atuye glimpsed Ononta, who resumed her hurried walk toward him, the bundled baby in her arms her only company.

His heart lurched. The foreign girl! She must have run out there all alone after all. But if he hurried…

Turning toward the nearing girl, he caught a glance from one of the men who were lining the trench, either one of the players or maybe just an onlooker.

"So what was that all about?" the man was asking, leaning closer, conspiratorial. "What's the thing between those two?" The eyes peering at Atuye sparkled with light mischief. "Or are your Bear People not able to make alliance between each other while attempting to do that with others?"

There was no malice in the beaming smile. He could see that. Only amusement, a good-natured provocation. They deemed him the most reasonable person among the unexpected visitors.

"It is not that," he said, forcing his limbs into stillness, while signaling Ononta with his eyes. She'd better come and help him get away from all that. "They are brothers, half-brothers. You know how families can be, sometimes."

"Oh!" The man laughed outright, a delightfully light sound. No hidden agendas there. "That's one squabbling a wise person would keep away from."

More chuckles erupted from all around.

"So where *are* you from?"

"We are from Teguenondahi." Sondakwa seemed to regain

enough of his equilibrium to join the conversation, eager to save his face surely, to cover the nakedness of his previous outburst, to pretend it wasn't that serious. "Certainly no village that." His smile flashed with surprising lightness. Again a remarkably fast recovery.

"I knew it!" exclaimed the nosy local from Ogteah's group, the one who had started it all. Turning to Ogteah, he waved his hands in the air in an obviously pretended accusation. "You are more involved than you pretended to be, oh mysterious visitor. In the Long Tails War as well, eh? Don't try to downplay it, brother." Shaking his head in a mocking reproach, the man beamed. "You interrogated our Attiwandaronk guest for half a night for a reason."

For a short moment Ogteah looked as though he would bolt away, the way his gaze darted toward the darkening trees adorning the edge of the flattened ground. Then the easy smile flickered, ridiculously similar to that of Sondakwa. One had to know the man well to detect the forced quality of it.

"Your Attiwandaronk guest was a fascinating man. One doesn't meet such people, not every day. I may have pestered the poor man with too many questions, yes. I admit to that crime."

The talk of Attiwandaronk guests brought the silhouette of Ononta to his side. He noted that without thinking, his full attention on his half-brother now, mind running amok. Something was wrong there, something didn't make sense.

"You kept him awake for half a night," claimed the local, laughing openly now. Yet, there was a fake tone to this laughter too, its pretended lightness not reflecting the open intrusiveness of the man's gaze. "No wonder the man looked relieved when we headed the other way."

Ogteah again seemed to be checking possible routes of retreat. It was too obvious, the way his gaze sneaked around, while more noncommittal words poured out of his mouth with admirable lightness.

Attiwandaronk! The word kept circling in Atuye's mind.

"So what is your thing with the Long Tails war?" continued the local probing, nose clearly on the trail of footprints, not about to let go.

"Like all of us, I'm curious about it." But this claim did not came out sounding convincing, and as the man turned his head toward the intensified drumming pouring from the sacred fire, Atuye knew he was checking more ways of retreat. As if in a dream, he kept watching, his mind swirling, reaching out, trying to grab the scattered pieces of information. The Long Tails war, and Attiwandaronk, *what has Attiwandaronk to do with any of it?*

And then it dawned on him, and he whirled toward Ononta, still dazed, not knowing what he wanted to do. "Where is the girl? Your friend, where is she?"

The abruptness of his advance made his childhood friend jump, and the baby in her arms began crying. Which shifted people's attention to them.

"She is... she is out there," mumbled Ononta, quailing most visibly, clearly wishing to be anywhere but on the receiving end of all those curious gazes. What his outburst didn't accomplish, the baby's intensified crying was doing now. "She... I'll go and find her. I... I saw her around, just now."

But there was no need to do that. A worried mother, the girl must have noticed the commotion surrounding her baby even if she couldn't hear its cries. Still dazed, he watched her rushing toward them, running up the incline, oblivious of everything else.

Attiwandaronk, she was Attiwandaronk, his numb mind kept repeating. And she claimed she knew his brother from the Long Tails war, that her man... Oh, but her man would be Attiwandaronk too, wouldn't he? The same person his brother was accused of asking too many questions?

He watched her reaching Ononta in one swift leap, taking the baby, almost snatching it from the girl's arms. The people around were shifting, chuckling, relieved, ready to go back to their business, amused by the silliness of this last interruption. Girls and babies was not the thing gambling men were interested in.

Then his eyes took in Ogteah. Frozen in the process of turning away, his half-brother looked like a deer caught in mid-leap by an arrow or a hurled stone. Stunned, disoriented, rooted to the place he was in the process of leaving, shocked. Frightened? Oh yes, *that* expression was difficult to miss. Such open dismay! Where had he seen it before?

The answer provided itself promptly. The girl, with the baby still wailing in her arms, stood there in the same pose of a frightened deer, about to burst into a wild run. Her eyes, glued to his half-brother, looked like two round bowls, too widely open and as panicked as his were, but holding no surprise. Hers had a measure of calculation, gauging her possible assailant's moves, preparing for every eventuality. Like an animal facing a hunter, knowing it hasn't been cornered, not yet, observing its possibilities – fight or flight? Somehow it was easy to imagine this fragile female doing either thing, running like a light-footed deer, or fighting in the way of wild cats, creatures smaller than the puma but sometimes as fierce, dangerous because of it.

As opposed to all this, Ogteah, looked like someone who might faint any moment, his face pitched and lacking in coloring, crumbling in its grayish pastiness, its unhealthy hue visible even in the deepening dusk. Again it was turning too quiet.

They all must have noticed. Out of instinct, Atuye moved to stand by the girl's side, noticing her shudder; and the fact that she didn't move away, sensing his presence, or so he hoped, reassured by it.

Ogteah came out of his dazed stupor as well. He watched the colorless lips moving, producing no sound. The stupefied expression was still there, engraved upon the familiar features.

"Are you well, brother?" the nosy local was asking, peering at Ogteah with what looked like a genuine concern. "You look as though you have been visited by a ghost."

That drew a few careful chuckles. A ghost! The word echoed in Atuye's mind, gaining power. The girl was speaking of ghosts as well. But could it be?

"You know this woman!" The words came out loudly, bursting out of his mouth on their own volition, with no regard to his will. Not a question but a statement. He *knew* that his brother knew her.

This seemed to bring Ogteah back to life as the air drawn in with much force hissed loudly, shattering the silence.

"What do *you* have to do with any of this?" he demanded hoarsely, challenging.

This made Atuye regret his outburst. He didn't know how to answer that. He didn't have anything to do with any of it until running into this girl such a short time ago.

"Come on, Little Brother, spill it all out!" Ogteah's roar caught him unprepared, made the wish to step back and away difficult to battle. The ferocity of the wild gaze, the uncontrollable fury of it frightening in itself. "Enough with your dirty little games. Spill it all out or I swear I'll cut your filthy treacherous throat before doing the same to her." He moved as though about to launch forward, but with no clear space to charge through, it remained just an impotent gesture.

The girl shuddered so violently, Atuye felt it rather than saw, although their limbs weren't touching. It gave him strength to contain the unseemly waves of panic, to retreat no pace, but to step aside instead, shielding her with his body. It was good to do something, to concentrate on doing it. The blazing ferocity of his sibling's gaze was something he preferred not to endure, not for the moment.

"What are you talking about?" demanded Sondakwa, another welcome interruption. The locals' gazes all around them backed the question. They didn't understand, and Atuye was painfully aware that he was in the dark as much as they were. Only the girl knew, her and Ogteah. The ghost of the Long Tails War? No, no, it couldn't be! And yet...

"You fought with the Long Tails, didn't you?" Now that his brother joined in he felt safer, safer to face, safer to confront. "With or against them?"

Ogteah looked more and more of a cornered animal, his eyes blazing fury, but his body motionless, as though glued to the same space with the strong mix of pine sap. He didn't seem to hear the question, or maybe his mind was not processing it.

Atuye pushed the unwelcome wave of compassion away. "Why won't you answer it? It is a simple question. Did you or did you not participate in the Long Tails War against the savages? *On what side?*"

Still no reaction. Only the vein pulsating on his brother's forehead let him know that the man was not a wooden figurine, this and the motion of the firm jaw that moved ever so slightly, its muscle quivering, throbbing.

"Did you?"

They all seemed to hold their breath, even the girl beside him. He could feel her most acutely, her tension and her warmth, coming in waves, like a wind on a spring day, promising coziness and danger and thrill, all rolled in one, an enchanting combination. But for that he had to shelter her, to protect her from the wrath of his brother. The man was disarmed for a moment, but why and for how long he didn't know.

"What are you talking about?" repeated Sondakwa, moving forward in a decisive manner, addressing him for a change, his face a study of irritation. "You don't make any sense."

Atuye swallowed, pulled back from his cloud of euphoria and into the reasonable world. The girl belonged to someone else, the man who already fathered children by her, and her claims concerning his brother, indeed, made little sense. And but for Ogteah's reaction...

"Ask him," he said firmly, facing his full brother while motioning toward their half-sibling, still a wooden figurine with no colors applied to it.

"I will," said Sondakwa. "But after you've stopped making this silly scene. Who is this girl and what has she to do with any of it?"

"Ask him that too," repeated Atuye, feeling more foolish with every passing heartbeat. But he must sound quite stupid, repeating the same thing again and again. If only Ogteah would come out of his strange, frightened stupor and do something already.

The wish came partly true when Sondakwa rolled his eyes, confirming the worst of Atuye's fears with this vividly showy gesture – oh yes, he made a fool of himself, he did – before turning to face their oldest of siblings.

"What is he talking about?" Surprisingly, his tone held none of the previous enmity or hatred, but only a matter-of-fact inquiry, even a hint of encouragement. How so? "What's gotten into you two?"

The words should have encouraged Ogteah. Instead, the man shuddered as though awakening from a dream. Or rather a nightmare, the likelier possibility if the expression in the familiar face was anything to go by.

The fire in the large eyes went out, replaced by a bleak, grim, blighted emptiness. A shrug of the sagging shoulders completed the gloomy picture.

"Nothing, nothing that you would care to hear," he said, turning around and beginning to walk away, not staggering but not charging either, his pace lacking in firmness, lacking in direction as well. It was as though the man began walking in order to do something with himself, with no particular purpose or aim.

CHAPTER 19

Where to?

He listened to the sound of his footsteps, shuffling upon the crumbling ground, his mind refusing to concentrate, focused on the rhythm they produced. Such a calming, pleasantly lolling sound. Better than the drums and the flute that were still pouring somewhere behind his back, refusing to dissolve in the night. All those celebrating people, were they still dancing or gossiping or flirting, or playing betting games? Or did they abandon their busy afternoon and all its pleasant activities, huddling in groups, passing on the news, astounded, or aghast, or maybe already rushing to pick their weapons in order to chase the filthy criminal, the man who had lied to them all?

Oh, but he needed to get away from here and fast! To hasten his step even now, as he walked, to break into a run, charge toward the fence and scale it, or just race along the palisade's corridor before his pursuers gained an advantage on him. To get down the river, snatch his canoe. But he needed his paddles and provisions, his things. It was all up here in the longhouse of his hosts, his goods and his tools, his weaponry even.

The bow, he needed his bow. Why didn't he leave it down there with the boat? And all the rest of his things. What had possessed him to carry in up and into this town? How stupid can a person be? He was here not on a friendly visit in the neighboring community. Had he forgotten his purpose while being accepted so readily, challenged with no difficult questions? How annoyingly damn stupid!

He forced his gaze off the ground, but the dark silhouettes of the longhouses towered all around, threatening, wishing him harm. He couldn't go on wandering about. He had no time for that. They would be questioning that little skunk Atuye and the girl.

On Mighty Spirits, the girl, that same nasty, hateful, treacherous snake, crawling from under the rock, flashing her poisonous fangs and just as one least expected it, the murderer, the deceptive malicious beast, the back-shooter. Where did she come from and why now, at the worst of timings? But of course. Of course! Snakes did that, waylay you and bite when you drop your guard, become complacent, too sure of yourself.

But how could she possibly know? How could she anticipate his appearance here of all times and all places? How did they all, when even he himself had decided to cross only when? Eight, ten dawns ago? It was all done on the spur of a moment, with the filthy attack on his village. Otherwise he would never have thought, never have …

He pushed the irrelevant thoughts away. It didn't matter, not now. However his brothers came to that knowledge, in whatever way they managed to find their filthy snake and make her tell and cooperate, they had done it, and all he could do was to try to get away, to charge into the woods, or maybe attempt to steal his own canoe and row away, by whatever means, using a stick instead of a paddle for all he cared. If they didn't organize the chase quickly enough, he might still have time to reach the river, jump into his boat, evade their attempts to prevent that, somehow.

The voices burst upon him before the silhouettes did, rounding the corner of the nearest longhouse, talking loudly, at length. Darting behind the wide façade's beam, he stopped breathing, his heart thumping in a wild tempo. Ten heartbeats instead of one, then some more. The air was swelling inside his chest, desperate to burst out.

The passersby swept on, their voices merry, footsteps shuffling. Lazy, unhurried. Just a group of people, youths, enjoying the post-celebration evening, the privacy of the abandoned town, up to no good. He remembered himself being part of such groups. Happy times of his youth. Well, no, not so happy. Bad, purposeless existence.

He let out a held breath, then tensed once again. They paused next to the thatched roof of the façade, speaking in hushed hurried voices. To slide deeper into the shadows became a necessity.

On the other side of the abandoned building the wind tore at him, surprisingly refreshing. Another longhouse stretched ahead, then another. If only he knew this town better, the layout of its dwellings, the location of the fence. They had entered it from the riverside – had it happened only two dawns ago? – but the fence must be stretching all around it, offering another opening or a few. This town was too large to have only one entrance.

Calculating his way toward the possible location of the palisade, he hesitated, the drumming pouring from the ceremonial grounds, soothing, suggesting a respite. Was he being chased or wasn't he? They may still be busy questioning the girl, or his brothers, discussing it all, trying to arrive to a conclusion. Most of the town must be still unaware of his alleged crimes. And if so, wouldn't it be wiser to walk openly now, not slink in the shadows like a proven criminal. He could find his way faster, could locate the longhouse that hosted him, collect his things and be gone before anyone as much as bothered to declare a hunt after him.

Still hesitating, he heard the youths on the other side of the building breaking into a louder talk, joined by new agitated voices. An argument? A brewing fight? He didn't need any of that.

Another heartbeat saw him slinking away, toward what sounded like the rustling from a more open ground. Tobacco plots? Oh yes, that would be helpful. Located near openings and fences, tobacco plots offered a certain route of escape. But where? Deeper into the woods? He didn't know its trails and pathways, not even the lay of the river.

The dark mass of the palisade towered to his left, unmistakable. He breathed with relief. Just to get to the other side of it, climb or find an opening, a missing pole. There must be such gap or breach somewhere around. This town was like any other.

From the vibrantly alive darkness he had left behind more voices were pouring now, a flicker of a fire or two. People were returning to their homes, done with the celebration. Did they hear about him already?

Struggling to pick his way toward the roughly carved poles tied by interwoven branches without tramping the gentleness of the early tobacco growths, he felt the darkness behind his back more alive than before, animated with voices. Abandoning the idea of following the dark mass until finding a gap in it, he ran his palms over the coarse beams, seeking protrusions. Like back in Arontaen!

He pushed the new wave of anger and frustration away. Was he to flee in this most ignoble of manners, chased and accused of every crime possible each time he stepped on his former people's lands? What a mistake! He should never have come here, never. And he hadn't learned anything of significance to justify this entire excursion. What would he tell the Wolf Man if by a chance he managed to come back? That the Rock People had not joined the Wyandot Union, not yet? That they resented the pressure to do so?

Well, such information may be of value to their future warriors' leader, but it didn't help him, Ogteah, not personally, not when it came to safeguarding his village, his woman and daughter and the child that was yet to be born. They would benefit from his recent adventures not at all, and if he died here – a likely possibility as the situation looked at the moment – she would be left with nothing at all, no support, no protection, not even a father to help raise his children. Oh, but how right she had been, arguing against his mission! A wise woman that she was. So young yet, so alluring and beautiful and delightfully silly at times, and yet she was wiser than him, more farsighted. It was different than on raids, different than when warring. Wandering the enemy countryside all alone he was chancing the exact thing that was happening to him now. Slim chance of meeting someone who knew all about him, but it did happen, it did, and at the worst of timings!

Oblivious to the rough wood and the multitude of splinters

that made it their business to tear at his flesh, he pushed his way up, reaching the edge of the entwined branches with surprising ease, the memories of Arontaen and its palisade making him smile grimly. This wall was nothing like that other one, not as invested. But for leading a raid upon this filthy town, to teach them a lesson, to avenge what happened to Lone Hill. Warmed by the idea of revenge and the distraction it provided, he slid between the sharpened poles, then paused for a heartbeat, catching his breath.

From his elevated perch he could see the darkness far away and below, quivering and alive, flickering with fires. Many sources of light now, some of them moving, in an alarming way. Torches? He drew his breath in sharply, pushing the surge of hatred that made his stomach constrict most violently. Not now. Later. When he was safely away, he would take his time fuming, loathing the people who forced him into this difficult, ignoble flight, wishing them harm. Two stupid hateful siblings and that little poisonous snake, the bad Long Tails *uki* who could not be killed, destroyed or got rid of in any other way. Was this girl a bad *uki*, after all? That would explain some things, most certainly.

The lights were moving again. Multiplying?

With grim determination, he pushed his precarious perch away, landing on his hands and feet, the jump not very high but painful nevertheless. No, it was not the time to wander back and try to brazen it all out. The girl was sure to spill her story by now, and backed by the little skunk of his youngest brother, she would be listened to. Believed, as well. These people knew not a thing about him, and his abrupt leaving of the ceremonial grounds was sure to brand him as guilty, nothing to doubt or question.

The river! He needed to reach the river and fast.

Helpfully, the moon broke from behind the surrounding clouds as he made his way along the outer fence, not daring to proceed close to it but keeping it in his eyesight, just in case. What did he know about these woods?

The lack of proper illumination irked. It was annoying to stumble through the nightly forest when all he needed to do was to reach his canoe and just sail. Would they try to chase him, the suspected spy, the disguised enemy? Or would they just shrug, take the goods he had left behind and proceed to forget all about him. Too much to hope for, but they had more important things to keep them busy, hadn't they?

The town still emanated sounds of lively activity, even though the drums seem to stop for good now. The forests around him kept quiet. Taking his knife out, just in case, he hastened his steps, careful not to trip over the multitude of obstacles, all these slippery rocks and protruding roots surrounded by prickly bushes aplenty. Oh, but those took pleasure in their determination to spring everywhere, to fail his step.

He cursed inwardly, then pushed on, determined. He would reach the river before midnight. The annoying lowlifes who were after him would not beat him to his canoe!

By the time he heard the familiar hum of a water body larger than a creek he was soaked with sweat and probably some night dew, flogged all over, exhausted by the necessity to push his way through the hinterland with no trail. The sounds of the river were promising, but not the upward tilt of the incline ahead. Trust it to bring him to this or that higher bank, away from the shore he needed and with no comfortable way down. He cursed loudly, beyond care.

The sounds of the forest all around made him clutch his knife tightly, the only weaponry he did have. It was Arontaen all over again! But how right Gayeri had turned out to be.

The thought of her made his stomach clench with a painful spasm. If he didn't manage to come out of this predicament, she would not even know what happened to him, would not hear a word. Left with the bad taste of their last quarrel, with the knowledge of him being wrong and not listening, acting recklessly, without a pause to think, not caring enough for his family, for her and the children, leaving them for the sake of adventure, and then not coming back – oh, but she would feel all of it and more, disappointed, hurt, bitter, let down. Oh Mighty Spirits, but he needed to get back, at least on that count!

The urgent rustling in the bushes to his left drew his attention, heralded a presence. Followed by high-pitched yapping and a faint bark, it made him freeze in his tracks. At this time of the seasons it promised only one thing – a cove full of cubs. Not wolf cubs, he hoped. Armed with a knife alone and barely able to see his own outstretched hand in the darkness, he had not the slightest chance against a pair of angry canines that must be prowling around, keeping their progeny safe.

The loud fussing continued. Coming from his right, the bulk of it, it gave him hope. Those cubs were tacked somewhere there, in a cave that did not stand between him and the river. Good! Slowly, he began backing away and toward his left, drawing in his original direction, toward the hum of the river.

When the greenery ended abruptly, opening at the moonlit cliff and the river speeding not so very far below, he was about to breathe with relief, but for his ears absorbing unmistakably low growling. Eyes darting frantically, taking in the ragged stony surface, only five, ten paces wide, with a lone, old, badly split tree cringing low above its edge, he focused on the growling silhouette of a fairly large creature, crouching low, ready to attack. Not a wolf, his senses told him, searching frantically for something to wield, a log, a stick, anything really. An angered mother coyote, judging by her loose belly, long enough from birthing her litter but not completely recovered.

Another sound drew his attention, a muffled whimper, coming from around the crumbling tree. Another danger? He had no time to check on any of it. The crazed coyote was charging, hissing strangely, in a low rumbling moan.

Involuntarily, he thrust his arm out, to keep the attacker away from his body, his vital parts, to slow it down until able to use the knife. It was there, slick in his other sweaty palm, launching forward already. But for a heartbeat of respite, the opportunity to regroup, to think his moves through.

The collision made him sway, slamming his back against the jagged rock to his left. A hurtful support but it helped. If he fell to the ground he would be helplessly overwhelmed, with his attacker mad with fury, set on the killing at whatever cost. The mother of the cubs back in the woods, for certain now.

He paid the thought of it no attention, his panic overwhelming, the frantic need to get rid of the insane creature uncontrollable, a terrified urge. The pain shot up his arm, sudden and piercing, distracting from the last of the reasonable thinking, the beast's jaws locked around it in a deadly grip. To slam it into another ragged surface seemed like the only practical course. He needed to get rid of the mad critter.

As his mind registered the loud, revoltingly wet thud, the strangled yelp, the sharpest of pains, all twirling in a flurry of panicked confusion, the weight of the creature was not on him or his arm anymore, its silhouette twisting upon the ground, screeching in bloodcurdling yowls.

Unable to fight the drive of his own previous charge, he went down as well, crushing beside the creature, again blind with panic at the mere proximity of it. Those cries and the clacking jaws, he had to get away from those, and just as his left arm was reacting strangely, refusing to accept any of his weight as he pushed away from the ground, the knife's handle cutting into his palm, reminding of its existence. The knife, his knife, it was still there! His mind clung to the words, not processing their meaning, not yet, but reassured by those. The next thing he knew he was plunging it into the meager pulsating fur, again and again, feeling it tearing, jerking revoltingly, plopping and screeching, such a terrible cacophony.

When his arm refused to rise again, he just sat there, leaning against the butchered carcass, indifferent to its stench, painting as noisily as the mad creature before, drained of the last of his strength. He couldn't even push himself away from it, let alone straighten up or even just roll aside. It was beyond him.

The sounds began penetrating his mind, returning gradually – the rustling of the forest, the hum of the river, the high-pitched desperate sobs up the lonely tree. The peacefulness of the night woods was back again, restored but for this soft whimpering.

He narrowed his eyes, trying to understand. Pushing away the butchered coyote, he put it all into the attempt to get up, successful only partly, half lying, half standing against the rock, its slippery raggedness reeking of gore.

"What in the name…?" To narrow his eyes didn't help, but his ears now told him that the whimpering came from the edge of the cliff, maybe the tree upon it, and that it was a human sound. "Who is there?"

The pitiful weeping stopped, replaced with a tentative silence, interrupted by loud gulping every now and then. Swaying badly, he went toward it, anxious to know all of sudden. The pain rolled up and down his arm, and he had to grab it with his other hand to maintain an upright position.

Later, he told himself, later. Later what? His mind refused to think about any of it.

The tree was tilting above the edge, as though observing the river below, not truly far but not an advisable jump, not with all the rocks adorning its bottom. In the split of the two wider branches, the silhouette of the child looked ridiculously small, hanging onto his precarious perch for dear life, or so it seemed. Grandmother Moon was shining with a renewed strength again, bathing the world in her silvery magic.

For a heartbeat they just stared at each other. Then another thundering hiccup brought the small thing back to life. His lurch had him nearly toppling off and into the river.

"Careful!" It came out in quite a shout, not reassuring at all. "Don't move, just don't move." He moderated his tone, trying to speak reasonably over the steady buzz in his ears, the way the world kept swaying lightly but constantly. Was it the wind? The annoying tree? He was leaning against it now, yes, making its tilt even worse. The child would fall out of it in the end, he reflected randomly, straight away into the river. "What... what are you doing here?"

The boy – he was so small, younger than his daughter even, or maybe of the same age – peered at him silently, gulping again.

"Where is your mother? Or father?" It was getting silly, this entire situation, with him clinging to the stupid tree, unable to leave its unreliable support and the child sitting up there, about to topple off and into the river. "Did you get lost? Are you from the town up there?"

Of course he was. Where else such a young thing would be coming from?

He wanted to shake his head to make it work, but to do that wasn't wise. That would see him crushing down and this time for good. If only this stupid arm would stop hurting so!

"Just come down that tree. It's not good for you to sway up there like a mad squirrel. This tree would fall any moment, or you would fall off of it yourself."

He paused, out of breath. The nausea, that was what irked him so, he realized. It was pressing his chest, rolling up and down it, in most annoying of manners. He had to sit down and rest. But for the stupid little skunk.

"Just get down, all right? Get your stupid carcass down here before I leave you here all alone."

A threat that he did follow through by sliding down the trunk and into the rocky earth. It made him feel infinitely better. The little thing would have to fare for itself for a while, until he gathered some of his strength back. Until his head stopped spinning and his arm stopped hurting so much.

He tried to wriggle into a better position in order to inspect it, the memory of the snapping fangs making the nausea return with redoubled strength. The damn thing sank quite a few of those in there, didn't it? The accursed sticking creature! But this was the last complication he needed now. And what if it was sick, stricken with real madness. Then he was as good as dead already, a terrible death, too. Oh Mighty Spirits!

The tree behind his back shook, trembling under the movement of a body heavier than a squirrel, yet as agile, apparently. In a heartbeat a pair of small moccasins swished by, the dark form landing beside him, jumping away for a fair measure, not trusting too close a proximity. But for the echoes of terror from his previous thoughts he might have smirked. The pair of huge eyes peered at him warily, dominating the small face, reminding him of something, not a pleasant memory.

"Oh, so you are a two-legged creature after all. How surprising."

To postpone the necessity to examine his wounds was not something to feel proud about, still he welcomed it, unwilling to deal with any more complications, not now. It was just too much, all of it, the discovery, the flight, all those people from his past coming to haunt him, then the crazy coyote. The worst of nightmares but not something he could hope to wake up from.

The boy was still studying him, all eyes and senses, ready to flee upon his slightest of movements. Ogteah forced his attention to his hurt limb. It was pulsating with pain and for a reason, he discovered, seeing the blood trickling, dripping down its sides, coming from more than one gush, even though it was difficult to tell with all the mud and gore smeared upon it, the remnants of the battle, or rather the butchery. How stupid he was to slay that coyote to such extent!

He clenched his teeth to stop more curses from coming out, the necessity to keep quiet essential, in case his pursuers were after him, somehow divulging his course after all. Also the boy would get frightened.

Glancing up, he saw the little one still poising on one leg, the other about to come up and into the air, a perfect ready-to-flee stance. He tried to wriggle out of his shirt, having no better bandage to stanch the bleeding, but the murmuring from the forested edge made him shudder, brought the little thing scampering to his side. Frozen, they listened to the rustling and faint grumble. The cubs, he reflected. They were looking for their mother, poor things. He took a deep breath, then glanced at his unasked-for company.

"You either go back up that tree of yours," he said in the most reasonable tone he could muster. "Or come with me. We don't need any more encounters with the rest of the coyotes that are ruling this part of the grove." These cubs, or their father, in case he was prowling around, he reflected, glancing at the dark trees, unsettled by his own words. More of the enraged, parental coyotes, in packs maybe? Oh no, he didn't need any of this. "Make up your mind until I wrap this thing around." To start cutting the decorated leather was too much to ask of his dwindling strength. The attempt to swaddle his arm in the entire wear seemed like a more realistic task.

"It hurts?" These were the first words of the boy, spoken in a squeaky hesitant voice, husky from too much crying. Carefully, the little silhouette leaned closer, studying the dark, glittering mess, a warm, surprisingly soothing presence.

"What do you think?" He forced his tone to be as light as he could, trying to sound amused, failing to do so but maybe only partly. As terribly as he felt now, he needed to make the child talk and feel at ease around him. There was no question as to the impossibility of leaving the boy all alone on his cliff, to huddle up his tree until someone else came, probably more forest predators. "That mother coyote was after you, wasn't she?"

He felt the small figure moving with his whole body, in vigorous confirmation.

"And you climbed the tree?" Biting his lips against the persistence of the pain, he wrestled with the uncooperative material, the shirt too large, full of wrinkles, thick and inflexible. "It's good thing that you did."

The boy kept studying his struggle with unabashed curiosity. "I climbed it before. When it became dark. It was scary down here after dark."

"What were you doing out here all alone?" Grimacing, he forced his throbbing arm up while leaning toward it, reaching for the improvised bandage with his teeth, trying to fasten it against the pull of his good hand, to encase the wound in a tighter grip. Maybe this would slow the bleeding, would stop it for good. Because if he went on bleeding like that, slowly but surely, on and on, his chances of surviving the night, let alone the prospective journey, were slim at the best.

"It's slipping again." The small hand caught the flipping side of the blood-stained material just as it escaped the bond that was achieved with too much effort, pulling it back firmly, with surprising determination.

"Oh, that helps." Relieved, Ogteah pressed the new tie with his good hand, resting for a moment. "This way maybe it'll stop bleeding." A glance at the boy rewarded him with the glimpse of a concentrated face, a funny version of the grownups' expression. "Where did you learn to be so efficient?"

The boy glanced back at him, still comically serious. "*Annen* showed me. When I had my hand hurt. She wanted me to help bandage it. She told me how to do it." The small face lit up. "She says I'm very good. In everything else too. She says I'm like a grown up man, help around."

"She knows what she is talking about." Clenching his teeth, he prepared for the effort of getting up. As much as it was tempting to stay where he was, to close his eyes and rest, just a little bit, it wasn't a wise thing to do. The activity around the mother coyote he had just killed was growing, joined by more grunting and grumbling. It wouldn't be long before more interested forest dwellers would be coming here, checking the situation, finding such tempting prey, a wounded man and a child, the smell of his blood ensuring the invitation.

"It was just like yours," the boy was saying. "All bleeding and hurting. And it turned huge. That huge." The small arms were widened, demonstrating how big something he was talking about was.

"What?" Catching the wobbly branch that provided anything but a steady support, Ogteah waited for the world to stop spinning. It was swaying but not as badly as he expected. Encouraged, he grinned at the boy. "Now we'll go down there. Before Grandmother Moon goes behind the clouds again."

His companion nodded thoughtfully, as though seeing the strength of his argument. Ogteah let the stupid branch go. "Is there a trail leading down there?"

The boy nodded readily.

"Then you lead."

"They'll put sticks to it," the boy informed him, when they reached the edge of the cliff and went alongside it, the little rascal leading with a practiced skill, a perfect guide, attentive and sure-footed.

Ogteah shook his head at the bizarreness of the situation. "What sticks?"

To talk helped. It kept his mind off the alarming way his wounded arm was reacting, sending sharpest pangs of pain every now and then in addition to the constant dull throbbing, the bleeding still there, persisting, soaking his improvised bandage despite the attempted pressure. It made it more difficult to walk, the need to cradle it in his good arm, more difficult to keep his balance. Neither did the light buzz in his head help, this floating sensation, like walking in puffy clouds; it made him wish to stop and lie down, to rest if only for a little while.

"The sticks," the boy was saying. "It hurts. When Father put it, it really hurt. And you can't climb trees this way." He halted when the trail forked and hesitated for a moment, studying the river that was closer now, rushing by with much force. "Father can put sticks to your arm when he comes. I'll ask him."

"Oh, this sort of sticks," exclaimed Ogteah, welcoming the brief pause in walking, fighting the urge to lean against the nearby tree. If he did this he won't be able to tear himself off, unless by sliding downwards to lie on the ground. To force his thoughts back to the conversation helped. "The splint. You mean what they put on your arm if it's broken."

The boy shrugged, then resumed his walk, the trail still clearly visible, despite the thickening vegetation.

"*Annen* didn't know how to put sticks to my arm. It was all huge, like that of a fat bear, she said. A really fat summer bear." The boy giggled. "Not a winter one." Then he sobered. "But Father put sticks to it. He said he must. He said my arm will be no good if he didn't."

"Oh, so you broke your arm." Reluctantly, Ogteah followed, encouraged by the intensified hum of the rushing water. "When did you have time to do that?" He could still hear the coyotes gnarling somewhere up there, yelping, mourning. The first summer's moon cubs, not old enough to present danger on their own, but not such helpless creatures either. They'd better reach the river and fast. Down there he might try to chance making a fire, to keep them warm and safe, while doing what needed to be done to the wound of this kind. He shivered and put his thoughts away from this and the rest of his prospects, concentrating on his step a heartbeat too late. As the muddy ground turned suddenly steeper, the moss-covered rocks slipped, rolling from under his foot. The entanglement of roots foiling his attempts to regain his balance, he threw his arms up in an involuntary attempt to catch something, anything, the pain in his damaged limb sudden and blinding, not softened by the blow from the wet earth.

Tossed and bounced, he rolled down the hill for what felt like eternity, hitting too many obstacles on his crushing charge down the river. It roared quite deafeningly here, but he listened to none of it, sprawling next to a rotten log that was lying across, helpful in its purpose of stopping his fall, of making the nightmare cease. Unable to catch his breath, he just lay there in a heap of crumpled limbs, the sounds distant, not important, penetrating his mind but barely, the boy's arm upon his side insistent, not enough to make him do something about it. Neither the feel of the damp earth nor the way it was jutting against his body bothered him. Only the intensity of the pain mattered, and the all-enveloping exhaustion. This and the certain sensation of relief – he wasn't forced to walk anymore.

"Are you good? Are you?" The boy's voice was coming in waves, annoying in its persistence, like a buzzing mosquito.

He tried to shake off the pressure of the small hand. "Go away."

But the words came out more of a groan than a speech, and the wave of overwhelming nausea that followed made him forget what he wanted to say. The vomiting lasted forever, it seemed, yet the moment he managed to breathe again he felt infinitely better.

Blinking against the world that stopped spinning gradually, the darkness focusing, losing its shimmering quality, Ogteah took a deep breath, then another.

"What? What are you saying?"

The attempt to push himself up using his good arm was crowned with success. The boy was huddling against him, pressing into his side with much force, threatening to upset his painfully gained balance once again.

"Stop that! What are you…?"

Then his mind focused as well, his senses warning him, that special prickle of the skin, that sensation of being watched with attentive, absorbed, careful eyes.

Freezing, he peered into the darkness, moving his gaze alone, probing with his senses, trying to catch a sound, anything. The moon was still strong but it didn't reach into their current location, the towering bank blocking its way, letting only mere slivers in. Not enough to see anything but maybe one's limbs, the most immediate surroundings.

One heartbeat of heavy silence, then another. The boy was just an inanimate form, radiating warmth but little life otherwise. Too terrified to react? Ogteah hoped he wasn't.

"We need to get to the river and fast," he breathed, hoping the boy was listening. Raising his tones for the benefit of whatever beast was watching them from the darkness, he went on, feeling better by the moment, the sound of his own voice reassuring, calming his frying nerves. "When I say run, you run. Together with me. Don't go too fast, make sure I'm still near, no more than a pace away. It's not good for you to be alone out there now. You make too tempting a target." The boy stopped breathing, now just a dark spot next to him. "Are you listening? You aren't too scared, are you?" Straightening into a more upright position, pleased to feel less of the previous dizziness, he patted the angular shoulder, so painfully small. But this boy was really too young for all this! "Don't be that scared. You are not a tiny forest mouse, are you? They didn't call you Tsonniatena the Mouse, did they?"

As expected that brought the fierce little creature back. "No! My name is Tsamihui! Tsamihui the Eagle. Father says—"

The low growling from the darkness opposite to where the hum of the river was coming from cut short the prideful tirade.

Ogteah jumped to his feet with little consideration to the protests from various parts of his battered body. His hurt arm being impossible to even think of bringing up, he waved the other one wildly, in mad fluttering.

The effort of shouting at the top of his voice came with blissful ease. He only hoped it was a wild cat, preferably not another mother protecting her litter. A mountain lion would see them both devoured and quickly, jumping or shouting to make them sound bigger and more dangerous or not.

"Scream something too," he hissed, fighting to catch his breath, his ears picking no sounds. "Yell and don't run until I tell you."

The darkness moved ever so slightly, like a breath of light breeze. He strained his eyes, pushing the boy behind his back. If still upon the cliff with the tree, he would have considered jumping, but here their options came to a wild run into the shallow water, nothing the adept forest dweller set on a hunt could not deal with, and easily. Still he had to fight the urge to do just that, to turn and run, as fast as he could, heedless of reason. Oh, but for a torch with a well-oiled tip, or just a burning stick, really.

Fire! If he managed to make their current assailant go, he would try to make fire, no matter how many others, forest creatures and humans, were after him. Their immediate survival was of more urgent concern and when he saw the size of their problem as it moved out of the shadows, still not attacking but just coming closer, either curious or merely hungry, he knew all the rest didn't matter.

CHAPTER 20

The screams were faint, coming from somewhere further down, below the elevated ground, crawling up their cliff like pre-dawn mist, muted but insistent, impossible to ignore.

Gripping his knife with too much force, Atuye suppressed a shiver. The night was deep, encompassing, and even though Grandmother Moon poured her light generously, ruling the cloudless sky, it was still uncomfortably dark beyond the blissful openness of their current sanctuary.

"He was here, I know he was," the girl was muttering, her voice broken with convulsive sobs.

She had cried her heart out, trembling in his arms, only a short time ago, while reaching this cliff and finding terrible things, that butchered coyote with yelping cubs, such a badly cut carcass, a revolting sight.

Yet, it wasn't what made the girl lose her fighting spirit, her impressively firm, single-minded willpower. The lack of their target, the boy they were searching here or at least the sights of him, did this. She was so confident, so efficient, so full of determination before. Like a wolf on a trail, a busy female coyote, slim, delicate, fit, perfectly adept, belonging there in the forest. If back in the town she had intrigued him with her outlandish ways, the fierceness of her reactions as opposed to the fragility of her looks, so obviously not belonging, so out of place, here in the forest she became one with it all, the trails and the trees and the surrounding bushes. Maybe with its inhabitants as well. Sure-footed and purposeful, she had led their way, not toward the shore the townsfolk used for storing canoes, for starting or finishing their journeys, but further upriver, unerring and confident, at home in these woods that weren't even hers to begin with.

Back in the town, after the awkward scene with his despicable half-sibling – a questionable person that the man used to be but never like this, lurking between them and the enemies, pursuing unclear motives and goals – he felt nothing but a grave embarrassment, which the girl's lack of cooperation didn't help. With Ogteah storming off in a puzzling fashion and him, Atuye, stuck in the middle of it, the initiator, demanded an explanation he could not provide, not with his own glaring lack of knowledge to the things he was accusing his brother of, the girl should have helped at least by repeating her story of bad spirits and warriors killed.

Instead, she kept shaking her head in refusal, shrinking under everyone's gazes. She wasn't about to explain, to help him out. A lack of loyalty that angered him, but not to the extent of turning around and leaving as well, his wish to protect her still there, overcoming the hurt. No, he couldn't let that matter go just like that. Ogteah was guilty, he was! Of what exact crimes he didn't know, but his flight proved him guilty, unarguably so. Didn't they see it?

Well, it seemed that they did, maybe, but not to a serious extent. They kept looking around, stealing glances at him or talking between themselves, more bewildered than angry, with Sondakwa – another surprise, as unpleasant as the behavior of the girl – growing outright indignant, taking their despicable half-brother's side all of a sudden, maintaining that enough was enough. There was no logic and no sense in Atuye's claim, his older brother maintained; no proof to be had for the wild, half-formed accusations.

Still Ogteah's abrupt leaving didn't help to restore everything back to normal. Soon thereafter people broke into smaller groups, then wandered off, even the players engaged in their rolling clay balls.

Angry over this mounting misunderstanding, wishing to find Ogteah and confront him again, with no witnesses and no public scenes this time – but he needed to know! – Atuye tried to convince the girl to scan the town first, make sure the child wasn't still inside the safety of the settlement's fence. With Ononta taking care of the baby, it would be a truly quick run, and he would have an opportunity to encounter Ogteah again.

However, this time, the girl was adamant, not about to comply with any more delays. Her child was out there, facing the dangers of the night forest and there was nothing that would make her stay inside, neither argument nor a physical force, if attempted. And yet, when on the edge of the ceremonial grounds a group of elders, one of them a member of Onentisati's Town Council, detained them for a brief questioning, there was little they could do but to stay and answer, even the reluctant girl. She couldn't just turn and leave, even though she looked as though she might. As a result of Atuye's urging, a few enterprising men had accompanied them, descending the river's shore, helping to search for the boy but also curious to see if the questionable visitor had sailed away in a hurry. That would decide their further actions. To chase or not to chase? And if yes, then for what actual reason or crime?

But of course, his outlandish charge cared not for any of it. Feeding her baby hastily before handing the quieted bundle back to Ononta, she had rushed into the night without an additional backward glance. And as eager to join the men who had gone down the river as he was, he couldn't let her go all alone.

Something the girl seemed to appreciate, even though she didn't show much of it. Scanning the ground like a wolf on a trail of footprints, she first made them go down the shore, along with the other descending men, then satisfied, or rather disappointed, with their lack of results, pursing her lips in the typical way of a female letting the man know that she knew he had been wrong all along, she had made them follow the turns of the shoreline before taking a smaller more hidden path.

By that time Sondakwa, disappointed with the lack of results as well but on a different score, had chosen to trail after them, making Atuye feel better. It was good to have his brother along, especially when in the dark unfamiliar forest and with nothing better than an eccentric girl for a guide, a wild thing bursting with too much determination and willpower and no hearing abilities at all. Such a strange situation, his irresistible fascination with her notwithstanding. He knew what it was by now, and he knew it was wrong, plain wrong.

And then, when they finally managed to reach the cliff she was looking for, a comfortably flat land overlooking the river, the place she had evidently hoped to find her wandering child at, she had suddenly lost her spirit. The way she had sunk desolately against an old tottering tree tore at his heart, and it felt only natural, even necessary, to take her shoulders between his hands, to try and give her of his strength. A simple gesture that unexpectedly released much emotion, her pent-up worry, agony, despair.

So determined and fiercely independent, and then suddenly this, he thought, his chest swelling with warmth, with the pleasure of holding her close, containing her grief. Not talking or trying to comfort. No point in mere words, even had she been able to hear any of it.

Sondakwa, evidently embarrassed and feeling out of place, had wandered off, inspecting the site. Mainly to pass time, to avoid letting them see his raised eyebrows, the derisive quality of his smirk, was Atuye's conclusion. Still, after some time, his gesturing grew quite insistent.

"Take a look at this thing."

From the cluster of rocks near the grove his brother was nodding at, standing alertly now, his club out and ready, came other noises, grunting and snarling, an occasional strangled yelp. Atuye made sure his knife was ready to slip out of its sheath. He should have brought his club as well, shouldn't he?

She didn't resist when he stirred her along, still hiding in his embrace, sobbing lightly. Poor thing. Yet, Sondakwa's discovery brought the warrior-girl back in a speed of lightning.

Oh, but did that coyote's corpse look gruesome, butchered so badly, so needlessly, in an exaggerated manner, torn into a terrible mess. As though a pack of wolves had feasted on it already, wolves armed with knives and not fangs.

"Ogteah?" they said simultaneously, looking at each other above the girl's kneeling figure. But why? Why would their brother do that?

She sprang to her feet, having done inspecting the ground, paying two grunting forms of clumsy cubs who were peeking from under the nearby bushes no more than a fleeting glance. Then it was back to the footprints that covered the dark mud all around. But for the resumed strength of Grandmother Moon!

Following her example, they had soon found themselves rushing back toward the tottering tree, diving into the bushes that apparently hid a small but well beaten trail, a deer path really. And just as they did this the shouts reached them, muffled yells, faint but somehow clear, holding puzzling vitality. No screams of distress.

"Down there by the river," breathed Sondakwa, eyes huge and wide open, glittering with excitement. "Keep an eye on the girl, then catch up with me."

Incensed, Atuye stared at the rustling outline of the vegetation where his brother's back disappeared before his words did. Annoying man! The girl stared at the greenery in question, her frown deep.

"What happened?"

The new outburst of shouts erupted. He thought he recognized the voice.

"Come!"

She didn't wait for his gesturing hand, but knelt to examine the patch of earth where the moonlight reached in force. For a fraction of a heartbeat he wondered, then realized that she couldn't hear what transpired.

Touching her arm lightly, he made sure her gaze leapt at him, startled and questioning. "Come, we need to hurry."

Her nod was brisk, matter of fact. But maybe it was better that she didn't hear. With all this terrible worry for her lost child... He kept his palm on her shoulder, pressing it lightly, while following into darkened path. In order to communicate fast, if needed be, he told himself, ignoring the renewed fluttering in his stomach.

When the trees receded once again, allowing the glimpse of the river, now very near and roaring strongly, he stumbled over entanglement of roots and might have tripped, rolling down and over the low cliff, straight into the yells and the commotion, heard most strongly here as well, but for the supportiveness of her grip. One hand clinging to a sturdy branch, she was clutching him with another, with surprising strength.

Busy catching his balance, embarrassed to no end, he had glimpsed the view of the shallow shore, all pebbles and dark shapes of bigger rocks, and his heart missed a beat. The scene unfolding before his eyes was surreal, its unrealism made stronger by the generous moonlight, silvery and flickering. The beast was impressive, long, sleek, majestic, crouching in the shade of a wide-branched tree, only a part of its body showing, hunching low, in an evident preparation for a leap but not moving its lower body, not about to charge, not yet.

Some paces away, maybe ten, maybe more, the most bizarre-looking figure hopped near the water edge, a disheveled, somehow disproportional form, jumping up and down, yelling frightfully, waving a long crooked-looking limb – a stick? – flailing it wildly, his other limb – another arm? – hanging awkwardly, in a shapeless bundle.

Atuye blinked, then heard the girl uttering an oddly sounding squeal before hurling herself down the steep incline with no trail from which he had almost fallen before, half rolling, half jumping, oblivious of reason.

For another fraction of a heartbeat he just stared, frozen in bewilderment, then his eyes caught a small figure huddling behind the man with the stick. The boy?

He didn't linger to ponder any of it. Gripping his knife with too much force, he pounced toward the nearest tier, measuring the distance. She would land between the deadly animal and its victims, and he would be better ready to throw his knife very accurately and very fast. Would it manage to hit its target, in the simmering darkness and from such unpromising distance? He didn't know, having no experience in this sort of untraditional warfare. Throwing knives, yes, like all boys did, but never toward a moving target. Still what else could he do under such circumstances?

Just as the girl landed, scrambling up and onto her feet nimbly, grabbing a twisted stick as she did – not much of a weapon but better than none – his eyes took in another figure entering the fray, running from the direction of the river, along the twisted shoreline. Apparently, Sondakwa had had enough time to reach the troublesome spot following a regular route. But it was getting too wild!

The thought that the majestic forest dweller evidently reflected, leaping to its feet before being swallowed by the darkness of the trees, gone as though never having been there in the first place.

His heart making wild leaps inside his chest, Atuye relaxed his grip on the knife, then hurried down the incline, but in a more careful fashion than her rolling down those tiers before. It was turning bizarre by the heartbeat and he wished he had had a little time to go away and think about all this in privacy. These were not the circumstances under which he wished to face his half-sibling for another questioning.

By the time he reached them, the peacefulness of the night had reclaimed its grip upon the narrow shore, with the moon dimming a little, hiding behind a filmy cloud.

From this closer proximity Ogteah looked even more grotesque than before, while facing his forest attacker, disheveled and smeared so badly he looked unrecognizable, practically naked but for a messed, half torn loincloth and a bundle of blood-soaked leather wrapped around his left arm. The other one still held the stick, in a way that suggested that he didn't find the idea of using it if need be ridiculous. Ready to defend himself? wondered Atuye. Against his brothers, this time?

Sondakwa, on the other hand, had his arms crossed upon his chest, his pose radiating confidence, delighted to no end. "You have some explaining to do, don't you, *Brother*?"

In the corner of his eye he saw the girl crouching in the shallow water, safely away from his brothers, pressing the child to her chest, oblivious of anything else.

"I don't owe you any explanations, you slimy piece of rotten meat." Battered as badly as he was, Ogteah seemed to lose none of his fighting spirit. "If you want to drag me up there and back into the town, you will have to fight me to do that."

"What a tempting possibility," drawled Sondakwa, pleased with himself. "It won't be much of a fight, though, oh Mighty Big Brother. Nothing satisfactory. I would rather have you recovered from that pitiful state of yours before it happens. Then it would be most pleasing to drag you anywhere you want to."

In response, Ogteah just spat, wavering but holding on. Even in the meager light of the fading night it was easy to see how ghastly he looked, so badly battered and with no color to his face, to the places where no mud or blood covered it.

"Well, all this fighting aside, let me check on your wounds before you faint here for good." It looked as though Sondakwa was making the same observations. "Don't want to deal with you all limp and lifeless, sprawling like a girl in her lover's arms."

"Shut up and go away," was Ogteah's response.

But Sondakwa's laughter shook the night. "You are in no position to issue orders, war leader. So drop that pitiful stick of yours and do as you are told."

For a heartbeat, a silence prevailed, interrupted by light sobbing coming from the boy. That pair was still huddling in the shallow water, holding each other tightly, not about to come out. Atuye shrugged, then made his way toward her. It was obvious who needed his help most. Not the pair of squabbling siblings.

"Is he well?"

She didn't hear his question, but the boy's movement made her look up as well. He watched stripes of mud crossing her lovely cheek, a scratch under her chin long and bleeding. Somehow those suited her, enhanced her wild beauty.

"Thank you," she was saying, voice trembling, pleasantly quiet for a change. "Thank you for helping me to find him. To save him!" She sniffed loudly and fell silent. The boy in her arms squirmed a little, squashed into inability to breathe, Atuye surmised.

"I did nothing," he said, not sure that his words were reaching her, hard to tell if she could read his lips in the darkness. "You found him. You saved him."

"The man with the knife saved," contributed the boy, managing to break free but not taking his chances by moving away from his mother's embrace. "He killed the bad coyote. And he scared the mountain lion off."

"Ogteah saved you?" He glanced at his brothers, still standing there and arguing, their poses unchanged. "How did you come to be with him here in the first place?"

The girl said nothing, biting her lips, while watching her son closely, with much attention. "You went to wait for your father, didn't you?"

The little thing scowled and said nothing, dropping his gaze. She rubbed her face with her free arm, a tired, desolate gesture.

"We'd better take you both back to the town," said Atuye, glancing at his brothers again. They stopped arguing and went toward the water line, Ogteah staggering in, tripping upon the slippery rocks, progressing with the agility of a bear awoken from his winter sleep too soon, not above using his good arm to help him along. Sondakwa followed closely, his moccasins plopping in the shallow water.

"I need to go back," she murmured, pulling the boy up and into the crook of her arm. Such a naturally graceful gesture, he reflected. "The baby. And Ononta. She must be worried sick."

He touched her shoulder lightly. "I will take you back now. Let me talk to them for a heartbeat." The boy was peering at him from under his brow. "Your mother was worried sick, you know. You shouldn't have done what you did."

A deepening scowl was his answer, but her smile made it up to him, such a wide unreserved beam, laced with open gratitude and affection. It took his breath away.

"I thank you for everything. Everything. You and Ononta are so wonderful, so kind!"

Somehow the mention of Ononta took the edge off his delight.

"There is no need," he muttered, his heart beating fast. "I did nothing special. Let me just talk to these two."

Hurriedly, he turned away. Next to another cluster of rocks, Ogteah was crouching awkwardly, dipping his arm in a shallow stream with an obvious reluctance. Free of mud and remnants of his clothing, he looked better now, more of a human being than a creature out of the wintertime tales.

Sondakwa was leaning as closely, studying his sibling's arm. At the sound of Atuye's approach he straightened up. "What's with the girl and her whelp? Are they good?"

Atuye just nodded, surprised with the atmosphere of strangely calm affability emanating from this part of the shore.

"Are you taking her back?"

"Yes." He hesitated. "And you two?"

Sondakwa's snort was loud enough to rival the roaring of the nearby rapids. "I'll stay here for a short while. See what that wild bear is up to."

Ogteah seemed to pay their exchange little attention, bringing his arm up from the water, grimacing direfully. "The stupid thing hurts like the underworld of the Evil Twin."

In spite of himself Atuye leaned forward, his curiosity getting better of him. Torn badly enough and oozing liquids, the disproportional swelling of his brother's hand was what made him shiver. So hideously deformed!

"All this mud does nothing but put more filth into that stupid arm of yours," commented Sondakwa thoughtfully, his tranquility once again out of place, atypical to the man Atuye knew. But he didn't see his brother so complacent, so *temperate* for a long time, if ever. Was it because their detested half-sibling was having a hard time?

Grunting something inaudible in reply, Ogteah slumped against the damp stone, letting his arm drop, his face again a mask with no color applied to it. Only his eyes were alive, gleaming with defiance, a painfully familiar sight, as always too obvious to miss.

"You know what has to be done with it, don't you?" Sondakwa got to his feet leisurely, decidedly relaxed, his voice having a dreamy quality to it.

A louder grunt was his answer.

"Unless you are willing to go back and see what the local healers have to say on the matter."

"I'm *not* going back there!" Ogteah's eyes flashed dangerously, his voice picking a growling tone.

Sondakwa acknowledged that with a thoughtful nod, looking like a faith-keeper called upon to deal with a difficult child. "Then we'll need to make fire."

Not a bad idea, reflected Atuye, watching his half-brother's suddenly tensing body. He was shaking badly enough, obviously cold, but somehow it was clear now that the fire was not about the warmth, not in this case. But then what?

He watched Ogteah straightening wearily, leaning to examine his arm anew, the torn flesh glaring back at them darkly, looking bad even in the merciful cover of the night.

"I won't leave you to enjoy the treatment all alone, Brother." Sondakwa drawled, again too innocent and good natured, exaggeratedly so. "It'll be my pleasure to help you, to do what is needed to be done."

"I bet it would," muttered Ogteah darkly. "Nothing will please you better than this."

"Oh, I can think of a few more pleasurable pastimes," admitted Sondakwa, unabashed. "But yes, this one would be among them." His smirk was decidedly open. "One can't leave one's own brother to treat his bad wounds all by himself, can one?"

An argument was piquing somewhere behind his back, and he glanced at the girl in time to see the little boy slipping out of her arms, fighting the insistent grip of her palm, as determined as his mother, and as stubborn. In another heartbeat the small figure shot toward them, paying little attention to his surroundings.

Watching the boy nearing the wounded, who by now was sprawling again, drained of power to stay upright as it seemed, Atuye sucked on his breath, understanding at long last. Such badly torn flesh needed to be stitched, cleaned most thoroughly, treated with ointments and brews, *attended by a healer*. Something his half-brother was determined to avoid. *Was he truly guilty of collaborating with the enemy, of fighting on the wrong side?*

He watched the boy slowing his step, nearing hesitantly, leaning forward with his entire body, shoulders hunched, hands stuck to his sides, as wary and as careful as a small rodent peeking out of its hole in the ground.

"Do you feel better now?" It came out in a squeaky whisper.

Ogteah opened one eye for a fraction. With the renewed strength of the moon it was easier to see how weary and bloodshot it was. "Ah, it's you, little one," he said, his lips twisting into a semblance of a grin. "Done fighting forest predators for tonight, aren't we?"

The boy relaxed visibly. "The mountain lion, he went away," he said after a little hesitation. "*Annen* made it go."

That wiped any semblance of a smile off the wounded's face. "Oh, yes, your *nnen*," he muttered. "I should have guessed!"

The boy hesitated, clearly taken aback. "Yes, *annen*," he confirmed, the frown in his voice amusing like only small children's can be when they try to speak like grownups do. "The mountain lion was afraid of her. She could hunt like a man. Father says so too."

"I know *that*!" growled Ogteah, the intensity of his voice sudden and unsettling, making one think of fury and violent deeds. He saw Sondakwa straightening up, himself stepping closer, just in case. Her boy was his responsibility, too.

In the corner of his eye he glimpsed her drawing closer, sensing the tension. It was good that she couldn't hear what they said, he reflected.

Ogteah lifted his head with an effort. "Oh, forget it," he said tiredly, reaching for the boy, who had taken a hasty step back in the meanwhile. "I didn't mean to frighten you. It's all right. This thing has nothing to do with you." The forced smile did not enliven his face, coming out like a twisted grimace. "Have your mother take you back to the town and don't run away from home anymore. Not before you are much older, eh?" This time the colorless lips stretched into a livelier smile. "Until you justify that hugely impressive name of yours, eh, Tsamihui the Fearless."

The boy was smiling again, all eyes and small whitish teeth.

"Now run along. Go back home and behave reasonably."

It seemed that the little thing would comply, taking a hesitant step back, then changing his mind again. "My hand was just like yours. It hurt. Really bad." The small arm jumped in the air. "But now it's good again."

Ogteah's laughter held a fair amount of genuine mirth now. "Then all is well." He sagged back into his previous slumber. "Now run, little one. It really *is* time."

With the boy gone, darting back toward his mother and up her arms, Atuye fought off his uneasiness. "Will you both stay here for now?"

"I won't!" stated Ogteah firmly, not bothering to open his eyes anymore. "The moment you reach that town, I'm off. So don't bother to send them anywhere around. They won't find me here."

"They are not after you, you suspicious man," said Sondakwa, back to his unusually sunny new self again. "No one is after you, but a few predators of this forest. So you can relax and take care of your wounds without running off like a spooked squirrel, whatever the crimes you must have committed elsewhere."

Ogteah's eye tore wide open. "You are lying to me," he said harshly, with not a trace of amusement to his voice. "They can't *not* wish to discover the color of my blood, knowing where I came from."

"Where *did* you come from?"

For a heartbeat, another bout of silence prevailed. *You truly don't know?* the suspiciously narrowed eyes asked. Then the wounded man's face closed with abrupt suddenness.

"It doesn't matter. I don't take my chances. Not with such ardency on some traitorous siblings' part to dig into any of it." A murderous glance shot at Atuye, burning his skin with the ferocity of it. "So much eagerness to sniff around in search of poisonous snakes lying under the rock, just for the chance of exposing me. Disgusting!"

With a dire effort, the man straightened again, looking as though about to attempt getting up or do something as unreasonable. Not a likely possibility, but Ogteah could be surprising in his resilience and occasional spells of stony willpower.

Atuye clenched his fists tight. "I wasn't busy uncovering anything about anyone! You are the one who did bad things, not me. So stop making me look like a traitor or something. I did nothing any decent person wouldn't have done." He felt his anger rising, welling like a river after the Awakening Moons melt the ice. It encouraged him. "This girl said you fought with the enemy. I didn't believe her at first. But now? Now I *know* that she was telling the truth. I know it! Your own behavior made me understand that." Ogteah was sitting very straight now, as motionless as the stone he was leaning against. Only his eyes glowed like a pair of coals, dangerously bright, but at this point Atuye stopped caring. "You were always like that, uncaring, indifferent, not loyal to your own people, your town, your family. So why should we be surprised now to discover your part in the wars that involved our enemies? I was stupid to doubt this girl's words at first. She didn't lie to us. You did!"

Momentarily out of breath, he paused, standing his brother's glare, detecting no more uncertainty, no more doubt or indecision. Nothing but the red-hot fury, the intensity of the powerless rage.

"Watch your tongue, young buck." It came out in quite an animal-like growl. "You understand nothing of it, and it is not your place to even try to. No youngster like you will be passing a judgment on me. Not anymore!" A quick lick of cracked lips stopped the tirade, but the blazing eyes didn't move. "As for your 'girl,' that poisonous snake, sweet little mother and all that, keep her away from my reach, well away! Whether it was you who fathered her brats or some other insane person who doesn't care for his own safety, make sure she doesn't cross my path ever again. The moment she comes into my reach she is dead. The very first moment, you hear me! If you want to save her worthless life, make sure I don't see her ever again!"

The darkness became heavier, more difficult to stand. Fighting for breath, Atuye felt it enveloping him, menacing and evil, such terrible sensation. The man in front of him, oh, but he wasn't a person, not human at all, a bad spirit, a rabid animal to be killed before it kills you. She had been right all along.

Before he could finish drawing even the shallowest of breaths, let alone decide what to do, Sondakwa, who had wandered off in the meanwhile gathering firewood, was between them, standing there firmly, not about to be moved.

"Stop it, both of you," he said stonily, with no trace of his previous lightness or amusement. "Just stop this stupid squabbling. You," the toss of his head indicated Atuye, "go back now. Just go. Take the girl and the child and leave that accursed shore. I will meet you up there in the town soon." The stern eyes bored at him with the familiar authority of a much older sibling, accustomed to giving orders, expecting to be obeyed. "Don't talk to anyone, or do anything until I come. Leave it at that for now." Another firm stare relayed a message. "Just do it now, Brother. Go."

He found it hard to make his cramped muscles work, his limbs stiff and rigid, not in a hurry to do his, or rather his brother's, bidding. To force his body into relaxing cost him more of his willpower.

"I do that only because you asked me to." Not very powerful parting words, but his mind refused to suggest a more appropriate reaction.

He turned away with another effort, not succumbing to the temptation of sneaking a glance at his wounded half-sibling. Whatever Ogteah was doing or about to do it wasn't his business, as long as he didn't try to harm *her*.

The sight of her helped, gave him direction. She was standing near the same cluster of rocks, cradling her boy, rocking him gently, monotonously. A touching sight. This alone gave him power to walk toward her firmly, with much determination.

"And you, you wild bear, lie still and stop yelling or jumping around." Behind his back, Sondakwa's voice rang with his previous calm amusement, enjoying himself. "For one who was so reluctant to let the townsfolk up there see the color of your blood, you go into screaming fits too readily, I say." Another soft chuckle. "Fancy getting all tough with one's little brother, threatening to kill sweet little mothers with children. You are incurable, man, just incurable. Mad criminal and worse."

He didn't hear Ogteah's answer to the derision-laced tirade and maybe it was a mercy.

CHAPTER 21

The fire was shimmering gently, spreading its soft, friendly glimmer. Huddling close to its blissful warmth, Ogteah reached for it, absorbing the good feeling. But for the prospect of the treatment the fire offered, he might have been more relaxed now, despite the nagging worry. Were they searching for him after all, combing their clearings and shores?

It has been some time since the filthy skunk called his youngest of brothers had left, taking his poisonous snake of a company along, leaving this shore cleaner, its air easier to breath. Enough time to reach the annoying town, probably. Even though it was darker now, with less moon to lighten their way. May they fall and break their necks, both filthy skunks!

"Not long now," drawled Sondakwa, his back upon Ogteah, a small mercy.

Busy separating some of the embers from the main body of their fire, he was pushing them away and into the pit he had prepared in advance, using one longish stick after another, each time his improvised tool burned for good. Efficient and busy, like a squirrel before the Cold Moons. Ogteah wanted to spit in disgust.

"Ready for the treatment, glorious warrior?" This time, his brother actually turned to face him, a smile of unconcerned delight spread all over his face. "My first time as a healer, you know. Exciting, isn't it?"

"Enjoy yourself." It felt strangely comfortable to sprawl there and talk as though they were back home, having traveled back in time, many summers and winters, again nothing but competing youths, grudging each other every bit of accomplishment or success, hating one another more often than not, but still sharing the same compartment in their longhouse, same bunk, same family. Fighting so often and with such abandon sometimes, and yet brothers, sons of their father, acting ridiculously the same. Or so people claimed, chuckling or outright laughing, to the great chagrin of Sondakwa's mother. Oh, but the silly woman detested him, a boy his father had had by another woman, a mysterious non-existent rival to battle every day of her life.

Back then, he didn't know, didn't fathom any of it, of course. On the rare occasions he had bothered to think about his adoptive mother's unfriendliness, her lack of warmth and her readiness to complain, he assumed that it was his fault, his frequent blunders and misconduct that made the woman into his enemy, even though her own much cherished son behaved in a ridiculously similar way. Still there must have been a reason, something rooted in him and his inclinations. She wasn't alone in her complaints.

He narrowed his eyes, watching the width of his half-brother's back, its muscles bulging, shifting in an impressive way. Not a fat bear he used to call him even now. A widely built man, yes, with a generous padding, but still a well fit, impressive, good-looking person, tending their much-needed fire that he, Ogteah, would not have been able to make on his own, not in his current condition. Stirring coals, generating a pretty show of sparks. Busy, immersed. Why was he helping him now? And why so good-naturedly, in such genuine manner, faking no pretended friendliness, no affection that would have fooled no one. Curt, spiky, amused, matter-of-fact. Why did he felt as though he could trust the man he hadn't trusted his entire life?

"Now we have that silly arm of yours washed again before burning it for good." Kneeling to pick a helpfully bowled piece of bark he had singled out earlier, while gathering firewood, Sondakwa trod his way among the slippery stones, coming back quickly, balancing his cargo in one hand. "Stretch it on that stone."

Clenching his teeth against the pain, Ogteah complied. The touch of the greasy rock was cold and unpleasant, but not like the pain the forced stretching out released. He shut his eyes as the cold water poured over the raw flesh, hard put not to groan, or at least curse aloud. An important thing to avoid doing while at the mercy of his life-long rival.

Sondakwa's chuckle made it clear that he was aware of it all. "It's nothing compared to the treatment ahead," he said, conversationally. "Those blazing embers do test a man's willpower, believe me on that. Help to tell the difference between a man and a yelping coyote, I say."

"Did you happen to enjoy any of it?" With the torturing touch of the cold water gone, it felt safer to unclench his teeth. His brother's back was upon him again, messing with the wet, dirty pile his tossed-away shirt presented.

"Yes, I did. Once. Not so long ago."

Pulling at what had once been a prettily embroidered sleeve, a shirt Gayeri had decorated through the previous Cold Moons with much investment, making their daughter help, teaching the little one how to do it, Sondakwa contemplated the muddied piece before putting his knife to work. It cut the stiff leather reluctantly, as though sympathizing with Ogteah, who was busy dealing with a renewed bout of anger laced with a fiercely painful wave of longing. But she had worked hard on this thing. His brother could at least have asked first.

"It was the first hunting party of the Cold Moons." Sondakwa's voice was even, pleasantly measured, a voice of a storyteller. "We were treading our way uphill, with no snowshoes as there were no blizzards as yet. It was terribly cold, like it's always before the snow comes and softens the freeze." Satisfied with the pieces he had wrapped around his fingers, to protect them against the burning, realized Ogteah, his insides shrinking some more, the man stirred the embers again, pushing with his stick, fishing out the most glowing-looking pieces. "And that raccoon, you see, it pounced on me just as I bent to examine some footprints. It was close to the cluster of thick bushes and I suppose it had something to guard there. Not a litter, because it wasn't the time. But maybe his prey. Maybe I interrupted the greedy little bastard's midmorning meal." The coal was glowing dangerously, held firmly between a pair of protected fingers. "Now stretch it and don't make a move, not a single flutter, not the smallest of jolts."

Easy to say! He found no strength to articulate even this shortest phrase, his eyes glued to the mess of his torn, ravaged arm, the coal glowing viciously, approaching the bloody mess with a measure of eagerness.

In the next heartbeat, his entire willpower was not enough to stop him from struggling, from the desperate effort to escape the pain. But for his brother's free hand pressing at his elbow, backed by the weight of his entire body, he might have managed to avoid the torture, to make it stop. As it was he just gurgled and chocked, fighting against his own instincts, the demand to keep still ringing in his ears, repeated or just echoed in his thoughts. Such a terrible ordeal.

When it was over, he had no strength left to even keep his eyes open, lying there with nothing but the pain rolling up and down his arm, spreading everywhere, biting viciously but not like the one that tore at his insides when the burning coals were eating his flesh away.

"Here, have a drink." The heavy footsteps were back along with the decisive pull of the ragged palm, dragging him up in the most unceremonious of manners. "Drink."

He wanted to tell the disgusting piece of rotten meat to get away from him, to leave him alone, but the rough edges of bark tucked against his lips, interrupted his line of thought, made him aware of the thirst. The water tasted good.

"Now lie back down and let me see if what we did was enough. With all your stupid tossing around it was difficult to see if I managed to cover it all or not. Those are deep holes that this mad coyote has left in that useless arm of yours."

"Leave me alone," groaned Ogteah, fighting against the push that sent him back sprawling. "Don't you dare to touch me again."

But the uncompromising force with which his arm was stretched anew left him with no other option than to clench his teeth in preparation to withstand more torture. He tried to think of something else, something good, unconnected. Gayeri, what was she doing now, in this same enveloping darkness? Sleeping,

ECHOES OF THE PAST

most probably. Or maybe not. Did she go out, all the way to the Great Sparkling Water shore, not such a long walk, the first turn of the trail that would start straight away after the palisade's corridor ended? Was she standing there now, waiting for him? Yes, she must be doing just that. *Holding their daughter in the crook of her arm, pushing the hair off her face with another, squinting with impatience, pursing her lips. A little angrily, yes, but not for real. Eager, expectant, restless, longing for him to come back. Loving him as much as before. Not hurt, not resentful.*

This time, the ordeal was shorter and more bearable. Or maybe those were his senses that went wandering. He tried to focus his vision, suddenly cold on the wet gravel. Sondakwa's arms were yanking him back up again, as unceremoniously as before. But was he a bag of provisions to be pulled and pushed at his brother's will?

"Leave me alone," he groaned, resisting the pull. "Take your filthy paws off me."

"Drag your filthy carcass back to the fire and I will let you be." The familiar voice again held mainly amusement. But had his filthy sibling developed a tendency to laugh on every occasion, the stupid skunk.

Yet, back near the dying fire, with Sondakwa now busy feeding it to make it come to life again, he felt infinitely better, still shaking like a leaf in the wind, but with less viciousness than before.

"You'll feel better soon," their self-appointed healer was saying. "Leave your arm like that. Don't let the wound touch anything."

Even to roll his eyes in response felt like an effort. He crawled closer to the fire instead, curling on the slick pebbles, keeping his burning arm away.

"Have another drink." The bark with more splashing water made him feel better again, gave him power to push himself into a straighter position.

"Thank you," he said after a while, when the dizziness receded a little, allowing him a glimpse of his benefactor, now sitting across the fire, throwing smallish sticks into it. "I'm grateful."

"You are?" Sondakwa's grin held a fair measure of exaggeratedly good-natured amusement, too much of it. "And here I was wondering…"

"Why are you doing this?" To follow the burning twigs as they curled into charred lines felt like the safer of courses. Such a pretty vision.

A placid shrug was his answer. "I wish I knew."

For some time they said nothing, letting the thickening darkness lull them into the night's tranquility. The moon was fading, heralding the nearing pre-dawn time.

"You are determined not to go back, are you?" Sondakwa did not take his eyes off the fire, watching it with deep fascination. "Cleaned by burning or not, you still would be better off letting a healer examine that arm of yours. It cries out for a good splint and probably various stinging ointments smeared all over it as well."

"I'll manage."

The thought of the prospective feat of survival made Ogteah shiver. But how was he to wander the woods, with no food, no supplies, crippled by a broken limb and with no boat he wouldn't be able to navigate anyway, because of the stupid arm. He would be in a worse situation than back in Arontaen, come to think of it.

"I'll manage," he repeated firmly, desperate to convince himself. "I'll tie a few sticks to that stupid arm and wait for it to get better." A glance shot at the mangled, misshapen, oozing mess of his limb did not reassure him in the least. He clenched his teeth tight. "It's swollen because of the treatment mainly. It'll get back in shape soon enough."

"Or so you are trying to convince yourself. Have plenty of experience at that, eh? At lying to yourself."

"Shut up."

Sondakwa's chuckle caressed the darkness. "You are hopeless, Brother, just hopeless. It's been some time since you left. How many, five, six summers? And we both have covered a considerable parts of our lives' journeys, eh? But here you are, as wild and as irresponsible as you used to be, running away from your crimes or misdeeds, breezing through when you don't." The face peering at him suddenly closed, the smile tagging at the corners of the thin mouth disappeared. "Or am I mistaking now? What did our brother talk about? What does that strange girl have against you, or you against her?" The meditative eyes narrowed along with the returning grin, in a reflective manner. "It can't be your usual misdeeds, can it? Both your reactions to each other were more passionate, more venomous and relentless than a simple playing around, then leaving her to deal with the consequences, these children alone, eh? That little thing that made her so worried, he isn't yours, is he? He looked nothing like you."

"What?" Forgetting his agony and exhaustion, he straightened up so abruptly his head spun and he had to fight for his balance not to crush straight away into the fire. The gnawing pain in his arm exploded with renewed viciousness, still his brother's words made him try to disregard that. "You... you are talking crazy nonsense. Oh Mighty Spirits, but this is the wildest, the stupidest, the most ridiculous thing I ever heard!"

"What? The claim that the boy looks nothing like you?" Evidently pleased with the effect, Sondakwa grinned smugly, in the familiar, highly irritating manner. "It can happen, you know. They don't have to be our replicas." A shrug, then the mischievous grin was gone. "Even though in your case it worked. Little Ondawa is a constant reminder to all of us, running around the town, a little you at the same age."

"Who?" He was still busy recovering from the previous shock. Oh Mighty Spirits, but how could his stupid, thickheaded brother assume something like that?

"You don't even remember?" The pointed eyebrows climbed high, the provocative smirk changed, filled with a generous amount of coldness. "You father them and move on, don't you? You are incurable, man, just incurable."

"Oh." He fought to reconcile his mind with another blow, this new attack coming too quickly after the previous shock and he wasn't at his best as it was. "I... I didn't know what she called him. I didn't..."

How to deal with that? The child Yahounk bore him, that first attempt at the settled life, he was still there, of course, running around the town of his childhood, like Sondakwa said. Oh yes, why wouldn't he? How old was he? It had been summers since he last thought about any of it, the plump round baby he had left behind along with the rest of his failure of a life. He was quite successful at keeping his thoughts safe from *that*.

"Yes, the boy you fathered by that fox of the Porcupine Clan." As expected, Sondakwa was not about to let him off without exploring the trial to its maximum. "A cute little thing, but wild. So much like you in his looks and behavior. His mother can't stop lamenting about it. The entire town is tired of hearing her carrying on." A wink. "Even my mother, and she is never averse to discussing your merits, or the lack of those."

"She would," he grunted, his stomach knitted in hundreds of painful knots. How old was this boy now? About six summers? A wild thing, his brother said, suffering constant harping, maybe, constant reproaches, knowing that he amounted to nothing much probably by now. Poor thing. "Has she taken another man? Does she have more children?"

Sondakwa's smile disappeared again. "It doesn't matter for now." A shrug. "Or maybe it does, but the night is running out for us and I have questions to ask. Answer those truthfully, and then I'll answer yours. How about that for an agreement?" A quick glance brushed past the blackness of the sky, with the faintest outline of the moon, by now almost gone. "We don't have much time." Then the eyes were upon him again, flinty and piercing, with not a hint of lightness or amusement, not anymore. "What was your part in the Long Tails War? Was it true what Atuye accused you of? What's your story with the deaf Long Tails girl?"

He knew it was coming. Since the moment he realized his brother would not try to drag him back to the town by force, but was actually willing to help, to take care of his wounds and stay, offering more help maybe – had he been counting on that? – he knew that the question would arise. If only he had more time to think, to prepare his lies.

The stories concocted for the Rock People, unaware of his past or family connections, were good for this town, but not for the rest of his father's brood. Oh, but he wasn't prepared to meet any of these, had no readily available tales. Where had he lived all those summers since Ossossane? In the Long Tails lands? Well, it could have helped, this claim, but for the accursed girl, the poisonous snake. Thanks to her he could not claim any of this, and there was nothing, nothing else, no plausible explanation.

"What were your dealings with the enemy from across our Sparkling Water? What is your connection with them?" Oh, yes, his brother was good, pressing his case as forcefully as he would have done himself, sensing his prey's uncertainty, his confusion, his indecision. Was he radiating all of it and more?

A glance at the flinty attentiveness of the familiar face confirmed the worse. Oh, but this one had a fair share of their father in him, even if it didn't show as readily on the surface as in Atuye's case. The subtlety, the strength of character, the sharpness of mind. But this one was more of a father than Atuye, come to think of it. Speaking of children being replica of their fathers. Oh, yes, Sondakwa was right, the likeness didn't have to show in a person's looks.

Father!

The memory of the narrow, wrinkled, dignified face invaded his mind's eye, the way he had seen the man last, not on the shore when arriving there with Gayeri – this one was different, distant, reserved, not trusting – but later on, on the night of his flight, at the wind-stricken bay attacked by the angry wind and nothing but the occasional moonlight to make the intimacy possibly, to prompt them into talking the truth. Oh, but how wise Father was, how patient and kind and perceptive, how creative in his desire to solve his, Ogteah's, lifetime problem while reaching the goal of making their people's lives better. He could almost hear the calm, measured voice telling him that he was too good to be wasted in this way, that the path he had been walking was wrong and that it was his, Father's, fault that he never made use of his son's unusual talents, unfitting for the regular settlement's way of life but perfect for the mission he was eager to entrust his offspring with. If only this man was still with them, alive and working, giving his clandestine messenger more directions and hope, taking to Sondakwa too maybe, convincing him to help along, or at least not to put hurdles, not to betray...

He focused on the face that was peering at him from across the fire, its eyes narrow and attentive, studying him intently, trying to see through him. He measured it briefly, satisfied with what he saw. Sondakwa was his father's son as well, despite his needless aggressions, despite the quarrelsome disposition, despite the easily igniting temper that he didn't know how to rule – a familiar trait this one! – despite all the prejudice. Oh, but they were more alike than different. People were right about them. And maybe this was why they quarreled so badly while growing up. But it didn't matter now, not anymore. They were grown men, with different lives, different goals. The old rivalry was gone, and maybe his younger sibling understood it faster than he did, staying to help on this forsaken shore when no one else would. And maybe, just maybe…

To talk his way out of his predicament in the best of the gambler's fashion was tempting. And yet, maybe he could get more out of it. Father's lifetime work, Father's desire. What if they managed to reach an agreement, to try and make their father's dream come true after all?

"What? Why are you staring at me like that?"

"Father didn't tell you, did he?"

The narrowed eyes were turning into mere slits. He watched the protruding jaw tightening, thrusting out in another familiar manner. There was no more amusement, no good-natured taunting, no friendly derision. A mask chiseled out of stone, a cold, hostile mask.

"Do not talk about Father with me." The air burst loudly through the man's widening nostrils. "You, of all people, have no right to mar his name with your lips."

He felt his own body going rigid, turning into stone. To straighten up was not an effort, not anymore. He didn't even notice himself doing it. Speechless, he stared at the hard, stormy face, the eyes not narrow anymore but blazing with fury, their hatred unconcealed.

"Father died because of you! He would still be with us but for the trouble you caused up there in the Cord People's lands. Do not talk about Father with me, unless you want to fight me, fight me for real."

The wind tore at them, coming from the riverside, vicious and furious, joining in their anger. Ogteah felt none of it, neither its cold nor its forcefulness. Numb, turned into ice. The dread was back, crawling up his spine, covering it with goose-bumps. But it wasn't true. It couldn't be. He might have been thinking that himself, blaming himself, yes, especially when the news had reached him at first, back in Onondaga Town, before the Long Tails War, before the acceptance. He had thought the same thing, hadn't he? And yet, it was different, his inner thoughts and fears as opposed to the open accusation. And from his father's son, the man who might have felt this loss more acutely, involved, there, maybe holding Father's hand, helping the Great Man into his new beginning, torn with grief, mourning.

The air proved difficult to draw in. He had to struggle to make it happen. The cold, oh, but it was truly freezing on this forsaken, wind stricken shore.

"Then there is nothing to talk about," he said, not recognizing his own voice, such a low colorless sound. "You can challenge me to a fight. I will welcome that gladly. But," his numb, swollen arm allowed only a one-sided shrug, "I won't talk about Father with you. I didn't mean to, anyway. I don't wish to discuss him with you any more than you do."

Again only the wind was left to shriek its annoyance. He took his eyes toward the blackness of the river, the hum of the raging water the only announcement to its presence in such a thick part of the night.

"He wasn't old," Sondakwa was saying, his voice as devoid of emotion now, as empty and dead. "He had so much to live for, to work, to achieve. He was the greatest of our people's leaders. He shouldn't have embarked on his Sky Journey so soon. And alone, away from home." The man's voice was fading, dissolving into the darkness.

His stomach was nothing but an empty ball carved out of wood. "Where… where did it happen?"

More silence. The unattended fire was dying together with the night.

"Somewhere out there. Among the Deer. In one of their filthy towns." A snort. "They made difficulties, played around like a young girl afraid of giving in. He had to travel there twice, before the Cold Moons and just as the snows melted. And that's *after* the Great Gathering. They said he was visiting there before as well."

"He did. At least in one town. There was a delegation present at Ossossane, one Deer town, or maybe even two." He didn't take his eyes off the dying fire, fearing to ask, to hear that Father had died all alone, surrounded by strangers, and the most ardent among his followers maybe, but no family, no sons or a daughter or a wife. "Who was with him when it happened?"

"Atuye. He was there with Father. He always traveled with him in those days."

"Oh." That was good news. Ogteah nodded numbly.

"He didn't die alone and among total strangers." After another heavy pause lasted for long enough to qualify as a silence, Sondakwa's words rang with more firmness, with a flicker of acceptance. "He didn't die a disappointed man." It was easy to imagine the wide shoulders lifting heavily, with clear reluctance. "After the Great Gathering he was different. Calm, amiable, at peace. He spent much time with Atuye, prepared him for his spiritual quest, took him hunting. Took him on his travels as well." Another heavy pause, but this time he sensed his brother's eyes boring at him, piercing the darkness. "What happened there in the Cord People's lands? What changed?"

Ogteah felt the calm spreading through his battered body as well.

"We had a father-son talk. It changed my life quite dramatically." His bad arm burst out with painful protests when he tried to shift it into a better position, the rest of his limbs numb with cold. "Maybe it influenced him somehow, too." This time drawing a deep breath proved a necessity. "He talked about my mother. It was something that weighed on his spirit for many summers. Maybe talking about her made him feel better, liberated him in a way."

Sondakwa straightened abruptly. "Your mother? Who was she?"

Ogteah grinned, surprised with an unexpected splash of amusement. But his brother wouldn't see that coming. "I'm not sure you want to know."

"Yes, I do."

"She came from the other side of the Sparkling Water, from the enemy side. Not a captive," he added hurriedly, realizing how his words might sound. "They were in love and she came to be with him, to live with him here." He grinned, remembering the stories. After the first shocking discovery back in Ossossane and all the wild speculation he and Gayeri had had on their way here, he had come to learn much about not only his mother, but his father as well, about the Great Man's younger days. The Onondaga War Chief and his woman were forthcoming with stories, plenty of fascinating tales from the old times. "He was a young warrior, about Atuye's age, and he was on their side of the Great Lake, escorting a delegation. There were some wild happenings, some reckless behavior and irrational deeds." He felt his grin widening, remembering the crinkling of the War Chief's eyes. "He knew their most powerful leader, the Onondaga People's War Chief from his earlier days. Another wild story." Shaking his head, he looked at his brother, then returned his gaze to the fire. "In the end he went back, with my mother and some other people. They traveled all the way to Ossossane, to work on the alliance of our nations, something he managed to achieve only later, much later in his life." He rubbed his face tiredly. "We don't have time for story-telling just now. But if we had, you would hear plenty of wild, implausible tales."

Sondakwa's eyes narrowed again. "What happened to her?"

"She died when I was born." He shrugged again. "Then Father left Ossossane and went back to our town."

"I'm not sure I'm ready to believe all that."

He tensed at the resumed hostility. "You may choose to believe whatever you want. I'm not here to convince you of anything."

"Then why *are* you here?" Again the challenge. He attempted to collect his thoughts anew. "Also why would he be sitting down to tell you all that, then mention not a thing to any of us, not even to Mother? He spent plenty of time with Atuye through this last season of his life. Why didn't he tell him a word of this?" The sharpness of the derisive snort cut the darkness. "Wasn't he busy enough in that Ossossane town to pour so many stories out to the son he barely knew or cared about?"

Oh, but the filthy lowlife was sharp. "I didn't learn any of it from him. Only the knowledge of who my mother was. The rest came from the Onondaga War Chief and his family."

And this was a sight worth seeing, he decided, watching his brother's face turning into a mask of astonishment, with his eyes widening into complete roundness and the mouth gaping into a perfect match.

He didn't try to hide the mercilessness of his laughter. "Should see yourself now, tough man. A very silly sight."

Sondakwa was still staring, moving his lips with nothing to show for it. "You what?" he forced out in the end, blinking.

Ogteah pushed the tide of inappropriate mirth away. The real hurdle was still ahead of him, to overcome or fail, sealing his fate.

"Father wanted me to go and live with the enemy, help to promote peace with our people, working together with him but from the other side." He hoped he wasn't overplaying it. "Having nothing to stay here for, I agreed to do that, to go and live on the other side with the neighboring Onondagas, to help him make them into our brothers."

His brother had been shaking his head for some time by now, not in denial or challenge, but in the way of a person who saw an arrow fluttering in his side and was just trying to grasp the meaning of it. Numb, not comprehending.

Annoyed ever so slightly, Ogteah shifted his stiff shoulder. "I know it sounds strange and implausible," he went on, trying to come across light, not passionate or even caring. "But you know how important it was to Father, the peace with the people from across. Alone against the entire nation, but he never gave up. He even managed to bring their delegation to our people's first gathering, a delegation from the entire Great League, composed of the five nations and not just the Onondagas. Father always got his way, didn't he? His strength and willpower were worthy of the Great Peacemaker himself."

"You do talk like an enemy would, I give you that." Sondakwa was still shaking his head, but now it was a controlled gesture, expressing his incredulousness. "Great league, great peacemaker. Those are their words, not ours. We don't think either of them great, or even worthy."

"Too bad as they both are, and were, great." He shrugged. "Father thought so. He never concealed his conviction of this."

"Father did not think the savages from across the Sparkling Water to be great or worthy," cried out Sondakwa, his fist bouncing against the nearby rock, making a smacking sound. "Don't try to twist it into something you want to believe now. Father invited the savage delegation to his gathering, yes, but he didn't make peace with them. He couldn't without the other leaders' agreement, and I'm not sure he wanted it badly enough to go on pushing this particular course."

"He wanted it badly enough to send his own son into the enemy's heartlands, to work on his behalf." This came out flinty, in a challenging manner. He moderated his tone. "Father wished us to have peace with our lifetime enemy. He didn't want an outright brotherhood, I suppose, even though he kept very close contacts with the Onondaga War Chief, and some other peacefully inclined leaders." Now it was his turn to lean forward, to hold his brother's unwilling gaze. "On their side, just like on ours, people are full of hatred and mistrust. They are suffering from our attacks just like we are suffering from theirs. You have to live on both sides to understand it, even though great men like Father or the Onondaga War Chief didn't need to." He licked his lips, craving a gulp of water. But it was thirsty work, to talk at length, to orate, even to no better audience than a spiky, sharp-tongued sibling on an abandoned shore. Still, his brother's reluctant attention triggered a reaction. If he did listen, maybe the others would too. "Our border settlements are suffering, ours and the enemy's. And for what? What goal or what reason? All this for no good purpose or case. And the warfare will become stronger, more intense. More organized as well." He shrugged. "Atuye didn't lie about me and the Long Tails War. I was there, a part of it. Never heard of such organized warfare before, with many hundreds of warriors on both sides. It was a sight to behold, Brother. But," he let out a held breath, "it is a sight I would rather avoid when it comes to our people. All our people. From both sides!"

A grimace that twisted Sondakwa's face was annoyingly familiar, that old derisive, goading spark, one eyebrow flying high, the corners of the wide mouth going in opposite directions, one climbing up, the other down. So much scorn. "You sound like a bad imitation of a faint-keeper, Brother. Stop that. It doesn't suit you. Makes you look ridiculous."

Ogteah stifled a curse. "Go jump down the steep cliff."

An outburst of mocking laughter was his answer. The old Sondakwa was back, not missed in the least. "So, living with the enemy, eh? Among all those savages? Must be exciting. The feasts on human flesh, of the captured enemy or even their own people. Must be tasting good, eh? The wild beast that you always were, I bet you are enjoying all this, enough to talk in the way you just did."

"Shut up and leave me alone!"

"Maybe I will, maybe I will." Squatting more comfortably, the man pulled a stick from the diminishing pile that was jutting against his upper leg. The embers he stirred generated a pretty show of sparks. "Better bring that fire back to life. It won't last you into the new day, but at least for the remnants of the night..." Springing to his feet, he tossed his improvised tool at Ogteah. "Take care of the fire until I'm back. Then we'll decide what to do."

He glared at his grinning sibling, his rage as intense as before, and as impotent. "Don't bother!" But for the stupid arm...

"I'll bother, I will. If for no other reason than to hear more of the wild tales from our current day would-be peacemaker." Then the laughter was gone, replaced with a light frown. "I mean it. I will be back, so don't crawl away or try to escape otherwise. With that arm of yours you won't manage anything but to kill yourself in this or that way." A quick peek into the graying sky. "It won't take me long to lay my hands on your canoe, but I have to talk to Atuye first, see what his plans are. So just wait patiently."

It was a reasonable suggestion, still he wanted to make sure. "If you give me away to this filthy town's authority, I will find a way to get back at you. Don't doubt that for even one single heartbeat."

A new outburst of hearty laughter answered his threat. "Empty promises, Brother. Of old, you were standing behind your direful threats, at least." Another wide smirk. "I will be back and with no company. Trust me on that. Fancy to hear more silly stories."

Ogteah shut his eyes in frustration. When he opened them again, Sondakwa's broad back was already dissolving into the darkness.

"To think of you living among the savages," the trailing voice was the last remainder, the open mockery of it. "Must suit you well, all things considered."

CHAPTER 22

The aroma of the medicine was thick, strangely pleasant in its heavy consistency. Ononta clasped the bowl to her chest, afraid to make it overturn.

"Where have you been all night?"

Her father's voice rang hoarsely, rasping with cough. He used to have a deep, beautiful voice, a wonderfully measured way of speaking, such a pleasure to listen to. But not anymore.

Her chest squeezed. "Drink the medicine, Father," she said quietly. "It's time."

He straightened obediently, doing this with an effort but on his own. At least that. She knelt beside him, ready to support.

"Did you manage to sleep through the night?" she whispered, unwilling to disturb the light snoring of the elderly woman on the mat beside the fire stones, another figure sprawling on the opposite bunk.

The opaque dawn spread evenly along the corridor, pouring its misty light into the shadowed compartments, but after the day of the ceremony and with the fields requiring no more attention than to keep the sown soil safe, the townsfolk, or at least the Deer Clan longhouse's dwellers, allowed themselves to sleep into the dawn. Even the women among them, such an unusual occurrence. Field duties or not, the midmorning meals needed to be cooked. Yet, no one seemed in a hurry to stir.

The wish to roll her eyes or, at least, groan aloud welled. Sleep, the luxury she hadn't enjoyed since the night before, when all was still simple and understandable, unpleasant yes, with no means to go home, but understandable and familiar all the same. The journey back home would happen, eventually. Either Father would get well, or someone else would come to escort them and help them along. Even the wild notion of her friend, the girl who wasn't afraid of anything and who could walk the woods, scan or navigate raging waters like a man, the girl who claimed that she, Ononta, should take it all into her own hands by taking her father and sailing home all by herself, made sense at the time. Oh, what blissful days those were, when she and Tsutahi had wandered away from the town and its gossipy eyes, working on her, Ononta's, surviving skills. She had almost believed that it would be possible. And why not? Tsutahi did make her practice, with paddle and other tools, did supervise her study of navigating one's way in the river, even though those were only the calmer parts of it.

It was all so pleasant and satisfying, so gratifying to be able to do things she was held to be too delicate or too precious to handle. Oh, yes, they would be surprised back home, even if they didn't come to rescue her. Her family, her uncles or cousins, did they forget her, or her father's, existence? And Atuye? Did she cherish a hope that he would sense her plight, somehow, would know that she was in trouble and in need of his help?

Well, he did this, came out of nowhere, the most welcome presence. Oh, but how astounded she was to run into him just like that back on the ceremonial grounds. Dazed, amazed, elated beyond reason. He came to rescue her!

Shaking her head, she held the bowl to her father's lips, making it as easy as possible for the sick man to consume its contents. He was not even wincing at the bitter taste or the repulsive smell anymore, used to drinking all sorts of revolting brews by now, his main nourishment these days. Still the fact that he sat upright and on his own was encouraging. Was he beginning to recover his strength?

"Thank you, Daughter," he whispered, his upper body shaking, holding the cough in. She hurried to reach for another bowl, full to the brim with fresh water this time.

"Drink this too, Father."

He shook his head, shutting his eyes in exhaustion, leaning his back against the bark of the wall. *In a little while,* the agonized twist of his wasted features said.

She put the bowl down, numb with tiredness, craving for the opportunity to crawl toward one of the vacant mats and fall asleep, for a whole moon preferably. Not to think of anything, people or children, or strange happenings, unusual behavior of friends she thought she knew or those whom she held to be her friends. Were Atuye and Tsutahi still arguing out there, in the spreading gray of the dawn, whispering ardently, with much gesturing? Or had the exhausted girl gone back to the longhouse of her hosts, to try and settle her children to sleep, the rebellious little Tsami who had made them all so worried at night? And what was about Atuye's brothers, both of them?

She shivered, then gave her attention back to the haggardness of her father's face, a mere shadow of his impressively broad, pleasantly wrinkled, brown façade. He was watching her, eyes narrow with sickness and exhaustion but glittering with attentive affection all the same.

"What troubles you, little one?"

She pressed her lips tight. "Nothing, Father." But her gaze dropped on its own, to stay on the soaked, rumpled hide that spread over the planks of his pallet, begging for thorough washing, if not a more drastic treatment.

"What did you do out there at night?" His voice trembled, struggling against the cough, yet holding enough fatherly authority to make her uneasy.

"I... well, my friend, her boy ran away and we were busy looking for him." She shivered at the mere memory. "It was so scary. He got lost wandering the woods and well, he was very lucky. The Great Spirits themselves were watching over him, to send good people his way and just as he was about to be devoured."

Oh, but Tsami's story did make the hair of her nape rise, the way he kept talking in a frantic rush, breathless and as though unable to stop. About that mother coyote, set on scaring him off that tree and into her fangs, so ugly and nasty and threatening, growling like a mountain lion and worse, determined to eat him right there on the cliff. His voice, usually light, chatty and boasting, so cute in its determination to tell everything that came into his head and to be listened to as well, now leaped to high-pitched hysterical tones, dropping to a terrified whispering every now and then, unable to stop, unable to relax, telling about the man who came to rescue him, only to be attacked and have his arm torn into pieces. He couldn't stop talking about that arm, and then the knife, and the coyote cut into shreds. It was difficult to take his entire story in, not with Atuye and the boy's mother talking in whispers above her head, as she huddled the little thing close to her and tried to make him feel better. He looked so ruffled, so discomposed and upset, not the Tsami she had come to know, to love and to spoil through the half a moon of their acquaintance. Oh, but the poor boy was so badly shaken!

"He was so scared, poor little thing," she said, peering at her father, forgetting her qualms. "And his mother, oh but she was desperate and afraid. And she is never afraid, not Tsutahi. Still this time she was just terrified."

Another memory that made her heart squeeze. Tsutahi, who could be angered into rushed actions, but who was never, never afraid, always acting, always grimly determined, in control, not letting anything, not even her lack of hearing, to get in her way, yet suddenly frightened senseless, terrified, twice over the same day. Oh, but she still didn't understand what it all had to do with Atuye's brother.

"Are they here now? Well and unharmed?"

"Yes, oh yes, thanks all the great and small spirits for that!"

Her father's eyes narrowed again. "And Atuye? Was he with you, looking for the lost boy?"

Taken aback by the open scrutiny of his gaze, she blushed. "He... yes, of course. He was very helpful. He and Sondakwa went out and helped her find Tsami. They were with her out there, in the woods, when I stayed to keep the baby."

Her resentment welled again, fueled by the mere sound of her words. At the time it felt natural to stay behind. When Tsutahi had tucked the little bundle into her hands, she didn't think anything of it. Her friend couldn't run all over the dangerous night woods clutching a baby to her chest, could she? And it was Atuye's duty to accompany her, man that he was. She wouldn't have thought of offering her escorting services even if there was no baby to keep an eye on.

And yet, the moment she took upon herself that less glorious of the duties, she had been forgotten so thoroughly, it hurt. Atuye turned all leader-like, giving orders, convincing the girl to be patient. Knowing her friend, Ononta didn't hold her hopes high as to his chances of success. But then the terrible scene with his eldest of brothers unfolded, and while watching it all with her breath bated and her stomach clenched, worrying about Tsutahi but somehow, somehow feeling bad for Atuye's brother as well – how cornered he looked, how beaten as some point – she knew that she didn't want to be left behind, caring for babies, dismissed as unimportant.

The feeling that didn't improve throughout the agonized waiting, pacing back and forth along the poles of the palisade and around tobacco plots, rocking the baby back to sleep every time he had awoken to demand the food she didn't have; spent, angered, exhausted. But it wasn't fair, it wasn't! Girls didn't rush into the woods on rescue missions fitting for men, yet Tsutahi was a young girl too, of her own age if not younger, and no one questioned her right to be in the thick of it. While she, Ononta, was left behind, dismissed as insignificant, with not a glance spared for her, not an encouraging word of comfort. And she was involved too, wasn't she? She did love Tsami, did worry about him! Yet, it was all about Tsutahi and her troubles. Come to think of it, it had been so through this entire afternoon.

Oh yes, since his sudden appearance, all Atuye did was to fuss around her friend, to fret about her troubles, shielding her against possible or even imagined threats, attacking his own brother and with most ridiculous accusations only because the girl said she might have seen him somewhere; dying too, of all things. Ridiculous, but Atuye believed her, while paying no attention to his childhood friend and her troubles, her sick father, her longing for home. He was as nice and as friendly as always, caring, patient, considerate, the Atuye she always knew, but his mind just wasn't there. He didn't truly care about her plight and her needs. Tsutahi's troubles gained the entirety of his attention.

And no, it didn't get any better when the night began wearing off and they came back at long last, Atuye, Tsutahi and the boy. Hugging the little thing with force, glad to be free of the hungry baby and his loudest of complaints, she had listened to the hair-raising tales spoken in a frenzied gush, the child terrified and excited all at once, shaken badly, overwrought; still a part of her mind dwelled on the grownups' ardent murmuring, with Atuye and the girl arguing passionately, in loud whispers, overriding each other, about perils of leaving, dangers of staying, and everything in between, with bad spirits or people or wounds mentioned more than once, and something about old wars. At some point his arms were pressing her shoulders in a comforting but also somehow not completely appropriate way, containing the girl's visible trembling, but Ononta wondered what Tsutahi's formidable man, Tsami's father, would have said if he had seen it. And he was yet to tell her, Ononta, something, to spare her a glance or venture a word of encouragement or appreciation. It wasn't as though she had slept snugly while they were out there looking for Tsami. But for her, Tsutahi wouldn't have been able to come along with them at all, not with the demanding screamer that her baby was.

Something the girl had actually understood and appreciated, unlike her childhood annoyance of a friend. She had thanked her, Ononta, lavishly and was still stealing glances full of gratitude and appreciation, mixed with affection aplenty. She did appreciate what Ononta had done. It was only that annoying Atuye who didn't care for anything his most loyal of friends felt or did.

"Listen to me, little one." Her father's withered palm wrapped around her wrist, dry and shriveled, startling her from her unhappy reverie. "This boy, Atuye, he is a good boy, a positive young man with great future ahead of him. I know you were fond of him, always." The weary eyes studied her, straining, narrow with an effort. "It's good that he came now, good that he worried enough to travel here and see for himself that no harm came to you despite our delay. I appreciate this young man's sense of responsibility, his loyalty, his devotion."

A brief pause ensued as the man fought down another outburst of vicious coughing. Ononta hurried to refill the bowl with more water.

"And yet, you must not act recklessly, out of longing or despair, little one. If you have feelings for this boy, leave it for later to decide, to act upon it when we are back home." The burning palm tightened around her wrist, surprisingly strong, encouraging, touching in its ardency to relay its message. "I'm sure your mother and the Grandmother of our longhouse won't be opposed to sending the customary cookies his way. They will be only too glad to do it, if you feel that this boy is the man of your future. It won't be difficult to convince them." Another barking cough cut the words short, the effort to dominate it tearing at her heart. "But wait... wait until then. Don't throw yourself into his arms out of loneliness and your longing for home."

Her cheeks were burning so fiercely, she was afraid the heat they generated would wake the other sleepers up. To tear her arm from her father's grip proved difficult, a feeble attempt on her part.

"I'm not... I don't..." she muttered, choking on her words, as though her own ability to speak was impaired with sickness of the chest. "I didn't... nothing inappropriate, I would never..."

The cracked lips were stretching into a semblance of a smile. "I know you didn't cherish any inappropriate feelings, nor did inappropriate deeds, little one. You are not such a little girl anymore, and your feelings are appropriate, all of them. It's just that I don't want you to decide, to do something in a rush, out of longing for home and your family and friends, *all* your friends, and not just one of them."

"I... I..." Wrenching her hands free at long last, she brought them to her burning face, wishing to run away, to think it all through again. Even her father, sick and fighting for his life, saw through her. Oh, how embarrassing! But she hadn't done anything wrong on this long night of the waiting. She hadn't done anything at all, while the others were busy acting, saving the boy, saving themselves. The tears were hot, streaming in unstoppable outpour, threatening to drown her. "I didn't, didn't do anything," she wailed, burying her face in the protective screen of her palms. "I didn't..."

His hands were trembling badly as they embraced her, the desperate effort evident in the rasping of his breath, in the strangled cough and the whizzing. Nevertheless, she snuggled there, in the familiar warm safety. Father always sheltered her, had always been there for her.

"I didn't, didn't do anything inappropriate," she whimpered. "And I didn't.... didn't think. Atuye, he is not what I thought... he didn't... I don't know what to do!"

The people around were stirring, awoken by their semi-loud scene, she was sure of it. Still to have Father's strength to rely upon was good, too good to leave the safety of his arms just yet. Even though they were trembling worse than before. She pulled away gently, helping him back into his previous reclining position, snatching a folded blanket and tucking it behind his back, to cushion the hurtful support of the hard bark.

"He came to take us back home, didn't he?" The viciousness of the cough was subdued after another drained bowl of water.

Ononta found it safer to just shrug.

"Do you want to go with him?"

Another shrug. But it was getting ridiculous, with her working her shoulders up and down, and her eyes drilling holes in the planks of the bunk he reclined on.

She forced her gaze up. "He will take us home, yes. You will recover faster in Mother's and our longhouse's womenfolk's care."

He nodded, shutting his eyes in exhaustion.

"I think you better try to sleep again, Father. The medicine, it will help you to do that now."

"Do not commit to this journey on account of me, little one," he muttered, overcome with the influence of the medicine, drowsy and sagging, not resisting her efforts to lie him down upon the wrinkled pelt. "I'm cared for and safeguarded here as much as back home. Do not let it influence..."

The murmuring trailed off, with his exhausted spirit drifting into the blissful oblivion, to stay there for some time, for the duration of the medicine's effect at least. Hopefully more, she thought. Oh, but he needed to rest and gather his strength back!

Splashing a little of the water over her puffy face, she made her way out hurriedly, before more inhabitants of their longhouse stirred from their dream worlds. No, no! To face any of them was to ask too much of her, not after the difficult night. The solitude of the crispy dawn and its freshness were what she needed the most, the lightness of the early breeze, the delicate tobacco plants wet with dew, caressing her fingers.

The nearest plots were where Atuye and Tsutahi had argued in the grayish of the pre-dawn mist, before the girl had taken her shaken, exhausted child back into the longhouse, carrying him in the crook of her free arm, tilting badly to do that with the baby tucked in the other. Was Atuye still there, pacing angrily?

Apparently, he was. Not pacing as expected, but arguing again. With one of his older siblings this time.

She neared them hesitantly, not feeling comfortable in his elder brother's vicinity, knowing him only briefly, a saucy, short-tempered, loud-mouthed man. Well, this time Sondakwa had been talking in surprisingly hushed tones, with urgency written all over his broad eager-looking face. It was as though he was anxious to convince Atuye of something, as though seeking Atuye's approval, or at least cooperation. Ridiculous!

At the sound of her footsteps they both glanced up, their frowns rivaling the grimness of the winter sky. She swallowed, but pressed on. Enough was enough, and she had earned her right to be a part of their dealings.

"Well, do whatever you want to, Brother," Sondakwa was saying, shrugging her presence off with an indifferent lift of his wide shoulders. "I won't be wasting my breath on any more talking. I have no time for this." The man's lips twisted contemptuously, just a thinly pressed line. "Go and dance your attendance on the wild fox, listen to her stories, bestow more children on her if you are that taken. I bet she will throw her man away for a treasure like you." The chuckle that marred the freshness of the morning air reminded her of the man she knew, if mainly by reputation, the scornful, quick to pick fights person.

Atuye's grim face, anything but relaxed before, stiffened into a dangerous mold, the harsh lines running down each side of his pursed mouth deepening, painting an alarming picture.

"Do not talk about her or me, or anyone else who is involved," he rasped in a low, growling voice. "Go and save our treacherous brother if you are so eager. It will serve you well to be betrayed by him later on, as I know he will do."

He drew a deep breath in a visible effort to calm himself. Out of habit, her heart went out for him. He was so eager to control himself, to behave in the most dignified manner, always. So different from the other boys, even though he didn't shrink from fights. Her childhood friend, the best of companions. Why was she so angry with him anyway?

"He is a traitor, he is!" Atuye was saying, his old earnestness flowing back, softening the atypical harshness. "He didn't deny any of Tsutahi's words, did he? He knows her; he told us so with his own lips! Therefore, her words proved truthful. Is it not enough for you? It is for me, you know." His arms came up, almost imploring. "Leave him to his own devices, if you feel it is wrong to turn him in, even though he is not even our full brother and not a real part of our clan or town and community anymore. Forget him on that stupid shore, if you must, but don't go with him, don't help him! It is against everything we were brought up to believe. It offends our common sense, if not our sense of right and wrong."

Sondakwa's eyebrows were climbing suggestively high. "Against what we were brought up to believe? Oh please, Little Brother. You must remember Father's lifetime ambition and work better than this!"

"I do remember Father's words, each one of them!" exclaimed Atuye, controlling himself no more. "He didn't believe in betrayal, and this is what Ogteah has done. By fighting for the other side he has betrayed everything and everyone, his family, his people, Father's memory, everything that is good and worthwhile to live for. You know it as well as I do," he added in a quieter voice, managing to regain some of his equilibrium back.

The achievement that Sondakwa didn't seem to notice. "Stop yelling, you stupid buck!" he hissed, taking a step forward, threatening. "Want to bring the entire town here in order to make me change my mind?" The air swished loudly, drawn in with much force. "Go away, Little Brother, go and do some growing up before jumping to judge your elders and betters."

Another sway forward didn't make Atuye retreat. Ononta felt her chest surging with pride. His elder brother or not, Atuye was not the type to be intimidated, not when he believed in something.

Sondakwa's mirthless grin reflected the same thought. "Just don't be tempted to do something stupid," he breathed, shaking his head as he did. "You will regret it dearly if you do, putting yourself in a most foolish light, achieving nothing besides this. Her allegations and silly stories of ghosts from that stupid war of theirs can't be proved. It will be her word against his, and think who will be listened to more readily. Not your wild fox, for certain." The man was turning away, still shrugging. "I will be taking his canoe, so you will have ours, to sail at your leisure with whatever human cargo you care to put in there." The narrowing eyes shifted to Ononta. "Talk some sense into your friend, will you? Have him taking you home as he intended at the first place. The only sensible way of behavior." The amusement fled, replaced with the previous sternness. "Forget what you heard here just now. And on the previous evening. It was all silly chatter, with no bones to it. Let Atuye take you and your father home. That will be the most sensible thing to do." His footsteps made a plopping sound on the wet earth soaked with dew. "Tell your wild fox to relax as well, Little Brother. Her bad *uki* won't be anywhere around to threaten her with more promises of revenge." His chuckle barely reached them, faint but still distinct. "I've yet to hear what she did to him that made him so thirsty for her blood."

Speechless, they just stood there, saying nothing, watching the wide back disappearing behind the poles of the fence, where the passageway between the two rows of palisade had begun. Atuye's breathing was coming in loudly, marring the crispiness of the newly born day. Tearing her eyes off the glimmering poles, she glanced at him, taking in the unnatural harshness of his taut features, the stiffness of his back, exaggeratedly upright, uncompromisingly straight, a statement.

"What was he talking about?" she asked quietly, perturbed. "Is it about Ogteah and what he did, what Tsutahi told us he did? But it can't be, you know it can't. You didn't believe her tales of him being dead, a wondering *uki* and all, did you?"

He whirled at her and for a wild moment she thought he would strike her, or at least wave his hands threateningly and yell at the top of his voice. Aghast, she just stared.

"Leave it, Ononta, just leave it!" he shouted, making the second part of her worry come true. "It has nothing to do with you!"

Two red spots were glaring upon the sharpness of his cheeks, and his eyes glittered wildly, not completely sane. She took a step back, but her anger kept rising, splashing in force, giving her courage.

"Don't yell at me," she demanded, pleased to hear her voice firm, even if unnaturally high, pitched in an ugly way. "I did nothing wrong. You were the one who acted wildly, arguing with everyone. It's not my fault, it isn't!" Her words began jamming into one another, colliding, their torrent impossible to stop now. "You act as though I do not exist and don't matter, and it is not right. I don't deserve... I don't..." The sobs were taking over again, and she stopped, hating her inability to talk reasonably when upset. Tsutahi wouldn't have broken into tears; she would be flaring at him, maybe even cursing him instead.

"Stop that," he was saying tiredly, in a more reasonable voice, not taking a step forward or attempting to comfort her with anything but the helplessness of his words. "Don't cry, Ononta. Please don't." He brought his arms up, at long last, but only to wave them in the air imploringly. It would have touched her, but for her own desperation and plight. "I... I'm sorry I screamed at you, I shouldn't have, yes. I'm sorry. But it all got so mad, so unreasonable, so dreadfully complicated." Another motion of his spread arms relayed his frustration most clearly. "I don't understand what is going on anymore. Your friend..." His face darkened, closed somewhat abruptly. "She didn't make any more sense than my brother did just now, her decisions as strange. And, well," he shrugged helplessly, bringing his arms down all of a sudden, to hang there as though he didn't know what else could be done with them, "I wish we never have come here, all of us, you and your father, as well. This town makes us all behave wildly. Even the bad *uki* that made your father sick. It's bad and I wish I knew how to make it right for all of us, those who deserve the goodwill of the Great Spirits."

She watched his pleasantly high forehead furrowing in the fashion she loved, his old sincere self again. "What will you do?" she asked quietly.

He shrugged with clear lack of enthusiasm. "I'll take you and your father home."

"And what about Tsutahi?"

His face darkened again. "She won't let me take her away from here. She is the most adamant girl I ever met."

And you just found it out now, she thought, not amused in the least.

"Will she sail on her own?"

"She can't!" He was peering at her, clearly upset. The girl must have stated the same thing, she reflected, her thoughts refusing to organize, floating in a strange haze.

"If anyone can do it, it's Tsutahi. She is the most independent person I ever met. She feels at home out there in the woods, more than many people I know of. She can find her way around any trail, any forest. She feels at home there like people in the corridors of their longhouses. The only place she feels bad at is in here, inside the palisade fence and in the longhouses."

He was listening avidly, drinking her words like a child told a wonderful story. For some reason it irritated her. Was his brother right in his taunting, in his baiting remarks about Atuye's possible willingness to try and take Tsutahi away from her man?

"It doesn't make sense," he said after a brief pause, when sure that she wouldn't be sharing any more revelations, she surmised. "Here among strangers, yes. But she can't be behaving in this way among her own people, her town, her longhouse and clan."

"That's how much you know." Suddenly needing to get away –

that privacy, didn't she go out looking for it in the first place? – she turned around, watching muffled silhouettes of people moving next to the bark walls, tending the morning fires. "I need to go back to my father, see how he feels."

"You just came from there," he protested, rushing to catch up with her, falling into her step, anxious to keep up.

Such a change, she reflected mirthfully. Who is running after whom now?

"I need to stay with him, keep him company. With your and her mess I left him for too long unattended." It came out as an outright accusation, but she didn't care. It felt good to feel so indifferent. No feelings, no anxiety, to nagging thoughts.

"I will be taking you both home," he repeated, not sounding highly convincing.

"I'm not sure about that," she retorted. "If Tsutahi will stay to wait for her man to return – now with your brothers gone it's a fair possibility, isn't it? – then I will stay here as well. I'm her only friend, her and Tsami's, and I will not be leaving them both behind."

He stiffened dangerously again, nothing but a rigid form walking next to her, emanating coldness. "And how would you propose to return later on, after her man bothered to return? If your father doesn't get better, you will be stuck here as badly as you are now, with your friend gone as well, leaving *you* behind."

"I'll manage," she said, glancing at the brightening sky, happy to see Father Sun gaining power, delighted to return to their world after his nighttime journey yet again, as elated as she felt about it and maybe as lightheaded now that the decision was reached. "She taught me to find my way in the woods, and she won't be leaving me behind as well. She'll make sure I reach home. She is a true friend."

CHAPTER 23

The filthiness of the last days receded the moment he spotted his brother's broad shoulders in one of the canoes that were kissing the slanting shore, progressing with the lively current. All the streams that drained into the huge water basin of Ossossane seemed to be the same, such forceful, energetic tides.

Pushing his way through the crowding people, Atuye tried to keep his impatience down, aware that he did so with less consideration than of yore. What happened to the polite, mindful youth, a warrior of little summers, aware of his junior status? He didn't know, didn't wish to try and find out what change. Too many things, and he wasn't ready to face most of those. Enough that on the day before, he was involved in a violent incident, the one that made the leader of their delegation, Honorable Tsineka himself, confine him to their camp for the rest of that day, while hinting that another such incident would see him being sent back home in disgrace. Oh Mighty Spirits, but was he turning into Sondakwa, or worse yet, Ogteah?

It was the same day upon which he had learned that his brother was on his way here, expected in Ossossane soon. One good turn, because the rest of it was so frustratingly bad.

Peering at the nearing canoes, he frowned, remembering the clearing and the bean game they were watching on that same accursed afternoon, idle and at ease, back from yet another hunting party and not required to attend the elders' talks.

"There is a good reason why our gatherings are held here in Ossossane. A very good reason, indeed," one of the locals was saying, perching on the trunk of a fallen tree, watching the players with marked disinterest. He was as young as Atuye, but more sturdily built, having a quality of an angry male deer to his posture, a dangerous specimen if aroused. Atuye hated the sight of him. "Think about it. First the gathering of two nations, an unheard of affair that the elders of our town worked hard to make happen. Then—"

"The elders of his town. Would you listen to that one?" Neither of the players bothered to straighten up, but one of the men chuckled loudly, waving his hand in the air, making the edge of the folded blanket quiver, threatening to scatter a pile of beans it hosted, still high enough as the game was in its opening stages.

"What's so funny about what I said?" The youth upon the log stiffened, his previously slightly bored indifference dissolving in the depth of his frown. Such lousy pretense, reflected Atuye, his insides bubbling with rage as well. The elders of Ossossane working hard to make the First Gathering happen? How ridiculous, how audacious!

"Your claim that it was that silly town up there that worked hard to achieve anything. That's what made me laugh." Leaning forward to examine his throw, the marked stones scattering upon the blanket in spectacular disarray, the player chuckled again, not bothering to look at the man he was goading. "The Ossossane elders won't work hard, no matter on what. They will rather go around and claim other people's achievements." Another good-natured chuckle. "Must be easier to do that, even if less fulfilling."

The reaction to the man's careless statement was mixed, from open amusement to dour scowls. Naturally, as his audience even if casually mixed, presented a thorough blend of visitors and locals, with the Bears and the Cord represented more heavily but not by much. The Deer and the Rock might have been taking their time traveling, leaving the others, more punctual Wyandot kicking their heels on the shores of the windy bay, still enough of the newcomers were already here, restless and wary, to a degree.

The Freshwater Sea, thought Atuye, shooting a glance at the hill behind which the wind was coming in gusts, fierce enough to make the tossing game into a challenge. Such a chilly, aloof body of water, formidable, grim, not very hospitable. No bluish friendliness of the Sparkling Lake, no lighthearted brightness. This northern Great Lake had watched the newcomers through a veil of barely hidden displeasure, not inviting or promising safety, not even after quite a few dawns spent upon its unfriendly shores. Why did they have to agree to hold yet another meeting here?

Honorable Tsineka said it was necessary to have a permanent place of gathering, the location that would make people think of the Wyandot Union with the mere mention of its name. The savages did it too, the old warrior claimed. They kept gathering in the exactly same place for many decades by now. They knew it was making their union stronger, permanently existing.

But why Ossossane? Atuye would ask. Why this presumptuous, haughty town that had given Father much trouble through the First Great Gathering of their people? It was so far away from their own lands and these of the Deer and the Rock; it wasn't situated as conveniently in between everyone as the savage league's capital was.

He would gather his courage and ask those questions, tired after yet another day of incessant rowing, then pitching a camp, helping around, never stopping to rest. It exhausted his physical power, this reluctance to rest and relax, but it gave him something he welcomed most eagerly – it left him with no time to think, to reflect, to remember. Such bliss. After the insanity of Onentisati, that Rock People's town that made everyone he knew behave unreasonably, with no logic and no sense, simple tasks of an escorting warrior looked like Sky World, so satisfying and bright!

Quitting Onentisati saw him finding the delegation he had abandoned earlier, at his brother's instigation, with much effort, a true investment on his part, hurrying to catch up with the people he shouldn't have left at the first place, rushing after them as though it was a matter of life and death. They must let him explain, they must understand. What he did was foolish, reckless, unfitting, to leave the way he had left, listening to the troublemaker of his elder brother. The price he was forced to pay was high enough, culminating in dreadful confusion, the terrible suspicion of his own inadequacy, lack of competence, even of courage and open-mindedness. Why had it all have to happen to him? Did he deserve it, his brother's and Ononta's disappointment, their barely hidden disdain at what they felt was his close-mindedness, his need to stick to the accepted way of doing things? Since stepping inside that accursed Onentisati he was made to question everything he believed in; he, who always strove to behave with logic and reason, to do the best by what he had been taught. And yet, those two dawns in that Rock People's town had proven him wrong, not in his eyes but in the eyes of the people he cherished. Sondakwa behaved unreasonably, and so did Ononta, but they made him feel as though it was he who should have changed his ways.

Ridiculous, but they stuck to their attitude, Sondakwa by taking their traitor of a brother and going away, never coming back, and Ononta by sticking to her resolution to stay, as adamant as she used to be yielding before. Such glaring change, brought about by none other than a strange foreign girl with outlandish ways and no hearing abilities, the mere memory of which still made his insides tighten in the most annoying of manners.

Had her wandering man returned by now? Had he taken her back home, leaving silly Ononta behind, all alone again? Would serve her right, that one. Another familiar thought that didn't make him ashamed anymore.

Concentrating back on the players and the man who was talking nonsense, such an annoying piece of spoiled meat, he pushed the thoughts of Ononta and her outlandish friend away. It'd been close to full moon, more than twenty dawns, since he had seen them last. Time to forget until he arrived back home. Then, if she didn't return as yet, a likely possibility, he might be inclined to go and rescue her, to behave with a courtesy she didn't deserve.

"Our elders did not claim achievements that weren't theirs and theirs alone!" The young man was no longer sitting, on his feet now and mighty upset, his voice rising high. "How dare you say something like that? Our elders did most of the work organizing that first gathering of our people and they did so now as well, sent messages and invited people in." The nostrils of his prominent nose widened fiercely, relating the depth of his indignation. "The Bear People were the ones eager to take the credit, to claim achievements that weren't theirs. That leader of theirs died conveniently fast, making it easy for their storytellers to let him have all the glory." The scornfulness of his snort shook the air. "And an inglorious death it was, so one hears. Dropping dead just like that, with no cause and no reason. Maybe he grew afraid of something."

That drew many voices to rise in protest or consent, the crowding men composed of many different elements, from all four nations this time. Kicking their heels for close to a quarter of a moon left them with no better option than to mingle and fraternize, to befriend each other even if grudgingly, to engage in throwing games and mutual hunting expeditions. A purposeful goal? Atuye would wonder from time to time. Yet, now he felt nothing of the sort, choking on the intensity of his rage, the all-consuming fire of fury. But how dared this man!

"Take it back," he cried out when able to control his vocal abilities, at long last. "Take back every word of what you said!"

Somehow his words overcame the general hum, or maybe he was shouting too loudly. He didn't know, didn't care. The face of the man who dared talking dirty about Father was very close now, startled but unafraid, not stepping back, not trying to avoid, eyes narrow, measuring, lips pursed. People around them fell silent.

"Take back what you just said," repeated Atuye, not recognizing his own voice but in the corner of his mind wondering where he had heard such a growling voice before. "Take it all back or I will be putting your words back there myself, with my fist if not my weaponry."

The young man was still watching him, puzzled.

"Come, relax both of you, young bucks," said someone, just a voice from the crowd.

"Yes, yes, go spill your bubbling somewhere else, do something useful." This time, it was the player, the one who had goaded the Ossossane rat before. "One can't even play a bean game in peace."

Atuye paid these words and their originator no attention,

daring not to take his eyes off his rival, who was glaring back as fiercely, not about to step aside, or to comply with the uncompromising demand, for that matter. It was time to back away. He was foolish, losing his self-restraint in such way. Foolish and unworthy. A somewhat familiar feeling by now.

The face in front of him twisted, reflecting derision, too obvious, too near the surface to miss. The youth knew what he has been thinking.

"No need to take the truth that hard. You better—"

The rest of the words crumbled, pushed back in by Atuye's fist. It crushed against his opponent's mouth, and he felt the pain most acutely, rolling all the way from his knuckles and up his arm, spilling into his elbow, setting it on fire. Such a strange sensation.

He tried to make sense out of it, his vision peculiarly clear, noting details, the brilliance of the grass still wet after the previous day's showers, the holes in the dusty earth, the man upon it twisting, marring its purity with unrealistically bright crimson sprinkles.

People were beside them now, many people. He shook their restraining hands off, paying them little attention, still fascinated with what was happening upon the ground. The youth he hit pushed himself up but was wavering on all fours, dribbling more crimson. Many hands leapt to help him to his feet.

"Are you all right?" someone was asking, a familiar voice. The man he had rowed with together on their last leg of their journey, a friendly presence.

"Yes, yes… I'm sorry… I shouldn't have…" This time his voice had no roaring or growling in it, only pitiful indecision. "I need to go."

"I'll take him back to our camp." His benefactor's words rang with enough firmness and authority to draw people's attention, he knew, not daring to look around, not now. The implications of what happened kept surfacing as his rage cooled into emptiness, leaving him more at a loss than before, with only a revoltingly bitter taste in his mouth. "I know him personally. He is a good boy, picked by our elder. He will behave and will not try to avoid the judgment."

The judgment? Oh yes, what he did warranted that, didn't it?

"What made you do this?" the man was asking, walking by his side easily, with no misgivings. "He was an annoying piece of excrement, I'll give him that. Still to break his jaw, or try to do that, was a bit harsh, wasn't it? Not worthy of you getting in trouble on account of it."

He felt it impolite to respond with no words at all. "What will they do to me?"

The man shrugged. "Maybe nothing. It depends on the injury of that other youth. If he didn't get hurt badly, then you will get away from it with no price to pay." The accompanied chuckle held enough mirth, caressing the heaviness of the afternoon air. It seemed that more rain was in store for them. "Our Honorable Elder won't be pleased, and certainly not with someone like you, a good, promising boy that you are. He was talking nasty about your father, yes, but it's still not a good reason to start shaking your fists. Not a respectable person's behavior."

Unless sons of our father, reflected Atuye gloomily, shaken to the core at the very thought. Was he becoming like Sondakwa or Ogteah? Oh Mighty Spirits, but what was wrong with him!

"Your arm is all right? You are holding it strangely."

"Oh, that!" He forced his mind to concentrate on the pain. It was still there, pumping around his wrist or maybe higher up, difficult to ignore. It provided welcome distraction. "I think maybe it got hurt, somehow."

"Let me see." By that time they were back in their people's camp, quite deserted at this part of the day but for a few loudly talking newcomers, a regular occurrence. People were arriving in this valley between the shores at the rate of tens and more per day, slower traveling delegators or just curious visitors. No one wished to miss the Second Great Gathering, larger than the first, more important. Four nations! Would their leaders truly manage to unite all Wyandot? Father would have been pleased to see that.

Father! The thought made his anger return with redoubled strength. But how dared they talk about Father like that, to not only take his achievements away from him, but to accuse him of… He clenched his fists tight, and welcomed the pain it brought to his damaged wrist. If only Sondakwa…

And now his brother was here, only a day later, leaping out of the smaller canoe, exuding health and wellbeing, the wideness of his frame as opposed to the cheerful agility of his movements impossible to mistake. Atuye didn't fight the urge to push forward. The rest of the new arrivals, twelve men all in all, sweaty and dust-covered, bearing witness to the journey behind, were dragging their vessels out, chattering between themselves.

"Little Brother!" As always Sondakwa held nothing back, forgetful of their previous quarrel or indifferent to it. Typical! "I was hoping to run into you here." A mighty pat on his back nearly pushed Atuye off his feet, reminding him how strong his brother was, so sturdily built, bulky but fit, never clumsy or running to fat. "What you've been up to, you wild thing?"

"I could ask you the same." Grinning with surprising ease – but it was good to see his brother and so far away from home! – he stabilized himself using his good arm against the nearest branch of a tree. "What are you doing here? I didn't expect…"

The circumstances of their parting back in Onentisati, those twenty or more dawns ago, surfaced, marring his elation.

"Me neither." Sondakwa's smile was wide, free of shadows or guilt. "And certainly not with the purpose I arrive here with now." The man shook his head, still chuckling. "The wildest storyteller…" Then he sobered all at once. "But that's for later, Brother. Not here in this clamor and the commotion. Do you think they have something worthwhile to offer us, the travelers? We rowed with no pause through the last day and night, and if someone here bothered to offer us a warm meal none of us would be opposed or offended. Would we?" His companions, still busy with their gear, nodded good-naturedly, none of their faces familiar, which was strange. Where *did* Sondakwa come from?

"Our mid-morning meal was good, made out of the fattest buck," he said, tucking his puzzlement away, for later consideration. "We hunted it not far away from the camp. It provided a welcome diversity." Glancing around, he frowned. "You will have to wait for our leaders to return, though. The women will not agree to warm those pots before it's time for the organized evening meal of the leaders."

"Oh, well, snacks will do nicely, for now." Another look at his companions. "Will you do without me, brothers?"

Their nods were brief, matter-of-fact.

"Come." A light sway of the formidable head invited Atuye to push his way out and away from the crowding. "Show me around that mighty camp of yours. They say it's a sight to behold, all our people gathering together. Larger than Father's First Gathering."

"They say that, yes." The familiar deep, rolling voice had had a calming effect. He felt like smiling for the first time since, oh since many dawns and nights. "It's been hectic all around, and people do quarrel more often than not. The warriors, that is." He shifted his wrist, now encased in a tightly wrapped piece of leather, to ease the pain. "The elders manage to have dignified talks, even though their veiled messages are shooting like arrows, quite a few per every few heartbeats, when they are in the right mood." Talking like that made him feel better, less of the useless hothead he was afraid he was turning into. "Not very peaceful meetings. Father would have conducted it in a better way."

Sondakwa's sigh was surprisingly loud. "Oh, yes, Father would have managed it better. I wish I hadn't missed the First Gathering all those summers ago." Then a light chuckle escaped the generous lips that were already quivering, twisting into a naughtiest of grins. "Plenty of stories about this gathering plagued my ears, too many if you ask me. The last half a moon was highly enlightening, Brother, very informative indeed."

Somehow he knew where this all was leading. "Ogteah kept you entertained while escaping Onentisati?" It still came with an effort, the need to utter his detested half-brother's name aloud, and with pretended indifference at that. Still, so far away from this town and all its citizens and guests the wave of blinding rage splashed like a small ripple. What did it matter what this criminal and a traitor of a brother did or told while fleeing Rock People's lands? With the Long Tails girl by his side it was important, vital, crucial. His brother was such a terrible threat to her, according to his own words spat in such fury and lack of restrain. And yet, she had turned away from his help and attention, preferring Ononta's company and friendship, choosing to wait for her man to return, as inconsistent as only women could be. Even though she looked so different, so unique. He pushed the thought of her away, all those disturbingly vivid memories.

"Oh, yes, Ogteah was entertaining enough through our journey eastward." Sondakwa's voice trembled with uninhibited mirth, his stride wide, displaying none of the protested hunger or exhaustion. If anything his brother looked atypically perky, full of high spirits and cheer. Atuye side-glanced him briefly. "Full of stories none of us ever heard, not even Mother. About Father and his younger days. Imagine that!" The heavily lidded eyes were dancing, watching Atuye with a fair amount of challenge. "He has his sources, that wild brother of ours, the storytellers we have no access to, no chance to interrogate but as war captives." A chuckle. "Remind me to make sure of that in case the efforts to reach all sorts of peaceful solutions go to naught."

"So where is he now?" Atuye's mind didn't go past his half-sibling as yet. "Did you escort him to our town, introduce him around, vouch for his good behavior?"

"Not quite." Again this playfully wicked spark. "He has a home to return to, you know? No time for touring childhood places and memories." The ensuing pause hung, heralding more revelations. "Poor man, to row all the way across our Great Sparkling Water and with that cracked arm of his. We fixed it with a pair of sturdy sticks, but you can imagine how useless it actually was. He kept having a bad time with it, even though the swelling was gone in the end." An innocent shrug. "I dropped him off at the best crossing point, next to the Cold Bay, where our warriors always start. Still, it left him with a full day of rowing at the very least."

He tried to place these words carefully, to put them together in the way that would make sense of this tale. Ogteah's broken arm, oh yes, it looked bad enough back on that shore, even in the darkness. It was torn cruelly, too. What did they do about that, to prevent it from rotting, a most realistic threat when wild animals and their fangs were involved? And the prospective journey, eastwards, toward their home, oh yes, it would be difficult to row with such an arm, impossible even.

"What all this has to do with our Great Sparkling Water? Who crossed it and why?"

Sondakwa's grin was one of the widest. "What do you think? Our brother, of course. He has to go home at some point."

The wide face beamed at him, so very close, familiar, unbearably smug, pleased with himself. Atuye stared at it for another heartbeat.

"What... what do you mean?"

"A nice sight your face is making now, Brother." Sondakwa's laughter was as loud as it was merciless, attracting attention of passing men. "Pity you can't see it."

Atuye swallowed hard. "Stop laughing. It's not funny. Why would Ogteah attempt the crossing? He never did this before. He never warred or bothered to be involved otherwise. Why would he..." But it was turning silly, his flood of questioning. He swallowed again.

"You know what, Little Brother?" Grimacing, Sondakwa resumed his walk, some of his inappropriately high humor gone. "For one who has accused the wild man of every sin possible, from masterminding the Long Tails War to all sorts of other ways of betraying our people – as though the Long Tails have anything to do with us, but that's a different matter – you are displaying much ignorance. If you didn't know he was living among the enemy now, then how did you come by all those bizarre accusations of yours?" The squinting eyes were peering at him, openly suspicious. "You were very quick with cries of treachery and bad deeds, but whatever that wild fox has told you, if it wasn't about Ogteah's current whereabouts, I'm not sure what it was." The full lips twisted derisively. "Never take sides with occasional women against your own family, however delectable and tempting some foxes may be. It isn't wise and it doesn't pay off in the future. Women come and go unless you move into their longhouse and even then you should never forget your family and your clan, the longhouse you belong to."

The wave of resentment was forming anew, with surprising promptness and strength.

"Don't give me unasked-for advice." But he had never spoken to his brother like that, never. He clenched his teeth tight. "Ogteah had fought in the Long Tails War and on the side of the enemy. For me it is enough to be disgusted with his treachery, even if our people weren't directly involved. The enemy of the Long Tails is our enemy as well. Our avowed enemy!" His fist still hurt when he bunched it. "I fought them only a short while ago, Brother. I risked my life in order to avenge our people. This is the same enemy our neighbors to the west and south had fought. It makes no difference if we were involved in their war or not. It does not!" Drawing a deep breath didn't help and he clenched his fists tighter, desperate to control the trembling, but the shaking was bad, getting the better of him. How dared his brother defend the despicable traitor's motives, and by such silly arguments. "If you say that the despicable traitor is living with our enemy, *actually* living among them, then he is a thousand-fold more detestable, vile, shameful person, a true poisonous snake and not just as disloyal as a feather drifting in the wind. There is nothing complicated about it, nothing to understand, nothing to accept. It is *that* simple!"

Forcing his legs to stop, as his brother had ceased walking for some time and was staring at him in what looked like a contemplative gaze, Atuye forced his face into a stony mold, standing the scrutiny, his own as unwavering, or so he hoped.

"It is that simple, eh?" Sondakwa's voice was unusually quiet, having disturbing gentleness to it. "And what if I told you that Father has wished it to be so, to have Ogteah living with the enemy, helping him to achieve his lifetime goal – the peace with the people from across?" The massive head shook. "What if I told you that we were thinking simply, while our brother did plenty of growing up since Father went to great lengths in order to save him, from his crimes yes, but from purposelessness as well? What if I told you that I'm ashamed at our own simple thinking, the sons of our father, deeming ourselves worthy while doing nothing, drifting no better than Ogteah before, contradicting Father's wishes when it was comfortable to just drift and do nothing." The smile tagging at the tight lips was small, mirthless and empty. "For one who has been striving to follow in Father's footsteps, you've been doing mighty nothing, Brother, since this Great Man embarked upon his Sky Journey, leaving us with no clear instructions. Well, he didn't do so in Ogteah's case." His shrug was fleeting, just a brief shake of the shoulders. "He left him plenty of work to toil with, plenty of proposed achievements. And I must tell you, I'm with him on that. I will be working to the same end, but on our side, talk and argue and make our leaders listen. If nothing else, Father's memory deserves that."

The wind tore at them as they reached the top of the hill and began descending the trail, the shore below their feet abandoned, glittering with crispy sand, dotted with fallen logs aplenty.

It can't be, thought Atuye, his mind suddenly blank, empty of thoughts, his chest fluttering with a matching void. It was simply not possible that Father would be behind all this, such subtle desperate impossibly intricate plan. No, even as great a leader as Father would not have attempted something as deviously complicated, as brilliantly bold. And how —

"His mother was one of the savages, apparently," went on Sondakwa, again in this casually conversational tone, as though relating unimportant gossip. "Would you believe that? A pretty girl from one of their nations, I forget which one, even though he told me their name. Not a captive, he claims, but on that I had my doubts. Until he told me the entire story, that is." The man's laughter roared, confronting the wind. "The wildest storyteller out of his mind and dreaming wouldn't have managed to come up with something as wild. Too bad Father isn't with us to confirm any of it. I would have felt better relaying it now. As it is…" The wide shoulders lifted, trembling with mirth. "He sounded very convincing, that wild brother of ours. Apparently, some of the people from the other side knew Father well, maintained contacts with him in some cases, like when he brought their delegation to the First Gathering. You have never asked how he did it, have you?"

Atuye tried to make his head work. "Father said something about it, yes. Before the Cold Moons, when we went hunting, just before I went on my quest. He had said something…" He tried to remember, the fragments of many such conversations, the blissful moons of having Father so open and communicative and mostly for himself blending in his memory, mixing. "He talked about the other side, yes, about some war leader or another. He said they had been reaching satisfying results. But," he shrugged helplessly, "he didn't expand on any of that."

The wind assaulted them with vengeance now that nothing stood between the mass of the waving grey and the intruders venturing into the shore.

"Wish he was still with us now," muttered Sondakwa, watching the agitated waves as though finding the view especially fascinating.

Atuye didn't even nod, his gaze soothed by the rippling endlessness, comforted by it.

"He was the wisest of men." Sondakwa's moccasin kicked at the broken piece of a rotting log, sending it rolling in a jerky dance. "So wise, so courageous. And we didn't even follow him the way other people did. We just took him for granted." Another kick at the helplessly scattered driftwood. "There is no excuse for that, no justification!"

Taken with his brother's atypically expressed feelings and plight, feeling closer to him than ever before because of that, Atuye touched the bare shoulder, pressing it lightly, relaying it all in this simple gesture. "What else did Ogteah tell you about Father?"

The massive shoulder shuddered under his palm, as though awakening from a dream. "Plenty of stories, Brother, plenty of stories. Enough to fill quite a few nights with storytelling, and I don't exaggerate when I claim that. But that we'll save for later, for a good night around the fire and with everyone else asleep or too busy to interrupt our talks." He could feel the chuckle rather than hear it, a soft, rolling sound. "I have much frustration ahead of me, much thankless work, nagging and talking to deaf ears. And even though Ogteah promised that our current leader and Father's follower, Honorable Tsineka, might be willing to open his ears, knowing much about his, Ogteah's, circumstances, if not all of it, I somehow doubt that the renowned leader would help me that readily. He has been mighty careful about the enemy since Father left. But with the benevolence of the Great Spirits, and maybe a bit of an active help on your part, Little Brother..." The amused eyes were upon him again, suggestive to the point of exaggerated, flickering with mocking pleading. As always Sondakwa was changing fast, too fast. "We could work together on this, try and ensure our people's wellbeing, the safety of the towns and villages that are closer to the enemy's side. They are suffering too, just like we are. That village you raided, it may be the same Ogteah lives at. What he told me about it fitted the description."

Atuye clenched his teeth again, not happy at the renewed flood of memories. It was not a brilliant raid and he didn't do anything outstanding in it, still he had fought and became a warrior, and now his brother's words took something away from even this unmarred achievement, made him doubt it. But for Ogteah's involvement in all this! Why couldn't his brother think of peaceful agreements with the enemy on his own, without their dubious half-sibling being a part of it? Hadn't he been entertaining such ideas on his own as well, even when on the raid and back home?

"We better go back. It's freezing on this forsaken shore and I could use this promise of a warm meal. Or at least the warmth those fires back there in that huge encampment might be offering." Over his serious or challenging musings again, Sondakwa turned around, clearly glad to present his back to the vengeance of the cutting wind. "We have plenty of time to talk about it all, to sound our doubts and opinions." The massive palm landed upon Atuye's upper back, making him nearly sway. "I won't be pressing you into joining me in this dubious undertaking, Brother. I have no clear idea how to go about it myself as yet. But I will wish to hear your thoughts on the matter, when you think it all through. You are a man worthy of listening to his opinions, Little Brother; you always were. And," another resounding pat, "not so little anymore, eh? I will have to grow used to taking you seriously, man. And not only because you are a living image of our father, but because inside you might grow into as great a man as he was."

He felt the warmth spreading, all the way through his chest
and down his stomach, to glow around his insides and color his
face in an inappropriately glaring hue. Like those fires Sondakwa
was musing about, the words warmed his inner being, soothing
its bruises, promising healing.

"I will try, try my hardest." He stumbled over his words,
licking his lips in an attempt to make them articulate his thoughts
better. "I... I'm honored by your words. Truly honored!"

"No need to get that agitated, man." Sondakwa's laughter was
soft and inoffensive. "I should have noticed it earlier, but you
were so very quiet and subdued, never offering an argument. It
took Ogteah and a wild girl to make you come out of your shell, to
show your true spirit. Like I said, you remind me of Father, all this
dignified reserve." Skirting around a pile of charred logs,
someone's old fire, the man chuckled again, more softly this time.
"Who knows? You may come up with better solutions than both
of us, me and our wild brother. He doesn't have a clear course, the
crazy man that he is. No wonder he is bouncing back and forth
between both our worlds, getting in trouble. You won't be
catching me doing the same, be sure of that. I'll stay on our side,
work on Father's ideas from here. Fancy espousing the way of the
savages! Oh no, not even if he promises the safest stay in that
inglorious village of his or their capital with the friendliest War
Chief ever, having a Wyandot woman for a wife, a woman from
Father's old town, imagine that! You will gasp when you hear all
the stories, you just wait and see. "

He was still chuckling, amused by his own words. Atuye gave
up on the attempt to collect his thoughts or impressions and just
drifted by, enjoying the sense of security his brother's presence
created. He didn't even know how much he missed him, that
spiky, sharp-tongued, short-tempered brother of his, how much
their last quarrel weighed on his own spirit. And whether he
decided to join in his case, that newfound mission and purpose of
his both older siblings, or should he find it too wild, too
farfetched, not practical in the least – was Ogteah truly living on
the other side, with the most bitter of his people's enemies and at
Father's request? – it was good to have his brother's love and

approval, his open appreciation, the sincerity of his words. *Father's image on the outside and the inside*, oh, but he would do everything in his power to live up to this generous praise.

"If you are curious about that little friend of yours," Sondakwa was saying as the top of the hill was back upon them, with the view of the flickering fires spread all over the valley, adorning it in prettiest of manners, "then she is well, back in Teguenondahi, all smiles and in great spirits. Her father is still alive too, having survived the journey. A terrible sight, if you ask me, nothing but a collection of bones wrapped in wrinkled skin, poor man."

He didn't notice stopping dead on his tracks, but when Sondakwa halted as well, turning to stare at him, he knew they must have stopped walking. "Ononta is back in Teguenondahi?"

"Yes, I just told you. She had arrived only a day or two before I left, about five, six dawns from now." The narrowing eyes were eyeing him shrewdly. "I thought you intended to take her home, actually. Back in that Rock People's town, I thought that was your plan."

Another attempt to collect his thoughts was not crowned with success. "I did, yes," he mumbled. "I wanted to. But she... well, all of a sudden she was eager to stay. For some reason. I didn't understand why." The memory of that conversation, this entire painfully confusing, terribly frustrating day, still hurt. He clenched his teeth tightly.

"I see." Motioning him to resume their walk, Sondakwa nodded sagely, again not his derisive, spicy, quick to pick on people's weaknesses self. "Well, you know how women can be. Impossible to understand in the best of cases. You must have done something that hurt her feelings, silly fox that she is, and that was that. And, come to think of it, I may have a fair guess what it was." A chuckle. "You did pay unduly attention to that other fox with the unruly child. You looked mighty taken with her, Brother, so maybe that's what made your easygoing Ononta grow fangs all of a sudden." His shrug was a light affair, relating the man's amusement, irritatingly so. "She'll get over it. By the time you are back, she'll be all affability, you just wait and see. Unless you don't care for her as much as we all thought you did, and then you are better off, Brother, free to look around, free to enjoy yourself. Eh, young rascal?"

This time the palm landing on his back was not as welcome as before.

"I'm not into any of it," he muttered, then cleared his throat, ashamed. "I'm not after Ononta, or anyone else for that matter. When I'll see someone I fancy I'll get busy listening to your advice." He drew a deep breath. "But until then keep it to yourself."

A hearty laughter was his answer. "Of course, of course, young buck. No unwanted suggestions or guidance, I promise."

"Who brought her and her father home?" he asked after a blissful spell of silence saw them advancing toward the commotion down the trail.

"That same outlandish fox of yours."

He felt his legs ceasing their progress once again, turning to stone at the mere mention. Tsutahi? But how? His heart was making strange leaps inside his chest.

"They came in two canoes, alternating the rowing, or so your girl told me. Naturally I was surprised, expected to see you around. But she said no, that she hadn't seen or heard of you since this same eventful day when I left." Shrugging, Sondakwa sneaked a wistful glance toward the fires. "The wild fox brought her entire brood along, the children and her man. Well, naturally they wouldn't manage without him. And I must tell you, Little Brother," the man's eyes sparkled with well familiar mischief, "it's good that you didn't pursue that girl, enticing that she might seemed to you. Her man, oh, he is just not the person to antagonize in any such way. Not the type to do that at all." The sparkle was gone, replaced with a light frown. "Remember us staying in that Deer People's town, just before we decided to sneak on our private side-mission?"

Atuye just nodded, numbed beyond any more lively reaction.

"Remember that Long Tail man who was urging us to make an alliance between ourselves? The one who had a gall to lecture us on our lack of prudence when dealing with our lifetime enemy, our lack of information and all that?"

He tried to make his mind work. Oh, yes, that Deer People's town, where their delegations had stopped for more than one day, when Sondakwa grew all restless and bored. There were people there, locals and visitors. Neighboring Rocks as well, yes.

"That tough looking bastard, all scars and limp and whatnot? Don't you remember? The Long Tail! The one who nagged on you about that raid, said you weren't prepared enough."

Oh, yes, that man. He remembered him well, a formidable, weathered, tough looking warrior, a person whose advice one tended to take, if for no other reason than to avoid angering such one into violent deeds. Even though the foreigner seemed to be in tightest control, observant and closemouthed until provoked with his favorite theme, the enemy from across. Well, the man was a Long Tail, after all.

"Yes, I remember that man. What about him?" The thought hit him and he stared at his brother, gaping. "No, it can't be. No!"

"Yes, oh yes. Her man, of all things. Now see why I'm glad you didn't develop more feelings for that delectable fox? Safer, huh?"

But Atuye was beyond even the simplest of reactions, neither amusement nor anger, not even the rightful irritation at his brother's continued probing of his possible infatuation, wild images sweeping his dazed mind, one more impossible than the other.

"It can't be. It can't! She is just a girl. And this man, he is old, and limping, and— he can't!" Bringing his arms to his burning face helped, mainly to keep his brother's twisting grin away from his view.

"Old? That man isn't old, you youngster. He is not that much older than me, I bet. He looks hardened and weathered, beaten by life yes, but well, Little Brother, that's what makes some girlish heads spin. Women like that, tough, seasoned warriors. Scars please them, young buck, so don't be reluctant to collect these."

He shook his head violently, pushing the words away, wishing to be alone, at least for a few heartbeats, to take it all in. But how was it possible? She was so young, so fragile, so small and delicate. How could a hardened warrior with evidently so many summers of warring and hard living behind him be allowed to take her and make her his woman, to force all those babies and children on her? What woman would give birth to one child after another, with not enough summers between each of those? Ogteah and Sondakwa were the only boys of their longhouse and the others in their clan to be barely one summer apart, but they didn't share the same mother.

Ogteah's mother! He welcomed the opportunity to channel his thoughts into different directions, anything but to think of *her* belonging to such an intimidating warrior and evidently a hard person. And Ononta said they didn't even live with the girl's family, somehow.

"Ogteah's mother, you said she was the Longhouse People's woman. How is that possible?" Oh, yes, this was the best of distractions, sure to prompt his brother into more storytelling and away from his, Atuye's, inappropriate feelings or weaknesses.

"Oh, that's a twisted story." As expected Sondakwa's eyes lit with renewed glee. "Took the wild man half a night to retell and I promise you, it won't bore you, this tale. But if you think this tidbit of information is odd," the conspiratorial gleam intensified, spilling out of the glittering gaze, "I wonder what you'll tell about a cute little niece of yours and mine, with another whelp of the savages on his way to be born and soon. All perfectly savage, Longhouse People children through and through. How about that?"

Again he found himself staring. "What do you mean?"

"Ogteah, the wild beast who could not stay with one woman for longer than it took the loose bastard to reach the peak and have all the pleasure. Remember that one, eh? Well," the mischievous smile was spilling, pouring from the beaming face, "apparently, the savage women do know how to handle a man, even a wild beast of our mutual sibling. He kept talking about her, could not shut up for one single day. Imagine that!" The man laughed again, so very pleased with himself. "And she keeps giving him children, another thing he couldn't stop talking about. I wanted to jump out of his canoe at some point; it was tiring, all this litany and praise, the excited reports on that little daughter of his, how she can do this or that. As though he invented this concept of being a father, you know. As though none of us had seen a child before, had not fathered several of those, he himself included." More condescending laughter. But this time Atuye couldn't help but join in. "So here you are, oh impeccable Bear People's man, an uncle of a savage little girl running all over the Great Lake's shores, the wrong side of it, with more wild nephews or nieces to come. How do you like that, *uncle*?"

"Like the thought of a snow in the middle of the Hot Moons," admitted Atuye, shaking his head in amusement he could not fight anymore. And just as he thought life couldn't become stranger. "Are you sure he wasn't lying to you? Inventing stories to cover this or that crime or transgression maybe? It would be more like Ogteah to do that, wouldn't it? More realistic than secret missions and new families among the enemies. I'm not sure—"

A hearty laughter cut his speech short. "I told you it would sound wild, and you didn't even hear the half of it yet. I spent five, no, six dawns listening to all that, until we couldn't delay any longer." The man shook his head, blowing the air through his nostrils. "It was a surprisingly interesting pastime, and yes, it all sounded wild, impossible, too unreasonable to make up in order to get away from something. He is not stupid, that brother of ours; never was. He would have come up with a more plausible tale if pressed to lie and make up excuses." A shrug. "Also your fox did claim to have seen him fighting with the Longhouse savages against her countryfolk. So here you have the testimony for his version of this tale." The wandering gaze hardened, fixed on Atuye, measuring him in a way, penetrating. "He has a good reason for hating her, so you know. If you ever run into her again, ask her about her part in that great battle of the Long Tails, about what she did while spying or shooting people in their backs." Another shrug. "But it's a different story, another implausible tale. She couldn't do half of what he accuses her of, not such a young fragile thing, but if he made this one up I would still be curious to hear what such harmless little girl did in a middle of a battle, any battle, to meet our brother and get such a lasting impression of him."

He pushed the thought of her away, for later consideration.

No, he wouldn't think about her now, fighting in battles – indeed, how so? – or belonging to the fierce Long Tail – did she back then? – or doing other implausible things. She had talked about Ogteah being killed by her man, a certain death too…

"Did he fight that Long Tail warrior out there? What did he tell you about that battle?"

"Plenty, but later, Brother, later. For now, let us hurry back to the camp and the fires of our people. The evening times are the best to catch our leaders mellow and willing to talk, to listen to unwelcomed suggestions and speculations. You know, this time after the meal is finished and the pipes are getting stuffed, just before the tiredness settles in, eh?" A light nudge of an elbow made Atuye grin. "We'll talk some more as the night progresses, Brother. Trust me on that."

You better, thought Atuye, following the decisive walk of his forceful sibling, shaking his head as he did. So busy and purposeful all of a sudden. Good for Sondakwa. But he wouldn't be lending any of this blatantly required support, not before hearing the entire story. He trusted his older sibling's judgment, but not blindly, not like Father's.

CHAPTER 24

The Wolf Man descended upon Lone Hill just as the heat of the midday set in, casting the entire village into a drowsy, slow, pleasantly dreamy mood. Most of the men were out there, fishing in small groups or hunting in larger ones, and but for his arm, Ogteah knew, he would have been required, or rather obliged, to join one of those.

Enough that his woman had neglected her field duties for two dawns in a row, having gone out there only this morning and with her eyes rolled and her prettily curved lips twisted in a grimace of barely hidden defiance. A sight that made him snicker and feel yet warmer inside, something he didn't think was possible since the evening of his return, those same two, by now actually three dawns ago.

Oh, but did she ran to greet him the moment the word had reached her, shortly after he had staggered in, exhausted by the long day of strenuous rowing, the crossing of the Great Lake being always the most difficult of challenges, taking sometimes the same time it took Father Sun to complete his journey through the sky, from sunrise all the way to his near disappearance. Did Father Sun get as tired by the end of each day, as exhausted, as eager to quit?

He had kept his mind busy with this and many other irrelevant questions, mainly to force it away from the tiredness and the dull but insistent pain in his damaged arm, the pain that grew into a real nuisance by midday and then into an outright torture as the heat began receding. He had to force his eyes away from it and not only his mind, as the terrible swelling that had been gone after the days of rest spent with his brother, loitering on abandoned shores and doing nothing but talking, was back now, impossible to ignore. By the time the currents intensified and the water changed its coloring, heralding the nearness of the shore, it was so misshapen and ugly he didn't want to look at it out of share disgust. But for his village being so near the sparkling giant of a lake! He had blessed all the great and small *uki* for making him settle in Lone Hill and not High Springs, or any other inland settlement. One more pull of a paddle and he would have fainted, he knew, just collapsed and given up, happily at that. It was too much to ask from a man, so much rowing and with a cracked arm at that.

However, his welcome back home made up for some of the pain. For the most of it, if one was to be honest with oneself. No, his fellow villagers did not try to hold back on their surprise and their joy at seeing him back, the genuineness of their affection. Amused and good-natured, a familiar combination, they flooded him with questions aplenty, patting his back, crowding and pressing, difficult to deal with in his current condition but still an encouragingly friendly presence.

He made a tremendous effort to hold on, to appear as vigorous as he could, to make jokes and engage in the spicy banter that was expected of him, but it was a challenge with the agonized waves rolling up and down his arm, and his mind busy searching for something to lean against, anything really. Even the tiniest tree would do. In the thickening dusk it should have proven easier to go on and talk to them and answer their questions and jokes but for that elusive support. Yet, when she had pushed her way through the crowding villagers, he knew it was her, even though it was difficult to see in the twilight and all the commotion. He could have told it with perfect certainty, even with his eyes shut and his ears clogged with moss. The racing of his heart and that familiar all invading warmth told him so. And then, all became well again.

It was difficult to hide his smile, even now, three days later, and facing the encounter he was not yet ready to face. The need to travel to High Springs he had put off with a certain amount of success, basking in her love and elation instead, letting her pamper and spoil him rotten, his arm needing much rest according to several local healers, to have the worst of the swelling gone before attempting to fix it in a splint. A professional one, this time, unlike the two sturdy sticks Sondakwa had managed to tie to his hand on the day after the treatment, already far enough from the accursed Onentisati, rowing along the shores of the Great Lake, heading in the direction of the rising sun leisurely, in no hurry.

Oh, but how annoyingly calm and breezy his brother was, how irritatingly sure of himself, brushing Ogteah's fears and impatience aside, perpetually amused now, a glaringly new facet to the restless skunk who was so easy to anger and throw out of balance, push into violent deeds, a life-time rival and adversary, now his unexpected savior, of all things. It had taken him an additional day or two to relax completely, to trust the conceited piece of meat with no reservations.

"So they say you are back!" The Wolf Man's beam was blinding in its radiance, rivaling the strength of the midday sun. "And just as expected, in a battered enough state to put the local healers to work, the wild beast that you are." The wideness of the smile was infecting, spilling from the sun-burned face, sweaty and flashed with unfailing health, bearing witness to much walking in an unreasonable pace.

Ogteah just grinned, glad to see the man despite his misgivings. Maybe he'd understand and accept, or maybe he wouldn't, but whatever his reaction would be it was good to be back and among his true people and friends. Here was his home.

"You don't look that much better, man," he retorted. "Have you run all the way from High Springs without stopping to catch a breath, or to make your needs in the bushes?" Measuring his visitor with a pointed glance, he sprang to his feet, his grin impossible to conquer. The rest that the healers demanded was a boring business. "You look this way, you know."

The Wolf Man grimaced, pushing himself forward unceremoniously, leaning to inspect Ogteah's arm. "What did they do to you? Tried to eat you alive? And they call us man-eaters!"

In his turn Ogteah glanced at his monster of an arm, not nearly as amused, hating the sight of it, the shapeless swelling and the grotesquely intricate pattern of scabs dotting it from inside and outside, interlacing, ridiculously glaring, an ugly sight.

"Something of the sort. Their forest dwellers certainly nourished the notion one night, several of them, one after another."

"Must be a story worth listening to." The man shook his head, losing some of his lighthearted humor, his grin gone. "Well, the news of your return caught me while loitering in Onondaga Town. Which saved me plenty of unnecessary walking."

"Then you must be starving."

Diving under the nearest bunk, Ogteah pulled out a basket lined with crispiest rolls of bread studded with berries, a treat he was presented with only this morning in exchange for his promise to stay in and rest just as the healers demanded. She had made him swear he would do as he had been told before rushing out and into the fields, unable to neglect her duties anymore. The Clan Mother of their longhouse displayed unusual tolerance by letting them spent two blissful days out there and in each other's arms, doing nothing for the community and in the pressing time of watering crops, but there was a limit to the leading woman's patience, even when so much passionately protested love had been involved. Gayeri didn't bother to hide her feelings, the depth of her relief at having him back and unharmed – well, relatively – the intensity of her remorse at having sending him off in the way she did. As though he had blamed her and not himself. How silly! But to bask in her unreserved love and adoration was good, as always, warming, fulfilling, reminding him why his life on this side of the Great Lake was worthy of every effort it required to keep them all safe, her and their children, and their countryfolk, his true people.

"Those are good!" The Wolf Man had sunk his teeth into his second cookie, devouring it with an obvious relish. "The women of your longhouse know how to spoil a man. Or was that your woman in particular? Not averse to having you back, is she?"

"It looks that way, yes." He chuckled, remembering her threats. "She made those cookies in order to keep me in, just like the old healer demanded. There is a price for this basket of wonder. But I know you are going to make me break my promise. So…"

However, his companion sobered at once. "What do they say about that arm of yours? It is broken, isn't it? Badly?"

He lifted his good shoulder, pushing the familiar wave of misgivings away. "It will get well in the end. Those things always do. They say it's only because of the rowing that it turned into such ugly monstrosity. Both healers promised that if I rest and do nothing with it, it'll return to its normal size soon, ready to be tucked into the sternest of slings." Another shrug seemed to be in order. "I had to cross our Sparkling Water at some point, and that arm, it didn't heal properly back then, not yet, even though it wasn't that ugly and huge anymore." He hoped his grin appeared as nonchalant as he wanted it to be, not as forced as he felt it was. "There is only so much activity you can do while in the heart of the Great Lake besides rowing and then rowing some more. And the stupid arm, it didn't like any of that."

"I can imagine." The penetrating gaze rested on him, deliberating. "Are you up to a stroll out there? I won't be able to stay and enjoy your village's hospitality, not this time. Have to head back before Father Sun is well on his way toward the western sky. Our highly esteemed Onondaga Town should not notice that I dared to sneak away when no one was looking. They better not, or some mighty influential leaders may get mighty upset with me." Matter-of-fact, the man glanced around, narrowing his eyes against a carelessly thrown piece of decorated leather at the edge of the upper bunk. "We'll make a nice snugly sling for you, to carry your arm in it."

"Don't even think of it." Grinning, Ogteah followed his friend's gaze, snatching the blanket he was sprawling on before, rolling it clumsily, determined to make the uncooperative leather behave. "Take your eyes off her favorite shawl and then we both may survive to eat more cookies this evening." The shawl was old and worn, made out of a very mediocre pelt to begin with, the small deer he had hunted for it being a poor specimen, holed with too many arrows; and yet, it was the reminder of their first days together, still on the other side, two fugitive, not sure about their mutual future; the days their love began blossoming for real. "If you don't touch it, she may be in a forgiving enough mood to make more cookies for you to take along before you depart. Otherwise, it's war."

"A fair warning." The Wolf Man shoved him aside, dealing with the blanket deftly and efficient, like he dealt with all challenges of his life. "We'll put that hugely impressive arm of yours in the neatest of slings, won't make it strain at all. If it's dangling by your side, resting, your promise won't be broken, and no angry women, or healers, will be tempted to punish you by withholding your tasty treats from you." The twinkle was back, twisting the generous lips into crookest of grins. "Here, stay still. I'll tie it in the way you won't even feel that silly arm of yours, won't even remember it exists."

An impossible promise to keep, as with every movement the damaged limb hurt, or at least, put him into this or that level of discomfort, still the improvised sling provided enough support and soon they had found themselves battling the heaviness of the heat, walking briskly, pitting their faces against the welcome touch of the occasional breeze, craving for more of such mercies.

"What is the goings in Onondaga Town? What are those meetings you are afraid to be seen missing all about?"

The Wolf Man's snort was noncommittal, dissolving in the hazy heat. "Some representatives came to nag on the Head of the Great Council, asking to summon the annual gathering earlier than was originally planned."

He couldn't help it. "And they can't do it without you holding their hands? How touching!"

A quiet snicker greeted his words. "Yes, yes, man of wit. I know you know that I wouldn't have been there but for a better reason." The decorations of the prettily embroidered moccasin swayed, kicking at a dusted stone, sending it flying. "The representatives' enterprise made it easier to gather a satisfactory amount of influential warriors, enough to justify spending our time in that presumptuous town, talking our days away." The merriment disappeared, replaced by a thoughtful nod. "Your return could not have been timed better. I'm certain you've learned enough to add to our talks and deliberations."

He felt the narrowed gaze brushing past him, brief and pensive, suitably intense.

"That I did."

Suddenly, he wasn't sure he had enough strength to go through it, not now, maybe not ever. He was so tired! All those happenings in that Rock People's town, his fright and his flight, the terrible night, the unexpected help – from his lifetime rival of a brother, of all things! – the days spent in relative comfort, sailing, talking, remembering, the shadows of the past not there, or maybe not interfering, as though the night on that Onentisati shore had cleansed them both, washed away bad memories and harsh recollections, old animosity and prejudice. It was good to talk about everything, to reminisce about bad incidents and laugh at those instead of growing angry, to snicker at the embarrassing ones. But Sondakwa turned out to be a fascinating person, not the frustrating, constantly incensed buck seeking to prove something, with his fists always ready, a perpetual annoyance. He was still sharp-tongued and irritatingly stinging, brutally honest and annoyingly ready to sound his mind, quick to see through pretense and swift to pounce on it, and in an unpleasantly condescending manner at that, making the most out of a person's blunders. Yet, now all these came accompanied with surprisingly broad thinking, deep comprehension, a fair amount of good humor, and most of all, an unexpected open-mindedness.

Why, his, Ogteah's, revelations should have shocked the man into leaving in the best of cases, turning him in, in the worst of it. Instead, his brother had sat listening to the tales from the other side – all carefully picked, nothing revealing, of course – as though it was only natural for a Wyandot man like Ogteah, a person with a bad reputation and criminal past behind him or not, to build his new life among the enemies of their people, hunt alongside their hunters, fight alongside their warriors, father children with their women, while being held to be a generally good, contributing member of the community. An impossible tale that made him doubt his own credibility, but Sondakwa didn't even bat an eyelid. A surprise!

On their last evening, upon reaching the bay where the crossing of the Great Lake was attempted most frequently, he had felt that he might have liked to prolong his stay and their conversations. But for the projected meeting they had agreed upon in a time for the moon to grow full and then shrink again, but for their plans regarding the future relationship of their people, he might have felt a genuine regret at parting ways with that brother of his, a person he hated the most once upon a time.

Their plans!

Easy to think those up while loitering on abandoned shores, musing and making jokes at each other's expense. Just like the tale of his adventures since the ordeal of Ossossane that didn't look too realistic when retold in the privacy of his former people's forests, their agreements and resolution did not look very practical here in Lone Hill, so far away from the places they had originated at.

Straightening his gaze, he measured his current company, assessing. Would their spectacular-looking, highly ambitious, up-and-coming warriors' leader let him talk about any of it, let alone consider it seriously?

"You may not like some of what I have to say." Licking his lips helped, but only a little. His mouth was suddenly as dry as an abandoned field in midsummer. "My journey, it has been enlightening, revealing. In more aspects than learning about whether the union of these people expanded and how badly. It was, well, it was an interesting journey."

"I see." The Wolf Man's eyes narrowed, his jaw, strong and protruding as it was, seemed to jut out some more. "Tell me!"

No helpfulness of small talk or, at least, a conversational tone. Nothing but the solemn, penetrating stare, the piercing quality of it. Ogteah couldn't help licking his lips again.

"First of all, let me tell you what you do want to hear, surely." To draw a deep breath helped. "Their union is, indeed, stronger than it was back in the days of my father, at the time when I left. The Bear and the Cord People seemed to be very solid and comfortable in their agreements, and even though the Deer had finally joined the proposed union no more than a summer or two ago, they are firmly in it now, or so the Rock People feel." He lifted his good shoulder in a shrug. "With a fair measure of resentment, I must add. They don't feel too good about the expanding Wyandot Union, those dwellers of the west; they don't like the way it has been conducted so far, and as you know, those are the people I went visiting, fortunate to establish brief contacts with them right away. One town, to be precise. Well," he made a face, amused but only very briefly, "it's been less than a full moon, and even though I intended to visit a few smaller settlements, the opportunity to travel with the people belonging to one of their main towns presented itself. So I grabbed it with both hands."

"Breaking one in the process." The Wolf Man's grin was fleeting but unmistakable, flickering with familiar affection. "Go on."

Ogteah shook his head, relieved. "Actually, these Rock People had nothing to do with it. It wasn't them who had made me do stupid things."

All traces of playfulness were gone again. "Who then?"

"I'll tell you that in a little while. But first," he drew another deep breath, unwilling to even talk about it. "The Long Tails. You said you suspected these Rocks having close contacts with our defeated enemy, aiding and supporting them as a part of the Wyandot Union or on their own. Well, yes, oh yes, they seem to keep very close contacts, with their Attiwandaronk neighbors at least, but not as a part of my former people's union. Not yet."

He let his gaze dwell on the group of children who were playing at the edge of the ceremonial ground, in the shadow of a huge maple tree, boys of various ages throwing sticks, aiming to hit rolling targets – the future spear throwers.

"You might be relieved to learn of the fate of our greatest of enemies, the leader of that monstrous force back in our Long Tails War. He is alive and well, limping all over those same Rock People's lands, and even the Deer ones, telling them about the might of our Great League, about our tactics that he seemed to learn very closely, about our strengths and how to deal with those, instructing them on what mistakes they should avoid making. Very helpful sort of a fellow."

His companion stopped dead in his tracks so abruptly, Ogteah had found it necessary to retrace his steps, hiding his grin at the incredulousness of the gaping gaze, the boldly outlined cheekbones protruding sharper, lips nothing but a thin line, barely visible, if at all.

"Your father warned us."

The wide opened eyes blinked. "How did you manage to overhear him?"

"To overhear?" He listened to his own chuckle ringing mirthlessly in the hazy heat. "I didn't need to creep around and crouch behind longhouses' corners, if that's what you imagined I had been doing. Oh no! I was privileged to talk to our limping friend, to ask him plenty of questions, to lead him on all I liked until our other fellow travelers' snores shook the night." He grinned at the memory. "It was easy to make him talk. He didn't need much prompting, that one. A talkative fellow when you quiz him on our Great League's matters."

This time, his chuckle rolled out more readily, the sight of his companion's face making the laughter come easier. The gaping mouth was an unbecoming sight when displayed on the strong, hardened features, under the spectacular warriors' hairdo and with the signs of regalia belonging to a high status warrior.

"You should see yourself now. Quite a sight. Careful that no mosquito should fly in."

The mouth shut with a clacking sound. "He didn't recognize you? How so?"

Ogteah tried to make hysterical laughter go away. "No, he didn't. Why should he? We didn't encounter him, none of us, until the last of the fighting. And then..." The inappropriate guffawing was gone with no more effort on his part. He swallowed hard. "Then he was busy fighting Akweks. He would have recognized him for sure. But me?" A shrug proved a difficult business. "When I rushed to hit his club with as many of my ribs as I could, well, he must have been busy, too busy to look whom he was fighting against, considering the fact that it was over in a few more heartbeats, or so your brother says." He shrugged again. "I admit that I understood all that later, much later. At first I was making a mighty fool of myself, shooting to my feet, grabbing my knife, readying to fight him the moment he neared. The people who brought me to their camp must have thought me to be a strange bird, a mad person roaming their woods. They certainly had these wondering looks on their faces. I'm afraid it took me many heartbeats to compose myself." He blew the air through his nose with much force. "Well, the main thing is that he is wandering all over the western Wyandot, as far as I was able to learn. Talking, listening, explaining. Stirring trouble for us, most surely. My brother said he met him in the Deer People's town some dawns after I had run into him, or so it seemed. He was talking about the dangers of our Great League up there, repeating himself."

"Your brother?" The Wolf Man's eyebrows were climbing high, one faster than another. "Are there more of your type out there? I didn't know."

"Yes, there are." Unable not to, he rolled his eyes, his companion's expression amusing in its suggestiveness. "That's another part of my story. I'll tell you about it too, after you stop making faces."

"I thought you said your mother died bringing you to this world."

"Yes, she did. The others came from the stupid fox my father took shortly thereafter."

"Shortly thereafter?"

"Yes, shortly thereafter. Sondakwa is barely a few seasons younger than me." He shook his head, suddenly perturbed. Father didn't grieve for too long, did he? Then he remembered. "My father, he wanted to forget. I suppose it was his way to do that."

The Wolf Man shook his head, as though getting rid of irrelevant thoughts, his eyebrows still arching, relating what he thought of such ways of dealing with losses. Nothing positive.

"What else about our mutual Long Tails friend, the persistent survivor that he is?"

"Nothing much." Another shrug seemed to be in order. "We

spent one evening in the same camp. Then the locals split. Most headed on toward the Deer People's towns, their original destination, while a greedy Onentisati man dragged me and some other of his fellow travelers back to his own town, set on laying his rapacious hands on the goods my canoe was loaded with." Smashing a fly before it managed to land on his injured hand made him feel better. "I wanted to go with our Attiwandaronk fugitive, to visit the Deer and see what they were up to, to hear him some more, to learn of his plans, but the greedy local was very insistent." Another fly caught his attention before he remembered. "Oh, and he hides his identity, that famous enemy of ours. Claims that he came from an unimportant village and never participated in the Long Tails War at all, not even as a simple warrior." He snickered, genuinely amused. "Much like I did, come to think of it. I kept claiming that I came from a small village of my people out there in the north, away from important happenings, politics and all that. At some point it became too funny, how we both claimed the same thing. It was amusing to provoke him into long, angered tirades, knowing all about his lies. He said he knew some Long Tails leaders to be able to relate their point of view. What a storyteller!"

"Why should he hide who he was? It's not like the filthy Rocks are inimical to the Long Tails, aren't they?"

"I don't think so, no. I kept wondering about that too. My brother promised to try and find out that."

"Your brother..." The thoughtful eyes narrowed again. "Now get to this part of the story, before we go back to our Long Tails friend. There are plenty of questions I want to bury you under, but first of all answer this. What has that brother of yours – a Bear People person, I presume – has to do with the Rock People and their Long Tails guests?"

Ogteah drew a deep breath, now less perturbed than before, more sure of himself. The Wolf Man would understand and maybe he would prove open enough to do something about it, to help him, Ogteah, along. If for no other reason than that he was his great father's son, and not a narrow-minded person for himself.

"Well, my brother, yes, this part of the story. I have two of these actually, the brood of my father from that other fat doe of his, and just to make the matters more bizarre, both managed to show up in Onentisati, that Rock People's town I was staying at, at the worst timing ever, and in the company... No wait, I don't want to complicate it even worse with irrelevant bits." Drawing another deep breath helped, the thought of the skinny snake, now a sweet little mother, still trying his temper to its limits. "Let me just say that not only did the Long Tail survived that battle. The filthy little thing with her murderous bow, she had made it out of there as promptly, in one piece, to thrive and blossom, and breed vigorously, an adorable little mother." Again the gaping mouth. He didn't pause to smirk, not this time. "Well, somehow she ended up with my brothers, or the youngest skunk among them. Don't ask me how, it's too complicated and looks like a game even the spirits wouldn't engage at while playing with us, mortal beings." This time his breath came out rather than in, loudly at that. He listened to the sound of it. "Anyway, one thing led to another, and here she was, exposing my pretense, the only one to know where I came from, and of course, unlike the filthy Long Tail leader, quick to recognize me." Incensed all over again, with the heedlessness of his flight as well, such a stupid decision, he rolled his eyes. "So I was bolting for their fence, eager to disappear into their woods, no weaponry, no goods, not even a paddle to try and get my canoe back. And well, I'm not sure I'll wish to repeat it all, even in ten summers from now, but in the end my brother – not the youngest skunk with his lusty eyes of a buck in heat for the treacherous fox – no, my other brother, the one with whom we used to fight and hate each other the most, all of a sudden decided to see reason. When I was in mighty bad shape, he helped me to get away, and... and he wanted to listen, about Father and his—"

Suddenly, he wished to bite his tongue off. But Father's secret mission of "friendly spying on the enemy or rather a possible future ally" was not common knowledge, not on this side of the Great Lake, thanks all the great and small spirits for that. And he was just about... Oh, but it was tiring, it was! These secret missions, half-truths or outright lies, the intricate net of politics he wanted to have no part of, not anymore. His previous life was meaningless, yes, a stupid, unworthy existence, still sometimes he missed its lack of complicity, the absence of more difficult dilemmas than the question as to the advisability of pursuing this or that pretty fox or getting away from this or that commitment. No weight of responsibility, of secret agendas and far-fetching plans that one could share only parts of, even with people one considered the closest of friends and family.

"What?" the Wolf Man was saying, peering at him again. "Have you seen a ghost?"

He rubbed his face with his good arm. "Nothing. I'm just tired." To meet the gaze of his companion took more of his precious strength. "Well, to make it short, while fleeing this accursed place full of too many Long Tails from our glorious past, I told him about my current circumstances, not about the spying, naturally, but about my life here, about our father's involvement and his desire to see the people of both sides living in peace." He grew another deep breath. "Naturally, he was aware of Father's attempts to make it work between both our people. They all heard about the delegation of which your brother had been a part of, those who traveled to Ossossane, to witness our First Gathering. But, well, to hear my version of it, my claim that the great leader had gone as far as sending his own son here in order to promote the very idea of peace, oh yes, that left him staring at me as stupidly as you did when I told you about the Long Tails lowlife." The grin came easier this time. "Just like you do now."

The Wolf Man was frowning, not amused. "I can understand why you made him think that. He wouldn't have helped you had he known the truth, siblings' connection or not. Or would he?" A shrug. "I wouldn't be turning my brother in had I known that he had been involved in the treason against our people, but..." Another shrug completed the sentence.

Ogteah sighed. "No, he wouldn't have helped. He would have been the first to hunt me down had he known the truth."

His companion grimaced thoughtfully and for a while the rustling of the tobacco plots not far away from where they stood interrupted the silence, gaining the fullest of their attention. Even the boys near the wide-branched maple stopped their stick-throwing activities, busy talking or squatting, their gesturing vigorous but unaccompanied by vigorous shouting.

"So what do you have in mind about that brother of yours?" The Wolf Man was still immersed in his study of the blossoming leaves. "Was that the part of what you suspected I won't like hearing?"

"Something like that, yes." He found the swaying plants of a great interest as well. "We spent quite a few evenings talking these matters over. Until that stupid arm of mine looked more fitting for traveling on my own." A skeptical glance over the deformed limb did not make him feel better. It didn't look as bad back then, not even on the night of the injury. "It gave us time to ponder matters of unions and peace and wars aplenty."

"I see." The spectacular warrior's voice rang calmly, expressionless, matter-of-fact. "What is he willing to do from his side of the lake? What *can* he do?"

Ogteah did not dare to let his breath out. "That would be up to you to decide, to think it over, to arrive at conclusions. People like you and your brother, influential people. I... I can run messages, pass information on, bring answers back." He cleared his throat, hating the way it was feeling, dry and helpless. "He, he will try to do the same, to accost people who matter. Father's old associates, you see? There is this man, Tsineka, he was one of the oldest and most devoted followers of Father, his right hand. He may be willing to listen, to try and do something, to help our efforts along. If for no other reason than to honor Father's memory. But maybe, just maybe..." The one-sided shrug began to annoy him. He tried to make his arm more comfortable in its cradle. It gave him something useful to concentrate on. "My brother is not a youth of little summers. He can make himself listened to and heard if he cares enough, and it seems that for some reason he cares now. Maybe he wants to honor Father's memory. Or maybe my tales made him curious. He will be heading for the gathering they are about to hold in that loathsome town of Ossossane again."

Another spell of heavy silence. The village beyond their backs was awakening with life, with women returning from the fields, spending there relatively little time in this part of the Hot Moons, when all the crops needed was weeding and little watering. He wondered if Gayeri had hurried back without detouring through the spring that would seal the womenfolk's daily activities with a good thorough washing. Did she miss him enough to skip on that necessity?

Squinting, his eyes followed more children spilling all over the flattened ground, trying to pick out the familiar flying garment and the angular run accompanied to it.

"Your brother may remember this old leader Tsineka. They might have come in contact back then. He was spending much time in my father's company, he said."

"Maybe." The Wolf Man let his breath out loudly, making a point. "Well, man of peace and grand visions, I better start thinking of my journey back. If I want to spare myself a walk through those night forests of yours, let us go and deliver you back, see if your woman is there and not too upset with us to give me little provisions, make my journey smoother." The twinkle was back, lightening the measuring gaze. "Although you don't look that badly worn out, you know, comfortable enough with that sling. Do you think you may be up to joining me, invading that haughty Onondaga Town for a few dawns at least? Might be a good opportunity to start accosting some of its influential visitors." The pointed eyebrows climbed again, suggestively high. "That same mentioned brother of mine is there now too. He might prove curious toward certain of your new ideas, even if to me they are sounding sadly far-fetched."

This time he didn't hesitate. "Well, yes, I'll come. And... I thank you. Your willingness to listen to any of it, to give it a chance..." The shrug came easier this time. Indeed, wrapped in a sling, something good and professional, arranged by a healer, he wouldn't have trouble dealing with the relatively short journey to Onondaga Town. And they did have good healers up there, the best among this nation's False Face Society medicine men.

"Think nothing of it." The Wolf Man was turning away

already. "I didn't agree to anything and I'm not sure I will be receptive to more of it, your re-established family connections or not. We'll see how it goes from there, what sort of communication you might manage to establish with that brother of yours, how far his contacts are reaching, how well your former people receive any of it. I predict you'll grow plenty of muscles while rowing back and forth across our Great Sparkling Water. Gathering plenty of frustration as well along the way." A smirk. "Your position won't be enviable, I promise you that much. But if you are willing to go to such lengths, to try and mend the matters between our people yet again, well, who am I to tell you to get it out of your head? A son of your father, you do honor him, and to the highest degree."

He hoped the burning sensation in his face didn't show, but just then a flurry of running feet made them look up.

"Father!"

No flying shawls or skirts bore on them this time, but the vision of a slick brown body adorned with nothing but a pair of moccasins and a wet swinging hair could not be mistaken.

He scooped her with his good arm, paying no attention to the vigorous protests of the other. To lift her up with the required drive was challenging, but he did his best to have her flight catch the momentum, enough to generate a wild squeal of delight. The attempt to prevent her from scrambling up and onto his shoulders was crowned with little success. Soon she was perching up there, observing the world from her favorite seat atop of it, her muddied moccasins dangling in his eyesight, his scalp hurting from the earnestness of her attempts to secure her position.

"You wild thing."

The Wolf Man was laughing his hardest. "What a climber! She'll put Takoskowa, the wild twin, to shame yet." His wink was directed upward, somewhere above Ogteah's head. "Make your father bring you along, when he is out and heading for High Springs, little one. I have a worthwhile challenge in mind for you, a boy who won't make your stay there boring or drab."

She stopped wriggling, busy thinking the offer over, of that Ogteah was sure. The splattered tips of both moccasins, still dangling next to his face, went absolutely still.

"High Springs is where the Great Council is?" she said slowly, suspicion in her voice.

The serenity of her tone made Ogteah snickered. A smaller version of Gayeri, one moment wild and playful, the other all seriousness and purpose. "No, that's in Onondaga Town. And you are not invited there. They like their visitors serious and dressed in more than a pair of muddied moccasins."

The Wolf Man guffawed. "Your father is right, but in High Springs we are not as uptight. So next time he is heading there, tell him the warriors' leader said to bring you along. He can't refuse his leaders."

Ogteah let one side of his mouth climb up. "That's what they think, those leaders."

Leaving the relative calmness of the ceremonial grounds, where more children were spreading now as well, they traded it for the commotion of the early afternoon village, the familiar clamor he had missed among so many other things.

"Is your mother back already?"

Her entire body moved with a shrug. He glanced at the Wolf Man, amused. Was his formidable company intimidating her? Rare were the times when she would go silent for as long as ten heartbeats, let alone if prompted with question.

"Think she'll be nice to our guest? Nice enough to pack some of those tasty cookies with berries for him to take along?"

Judging by another wink of their prospective warriors' leader, the girl must have been studying his intimidating company openly, safe in doing so from the security of her father's shoulders. "Your mother may not like me taking your father away again, but you tell her that it is so because your father is an important man that our elders and leaders wish to consult, ask questions, hear his opinions. Tell your mother that it's because he is a very important man."

"Mother is washing in the spring. She said to go and look after Father until she is done."

"Wise, very wise," agreed the Wolf Man gravely, making Ogteah's attempts to control his laughter more difficult. "Your father needs looking after. The moment you left for the fields, he was out and about, I can tell you that. Like those mischievous boys, you know."

"Stop getting me into more trouble than I'm already in." To elbow his companion with one hand disabled and in a sling and another securing the unstable rider upon his shoulders turned out to be an impossible challenge. He patted whatever he could manage to reach of his daughter's side, instead. "Don't listen to him, little rascal. Help us convince your beautiful mother to give us plenty of tasty treats and wait for me with more upon my return. Make sure she is not angry or sad while I'm away. Think you can do it?"

She was considering it soberly. He could feel her concentration, seeping through her once-again-motionless limbs. "What tasty things? Like porridge with sweet maple?"

He could hear his companion chuckling again before turning to answer some passerby's greetings, a group of elders clearly expecting him to come nearer and pay his respects.

"Yes, like sweetened porridge and bread with berries." He shifted to find a better position, his shoulder responsible for the slinged arm protesting with dull but persistent pain. "But mainly make sure your mother is not sad like the last time, eh? In three, four dawns I'll be back. Keep reminding her of that."

"When you were away she was sad, yes." As though sensing his discomfort, she began climbing down, with little consideration to his readiness for such feat.

He gritted his teeth, dealing with the challenge of catching her, preventing her from falling off, breathless with pain for a moment. "Why won't you..." He pressed his lips tight, swallowing the angry words back. "Careful, little one. When my hand is good again, you can jump all over me like a squirrel who ate a wrong plant."

She was settling in the crook of his good arm, pressing close, as though seeking his warmth, or maybe this same reassurance he was trying to convey to Gayeri through her. The sight of her little face screwed into a troubled expression, a funny imitation of a grownup's panted concern, made his heart squeeze. She suffered from his moon-long absence as well, poor thing.

"I will come back very quickly this time," he said, pressing her close, melting inside. "Three, four dawns. Count them, will you? Every time you wake up with the first rays of Father Sun, make a count. Mark that beam of our bunk, the one closest to the fire, eh? Make a tiny little cut so Mother or Great Aunt won't see it. I'll give you a piece of flint for that."

She was wriggling wildly, trying to break free in an attempt to see him better, he knew.

Helping her to make herself comfortable back in the crook of his arm, he smiled. "How about that?"

"Yes, yes. Will you? You'll give me flint? All for myself? To make cuts? Each dawn?" Her face peered at him from below, shining as though he had given her the most wonderful of presents, a star from the nightly sky or at least a huge grizzled bear's pelt all for herself.

He swallowed, then pressed her back into his chest, needing a heartbeat to compose himself.

"Only when Father Sun comes, yes? Only then?" She was still chattering, her voice muffled, tickling his chest. "The moment I open my eyes, yes?"

"The moment you open your eyes and see a good opportunity to make your cut without having your Great Aunt fussing around, protesting about you cutting anything at all." The laughter restored his composure and, bouncing her higher up in her new seat, he resumed his walk, glancing at the Wolf Man, who was still hopelessly caught, unable to escape the dignified elders' company without committing bad crime of impoliteness. Which of course left him, Ogteah, to prepare their journey, short and undemanding that it was. What pleasure was there in walking on an empty stomach?

"Let us go and find your mother and make her feel better too, eh, little one? She deserves that, a good treatment, the best treatment ever, because she is the greatest woman that ever lived, aside from the Sky Woman maybe and her daughter, the mother of Celestial Twins. Oh, and aside from you, too." He winked at her, bouncing her again, drawing a flurry of giggles in return.

"Then, just before I go, when the warriors' leader comes to fetch me, I'll slip that flint into your palm and you will hide it the best you can. And we'll find the place you can make your marks. First thing, we'll do that."

Maneuvering his way between the longhouses, now bursting with life and babbling, he answered people's greetings, retuning grins or exchanging joking remarks, at peace once again, content now.

The foray into his former people's lands, a desperate undertaking in the beginning, now lay behind him, promising to turn into a greater achievement than either he or anyone of the originators of it could have planned or hoped for. A possible peace, or at least some sort of agreement that would stop the fighting, stop the meaningless raids, keep his family safe, oh what an alluring prospect, worthy of his efforts, of all the hardships and sweat. And didn't his people deserve it, his people from both sides, his family, Gayeri and the little ones, but also his brothers and their children, and that boy that was a fruit of his loins whether he stayed to raise him or not. They all deserved lives with no constant fear, no constant readiness. They all deserved better.

The smile was turning too wide to hide, and he paused in the storage room of their longhouse, wishing to compose himself, unwilling to discuss any of it as yet, not even with Gayeri, wishing to think it all through. Could it be that he wouldn't have to choose after all? Could he and Sondakwa take their barely formed ideas past the talking stage and into a more realistic phase? Because if they managed, even partly, then their father's and the War Chief's desire could still bear fruit, despite all the deaths and the failures. And then he wouldn't have to choose between his current and former people, between various family members on both sides. Oh Mighty Spirits, but for something like that to happen!

"Mother!" Slipping down and away from his arms, the little rascal was bolting toward the light of the corridor and out of the storage room's semi-darkness. "Father said three or four dawns, he said he will not be away for long if you make a sweet porridge with a lot maple in it!"

His grin stretching to impossible lengths, he shook his head, then hurried after the squeaking shouts, eager to catch up with this flood of irrelevant information, if for no other reason than to explain it better. Also to hold his woman close and feel her warmth, her love, her belief and trust and devotion, something he missed so badly while out there and doing all the wrong things.

Oh yes, for these two women of his life he would try his hardest. And his brother would do his part, such an unexpected ally. Who would have thought, of all things? Shaking his head, he emerged into the regulated commotion of the corridor, still grinning.

ABOUT THE AUTHOR

Zoe Saadia is the author of several novels on pre-Columbian Americas. From the architects of the Aztec Empire to the founders of the Iroquois Great League, from the towering pyramids of Tenochtitlan to the longhouses of the Great Lakes, her novels bring long-forgotten history, cultures and people to life, tracing pivotal events that brought about the greatness of North and Mesoamerica.

To learn more about Zoe Saadia and her work, please visit
www.zoesaadia.com

Made in the USA
Lexington, KY
11 August 2019